An Almost Perfect Ending

The Torch Singer
Book Two

Books by Robert Westbrook

Howard Moon Deer Mysteries
Ghost Dancer
Warrior Circle
Red Moon
Ancient Enemy
Turquoise Lady
Blue Moon
Hungry Ghost

Coming Soon!
Walking Rain
A Howard Moon Deer Mystery

The Torch Singer Trilogy
An Overnight Sensation
An Almost Perfect Ending
The Saint of Make-Believe

Left-Handed Policeman *series*
The Left-Handed Policeman
Nostalgia Kills
Lady Left

Other Books
Intimate Lies:
F. Scott Fitzgerald and Sheilah Graham – Her Son's Story
Journey Behind the Iron Curtain
The Magic Garden of Stanley Sweetheart

An Almost Perfect Ending

The Torch Singer
Book Two

Robert Westbrook

SPEAKING VOLUMES, LLC
NAPLES, FLORIDA
2021

An Almost Perfect Ending

ISBN 978-1-64540-472-9

For Gail, again, always

Part One

All That Slips Away

One

California: April, 1954

She remembered it afterwards as the last best day of her life, that night at Ciro's when she sang her heart out and the world adored her.

Her name was huge on the marquee outside, ablaze in lights so that all Sunset Strip knew she was there: SONYA SAINT-AMANT IN PERSON!

She was no longer as famous as she once had been. By 1954, the Ooh-La-La Girl of 1944 had gained weight and her hazel-green eyes no longer blazed so brightly. But her name was still synonymous with sex, her voice was strong, and she believed the good days would last forever.

Standing in the blue beam of a spotlight, she sent her low smoky voice out into the room as half-seen couples glided by on the dance floor, many of them showing off with elaborate dips and twirls. From the stage, the tables with their white cloths and candles seemed to be floating in the darkness like stars in the night sky, small islands of light.

There was an expensive, late-night smell of cigarette smoke, perfume, mink, and liquor. A sea sound of murmuring voices punctuated by sudden sharp peals of laughter. Above all, there was a sense of anticipation that magical things could happen at Ciro's tonight. Contracts signed, love affairs sealed, fame won, fortunes lost. Who could say?

Joan Fontaine was in the house this evening. And Alan Ladd. And Bugsy Siegel, the gangster. And starlets and gossip columnists and press agents and producers. And some people no one knew at all, the moths who were always eager to circle the flame of other people's celebrity.

That was Ciro's in 1954. More of a clubhouse than a club. A place where show people could gather and flaunt what fun it was to be an insider. And tonight they accepted Sonja Wojtkiewicz as one of their own, the girl from Krakow, Poland, who had transformed herself into Sonya Saint-Amant.

She stood on the stage with a microphone in her hand and a five-piece band behind her: piano, bass, drums, saxophone, and clarinet. It was the Ciro's house band rather than the group who usually backed her (Buddy Kanin and His Orchestra), but they were good. They could play any tune in any key without thinking twice. To be a success in show business, you had to make it look easy, and these boys were so easy they almost seemed to float away.

She performed two sets, as specified in her contract. The opening set began at ten-thirty and the first few numbers were slow getting off the ground. Music was like that. Sometimes the magic was there, other times it wasn't, no matter what you did to goose it along. It wasn't until halfway through "If I

Loved You" that the glow kicked in. The spark when everything lit up from inside and suddenly you slipped into an enchantment where nothing could go wrong. By the time she got to "Ain't Misbehavin'," she had the audience loving her as much as she was loving them. "Ain't Misbehavin' " was a song she'd once had trouble with, back in the days when she was struggling, but she had it figured out now. She sang it so slow and sexy that everyone in the room knew that misbehaving was what Sonya Saint-Amant was all about.

When she was finished, the room went wild.

"Sasha!" someone shouted from a back table. Sasha was Sonya's nickname, what everybody called her. Just like Gary Cooper was Coop and John Wayne was the Duke and Robert Wagner was R.J. It was important to have a nickname in Hollywood. It meant you were famous enough so that people wanted to claim you as a special pal.

"Hey, Sasha, you can misbehave with me any time!"

It was a loudmouth actor, a pretty-boy from a TV western, and he was drunk. Sasha thought she might have fucked him once. But maybe that was somebody else.

The evening just kept getting better. "My Funny Valentine," "They Can't Take That Away From Me," . . . by the time she finished the first set with "Satin Doll," the glow was so hot inside of her, it was like she was burning. That's what it meant to be a torch singer. Sasha was a girl on fire.

And the second set was better still. Sasha had a Little Secret. She had smoked a marihuana cigarette in her dressing room between sets. Reefer wasn't something you wanted to talk about in 1954, though all the jazz boys had been doing it for years. A sax player in Buddy Kanin's orchestra had introduced her to reefer a few years ago on tour and from that time on she never performed without it. It made you feel that music was a living presence all around you. It filled the world with poetry and sound.

"Little Girl Blue," "Stormy Weather," "How High the Moon," on and on. She saved the best for last, "I Believe in Tomorrow," the song that had made her famous. It was Sasha's theme song, written for her voice alone, an anthem of hope and courage that had worked its way down deep into the national mood of war-weary America in 1944. Even now, a decade later, it was music that had the power—with a drink or two—to make tough men cry.

The applause went on and on. They made her sing three encores. They loved her.

For Sasha, there had never been a better night.

Until she drifted backstage to her dressing room and found the past waiting in ambush.

*****

Sasha kicked off her shoes and poured herself a big slug of vodka from the bottle on her makeup table. These were the priorities when you got off stage: get comfortable, pour yourself a drink. Her feet hurt, her neck was sore, her body stank of stale sweat. You leave yourself behind when you're performing. But there's always a hard landing waiting afterwards in the dressing room.

"You were good tonight!" she told the three-way mirror on her dressing table. "You knocked 'em dead."

With a frown, she moved closer to the glass for a better look. Her face was ashen and the makeup didn't completely hide the dark circles beneath her eyes. This was worrisome because being beautiful had always been the foundation of her success. But she had knocked 'em dead tonight, that was the main thing. It almost seemed like revenge for something, to knock 'em dead, though she wasn't exactly sure revenge for what.

Sasha unzipped her dress—a slinky white evening gown— and she let it fall in a heap on the floor. The dress had been tight and it was good to be free of it. But that was the moment the past found her. She was standing in her slip when a movement in the three-way mirror made her catch her breath and spin around.

"Goddamn!" she cried. "How did you get in here?"

Ex-NYPD Detective Ricky Bolano was sitting in an armchair deep in the shadows of the room. He was a slight man with a gaunt, wolfish face. His skin was sallow, as though it had been pickled in the yellow-brown residue of cigarette smoke. He might have been forty or sixty—you couldn't tell his age, he gave nothing away. His legs were crossed and his hat, a fedora, rested on his knee.

Sasha's throat went tight at the sight of him. She had first met Detective Bolano in a movie theater on Sixth Avenue in 1943, and the memory wasn't a pleasant one.

"You can pour me some of that," he said, nodding at the vodka on her the dressing table. He spoke so softly you had to strain to hear him. "Though I would have preferred bourbon, if you'd had it."

"How did you get in here?" she demanded again, hoping if she put on enough bluster he wouldn't see how frightened she was.

He shrugged. "Oh, I got friends. Friends who owe me a favor or two. Even in a swell place like this."

"Get out! You have a goddamn nerve coming into my dressing room!"

He gave her a long look but didn't move from the chair. "It didn't take much nerve really. You'd be surprised how easy it was. I liked the show, by the way. Only one criticism. You're doing 'Satin Doll' too fast. You gotta pull back on the tempo. Make the rhythm more stately. Know what I mean?"

He began to sing it for her in a tuneless monotone, a few bars, the tempo he had in mind. In Hollywood, even the thugs were critics. Sasha kept the anger from her face. Ricky had hit her hard once and her body retained a physical memory of him.

"You can give me that drink now," he said. "You should know I don't like to be kept waiting."

Sasha poured a few fingers of vodka into a water glass and kept her distance as she handed it to him.

"You seem kinda edgy, doll. Do I make you nervous?"

"What do you want?"

He smiled blandly. "It's rent time. Time to pay up or shut up. Know what I mean?"

Sasha worked to keep her voice even. "I gave you money four months ago. You said that was it. You said you would never come back to bother me again."

His smile was almost sympathetic. "You see, that's one of my faults. I lie sometimes. Because here I am again needing money. But I'm going to be nice because I liked your show so much. I'm only going to hit you for a grand."

"A thousand dollars!"

"That's right. A cool grand and you won't see me again for . . . well, until the next time I need money."

"I don't have a thousand dollars, Mr. Bolano."

"Sure, you do. Don't try to fool Ricky, because Ricky knows all. Why, you're getting a thousand bucks just for this one lousy gig. Which makes it easy. You pass that dough my way and it'll almost be like I was the one on stage."

Sasha lit a cigarette and tried to think of some way out. Ricky was sucking her dry. He was a disease that was slowly killing her. But she didn't know how to stop him.

"The money from tonight is already gone," she told him. The truth, unfortunately. "I'm in debt to my manager and the check is going straight to him. I'm broke, Mr. Bolano. If you know so much, you should know that."

He took his vodka in a single swallow and nodded. "Broke? Well, sure you are, doll. You go through money like there's no tomorrow. You don't know how to budget, that's your problem. You got no self-discipline. But lucky for you, you got resources. For instance, there's the money your boy makes. All the dough from that dumb TV show he's in. I bet you've been socking that away for him, haven't you?"

"I will not touch my son's money," Sasha answered tightly.

"Sure you will. His bank account's in your name. He doesn't even have to know."

"I won't do it."

Ricky put down his empty glass on the coffee table and rose slowly to his feet. Sasha backed away warily.

"Now I want you to pay attention," he said. "You're not the only person I can make trouble for. You think CBS is going to keep little Jonathan on that show once word gets out that his mother was arrested for whoring in New York? I don't think so. I don't think having a whore for a mother would do a thing for the ratings, you see."

Sasha didn't dare answer. She only stared at him with intense loathing.

Ricky shrugged. "Hey, get the money somewhere else then, I don't care. Get it from your fancy boyfriend Max McCormick if you like. You see, I know all your secrets. Even the reefer you smoke. So just get the money. I'm going to give you a week just because I'm such a patient guy. I'll phone to let you know when I'll be coming by. And don't even think of funny stuff because there's an attorney who has instructions to open a certain envelope in a certain safe if anything happens to me. Are we clear about this?"

Sasha nodded.

"Don't nod. Say yes. Say yes, Ricky, I'll have a thousand dollars for you in one week's time."

"Yes, Mr. Bolano, I'll have a thousand dollars. In one week's time."

"Okay, then. Well, I've got myself a long drive back to the Valley, so I guess I'm off." He smiled. "Unless you'd like to suck my dick for old time's sake. Whad'ya say, doll?"

"Go fuck yourself!"

Ricky laughed. "Go *fuck* myself?" he repeated. "Is that what you just said? *Go fuck myself*? And here I've been so nice. I guess you want some slapping around. Is that it? Do I need to teach you a lesson?"

She stared at the floor and didn't answer. Her heart was beating fast.

"Is this what you want?" He gave her a light slap across the face, open handed. It wasn't hard, but it took Sasha by surprise and she stumbled backward against her dressing table.

He slapped her again, this time on the shoulder. "Some broads enjoy getting beat up. It turns them on, I guess. Is that you, Sasha? Want me to beat you up?"

"No, please."

He slapped her playfully on the other shoulder and then the first shoulder again. Each hit was just a little harder than the previous one.

"I could break your arm, for instance," he said. "I could really mess you up. Unless you'd like to apologize, of course. For telling me to go fuck myself."

Sasha found herself buffeted, reeling from side to side as he continued to slap her shoulders and arms. She hated that she was dressed only in her slip. It made her feel especially vulnerable. Without further warning, he hit her hard, an open-handed whack against the side of her face. She tumbled backward, knocking over the dressing table chair. Ricky wasn't playing anymore.

"You gonna apologize now?"

"I'm sorry!" she cried.

The blows were coming faster now, one after another. He kept slapping her shoulders, her face, the top of her head, everywhere. She tried to protect herself with her arms, but there was no way to fend him off.

"So don't you ever tell me to fuck off again. You got that, bitch? Ricky Bolano does not tolerate whores telling him to fuck off."

"I won't! I promise!" she cried.

He grabbed her hair and pulled her violently to her knees. "You're going to suck my dick now, aren't you?"

"Oh, please . . . don't!"

He kicked her.

"Maybe you think you're too good to suck my dick? Is that it?"

For Sasha, it was like being caught in an ocean wave. The blows seemed to come from everywhere, rolling her round and round in a swirl of pain. There was a taste of blood in her mouth and mucus and slime and tears. She tried to get away from him by curling into a protective ball on the floor, but he yanked her back to her knees. She found his penis pressed her face. It was half-hard. A disgusting sweaty, fleshy, smelly thing.

"Suck it!" he ordered. "Suck my goddamn dick."

Sasha was about to do it. There wasn't any choice. She had always done what was necessary to survive. It was how she had escaped Nazi Poland in the worst years of the war. You did what you had to do, that was her core belief. She closed her eyes, she didn't want to see her shame. But just as she was about to take his cock in her mouth, a hot stream of urine began raining down on her from above. Sasha was so disoriented that it took a moment to understand that ex-NYPD Detective Ricky Bolano was peeing on her.

"You see, actually, I don't let whores suck my dick," he said in his angry whisper. "A slut like you, I'd probably get some disease. Now you got a week to get my fucking money or you'll be sorry! You got that? One week!"

He kicked her one last time with the pointed toe of his black Italian shoe. Then he turned and left the dressing room, leaving Sasha sobbing on the floor, broken and humiliated.

*****

The sky in the east was hinting at a sullen November dawn when Sasha eased her car up her driveway in Beverly Hills. It was an expensive car, a cream-colored '52 Cadillac convertible with leopard skin seats and white-wall tires. Cars were important in California, you had to show people what a success you were.

Gino, the headwaiter at Ciro's, had given her a bundle of ice wrapped in a linen napkin which she held pressed against the swelling that was rising on her chin and around her left eye. She told Gino that she had slipped and fallen, and he had pretended to believe her. A headwaiter at Ciro's saw pretty much everything. He had offered to call a cab so that she wouldn't have to drive, but Sasha said she would manage. She didn't want a stranger, a taxi driver, to see her in this humiliating condition. She wanted to be alone.

She sat in her driveway for nearly ten minutes with the ignition off, the engine ticking, working up the will to move. She hurt everywhere. She was more than halfway drunk and she couldn't stop crying.

"Bastard!" she kept saying over and over to herself. "Fucking bastard!"

Her son, Jonno, had left the outside light on, a yellow bulb in a wrought-iron lantern that lit the white stucco portico with a splash of color. Sasha was proud to own a house in Beverly Hills, even if it was only in the flats, closer to Santa Monica Boulevard than Sunset. But this morning the big house looked down on her in mockery: to have come so far in life only to be at the mercy of a cheap crook like Ricky Bolano.

She found the resolve at last to open the car door and stand in the driveway. Her balance was precarious. Setting herself in motion, she wobbled uncertainly along the footpath that crossed the front lawn toward the front door. Her hand shook so badly it took several tries to fit the key in the lock.

Once she was inside, she locked the door behind her, determined that nothing else would hurt her. From the foyer, Sasha climbed the stairway that curved to the upper floor, one step at a time, pausing occasionally to catch her breath. The house was Hollywood Moorish with a wrought-iron banister and blood-red Spanish tiles underfoot, built in the Rudolph Valentino era.

She hesitated when she reached the top landing, holding the banister for support. She had intended to continue toward her bedroom, but now that she had come this far, she thought she would rather die than be alone.

She made her way across the landing and slipped in the door to Jonno's bedroom as quietly as she could so as not to wake him. The room was dark with only a dim line of light from the edges of the curtains. She bumped against his desk, banging her leg in a place that already hurt. "Fuck!" she said, forgetting to be quiet. Sasha adjusted her course and stumbled onto the bed. Jonno was asleep on his side with a blanket up around his shoulders. She kicked off her shoes and stretched out alongside him on top of the covers. She knew he didn't like her creeping into his room when he was asleep because she had done this before, usually when she was drunk. He had made it clear that at the age of eleven he was too old to be sleeping with his mother. Still, she couldn't help it, not to-night. There wasn't anyone else who loved her.

Jonno moaned softly as she put her arm over him but he was asleep again in an instant. It was astonishing how children slept, the easy peace of their rest. She herself had not slept well for years.

Even now—beaten, exhausted, drunk—Sasha didn't fall asleep immediately. Lying in the darkened room, listening to

Jonno's breathing, she wondered with all her might what she was going to do about Ricky Bolano.

She fell asleep with the question rolling in her mind like a pebble washing in the surf. She didn't wake until the early afternoon and the question was still there, rolling, washing, looking for an answer.

The sun was streaming in the edges of the curtains and Jonno was long gone. The studio car would have picked him up hours ago for his morning commute to Paramount. Sasha sat up in bed and found a cigarette from her handbag on the floor. Her body hurt everywhere, even worse than the night before. She wondered if Jonno had been angry when he woke and found her asleep on his bed. She hoped he knew how lost she would be without him. Her one ally in a merciless world.

At least she knew what she was going to do about Ricky. The answer came as she held the flame of her silver lighter against the tip of her cigarette. She was going to kill him.

She didn't know yet how she would do it. But she knew she would find a way. There was no other solution.

Just a small murder and she would be free.

Two

I wasn't happy to wake up and find my mother passed out drunk in my bed. It wasn't my idea of "normal," an imaginary state to which I aspired. It wasn't how mothers were supposed to behave.

My radio alarm woke me at exactly 6:15 with "Mr. Sandman," a big hit from the Chordettes, a girl band of the time that roused me from sleep with the cheerful wish that Mr. Sandman would send them a dream. I appreciated the sentiment. I liked dreams. But there was an awful stink in the air, a pungent aroma of pee. I'm not at my best in the morning, so it took me a moment to realize something was wrong.

At first I thought it was me, that I had wet my bed, something I hadn't done since around the age of five. Then I became aware of my mother's arm draped over my waist and the rest of her body curled around me like a spoon. She was snoring and a blast of vodka-breath cut through the stink of pee like a midnight breeze from a bar. I wiggled loose from her embrace and got out of bed in a foul mood.

"Fucking hell!" I muttered. At the age of eleven, I used the word fuck frequently, often in creative combinations.

Standing by the bed, I gave my mother a closer inspection and noticed the black-purple bruises on her face and arms. I was concerned but not overly sympathetic. I assumed it was her fault, that she had walked into a door or tumbled off a stage. My mother's private life had become increasingly a thing of wild tabloid antics, but this was definitely a new low. I regret now that I assumed she was the one at fault, another drunken escapade. But what else was I to think? I was grumpy, the studio car was due in less than an hour, and I only wanted to get away.

I gathered my clothes and headed to my bathroom in the hallway at the top of the stairs. I brushed my teeth, dressed, used the toilet, and avoided my bedroom for the rest of the morning, wishing to spare myself the sight of my sodden mother snoring like a pig.

Claire, our maid, was busy getting breakfast together downstairs in the kitchen: fried eggs, bacon, toast, a glass of orange juice. Claire was a big, comfortable Colored woman who slept in a room next to the kitchen five nights a week. The other two days, Sundays and Mondays, Claire returned to her own home in Inglewood where she had a husband and two daughters. I had never met her real family but—believing myself to be the center of the universe—I assumed she loved me more than she loved them. I had a lot to learn.

"You sleep well, honey?" Claire asked as I bedraggled my-self to the table.

"Oh, sure," I grouched. "Until I woke and found my moth-er passed out on my fucking bed!"

"Jonathan Saint-Amant! Don't you go saying words like that!" Claire was fond of me, I think. But she didn't approve of me one bit.

"You gotta understand how hard your mama's working," Claire said while she finished cooking my eggs. "My Lord, singing 'til all hours at those club places! Why, Jonno, I don't think she got home this mornin' 'til close to dawn."

"Right," I said skeptically, staring at the plate she set down in front of me. The two orange eyeballs of my eggs stared up at me like a reprimand, too sunny by far for the way I was feeling. It didn't seem to me that working hard was any excuse for my mother to come creeping into my bed stinking of pee. That was booze, not work.

Claire and I didn't do much more talking because I was on a schedule, my morning rush, and I had to stay focused. I wasn't just any kid, after all. I was a star. A child actor on the hit weekly TV sit-com, *What A Life!*

Lucky me, you might say. How glamorous! Or maybe not.

The studio station wagon came for me at precisely seven o'clock, pulling up the driveway with a little honk of the horn. Penny was already in the back seat, reading a script and studying her lines. Penny lived in Brentwood, which was farther from the studio than I was, so she got picked up first. She was almost fourteen and she played my older sister on the show. Five days a week the studio car ferried us back and forth to Paramount together. I'm sure that Mort Jenkins, the show's producer, thought this would be a good way for us to bond.

Penny was dressed in her comfortable at-home clothes: yellow pedal pushers, a pink sweater with a white blouse underneath, penny loafers on her feet. The Fifties were a time of hideously bad taste so I didn't much notice how the colors clashed. Personally, I thought she looked great. Her hair was blonde and it was tied back in a perky little ponytail that I always wanted to grab. She had a cute little snub nose, her skin glowed like sunshine, and she smelled fresh as soap. Basically, I wanted to eat her. I wanted to lick her with my tongue, head to toe, as though she were some kind of girl lollipop.

I need to confess something from the start: Penny wasn't the innocent creature she pretended to be on our TV show. She had seduced me a year earlier and had turned me into a kind of sex toy to satisfy her genital needs. Vibrators didn't exist back then (as far as I knew), but that was more or less the hole I filled, metaphorically speaking. Basically, it was innocent kid stuff, a show-me-your-thing and I'll show-you-mine sort of situation. A preadolescent affair rather than an adolescent one. It wasn't supposed to be anything more than that. But I was foolish, I fell hard. I believed I loved her. I believed I loved her more than I had ever loved anyone before or since.

An Almost Perfect Ending

I'm not saying I was some slick eleven-year-old Casanova. I wasn't. I was so raw and thunderstruck by the erotic girlness of her that I could barely speak in her presence. Fortunately, it wasn't eloquence that Penny required of me.

"Hi!" I smiled goofily as I slipped into the seat next to her. Not only was she three years older, she was bigger also: a foot taller with an extra twenty pounds. Some of those extra pounds occurred in parts of her body that I found fascinating.

"Hey, did you see *I Led Three Lives* last night?" I asked as she continued to study her script. *I Led Three Lives* was a hit TV show about an average American guy, Richard Carlson, who pretends to be a Commie so he can spy for the FBI.

"Hmmm," she grunted, her eyes on the script.

Our driver was a lanky middle-aged cowboy named Burt who had come to L.A. from Montana hoping to star in Westerns. It never happened. As with a lot of people, fame and fortune passed Burt by. The closest he ever got to Hollywood celebrity was driving two bratty child actors back and forth to Paramount. He didn't seem to mind, as far as I could tell. Mostly, Burt ignored us, listening to sports on the car radio and not paying much attention to what Penny and I were doing in the back seat. Which was a good thing, all in all, since often what Penny and I were doing wouldn't bear adult scrutiny.

But not this morning. Today Penny ignored me. She kept studying her script and didn't seem interested in me in the least.

"You'll never believe what happened," I said, trying to snag her attention. "I found my mother in bed with me this morning when the alarm went off."

It worked. Bed, I believe, was the magic word. Penny's eyes rose from the script and turned my way with faint interest.

"In *bed* with you? Like, under the covers?" she asked. "*Naked*?"

"Not *under*. Jesus! She was on top, naturally. Totally dressed. But wow, was she boozed-up! Her breath was enough to sink an aircraft carrier."

Penny's eyes were gray, the color of early dawn. They glittered briefly. "So does she do that often? Get in bed with you?"

I shrugged. "Not really. I mean, sure, it's happened. But not, like, every night."

"Does she . . . touch you?"

"For chrissake, Penny! She's my mother!"

"That doesn't always mean anything."

"Why, sure it does," I said stoutly.

"No, it doesn't" Penny assured me, turning back to the script.

An Almost Perfect Ending

I watched her profile intensely for clues, but her face was deliberately blank. Outside, the low buildings of Melrose Avenue drifted by in a slouchy haze. A few decades in the future, Melrose would become a fashionable part of town, but it wasn't yet, not by a long shot. We had maybe another fifteen minutes before we got to Paramount.

"So, look, what about doing something this weekend?" I suggested. "We could go to a movie?"

"I can't," she answered without looking at me.

"How about a sleepover?" I asked optimistically. We had done sleepovers before and they were about as close to heaven as I could imagine heaven to be.

But Penny shook her head. "I'm going to Palm Springs with my mother and her new boyfriend."

Palm Springs? I didn't like this. Plus, it seemed to me that she might have said this at the start.

"So where are you going to stay?" I asked, trying to pin her down.

"Jonno! I got to study my lines!"

"You didn't do that last night?"

Her gray eyes flashed my way in exasperation. "No, I went to a party. Now for gosh sake, Jonno, shut up and let me learn my lines."

A party? I liked that even less than I liked Palm Springs. I wanted to ask her what sort of party, and where was it, and who was there. But I wasn't entirely stupid so I kept my mouth shut.

We drove the rest of way to the studio in silence. I opened my script and pretended to study my lines too, just to have something to do. But all I could think about was Penny sitting next to me, so close yet far away. I listened to her breathing. I inhaled the warmth of her body. I remembered a time we had taken a bath together and how afterwards she had stood naked near the sink, her body all rosy and still a little steamy from the bath. She had let me dry her with a small hand towel. Just the thought of it now gave me a boner, which I did my best to hide with my script.

Oh, Penny! How I longed for her! Just as we were driving in through the Paramount gate, I let my left hand drop casually onto the upper region of her right leg. She gave no indication that I was touching her, but she didn't push me away. Love is never easy. But the universe grants us small favors from time to time, for which we must be grateful.

*****

I had the featured part that week on the show. In the story, I lose an envelope full of money that I'd collected as class treasurer—$25 to throw a surprise birthday party for a teacher—and I have to go through all sorts of shenanigans to get it back. Eventually, it turns out I'd left the money on the school bus, which the driver found and gave to my father, who's had it all the time, keeping me in suspense in order to give me a lesson in responsibility. It was a typical situation for our TV family, week to week. We always managed to get in to huge amounts of silly trouble, but everything turned out well in the end because we were good Americans—Mom, Dad, Penny, and me—and God smiled down on the well-scrubbed innocence of our 1950s lives.

I was good with lines. I didn't have to spend hours memorizing scripts the way Penny did. Making up things has always come naturally to me. Still, I had to concentrate on being cute and funny. I was aching for Penny, but I did my best to put her out of mind until we broke for lunch at 12:30.

Penny and I had our established routine. We always had lunch together in her dressing room and often we got into some mischief afterwards if there was time. I hurried to the commissary and picked up a tuna sandwich for her and a turkey club for me, and then I ran back to Stage 17, hoping to have as much time with her as possible. But when I got back to the sound stage, Penny wasn't in her dressing room and I couldn't find her anywhere on the set.

I was wandering through the darkened set, looking for her, when I came across a camera grip I knew—Matt, who was in his early twenties and sometimes threw a football around with me in the alley outside Stage 17. He was on his knees with a screwdriver, tightening one of the wheels on a camera dolly.

"Hey, Matt, have you seen Penny?" I asked. Trying to seem casual, like my entire life didn't rest on the answer.

"Sure, she passed through here a few minutes ago. She was with some kid," he answered without looking up.

"Some . . . kid?"

"A teenager. I've never seen him before."

Did a shiver of premonition tingle up my spine? Did I know my world was ending? Yes and no. I didn't want to see it.

I prodded further and managed to get a description of this unknown teenage person. According to Matt, he was tall, blond, maybe sixteen-years-old, good looking. He and Penny had been laughing together as they passed through the set on their way outside to take a look at his car.

It's nothing, I told myself. Penny was probably only being polite. Why should she care about a blond, tall, good-looking, sixteen-year-old boy with a car? Nevertheless, I felt as though an icicle had just pierced the very center of my heart.

*****

The situation didn't improve in the afternoon. I had a brief scene later in the day with Penny in which she turned on pretended interest while the cameras were rolling, but then continued to ignore me as soon as the scene was over.

It was like I was no longer her best friend. Nor had ever been.

Later, when the workday was finished and it was time to drive home, Burt informed me that I would be riding alone this afternoon since Penny's mother was coming by to pick her up. Apparently, Penny was going to some kind of press function at the Ambassador Hotel to which I hadn't been invited. I should mention that she was a bigger star than I was. I was still only a kid actor, while Penny was growing up fast, leaving me behind, starting to get her photograph in teen magazines.

I sat silently in the front seat of the station wagon barely noticing the passing streets as Burt drove us to Beverly Hills. It was like someone had put me in a deep freeze. I was numb all over. My stomach felt like I was on an elevator that was going in one direction only: down, down, down.

It was dark by the time we pulled up to the curb in front of my house. My mother had arrived home only a moment earlier and was in the driveway getting out of her car. With more important things occupying my brain, I'd forgotten all about her, how I'd woken up this morning to find her in my bed stinking of pee.

"See you *mañana,* pardner," Burt said as he dropped me off.

"Sure," I answered bleakly. I slouched my way up the driveway, feeling like some kind of squashed bug. My mother hadn't seen me yet. She was wearing huge sunglasses, even though it was dark, and a hat with a wide floppy brim that hid half her face. I assumed she was coming from some place where she hadn't wanted to be recognized. As I came up behind her, she was reaching through the open car door for something in the front seat.

"Hi," I said unhappily.

My voice startled her. She jumped and stood up straight, almost guiltily, and made a grab for something that was fumbling about in her hand. It was a book and somehow in the surprise of me coming up behind her, she had lost her grip on it. She did a little juggling act but it fell to the ground with a plop.

"You shouldn't startle me like that," she said.

The interior car light lit her face and I got a better look at her. Even with the floppy hat and dark glasses I could tell she was in bad shape. She was wearing a lot of make-up—powder, some rouge on her cheeks—but it didn't entirely hide the puffy dark bruises on her face. The way she moved was like an old woman.

I picked up the book she had dropped and was surprised by the title. *Famous Murders*, it was called. *How They Did It, And How They Were Caught.*

"Gee, Mom," I said, "What are you reading about murder for?"

"I'm interested, that's all," she told me irritably, reaching for the book.

I didn't give it to her right away. "But why?" I insisted.

"Everyone likes a good murder," she said. "That's why they write about them. Now give me my book."

It wasn't like my mother to go shopping for books, especially when she looked as though she'd had a rough night. I'm not saying she was illiterate. She made a point of reading bestsellers, particularly ones that Max gave her. But this didn't add up. I sensed wrongness here. I sensed evasion.

"And you look all beat up," I told her unkindly. "What happened to you last night?"

"Never mind," she snapped. But we knew each other very well, my mother and I—too well, you might say—and when she saw I wouldn't be put off, she changed tactics. She tried a reassuring smile, but her lip was cracked and swollen, and it wasn't what you'd describe as a sunny smile. "Darling, everything's fine. I tripped over a chair, that's all. I don't want you to worry about a thing."

Right. First Penny disappears with some jerk who's sixteen and handsome and owns a car. Then I find my mother looking like she'd been run over by a truck, fumbling about in the driveway with a book about murder.

Life was great in sunny California, our paradise by the sea! What was there to worry about?

Three

From the beginning, my mother and I were thick as thieves. I was her Little Man, that's the awful thing she called me, the role I played. Not only was I her Little Man, I was her bartender, confidante, and all purpose guardian of the gate.

"Jonno, we're artists, you and I, free from bourgeois prejudice!" she liked to proclaim, usually when she wanted me to do something of a dubious nature.

Due to this lack of conventional restraint, I spent a good deal of my childhood helping her juggle a chorus line of men, all of them doing their best little dance to gain entry to her bedroom. I was the messenger, go-between, and often the look-out as well. As far as my mother was concerned, I was a kind of all-purpose Cupid, minus wings. It shocks me now, of course, to remember these things from the vantage of a more knowing age. But at the time I took it for granted that, in a horny universe, adults were incapable of keeping their hands off each other and this was a service all children performed for their parents. My mother often told me that she had acted as lookout for her own mother, the opera star, back in her mythical Krakow childhood.

When it came to lovers, Zachary Wise was first in line— my godfather, as I was encouraged to call him. A make-believe designation since he was Jewish, like my mother, and had certainly never stood at a stone font while some priest doused me with water. But he was rich, he owned a movie studio, and frankly, we needed him. Godfather Zach generally visited in the afternoons and he never stayed for more than an hour, being a busy man.

Uncle Max was next in line, and he usually arrived after dark, sneaking up the stairs when I was supposedly asleep. Somehow these honorific titles—godfather and uncle—lent my mother's polyandrous existence a kind of respectability, at least in her eyes. A family affair, you might say.

Luckily, Godfather Zach didn't know about Uncle Max. These things are impossible to say for certain, for Zachary was no fool. Still, he pretended to believe Sasha's roving days were over and that she belonged to him alone, eager for his attentions whenever he could take time away from his studio and his wife. As for Max, though he knew in theory that he shared my mother's favors with Zachary, he took the ostrich approach to the matter, head in sand, and did his best to avoid thinking on it directly.

I know Max suffered, for it was the sort of situation to make a sensitive man sigh and shake his head and drink more than was good for him. But he didn't wish to know the specifics and if there was angst to be had, he believed he deserved it. He blamed himself. He had been weak and indecisive; he had abandoned my mother on the *Mauretania* and had left her in New York to make her way in the world alone. So how could he complain if she had found another protector?

I'm sure my mother loved Max in her way, as much as she was capable. He was her romantic ideal, a dreamy, poetic man. I imagine they flew into each other's arms when they met again in California in 1944, shortly after my birth—at the Polo Lounge, as it happened, spotting one another across a crowded room at a cocktail party. They had themselves a merry romp that lasted several years: love, laughter, and plenty of sex. But by the time I was old enough to bear witness to the tale, their ship, so to speak, sailed on stormy seas.

Max and my mother were the sort, of course, who enjoyed drama, the stormier the better. It's the curse of the Hollywood kind to prefer drama to peace of mind, and, as the years progressed, their affair took on an operatic quality, careening down a bumpy road of jealousy, imagined slights, misunderstandings, miscommunications, betrayals, and other miseries of the heart. They broke up every six months or so, always with a good deal of noise—shouting, tears, and often glasses of vodka flying across the room—only to reunite some weeks later, generally with an equal racket (more tears, vodka, flowers, and occasional bottles of French champagne).

Usually, it was Max who would break off the affair, unable to stand the strain. He yearned for what he liked to call "the simple life," the mythical existence he might have had if he'd never met my mother on the *Mauretania*.

"It's all too complicated, Sasha!" he would tell her miserably. "I can't work, I can't think, I can't sleep, I can't go on living this way!"

"Then *go!*" my mother would scream. "And don't bother coming back, because I don't ever want to see you again!"

Yet he'd be back sure as clockwork a few weeks later and they would have a jolly time making up. It's worth noting that he never offered to leave Mina—"she needs me," was his constant refrain, referring to her delicate psychological condition. My mother pretended to be hurt that Mina always came first, but in fact I don't believe she wanted Max to divorce his wife any more than he did. She enjoyed her independence far too much.

"Men are such fools, Jonno!" she would tell me merrily. "They can't look truth in the face. So we must give them little white lies!"

Naturally, I was exempt from this rule. I was treated to the unvarnished truth, she assured me, because I was special. Of course, I wasn't a man at all but rather her Little Man.

As for the unvarnished truth, this was a complicated matter due to the fact that my mother liked sex and she didn't see why she shouldn't have everything she wanted. Why be a Hollywood star otherwise?

And so, along with Max and Zachary, there were stray cowboys, tennis pros, oil tycoons, pool boys, and lusty leading men who occasionally paid visits to my mother's bedroom.

This entailed quite a bit of traffic up and down the stairs, which led to occasional problems. Unfortunately, romantic assignations can easily become confused when there's a gaggle of too many players on the field. Lovers can get their times wrong, their appointed slot, they can even show up unexpectedly without calling. But this is where I came in.

"Jonno," she would say, "would you be a darling and keep an eye out the window and let me know if you see a Rolls Royce pulling up the driveway?"

The Rolls in question, a 1949 Silver Cloud, belonged to Zachary Wise, the one lover who couldn't be crossed. I was glad to do her bidding, for these small tasks made me feel important; they guaranteed me a central place in her affections and they gave me a ringside seat to the drama.

"Mom, Zachary's here!" I would cry, pounding on her closed bedroom door. I remember one time hiding a half-clad saxophone player in my bedroom closet until Zachary had come and gone. I enjoyed playing my part. The only bit I minded in this instance was that the sax player chain-smoked cigarettes in my closet, fearful that he was going to be caught and beaten to a pulp, and for months afterwards all my clothes smelled of tobacco.

"Darling Jonno, promise me that we'll keep each other's secrets forever!" she made me swear. "You must promise that you'll always be my Little Man!"

An Almost Perfect Ending

Of course, I promised. I promised fervently, with all my heart. Even then, I suspected this wasn't the usual arrangement between mother and son, but I was flattered by her confidences, pleased that she couldn't do without me.

I'm a wiser man today. But at the time, I wouldn't have had it any other way.

*****

Once a year at Christmas, my mother and I were required to pay a formal call on Zachary Wise at his home, a gloomy old mansion that stood behind a high wall north of Sunset Boulevard. We were always on our best behavior during these visits, though my mother generally tanked up on vodka beforehand in order to get through the ordeal. I can't say I enjoyed the visits, but I knew they were necessary.

"Well, Jonno, how's school?" Zachary would ask, every year the same question, turning his focus my way for a moment or two.

"Oh, school's just fine, sir," I would answer, my annual lie.

"You're learning a lot, then?"

"You bet. English and Social Studies and Latin, all sorts of interesting things."

"Latin? Well, how about that! Say something in Latin for me, Jonno. I'd like to hear how those old Roman fellas used to talk."

35

The particular Christmas I'm remembering, I was still at Black Fox, a few months before I became a TV star. "*Per ardua ad astra*," I told him in all seriousness. "*In hoc signo vinces*."

"Which means?"

"Through adversity to the stars," I answered. "By this sign shall you conquer."

Both Latin phrases were from the front of the Pall Mall cigarette package, which is how I happened to know them. I'd begun smoking at an early age. But Zachary Wise was a nonsmoker so I guess I impressed him. After asking about school and sports and my life in general, he would reach for his wallet and give me a crisp hundred dollar bill, which was a lot of money for a kid back then, not the chicken change it is today. Still, I was never entirely easy with him, and I was always glad when my mother and I got in her car and drove home.

Then in 1954 something awful happened. Zachary Wise came down with a bad case of lung cancer. He was mortal, after all. He didn't smoke, he didn't drink, he swam thirty laps in his pool every morning, he was the first person I knew who ate only organic food. So it didn't seem fair. I suppose it was secondhand smoke that got him, having affairs with people like my mother who blew bad air his way.

"Can't they just put him in an iron lung?" I asked my mother. I knew about iron lungs because they were big back then due to polio. It seemed inconceivable to me that modern science in the futuristic year of 1954 couldn't solve such an elementary problem as human breath.

"I don't think an iron lung would help," my mother said thoughtfully. I'm sure she was weighing her own options, wondering what life would be like without Zachary as a protector. "The doctors say he has only six months to live."

I didn't like thinking about death, a subject we avoided in California. But then one Sunday, my mother said that Zachary was sinking fast and we needed to pay what might be our final visit to his home.

I tried to beg off. "Oh, Mom, please, I don't want to go!" I pleaded. "I mean, yuck, it's awful!"

"We have to go, darling." My mother scrunched her nose and made a cute face, which was one her strategies to get me to do what she wanted. "He's your godfather. Besides, maybe he'll leave you something in his will."

I hate to admit it, but the idea of "something in his will" lit my reptile brain with a faint flicker of interest, enough to overcome temporarily the distaste of death. So I dressed in my good blue suit and hideous red-and-gold striped tie and together we made our way to Sunset Boulevard a few blocks away.

Zachary's house was a faux-English country manor that sat on a hill at the end of a long driveway, a heavy, tomb-like place where every blade of grass was perfectly cut and the stillness was profound. As far as I was concerned, it already had the look of a home where the owner had died. My mother parked near a stone fountain with a statue of a naked little boy in the center who was peeing from his marble dick into the pool below. Quite disgusting, really.

"Mom, I think I'll wait in the car," I said.

"No, you won't!" she told me. Her eyes went hard, the pretty manner was gone, and she was determined to have her way.

Zachary's wife was a steely-eyed matron with a thick waist, a proud bosom, and gray hair that was starting to turn blue. She met us at the front door with an icy blast of disapproval and a scowl so fierce I would have turned and made a run for it if my mother hadn't been gripping my hand so tightly. It was easy to see why Zachary sought pleasures in other beds than his own. Officially, my mother was only an actress under contract in Zachary's studio, but I imagine Mrs. Wise had her suspicions. She literally raised her nose at the sight of us on her doorstep. Still, she knew her duty. With barely a word of greeting, she showed us into the living room and then allowed my mother upstairs to where the great man was dying.

"I need to talk to Zach alone for a few minutes, then I'll send for you," my mother whispered, giving my hand a squeeze before she climbed the stairs to the upper regions of the house.

An Almost Perfect Ending

Mrs. Wise lingered with me in the living room for a few minutes, probably to make sure I didn't steal the silver, but finally she left as well. Alone, I sat on a huge sofa and killed time by listening to the ticking of a grandfather clock from somewhere in the house. Tick-tock, tick-tock. Not exactly a fun afternoon.

I was half asleep some time later when an ancient butler came to take me upstairs. He led me down a long corridor to a closed door, and when I stepped inside, I was surprised to find Zachary and my mother in the middle of a quarrel.

"God damnit, Sasha, I'm through getting you out of jams!" Zachary was saying as I came into the edge of the room. I stopped in the shadows, half-hidden by a huge Chinese urn. "If you were dumb enough to get yourself arrested for whoring, you'll have to deal with this blackmailer yourself."

"But, Zach, it's a lie! I didn't do anything. I was sitting watching a movie, that's all, when this man sat down in the next seat and propositioned me. When I told him to go away, he got angry and said he was a policeman and I was under arrest. That's all that happened—I swear to you on my life, Zach. But now of course it's his word against mine."

"Oh, Sasha, please! If you're innocent, why have you been giving him money all this time?"

"Because I had to! If he goes to the papers with his story, who's going to believe me? Oh, Zach, and he keeps coming back saying he wants more and more to keep his mouth shut. I don't know what to do."

Zachary closed his eyes, momentarily too exhausted to answer. His bedroom was huge and gloomy and old-fashioned, like everything else in the house. There was a canopied bed at one end and a sitting room arrangement near the French doors that led to a small decorative balcony, not the sort of balcony anyone ever used. The walls were crowded with musty old paintings, dark scenes of virgins, satyrs, and half-naked people from another age.

Zachary was seated in a big armchair, dressed in a silk dressing gown with a throw rug over his lap, and he didn't look well. I was shocked by his appearance. He had always been a rugged, vital sort of man, but now he was shrunken and frail. His fabulous suntan was all that remained of his former self, a kind of brown-yellow smear that had survived the ravages of his disease. As for my mother, she was pacing nearby on an oriental carpet, too worked up to remain in one spot. Neither of them took any notice of my arrival.

"Sasha, Sasha!" he said at last wearily. "You should have come to me right away."

"I know, darling. But I didn't want to bother you when you're sick. And I was frightened. Even though none of it's true, I was afraid of what you'd say."

Zachary sighed and shook his head. "For chrissake, Sasha, sit down—you're making me dizzy with all your pacing. Now, tell me this guy's name again."

Dying of lung cancer, I can't imagine Zachary was thrilled to be confronted with this new problem from my mother's past, but he had always been her protector and he seemed resigned to continue that role now. The way Zachary ran his studio, he was more like a feudal lord than a businessman. That's how things worked back then in Hollywood, once upon a time. A town held together by allegiance and alliance.

"His name's Ricky Bolano," my mother answered, seating herself on the edge of an elaborately carved wooden chair that looked like a throne from some Germanic fairy tale. "He was a cop in New York, but now he calls himself a private eye. You must believe me, Zach. I'm absolutely innocent of this terrible thing he's saying."

"Sure, you are. So what do want me to do? Kill the jerk? Is that what you want, Sasha? Put out a contract on him?"

My mother studied Zachary intently. "A contract?" she repeated delicately. "Is that something . . . well, something you could *do*, Zach?"

He laughed soundlessly. "I'm not saying I can do it. I'm asking if that's what you *want* me to do?"

My mother kept staring at him. She didn't speak for a long moment. Her eyes seemed to narrow with a strange intensity I had never seen before.

"Yes," she said at last. "Oh, yes, kill him, Zach! You see, it's the only way. He's like a nightmare that won't go away. Oh, please, Zach. I'm terrified of this man. If you do this, I'll never ask anything else of you ever again. I swear I won't."

Zachary stared back at her. "For chrissake, Sasha! You're seriously asking me to have this guy whacked?"

She nodded slowly. "He beat me up, Zach. He's sucking me dry. Oh, darling, you can do this for me, can't you? You know people, I know you do. The sort of people who . . . well, *do* things like that. You just need to tell someone, and that someone will tell someone else, and no one will ever know. Please, Zach. It's the only way I'll ever be free."

Zachary gave a dry little laugh and closed his eyes. He looked tired. "Let me think about it," he told her. "Maybe I can come up with something. But it won't be until I get back from Denver at the end of the week. The premiere of *Rodeo* is Tuesday night."

"Denver? Zach, what the hell are you talking about? You can't go to Denver in your condition!"

"Sure, I can. I've got to. Anyway, I got my plane. All I gotta do is get myself driven to the airport and they'll meet at the other end. I'll be fine. And when I get back, I'll see what I can do about this Ricky idiot for you. Okay? I'm not promising anything, mind you."

"Oh, Zach! I'd be so grateful. But darling, please don't go to Denver. Can't you send someone in your place?"

"No, I can't send someone in my place," he answered grouchily. "No one can deal with all the crap except me. *Rodeo* cost me twenty million dollars and it has to be a hit or else, no two ways about it. I don't know what the hell's happened in this town, why everybody is so incompetent all of a sudden, a bunch of assholes. It never used to be like that."

Rodeo was Zach's new picture, a Technicolor extravaganza in a new big-screen format called Cinemascope that had been filmed almost entirely in Colorado, which was why the premiere was taking place in Denver rather than L.A. There was going to be a parade down the main street, a ton of reporters, all the stars were going to be there, a very big deal. Television was eating into movie profits in 1954, keeping families at home, and studio bosses like Zachary Wise were gambling that Cinemascope would lure audiences back into theaters. Television, of course, was seen as the enemy back then, a threat to the established order. Which was perhaps why Zachary at last turned his gaze my way, sensing my presence in the shadows of the room.

"So, Jonno, how are you?" he asked without enthusiasm.

"I'm fine, sir."

"Good, good . . . stay a while, Jonno, I want to have a word with you. Sasha, you go wait downstairs. We'll talk this weekend when I get back from Colorado."

One thing about being a studio boss, you can dismiss people whenever you like, even people like my mother. She kissed Zachary dutifully on both cheeks, which he endured with grumpy bad humor. Then she flashed me an inquiring look and left the room, leaving me alone with Zachary. He had never asked to speak to me alone before so I was mystified and nervous.

"Sit down, Jonno," he said when my mother had left. "Did I tell you? I saw that show of yours the other night, *The Good Life*."

"*What a Life!*" I corrected, taking a seat on the huge armchair that my mother had vacated.

"Whatever. Normally, I don't watch television, I hate that damn little box. It's going to destroy this town with smallness, just you wait and see. But I was curious to see you. Wanna know what I think?"

"Yes, sir."

"What I think is you should put your money in the bank and forget about acting. You're not cut out for it. You listening to me?"

I was listening, though I didn't much like what I was hearing. It wasn't that I thought I was a great actor. But I got plenty of fan mail, mostly from twelve-year-old girls who said I was terrific, and my own opinion was that I wasn't half-bad.

"It's not that you're terrible," he said, seeing my disappointment. "What it is, Jonno, you're not hungry enough. You don't care about it a hundred and ten percent. See what I'm saying? You don't live to be in front of a camera, and as long as you don't have that kind of drive, you're better off in another profession. Leave acting to the idiots who can't do anything else."

"Yes, sir." I nearly told him about my plans to be a rocket ship pilot, but I decided to keep that to myself, sensing he might nix it too.

"Remember what I'm telling you, Jonno. But that's not why I wanted to see you alone. I want to talk about your mother."

"My mother, sir?"

"Yeah. She's drinking too much and you're going to have to take care of her when I'm gone."

"You mean while you're in Denver, sir?"

"No. I mean gone-all-the-way-gone. Now, listen to me. Your mother is a wonderful woman, I love her to death. But she's spoiled and foolish and too damn tricky for her own good. If it hadn't been for me helping her, she wouldn't have gotten anywhere in this town. Sure, she's a looker and guys like that. But that'll only take you so far, and in a few years when her looks go, she'll be all washed up. She lives in a world of make-believe and that's fatal. Are you getting me?"

"I think so, sir," I answered, though I was confused. I had always thought make-believe was what Hollywood was all about.

He raised an instructive finger. "Fool the public, but never fool yourself. And above all, *never* believe the lies your press agent is saying about you. Remember my words, Jonno. You gotta keep your head in this town. You listening to me?"

"Yes, sir."

"Good. Now go to my bedside table and bring me the box that's there. I have a present for you."

I was glad we were getting down to more enjoyable matters. I liked presents, especially when I was on the receiving end of one. I stood and walked across the room and returned with a wooden box that I found on the bedside table. The box was dark and old, made of closely fitted slats that were of slightly different colors, all of it pieced together like a puzzle. It was rectangular, maybe eight inches long and four inches across, and it was heavier than it looked.

"Open it," Zachary told me.

I sat again in the chair and examined the box more closely, but I was stymied. There was no latch, no knob, no apparent way to open the thing. There wasn't even a seam to indicate a lid. I turned it upside down and examined it from every angle. I pushed on the top and on the bottom, but nothing moved. I couldn't see any way to get inside.

I looked up at Zachary and saw that he was smiling at me.

"Can't open it, huh?"

I shook my head.

"Well, keep trying," he told me.

I did as he said. I kept trying, but I couldn't get anywhere. The box had four slick surfaces that were all the same and it wouldn't open, no matter what I did. Finally I asked, "Is there a trick?"

"A trick?" he repeated. "I guess you could call it that. The trick is to be clever, just like you have to be in life. The trick is to be smarter than everybody else."

"But what's inside?"

His smile became cagey. "Naw, I'm not going to tell you. That would spoil the fun. Besides, I want to see how smart you are—and if you're *not* smart, then you're not getting anything. Not from me, anyway, because I don't like dumb people. So you'll have to figure out how to open the box or you'll never know what's there. Take it home and work on it. I'm betting you'll get it sooner or later. But maybe I've misjudged you."

I smiled back. "What if I just get a saw and cut it open?"

"No, I wouldn't do that. That would be cheating. And besides, you might destroy what's inside, and that would be a shame. Now, that's all I'm going to say on the subject, the rest is up to you. I'm tired and your mother's probably going crazy wondering what we're talking about, so you'd better get down to her. Make me proud, Jonno. I'm counting on you to take care of her. Don't let me down."

He insisted on kissing me goodbye. He kissed me on the lips, which I didn't much like—it wasn't like kissing Penny, that's for sure. But I endured it with good grace because I sensed that this goodbye was forever and I would never see Zachary Wise again.

*****

Two days later, Zachary's twin-engine Beechcraft crashed into the side of a 14,000 foot peak in the Rocky Mountains on a perfectly clear day, and he never got to Denver to see the premiere of his movie after all.

Pilot error, they said. And when they found the wreckage high in a snowy forest, they discovered it was Zachary who had been flying the plane. At the last moment, he had told the regular pilot to stay behind in L.A., saying he wanted some time alone, just him and the blue yonder. He had a pilot's license so this wasn't entirely out of the question, though it seemed odd that he should fly by himself when he was ill. Nothing was ever proved one way or another, but I've always had my suspicions that he simply decided to beat cancer to the punch. Zachary was a man who liked to be in charge. He would have wanted to meet death on his own terms, as he had done with life.

Financially speaking, the plane crash was a lucky break for his widow. With the publicity surrounding Zachary's death, and a big Hollywood funeral where all the A-List people came out, *Rodeo* ended up making huge amounts of money. I've always imagined that Zachary would have liked that, smiling down from the clouds.

As for myself, I kept Zachary's present, the wooden box, on a bookshelf in my bedroom where I forgot about it for a number of weeks, occupied with other matters. (Penny, Penny, Penny!) At first, my mother had been curious about the box, just like I was, but she couldn't open it either, and, in the end, we both decided it was probably only a joke, Zachary's odd sense of humor. He was crazy, after all, like all the other Hollywood tycoons of the time—Sam Goldwyn, L.B. Mayer, Daryl Zanuck, Jack Warner, all of them as eccentric as they pleased, back before movie studios became just like any other big corporation, with a CEO in charge rather than a god.

But Zachary's death left an unsettled impression, a feeling that life was a frightening business with a bad end, and I couldn't get him out of my mind. Where was he now? I wondered. Could he be out in space somewhere watching me? I became transfixed by his death, the mystification of it, the Big Questions that lay beyond our sunny California shore.

So finally I picked up the wooden box again and began to play with it, running my hands over every surface, as though it might provide some clue as to where Zachary had gone. It took me nearly three more weeks of fiddling before I got the box open. I came upon the answer in a purely accidental way, finding one of the closely fitted slats on the front that moved when I pushed it in a certain way. Suddenly the top sprang open. Just like my eyes did when I saw what was inside, Zachary's final present to me from the grave.

Inside the box, there was a gun wrapped up in a soft cloth. I knew what it was immediately from the shape, but it took another moment to unwrap the cloth and see exactly what I had—not just any pistol, but a silver .38 revolver with six silver bullets in the chambers, the sort of bullets the Lone Ranger used. I only discovered the caliber later, but I knew the gun was real when I picked it up and felt its solid weight.

But there was more.

Underneath the revolver, in a plain white envelope, there were twenty $500 bills with President William McKinley on the front, ten thousand dollars in all. My arithmetic was never very good, so I had to count the bills several times to be sure. It was an astonishing sum.

Zachary had written a few words on the back of the envelope in a spidery hand:

"Dear Jonno, put this away for a rainy day because life is a crap shoot and you never know. Z."

And that was it. Ten thousand dollars and a pistol with silver bullets. A crazy present from my crazy Godfather Zach.

The gun fascinated me and I spent a few hours pointing it at imaginary bad guys and saying bang-bang. I hadn't heard of Chekhov yet, or his famous rule about storytelling: that in any drama, when a gun appears in Act One, it needs to go off by the end of the play. But I felt something portentous as I held it in my hand. The power it had. Its potential to change the world in an instant.

Once I'd finished saying bang-bang to bad guys, I put the wooden box away with the gun and the money inside on the farthest shelf high up in the very back of my closet, out of sight, out of mind. I didn't tell my mother. I didn't tell anyone, not even Penny, and generally I told Penny everything.

I liked having a secret, and whenever I thought about the gun and the money, I felt a small thrill knowing what was hidden in my closet: the power to buy, and the power to kill, which is a potent combination.

It made me feel like a boy in charge.

And the rainy day did in fact come. Only it wasn't a day, but rather a night: a dark and stormy night that was waiting just two years away.

Four

Sasha often said she'd kill for a good night's sleep. But sleep eluded her, that simple, natural, healing thing.

Nothing helped, not vodka, nor pills, not even an athletic tumble in bed with whichever passing cowboy or sax player was in favor at that moment. Her mind kept ticking no matter what, whether it was three o'clock, four o'clock in the morning, hatching plans, worrying. Her mind refused to quit.

She had suffered from insomnia before, but the curse of sleeplessness got worse after Zachary's death. Often she fell asleep right away only to wake an hour later, dry mouthed and anxious, with the ghostly specter of memories and regrets swarming around her bed. She had begun to dread the night, the long hours. The only rest came in the morning, after the sun had risen, after she had worn herself out. As a result, she began sleeping later and later into the day, sometimes well into the afternoon, waking with a logy feeling that life had passed her by.

Among Sasha's worries, Ricky Bolano was still at the top of the list. It appeared that Zachary had kept his promise and had dealt with Ricky before his plane had crashed, but Sasha couldn't be sure. That was the terrible thing. Zach had left no word of what he'd done, if anything, and she didn't know. She had given Ricky a thousand dollars a week after the terrible night at Ciro's—money, I discovered later, that she had taken from my bank account—and she hadn't heard from him since then. Sometimes, trying to fall asleep at night, she visualized Ricky with a cement block chained to his leg at the bottom of the ocean, his body undulating in the currents as fish swam by. It was a pretty picture. But Ricky had left her alone before, sometimes for six months at a time, and doubts continued to nag at her.

Then there was the equally disturbing question of her career, which had begun a downward slide even before Zachary's death.

You'd think that once you became a star, that would be the end of it. A guaranteed happy ending. But Hollywood wasn't like that and by 1954 everything Sasha had worked for was in danger of slipping away. It wasn't one particular thing. She sang as well as she had ever sung before. Even her good looks were holding up, as far as the paying public could see, with only a small amount of wear and tear. But it was a new decade and fashions had changed. In California everything old was pushed aside and no one cared anymore for the songs of the 1940s. More worrisome still, there was a new crop of pretty girls younger than herself who were demanding their moment of fame.

As long as Zachary had been alive, he had been able to shield her from these hard facts. With a single phone call, he could get her a week in Vegas at the Sands, or a cameo in a picture, or a new contract with a record company. But now he was gone it seemed to Sasha that he had taken all her good luck with him to the grave.

Six months after Zachary's death, Sasha found herself so worried about money that she was considering raiding my savings account again in order to pay a number of bills. She owed money all over town—to the grocers on Roxbury Drive, the cleaners on North Canon, the liquor store on Doheny, a bar bill at the Brown Derby, her hairdresser at Elizabeth Arden, on and on. She even owed two weeks salary to Claire, the maid, and had been forced to reduce Claire's hours to three days a week.

Sasha was astonished how much money was needed to run a Beverly Hills household. No one gave away anything for free, that was for sure. And where would the money come from if she couldn't sleep, couldn't work, and no one cared that she was a girl with poetry in her eyes?

For Sasha, these anxieties swirled around her like a cloud of mosquitoes, making it hard even to think. Somehow she needed to come up with a Grand Plan. A single role in a picture and she could get herself back on a solid footing. Even a stint at the Sands or the Macombo would be a considerable help. But a week arrived when she had no work at all. She didn't have a thing to do with herself, not even a rehearsal, until the following Thursday when she had a four-day stint at the Biltmore Hotel in Santa Barbara.

An Almost Perfect Ending

The Biltmore was a fine hotel, very posh, and she would be given a suite with a view of the ocean during her stay. Still, to sing in the lounge of a hotel . . . in Santa Barbara! For Sasha, these facts alone made her situation depressingly clear. There was only one bright spot in her calendar. Later that summer, in July, she was scheduled to tour the country. She and her band would travel in a bus for nearly two months, crisscrossing their way up and down America, west to east.

In past years, her tours had included only the largest venues in major cities. This summer she was set to perform at state fairs and small towns, many with names she didn't know. This was a disappointment, yet it seemed to her there might be an opportunity here in disguise. Americans liked the expression "grass roots." Personally, Sasha preferred palm trees if one must have vegetation, but in this case a grass roots tour of America might be just the thing to give her career a boost.

"All I have to do is hold out until July," she told herself firmly.

And perhaps raid Jonno's bank account to cover just a few temporary embarrassments.

*****

Sasha was plotting her course one afternoon, pacing her bedroom with a cigarette in hand when her phone rang. It was

Sol Weintraub, her manager, calling to suggest that she stop by his office the following day.

"Why, of course, darling!" she replied with a gush of enthusiasm. Sol never called these days unless there was money involved. She was certain he had good news for her. A job, a record deal, maybe even a movie.

"Let's make it two o'clock, shall we?"

"Oh, yes, Saul! Yes!"

She put down the receiver with a familiar glow spreading through her body, the radiance of being a winner on life's fabulous playing field. Everything was going to work out after all!

Sasha drank too much, she couldn't sleep, she lived a jaded life in a jaded town. But at heart, she had never lost her innocence. Despite everything, she remained a true believer in her own fairy tale: that life could change in an instant with a phone call. Or perhaps a chance meeting with a stranger on a bench.

"You know what? I'm not going to drink tonight!" she told herself, flushed with purpose. "Not a drop! I want to be fresh for Sol!"

It was a bold promise. And in fact, she nearly succeeded. She waited until ten o'clock before pouring herself just one small glass of vodka. And then one more, because the first had been so small. And finally another, because she really needed to sleep tonight in order to look her best tomorrow, and she was certain that vodka was better than pills.

She told herself that liquor was only a temporary measure for a girl whose nerves were shot. But once Sol told her his good news, it would provide just the push she needed to go on the wagon for good.

*****

Sol's office was on the Sunset Strip not far from Schwab's, on the ground floor of a mock-Tudor building with heavy wooden beams. At ten minutes to three on the following afternoon, fifty minutes late, Sasha passed through the reception area, smiled frenetically at Sol's middle-aged secretary, Ruth, and went quickly into the inner office.

"Sol! Darling!" she cried brightly, doing her best imitation of a woman without a care.

Sol Weintraub was a dignified Jewish gentleman with a sad, thoughtful manner, kind eyes, and a fuzzy shock of gray hair. He stood from his desk, impeccably dressed in a dark suit, and greeted Sasha with a kiss on the cheek.

"Good to see you, Sonya!" He always called her Sonya, shunning the informality of her nickname. He took her hand and gave it a friendly squeeze. "Sit, sit," he said, indicating an armchair that faced his desk. Sol's office was comfortably old-fashioned, cluttered with papers and books on every surface. "And how is Jonathan?"

"Jonno's marvelous," she told him. "I'm so proud of that boy. They're giving him bigger and bigger parts on his show. And how's Dwight?"

Dwight was Sol's son, a priggish little monster with pimples who always spoke to Sasha in sarcastic tones. He was in his second year at Stanford and it was obligatory to spend a few minutes pretending interest. It always amazed Sasha how in Hollywood you had to act as though you were having such wonderful fun that business was only a secondary matter.

"I'm so glad you suggested a meeting," she said once the preliminary fluff was behind them. "Because I've had the most wonderful idea for the summer tour, Sol. What if we convince Capitol to release a live recording? It could be called 'Sonya Saint-Amant Sings to the Heartland.' Capitol can send along an engineer and whatever equipment they need. It will be less expensive than recording in L.A., and audiences love live performances, the spontaneity of it. Sol, I just feel in my bones that this is exactly what I need to give my career a boost!"

Sol listened thoughtfully, nodding from time to time, holding the palms of his hands together close to his mouth, as though he were praying.

"Hmmm, well, a live recording," he said, when Sasha's gushing came to a momentary pause. "Yes, I can see what you're saying. The problem is Capitol didn't make money on your last two albums, Sonya. And, in fact, our contract with them lapsed two months ago and they didn't wish to renew. I think I told you this at the time."

"Yes, yes . . . but I'm sure they'll be interested in a concert performance. I was thinking I'd sing all my great old tunes, maybe even a new arrangement of 'I Believe in Tomorrow.' "

Sol nodded sadly. "Yes, well, I don't know what to say. Look, my dear, I wish there were an easy way to tell you this, but the reason I suggested this meeting today is that the tour is off. You see, we've had to cancel."

Sasha's smile remained frozen on her face. She wasn't certain she had heard correctly.

"But we're all set for July . . . July eleventh, isn't it? Santa Rosa is the first date, I believe."

"No, no, listen, that's what I'm trying to tell you. The whole thing is off. I'm sorry, but it's been cancelled, Sonya."

She couldn't speak at first, only stare in bewilderment. "But we're all set," she repeated. "I've even found a place for Jonno. He has a six-week break from his show so Mina's going to take him to New York. The tour can't be off!"

Sol kept shaking his head mournfully. "You see, the ticket sales just weren't there, my dear. This wasn't my decision, I assure you. It's the venues, they're the ones backing out. They didn't see how they were going to make any money."

"But of course the ticket sales aren't there!" Sasha was suddenly angry. "It's still nearly three months away. Who buys tickets for a concert three months in advance?"

"Like I said, this isn't my decision. There's just a sense that you don't have an audience these days. It's nothing personal. It's 1954, Sonya. People want a new kind of music, that's all. They want rock and roll. You're considered . . . well, old-fashioned."

"But this new music, it's awful!" Sasha complained. "It makes me want to put cotton in my ears!"

"Personally, I couldn't agree more. I can't stand that music, it's just a lot of noise as far as I'm concerned. But all the venues, it's what they want. They want music the kids can dance to."

"Sol! Six months from now, no one will want this rocking and roll. It's only a passing phase!"

"Sonya, the Charleston was a passing phase. So was the waltz. These things come and go and you have to be philosophical. After rock and roll, there'll be something else. But it'll be something new, it won't be like the music from the nineteen-forties. That's all done with now. You have to understand the times, Sonya. This is a country that only wants what's new."

Sasha felt a haze of anger and depression engulf her. She wished Sol would offer her a drink.

"But Sinatra, Crosby . . . I could name plenty of singers from the Forties who still sell records."

"Yes, of course. But these are performers with a huge following. Plus, they have their movie careers. You've never had that kind of big career, Sonya. You didn't really make it in the movies. I don't know how to put this to you to make it any easier, but you can count yourself lucky you had ten good years in show business. That's more than most people ever get. Meanwhile, you're still a young woman. Get married, Sonya, that's my advice to you. Find yourself a nice man. Put this crazy business behind you."

Sasha stared at him coldly. "You're saying I'm finished?"

"Let me be honest with you. Sure, I'll be able get you jobs for a couple more years. But they won't be good jobs. A few nights in the lounge of some hotel. Maybe a week now and then in Nevada—but it won't be Vegas, it'll be Reno. That's what we're talking about here, Sonya."

Sasha put a cigarette to her lips and Sol quickly brought out his lighter. "The band is going to be disappointed," she said blowing smoke.

"Don't worry about them. Buddy and the boys already have a new tour lined up with some kid. I think he's seventeen years old."

Sasha laughed bleakly. "Well, that's loyalty for you!"

"Honey, I keep telling you, it's nothing personal. Show business is a hard business, that's a fact. Now there's one more thing I have to tell you, and you're not going to like this either. On Friday I had some guy from the FBI come in and ask about you. He wanted to know what your political leanings are, if you're a Red."

For Sasha, it was as though a horse had kicked her.

"The FBI?"

"Yes, that's what I said. Naturally, I told them you weren't political, not in the least. But I just wanted to warn you, that's all. They, uh . . . well, they were particularly interested in your friendship with Max McCormick. Look, Sonya, if I can give you some advice, lay off seeing Max for a while. You know, I've never interfered with your personal life, but this relationship is going to hurt you. Everyone knows Max is pink. And if he ends up getting blacklisted, people will start thinking you must be pink too. So be smart, Sonya, and keep your distance."

Sasha puffed on her cigarette, overwhelmed. It was too much to absorb all at once, her tour cancelled, the FBI asking questions about her. And now Max . . . no, she didn't believe it!

She stood abruptly to her feet. "Find me a song, Sol."

"I'm sorry?"

"All I need is one good song. That's what made me in the first place. I need another song like 'I Believe in Tomorrow,' a beautiful ballad. Surely you can find me one goddamn great song, Sol. That's all I need, and everything will be fine again."

Sol rose to his feet, shaking his head. "Well, I'll try, Sonya. But it's not so easy."

"I don't care if it's not easy. None of it's ever been easy. Goddamn it, do you think I've come this far to give up now?"

"All right, my dear," he said softly, looking down at his desk. "I said I'll try, and I will."

"And one more thing. Max McCormick isn't a Red. That's just plain ridiculous!"

Sol raised his eyes and looked at her sadly. "Oh, Sonya, Sonya. Of course he's not a Red. None of them who are getting blacklisted are Reds. That's just an excuse."

"An excuse for what?"

Sol could only shake his head. "Who the hell knows? I wish I could tell you."

Sasha turned and marched quickly from Sol's office. She managed to hold off her tears until she was inside her car in the parking lot behind the building. Then she wept bitterly, her head bent over the steering wheel.

The world was so difficult she couldn't bear it. She knew she had to fight back, but for the moment the forces gathered against her appeared so overwhelming she didn't know where to start.

Five

Driving back into Beverly Hills along the Sunset Strip, Sasha passed a billboard with the heads of Grace Kelly and Jimmy Stewart towering like gods high above the traffic. It was an advertisement for *Rear Window*, a new Hitchcock picture that had only been out a week and was already a huge hit.

It didn't seem fair that Grace Kelly should have such luck to be a big star when she came from a wealthy family and didn't need the money. Lots of men had told Sasha that she was prettier by far than Grace Kelly. So why wasn't *she* on that billboard above Sunset Boulevard? Why wasn't it *Rear Window* with James Stewart and Sonya Saint-Amant?

Sasha had never understood why her movie career had fizzled after her initial success. After *Underground*, Zachary had put her in the lead role in a romantic comedy, *The Blonde Next Door*, but the picture had bombed with audiences and critics alike. Ironically, Sasha was a perfectly convincing actress in ordinary life, but on screen she came off as patently false. Over the next few years, Zachary had given her several smaller roles until finally calling her into his office one day to suggest she concentrate on singing and leave motion pictures alone.

But that was years ago, and she had learned since then. She saw now what she'd done wrong, declaiming lines in a stilted operatic style as though she were on stage. In pictures, you only had to whisper and the microphone picked up every small nuance. She understood this now. If only she had another chance, she was certain she could be a success.

But who would give her that chance?

Max! she thought. They had been fighting, she couldn't remember why, but now the memory of him came rushing back, his face, his smile, his gentle humor. Surely, Max would give her a role! One good movie and the world would fall in love with her all over again, just as it had eleven years ago.

She had never asked Max for help before, and she was certain he would do it. Max loved her. Max wouldn't let her down. And wouldn't it be fun to work together?

Sasha was thinking Max . . . Max was the answer to everything! . . . when she remembered the cause of their most recent quarrel. Max had heard a rumor that Sasha was having an affair with Victor Mature, the actor—absolutely untrue, as it happened, there had only been a small flirtation at a party. But she and Max had both been drinking and the quarrel got nasty fast. He had called her a slut, she had slapped him, and finally with a good deal of shouting, he had stomped out of the house.

Two days later, she had received a note from Max apologizing for his harmful words. But the tone was coldly formal and he suggested they didn't see one another for a while. She had been glad and sorry, all at the same time, for by 1954 she loved Max and despised him in equal measure.

Sasha was pondering these matters with such intensity as she drove home on Sunset Boulevard through Beverly Hills, that she clipped the rear bumper of the car in front of her as she was making a left turn onto her street. The jolt wasn't hard, but it was enough to bring her back sharply into the present. Unfortunately, there was a motorcycle cop in the opposite lane who had seen the small collision and he gestured for her to pull over.

"*Merde*!" she swore, reverting to the long-ago French of her childhood. This was all she needed, a ticket and possibly an expensive repair bill. Sasha made her calculation quickly. There was a grass divider separating her from the policeman and he would need to continue east in the wrong direction for at least another block before he could make a U-turn and come after her. Sasha didn't hesitate. She gunned her Cadillac and sped down North Maple Drive, determined to get away. It was a purely instinctive reaction to danger, an overwhelming desire to escape.

She raced down the quiet tree-lined street, aware of a siren following in the distance. Luckily, the street was empty of traffic and she didn't have far to go, only a block and a half to her house. She made a dangerously fast turn into her drive-way, left the engine running as she ran to open the wrought-iron gate, then drove on through into the backyard and closed the gate behind her. She'd always been good in a crisis, knowing what to do, and she was pleased with herself. But she was glad there was no one at home to see her. Jonno was at the studio, Claire had the day off.

Flushed with adrenalin, Sasha kicked off her high heels and walked across the lawn to the swimming pool. Impulsively, she hiked up her dress, pulled off her nylon stockings, and sat at the edge of the pool with her bare feet dangling in the water.

Sasha was enormously proud of her swimming pool, though she hardly ever swam in it. The pool always made her think of her darling Julka, how delighted he would have been to see it. What a laugh they would have if he were here! Of course, Julka wouldn't actually swim in the pool either. Glamorous though they were, swimming pools just weren't a very Polish sort of thing.

"Oh, Julka!" she said aloud, dispiritedly. "Look at me!" It seemed to Sasha that she had come so far, and yet nothing had changed in the least. Here she was still struggling to outwit the world, running from danger as fast as she was able.

She found a cigarette from her handbag, lit the end with her lighter, and exhaled across the turquoise waters of her pool. It had been fun getting away from the policeman; she had enjoyed her small triumph. But now her problems came crowding back.

Sasha was frowning intently behind her dark glasses, sitting at the edge of the pool with her feet in the water, when she heard a sound behind her. She turned and was startled to see a motorcycle cop walking up the driveway into her backyard.

She hadn't escaped after all.

The policeman was dressed in dark blue with high black leather boots that came nearly to his knees. He was young and good-looking in an oversized, beefy sort of way. Unfortunately, there was a huge revolver on his hip and he didn't look amused.

"You're in big trouble, lady," he said as he came closer.

Impulsively, Sasha slipped into the water and paddled out to the middle of the pool. It was a foolish thing to do, but the stress of the last few days had made her giddy and she didn't care.

"Hey, get out of there!" he told her. "You're going to jail, lady. Do you know how many laws you broke? Leaving the scene of an accident, evading arrest. And that's just for starters.

"I'm a bad girl, Officer," she taunted. "And if you want me, you'll have to come and get me."

"Get out of that pool right now! You're only making it worse for yourself."

She splashed water at him. "Don't you know who I am? I'm famous. I'm Sonya Saint-Amant."

"I don't care if you're Rin Tin Tin. Now, get out of that pool!"

She laughed and undid the button at the back of her dress. "Want me to take my clothes off? I bet you do. I know what you boys are like."

She lifted her dress over her head and let it float off soggily on the surface the water.

"What the hell are you doing? You stop that now!" he told her.

"The water's fine, Officer. Come on in, why don't you. I won't tell, honest."

She took off her slip slowly and then her bra, making a show of it.

The young policeman glowered at her, his hands on his hips. "Put that back on! I'm not going to tell you another time!"

But Sasha knew she had him hooked. She saw the look in his eye. Men couldn't resist her, that was a fact. She had known this from the time she was twelve years old. It had always been her best card to play.

"You know something? You're very handsome, Officer," she told him in her sexy little girl voice, a completely phony construct that never failed to arouse. "You could be a movie star, I bet. I could help you get a screen test. If you're nice to me."

But he shook his head and refused to play.

"This might surprise you, lady, but no, I don't want a screen test. And I sure don't want to screw some broad who used to be famous back when I was a kid. Now, I'll tell you what. Get out of the pool and I'll overlook the last few minutes. Okay? Just so that neither one of us is embarrassed when we get to the station."

Sasha stared at him in disbelief. No man had ever turned her down before. *A broad who used to be famous back when I was a kid!* She forced a laugh, as though she didn't care, but her cheeks burned with humiliation. As the officer stood watching, she gathered her wet clothes from where they were half-floating nearby, covered her breasts, and climbed out of the pool.

He felt sorry for her, that was the worst of it. She walked past him with averted eyes, but she felt his pity. He was even more embarrassed than she was.

He let her change into dry clothes and fix her hair before he called for a squad car to take her away. That was decent of him, she supposed. She knew from experience that cops could be worse. But riding in the back seat to the police station in the basement of the Beverly Hills City Hall, she had a sense of déjà vu so complete it was like being caught in a loop of film that was destined forever to circle round and round.

Here she was again riding off to jail, the girl who always got it wrong.

An Almost Perfect Ending

At the police station, she was photographed, fingerprinted, booked, and told she could make a single phone call. But that presented a new problem.

Who was this one person she might call? Who would help her?

There wasn't anyone. Zachary was dead, Max was angry at her for flirting with Victor Mature, Sol believed she was washed up. She couldn't think of a single person who wouldn't be embarrassed to receive her call. No one who would help willingly, without question, without judgment.

It wasn't until she was being led down the hall toward the jail cell that she remembered the card with the private number that Jonno had brought home from Paramount ages ago.

Fred! she thought, frowning intently.

Could Fred help her? Was it possible? On the *Mauretania*, Fred Landson had been the road not taken, and here he was again. The practical choice she had shunned for a more romantic go with Max.

And what had *that* gotten her?

Fred was a Congressman now. Fred was rich. And Fred still carried a torch for her after all these years. Sasha ticked off these attributes like wishes on a list.

Wasn't it funny how life kept backing up to give you one more chance at the lessons you had never learned?

Six

I should have been paying more attention to the wreck my mother was making of our lives. But I had other worries just then and I took my eye off the ball. My darling Penny was slipping away and I could barely think about anything else.

It was age that defeated me, the simple bad luck of time. I was still eleven, struggling to catch up and become twelve, while Penny was now a precocious fourteen. There was nothing I could do to close the gap that was widening between us.

My immediate problem was the handsome sixteen-year-old idiot who had whisked Penny away from me at lunch that day on Stage 17. I knew his name by now—Bobby Bradshaw—and I had met him, too. Not only was he good-looking, he was smooth and easy and so self-confident that he deigned to be friendly toward me. "Jon-Jon," he called me, for some reason of his own. He seemed to find me amusing. He was everything that I was not. Worst of all, he had a driver's license and a fabulous car. How could I compete?

Bobby was the son of a big shot executive at Paramount, and he seemed to think this gave him the right to come swaggering onto our set whenever he felt like it. One Friday afternoon, I overheard him invite Penny to go surfing with him that weekend at Malibu, and to my dismay, she said yes. He smirked and strutted and said he'd pick her up in his jalopy, a

'48 Chrysler Town and Country convertible with woodie sides and white sidewall tires, which was about as cherry as cars got back then. My shoulders slumped, my world turned dark, and I knew I was doomed.

I didn't lose Penny all at once, but in slow motion, a gradual fade-out in which I struggled hopelessly to hold on to what I couldn't have. It was like trying to keep water from leaking through your fingers. Some days she seemed just the same as before, my best friend and naughty playmate. But other days her eyes glazed over when she saw me and I was left behind in the cold wake of her disinterest.

There is no sorrow so momentous as the first time your heart is broken, and it left me blind to other matters. So I wasn't prepared for the note I found when I came home from the studio on a Thursday night in April, my soul crushed, my eyes lowered.

I stumbled inside the front door so deep in misery that it was several minutes before I discovered that my mother wasn't home despite the fact that her car was in the driveway.

"Mom?" I called. I walked upstairs to her bedroom, but she wasn't there. She wasn't upstairs, or downstairs, or in the backyard, or any place I looked. I supposed someone could have come by to pick her up and take her to a picture or a party. She didn't always keep me up to date with her plans. Yet a tingle of concern wiggled through my brain. Something didn't feel right.

I didn't find the note for another fifteen minutes, not until I went downstairs to the kitchen to make myself a peanut butter sandwich. The note was waiting on the kitchen table.

"Jonno darling don't worry but they're taking me to the station," I read in my mother's free-form scrawl. "Nothing serious only a car accident, nobody hurt. I'm fine just wait for me at home. XXXXXX, Mom."

I studied the note in dismay, doing my best to parse the information. Which station? I wondered. What sort of car accident? I couldn't even be sure who the "they" were who had taken her to this unspecified place.

As I stood baffled with the note in hand, I heard the phone ring in the den downstairs. I made a dash from the kitchen and picked up on the fourth ring. It was my mother.

"Mom!" I exploded. "What's going on?"

"Jonno, listen carefully because they're only letting me make one phone call. I need you to be very grown up and do something important for me. I want you to call Congressman Landson. You remember Fred, don't you? You met him when he came on your show and he gave you a card with his private number on it."

"Mom—"

"Just listen, darling. The card's in the drawer by my bedside table, and I need you to phone and tell him that I'm in a small jam with the police. A silly misunderstanding, really. But if he could talk to the officers here and explain what really happened and convince them to drop the charges, I'd be very appreciative. That's the phrase I want you to use. *Very* appreciative. He can interpret that as he wants."

"Mom!" I cried. "You're in *jail*?"

"I told you, it's only a silly misunderstanding. I was making a left turn from Sunset when I brushed against some little car. Honestly, I barely dented the rear end, such a small thing I didn't notice. I had just come from seeing Sol and my mind was on other matters. So I kept driving—in absolute innocence, I swear, Jonno! But now they're saying I left the scene of an accident. That's what I want you to tell Fred. That it's all just such a silly mistake, something I'm sure an important person like him can fix with a single phone call. Tell him I'm at the Beverly Hills police station. And remember to say I'll be *very* appreciative."

I absorbed this information in silence, working my way through the fibs and evasions. I couldn't imagine how you could dent the rear end of the car ahead of you without noticing you'd been in a collision. But I could see the line she was taking and I thought it might be a good one. My problem with the strategy was Fred. It was maybe six or seven months since he had been a guest on my show, summoning me into the back of his limousine for a chat, but I remembered too well how creepy he was.

"Mom, I don't think Fred's a good idea," I said. "Isn't there somebody else I can call? What about Sol?"

"No, darling. Just do as I say. You know how cops are. They're not going to listen to Sol. They don't like people in show business. They're jealous, you see. We make so much more money than they do. Our lives are big and grand while theirs are small and boring. So when they have us in their clutches, even if it's for just the tiniest thing, they squeeze you for everything they can get. But they can't do that with a Congressman. They'll listen to Fred. They'll do what he tells them."

I could tell that my mother had done some thinking about this, but I still believed she was making a mistake.

"But, Mom, Fred's weird," I objected. "And he's stuck on you in some creepy way. If you give him any encouragement, he won't go away."

"Jonno, believe me, I can take care of Fred Landson!" She tittered briefly at the thought, that a man like that couldn't be handled by a woman like her. "Look, it was silly that I wasn't paying better attention to the road. But accidents happen and Fred is the best person to help. Now, I have to go, darling. But I'm trusting you to do this for me. You have to be my Little Man."

I put down the receiver hard. Slammed isn't exactly the word, but I was momentarily fed up with my role as Little Man.

What about *my* life? I wondered. Didn't I have the right to have a crisis too? Meanwhile, I hated to think of my mother in

76

jail but I didn't think Congressman Landson was the answer. It wasn't just that Fred was a weird guy with a fake hand that he kept hidden beneath a black glove. His real hand had been shot off in the war, so I guess that wasn't his fault. But there was something else I couldn't quite put a name to that bothered me more, a feeling that we would regret it if my mother gave Fred even the smallest opening into our lives.

I paced around the house and thought about these matters as hard as I could. The main point, of course, was to get my mom out of jail as quickly as possible. But I didn't know the best course of action. And I didn't want to make a mistake.

Still undecided, I wandered up to my mother's room and searched her bedside table for the card I'd given her with Fred's phone number on it. I found the card in the drawer where she told me it would be, but the sight of it brought back too clearly the afternoon when I'd sat next to him drinking Dad's Old Fashioned Root Beer on the dove gray upholstery of his limousine. The guy was definitely spooky.

I lit one of my mother's cigarettes from her bedside table. I'd been smoking on and off for years, though I didn't inhale—that treat was waiting in my future. Nevertheless, holding a burning cigarette in my hand made me feel grown-up. And I needed that now, since grown-up things were expected of me.

I thought and thought. And in the end, I didn't phone Congressman Fred Landson as my mother had asked me.

I took fate into my own hands and caused it to bend in a different direction.

Seven

It was a very different sort of jail than the one where she had spent a night in New York City in 1943.

That jail had been full of noisy women—whores, drunks, drug addicts, twenty or more in a single holding cell, some of them vomiting in the corners. It had frightened Sasha half to death back when she was seventeen years old, freshly arrived in America. Or had she been nineteen then? Twenty-two, more likely. Sasha had gone through so many made up ages, she couldn't keep track any more of how old she'd really been.

This jail eleven years later in Beverly Hills was different: five clean cells all in a neat row, each with a bench and a wash basin and a locked door with bars leading out to a long corridor. The cells clearly weren't designed for long stays—serious criminals, not many in Beverly Hills, most likely were transferred quickly to the L.A. Sheriff's Department downtown. But these were cages nevertheless, no way out, and what Sasha felt most was the eerie quiet. There was only one other inmate in the entire place, a man in a wrinkled suit two cells away. She could see him through the bars asleep on his bench and hear the monotonous rhythm of his snoring. The sound added somehow to the sense of endless waiting.

Sasha sat primly on her hard wooden bench, her back against the jail bars as the slow minutes passed. It seemed forever since she had spoken to Jonno. An hour? Two hours? The jail had no windows to the outside world so there was no reference point, no way to know. They had taken her wristwatch at the main desk outside, along with her personal belongings. They had done that in New York City, too, and they had stolen her money. Sasha wondered if that would happen here as well.

She felt numb and bored and helpless. Like she was a child again and had never been a famous star. It had all been a dream, perhaps, because here she was again, the real her: Sonja Wojtkiewicz, the girl who always ended up getting into trouble.

"Hey! Who the hell are you?" a voice demanded. "You look familiar."

It was the man two cells away. He was awake now, peering through the bars at her. He was dressed in a tan suit that looked as though it might have once been expensive, but his tie was askew and he sounded drunk. "I said, who the hell are you?" he repeated belligerently.

She glared at him briefly then turned away without answering.

"Hey, you're that sexpot, aren't you? The one who's always getting into a jam?"

He'd pegged her perfectly. The sexpot who was always getting into a jam. But she still didn't answer.

"I'm a famous writer," he told her. "I wrote *Gone With the Wind*."

She snorted with derision. Like everyone else in Hollywood, Sasha knew that writers were lower than toads in a swamp. They had silly big egos, but they didn't count.

"You didn't write *Gone With the Wind*," she told him. You're not Mary Mitchell."

"Margaret Mitchell," he corrected. "You're not very bright, are you? Good thing you're sexy."

She sighed and looked away again, hoping he would shut up. Where was Fred? she wondered. Why hadn't he come for her? Or sent someone. That would be all right, too. Someone from his office. Someone with the power to get her out of this place.

More endless minutes dragged by. The writer two cells away continued to stare at her in owlish silence and Sasha tried to ignore him.

"Anyway, I didn't write the book, I wrote the movie," he told her, continuing his thought. "You saw the movie, didn't you? I was hot shit for a while. Big money. I had a house with a swimming pool. Gable and me, we were pals. We used to go out drinking together. But then he dropped me, I don't know why."

"Shut up!" she told him. She couldn't stand it anymore, listening to a drunk has-been writer through the bars of a jail cell. "Just shut up and leave me alone!"

"Okay, okay. No need to get on your high horse. Christ almighty, you'd think you were somebody. But you're not. You're nobody at all."

Sasha did her best to tune him out, but she felt him staring at her and it was disconcerting.

"You ever read *War and Peace*?" he asked after a while. "I wrote that, too. The book, I mean. L.B. Mayer brought me to Hollywood to do the screenplay, but the picture got bogged down in bullshit. Know what I mean? They ruined my beautiful story, and that's why I became a lush. But I'm not finished yet, not by a long shot. I'm going to write another book and it's going to be even better than the first. I'm going to call it *Anna Karenina*."

Sasha groaned and stretched out on the bench on her side, closing her eyes and covering her ears with her hands. She couldn't stand it anymore, to be trapped in this Hollywood version of hell.

Oh, Fred, come save me! she prayed. *Why aren't you here?*

But no one came and time seemed to slow to a stop. In the tedium of her jail cell, Sasha hugged her knees and fell sleep.

*****

She was still asleep, curled on her side in a fetal position, when she was woken by the sound of her cell door clanging open.

"Someone's here for you," said a policeman. Sasha sat up groggily and found an elderly officer studying her in a not unkindly way. He had white hair and a big stomach that dropped over his belt. He looked harmless, more like somebody's grandfather than a cop. "Please come with me, Miss Saint-Amant."

"Thank, God!" she muttered. Sasha didn't know how long she had been asleep, but Fred was here at last and she was getting out. She followed the grandfatherly policeman from her cell down the hallway. The writer, whoever he was, was no longer there and she wasn't certain if she had only imagined him. But it didn't matter. She was getting out.

Walking from the jail toward the front desk and lobby, Sasha tried to prepare herself for Fred, putting the right expression on her face and rehearsing what she would say. "Oh, Fred, darling, thank God you're here! It's incredible, the incompetence of these awful people! Of course, I would have stopped if I'd known I'd been in an accident. But honestly, I was thinking of other things and it was such a small bump I didn't even feel the collision!"

She had talked herself into believing her made-up story. It was more logical, really, than what had actually happened. The words were ready to roll off her tongue as the elderly police officer held open the final door to freedom and stood aside to let her pass.

"Now, I don't want to see you here again, Miss Saint-Amant," he told her quietly. "You behave yourself from now on."

Sasha hardly heard him. Her focus was entirely on the familiar figure of the man in the waiting room. He had been sitting on one of the hard chairs but rose when he saw her.

The words were already on her tongue. "Oh, Fred . . ."

But it wasn't Fred. It was Max. He looked tired. His face was pale in the harsh light of the police station. She was surprised to notice—really for the first time—that he was no longer young. His hair was thinning, his stomach had an outward bulge, the years had taken their toll. But everything about him was familiar and comfortable, even the tweed sports coat and flannel trousers that made him look more like a college professor than a movie director.

"You!" she cried. "But what . . . how . . ."

"Jonno phoned me. It took a few hours to reach my attorney and get everything sorted out. But it's all settled. You're going to have to pay a small fine, but you're free to leave now. I have my car outside to drive you home."

Sasha felt an initial gush of anger. She had told Jonno to call Fred not Max. How dare he disobey her! But Max was here . . . *Max*! Sasha melted. Everything in her that was hard and angry went soft.

An Almost Perfect Ending

He was studying her with grave concern. "Ah, my naughty girl!" he said gently, smiling his sad smile.

"Oh, Max!" she cried. "Thank God you're here! They say I ran from an accident. But I swear, I'm . . ."

Innocent was the word she was after. But as Max stood regarding her with his dear kind eyes, she couldn't finish the sentence. The tears exploded, and she wept like a child out of control.

Max took her in his arms.

"Sasha, Sasha," he said, holding her. "Let me get you out of this place. Let me get you home."

Eight

It was four o'clock in the morning, the hour of the wolf—that's what people called it in Poland when she was a child. When night was over, but dawn had not yet arrived, and you were caught in a limbo where every shadow became exaggerated, every thought. People committed suicide at four in the morning. Or found God.

Sasha remembered hearing wolves once, in a forest outside Krakow, late at night in winter when there was deep snow on the ground. Their lonely, terrifying call. She must have been six or seven. A rich gentleman friend of her mother's had taken them to the mountains and Sasha had been unable to sleep. The wolves, she remembered, had begun to howl all at once, a whole pack of them not far from the frost-covered window of her room in the little chalet where they were staying. Sasha had hidden herself under the covers, terrified.

You had to be born in Poland to know the terror of wolves. Though Los Angeles had its perils, too.

Max lay on his back in bed next to her with his eyes closed, breathing evenly. There was one candle still burning on the dresser table. The sheets and blankets were in disarray from their love making. Sasha felt a warm contentment in her body. Sex between them was no longer as urgent as it once had been, but it was deeply comforting and Sasha wished they could remain like this forever. For just this moment, she was at peace. She wanted nothing more. But eventually the worries came trickling back. Her cancelled summer tour. The unpaid bills waiting on her desk downstairs. Everybody wanting money she didn't have.

She sat up carefully so as not to wake Max and reached across his chest to the pack of Lucky Strikes on the bedside table.

"I'm awake," he said softly, opening his eyes.

"I was hoping you would sleep. You looked so tired, Max, when I first saw you tonight."

"I've been working like the devil," he admitted. "Four pictures this year, one after another. It takes a toll."

"You should take time off, darling. When the studio calls next time, just tell them no."

Max smiled at the thought. "Unfortunately, Jack Warner doesn't like the word no. Not from someone like me. I'm not a big enough fish in the pond. You start telling people no in this town, and before you know it, your phone stops ringing and you're sunk."

"I hate Hollywood!" she told him moodily.

"Sure you do," he agreed. "But where else are you going to make the sort of money we do just to play at make-believe?"

Sasha lit her cigarette and exhaled a stream of smoke across his chest.

"A puff?" she asked, lowering the cigarette to his lips.

"I'll have one of mine," he told her, sitting up in bed. "Your Luckys make me cough."

Sasha remembered how at the beginning of their affair on the *Mauretania* they had always shared cigarettes, passing them back and forth, her lips to his. Now they preferred different brands—Luckys for her (loyal to the sponsor of Jonno's show), while he smoked Pall Mall which he said weren't so harsh on his throat.

"God, the sawdust we smoked in Poland during the war!" she said for no particular reason. "Sometimes we tore pages from books to use for the paper."

"Don't tell me you're nostalgic for Nazi Poland?"

"No, but at least you knew where you stood. Here in L.A.. . . everyone smiles, they say they love you. But they'd trample over you in an instant if they thought it would get them anywhere."

Max climbed from bed and walked naked to the dresser near the window where there were two bottles and an ice bucket. Sasha watched critically as he poured vodka for her and a glass of whiskey for himself. He had gained weight and his body sagged in places it had never sagged before. These days he looked better with clothes on. The realization gave her a touch of four-in-the-morning sadness. How time passed and washed everything away.

"What's going through that sharp brain of yours?" he asked, carrying the glasses back to bed. "I can see you thinking."

"Nothing really. Just how we've known each other all these years. So many years, Max. Doesn't it make you . . . sad?"

"Sad?" He snuggled back under the covers and they touched glasses, as they had done so many times before.

"Oh, Max, don't you ever want to go back to the person you used to be and start all over again? Wouldn't you like to be some different person altogether?"

He regarded her more closely. "What's this about, darling?"

Without warning, she began to cry again. It was that sort of night. A night of tears. "I'm just such an awful person!" she told him. "I *did* run away from that accident! I wasn't paying attention. That part's true. I was driving along Sunset thinking all sorts of things and suddenly there was a crunch and I'd run into the back of someone's car. Then I saw a motorcycle cop in the opposite lane waving for me to pull over and all I could think was to make a run for it and get away . . . why am I like that, Max? What's wrong with me?"

"Shhh," he said soothingly, holding her in his arms as she cried. It was a dangerous embrace with two cigarettes burning. "It's all right . . . you'll have to settle with the man whose car you hit, a small repair bill. But that's all. Actually, he was quite thrilled to discover he'd been run into by Sonya Saint-Amant. I'm sure he'll be dining off the story for months."

"And they'll all be laughing at me and shaking their heads with indignation! Oh, I wish I wasn't such a bad person!"

"No, you're not bad. You're naughty, that's all. You're . . ." He searched for the right way to put it. "You're rather like a cat I once had as a child who was always getting caught up a tree. I'm not sure you've ever been entirely house-broken. But that's why I love you."

"*Do* you love me, Max?"

"Of course, I do. Don't you know that by now?"

Sasha sat up from his embrace, remembering further worries.

"Max, tell me something. Were you ever a Communist?"

He looked at her and laughed. "Good God, you're suddenly interested in politics?"

Not in the least. But *were* you?"

"A Communist? No, of course not. It was all the rage, you know. The smart thing to be back in the Thirties. But I always found it dreary. All those Five Year Plans and humorless people discussing dialectical materialism at boring meetings that went on forever."

"Then you went to meetings?"

"Once or twice. I was curious to see for myself what it was about. But I decided pretty quickly it wasn't my cup of gin. Why do you ask?"

"Oh, it's horrible! I saw Sol yesterday—that's where I was coming from when I had my accident—and he said the FBI's been coming round asking questions, wanting to know what my political leanings were. And they asked about you as well."

"The FBI? Well, I wouldn't let it worry you. My guess is you'll pass muster as suitably American."

"Max, I'm frightened! Sol said that I should be careful about seeing you. That people would start thinking I was a Commie too if we were friends."

He laughed again. "Let's just hope they don't find out we're having sex. Communism is catching, you know. You can get it from someone in bed. In fact, I'd say that's the main way Communism spread in the Thirties."

"Darling, it's not funny! People are getting blacklisted. Their lives are being ruined!"

His face became serious. "You're right," he agreed. "That's not funny in the least. It's despicable and terrifying."

"Thank God, you were never a Communist! That means you're safe, Max! Aren't you?"

"Not so fast," he warned. "You see, I voted for FDR. I even met him once or twice. And that might count against me."

"Were you . . . ." She lowered her voice. "Were you ever . . . a socialist?"

Robert Westbrook

He nodded. "Mmm, afraid so. For about six months once when I was a sophomore at Harvard. Utopian socialism has a certain attraction when you're young and idealistic. You read the wrong books—the Bible, for instance—and suddenly you start thinking the wealth of the world should be for everyone, not just for a few people to have it all. Before you know it, you start believing in labor unions and rights for Colored people and all sorts of dangerous ideas. Luckily, I grew up. Now I know that life is for the rich and the tricky and everybody else can go to hell."

"You shouldn't talk like that."

He patted her leg in a reassuring way. "Don't worry. I only say reckless things when I'm in bed with beautiful women. It's my way of showing off."

Max was only being funny, she knew that. But the blacklist wasn't a joking matter and Sasha felt a gnawing anxiety. These days the smallest whiff of un-Americanism could destroy a career. It didn't matter how famous you were. Even a great star like Charlie Chaplin had been forced to flee the country for England.

"Max, I want you to promise me something. I want you to promise that if the FBI comes asking questions, you won't make jokes or give any of your smart answers. You'll be cooperative."

He smiled. "Aren't I generally cooperative? When have you ever had trouble with me?"

"Be serious. You know what I mean."

Max sighed and shook his head. His eyes had lost their twinkle. "Yes, I'm afraid I do. Sasha, listen to me. If you go along with this witch-hunt of theirs, then you become complicit. You help it along. So somewhere along the way, someone has to stand up and say no."

Sasha tried to speak calmly, but a note of irritation had come into her voice. The matter was so clear to her and she didn't see why he was being difficult.

"Look, Max, you're not a sophomore at Harvard any longer, you're in the real world. So if people come asking questions, you have to promise me that you'll tell them what they want to know."

"I should name names?" He looked at her coldly. "Is that what you're suggesting?"

"Yes, I am." Sasha's irritation was quickly turning to anger. "Don't be a fool, Max. Otherwise those bastards will blacklist you and ruin your life. When all you have to do is—"

"When all I have to do is rat on my friends," he interrupted. He was becoming angry himself now. "When all I have to do is tell them the names of people I knew twenty years ago who flirted with a youthful idealism that's no longer in vogue. Is that what you're saying, Sasha? That I should be a stool pigeon?"

"It's not being a stool pigeon to save yourself! You have to do it, Max! Why not?"

"Why not? Because it's despicable, that's why. It's dishonorable."

"Goddamn you! This isn't some silly schoolboy honor code! You *must* cooperate. For God's sake, make up names if you have to! What does it matter?"

"What does it matter? Sasha! I might end up getting an innocent person sent to prison."

"Darling, listen to me. If people are asking questions about you, somebody must have named *you*. Don't you understand? You have to go along, everybody knows that. There isn't any choice."

Max shook his head. "Sure, there's a choice. That's what life's about, choices. You think I could live with myself if I went along with these Nazi stormtroopers? You should understand this better than anyone, Sasha."

"Of course, I understand! For chrissake, Max! You think we walked into the Gestapo and told them how wonderfully moral we were so they should leave us alone? We lied, we hid ourselves, we did anything we had to do to save ourselves. So don't play noble. You do whatever you must to save yourself! Do you hear me?"

"*Play* noble? Is that what you think I'm doing?" Max regarded her distastefully. This wasn't a conversation any longer, it was the clash of two opposing world views. Sasha didn't understand herself why she was so angry. It seemed almost a personal rejection that Max should refuse to acknowledge what to her seemed obvious: that you had to do what was necessary to get by.

Max shook his head. "It's funny, isn't it? We've had this conversation since we first met. Ever since that afternoon on the *Mauretania* when I saw you cheating at cards."

She flushed and turned away. "You'll never forgive me for that, will you? I told you at the time. I didn't have any money. I had to—"

"You had to survive. Right. I got that Sasha. I got it then and I got it now. And what did I tell you about me?"

Her eyes blazed at him. "I remember you said you were a dinosaur. You said you didn't care about surviving. But I won't let you be a dinosaur, Max. I won't let those bastards destroy you, I swear I won't!"

Max laughed. He got out of bed and began gathering his scattered clothes from the floor and an armchair.

"What are you doing?" she demanded.

"I'm going home. It's nearly morning and I have to put on fresh clothes and be at the studio at eight."

"Oh, Max! Then stay here. I'll shut up, I promise. I'll let you get some sleep."

He shook his head wearily. "No, it's best I go. We're just too different, Sasha. We always come up hard against the same wall. It's never going to work."

"Then make it work. If you love me, you need to fight for me."

He shook his head again, more sadly than before.

"No, I'm not really much of a fighter, I'm afraid. At heart, I'm a very boring fellow. I just want to make movies and have the world leave me alone."

"You won't be making movies if you get blacklisted!" She couldn't resist getting that in, another dig.

Max was dressed now and he came over to the bed to give Sasha a kiss. But she turned her head away.

He paused to regard her. "Goodnight, Sasha," he said after a moment. "We'll talk again in a few days. All right?"

Sullenly, she refused to answer. She listened as Max left the room, closing the door behind him. Until the last moment, she thought he might apologize. He might give way and say she was right after all: that you had to do what was necessary to get along. You couldn't sit on your high horse and follow some silly schoolboy honor code that had no place in the real world. But he said nothing. He didn't apologize. She listened to his footsteps down the stairs and then the front door open and close. A few minutes later, she heard his car start up in the driveway, his old Packard. Then headlights swept against the curtains of her window and he was gone.

Alone, Sasha felt an enormous loneliness well up inside of her. She knew that she had driven Max away. But how could he be so stupid? It infuriated her. Just recently the actor John Garfield had been found dead in New York City, a broken man, ruined—unable to work because of the blacklist. If a big star like that could fall victim to the witch-hunt, it could happen to anyone.

"Goddamn you, Max!" she said bitterly to the empty room.

*****

She was still angry when she woke alone in bed later that day, at nearly two in the afternoon.

Sasha used the intercom to call Claire downstairs to bring her coffee, forgetting that Claire wasn't in today. Her hours had been reduced as a necessary economy.

"Well, I can just make my own goddamn coffee!" she swore as she climbed out of bed. "I can take care of myself!"

And that was what was important, after all. You had to take care of yourself. Smart people survived. That was life's only rule. And if Max didn't understand it, he could go to hell.

Sasha made her coffee, she took a bath, and then she set about getting her life in order. She couldn't afford Max, it was as simple as that. She didn't have the luxury to fall for a dreamer. Zachary was dead and she needed someone who was strong and rich to protect her.

Bustling about the kitchen in her bathrobe, Sasha made herself a small breakfast, two pieces of toast and half a grape-fruit. Then she poured herself a shot of vodka and returned upstairs to find the card in her bedside table that Jonno had given her.

Jonno had meant well, phoning Max rather than Fred. At heart, Jonno was a romantic . . . just as she was, too, in her way. It was wonderful to be a romantic. It was the reason she was a singer rather than a secretary. But her career was failing and in the end you had to be practical.

The shot of vodka had filled her with a glow of determination. She picked up the telephone and dialed O.

"I'd like to make a person-to-person long-distance call to Washington, D.C.," she told the operator, practicing her brightest happy-happy voice. "My name is Sonya Saint-Amant and I wish to speak with Congressman Frederick Landson . . . yes, that's right! I'm the famous singer. Aren't you nice to notice!"

Nine

I became aware only gradually that my mother and Congressman Landson were involved in a long-distance courtship, talking most nights on the telephone, L.A. to Washington. My focus, as I've said, was entirely self-centered, *chez moi*. Obsessively focused on my aching, breaking heart.

I was in such a bad state that I had started writing poetry. It wasn't great poetry at the age of eleven, but at least it rhymed (as opposed to the poetry I wrote at a later phase of my life). I rhymed "fool" with "cruel" and "pain" with "rain" and mangled awkward syllables like "heart" and "apart" so that I could force them onto the endings of alternating lines. Awful stuff, really. But I meant every feverish word with a sincerity that was frightening, and the egotism of the effort brought some relief.

When I wasn't writing poetry, I spent my evenings listening to sad songs on the radio and reading science fiction, escaping to distant planets. As a result—having gone essentially missing from Beverly Hills—I'm not the best person to narrate my mother's drama at just this point. Nevertheless, it was impossible to miss entirely what was happening. I'd pass the downstairs den, or one of the other half dozen places where there were telephones in the house, and find her sitting with a drink in one hand and the receiver in the other, speaking in a fakey-fake voice I barely recognized.

"Oh, Fred!" she would coo with a titter of phony laughter. "Or should I call you *Mister* Congressman, now that you're such an important fellow?"

Yuck! Then one awful Saturday, when Penny was busy surfing the foamy waves of Malibu with Bobby Bradshaw, and I was collapsed on the living room sofa in a state of suicidal despair, my mother came to me with an odd request.

"Darling," she said, "I want you to do something. Fred's in town for a long weekend and he's asked if he can take you fishing tomorrow. I'd like you to go."

"Fred?" I repeated. "*Fishing?*" With more important matters occupying my brain, I couldn't even remember at first who Fred was, or make any sense of this at all.

My mother settled alongside me on the sofa and took my legs in her lap. She was very physical, forever touching me. Which I had liked when I was younger, but not now.

"Darling, Fred wants to take you out on his boat. Won't that be fun?"

I sat up and stared at my mother in dismay, unable to speak. The thought of going fishing with Fred was beyond awful. It belonged to a whole new category of dread.

"You're joking," I managed, once my lips regained their ability to speak.

"Not at all, darling."

"But *why*?"

"There's no why about it. He wants to get to know you better, that's all. He knows you don't have a father around and he'd like to do something nice for you. Personally, I think you'd be very ungrateful not to accept."

I was starting to get it. "Mom, I see what you're up to, but forget it. Look, he's not going to be your next Zachary Wise. You're wasting your time on him, I promise."

"Oh, yeah? Well, you listen to me, Mister Know-It-All— he's offered to get me an orange juice commercial on television, if you really must know."

"A *commercial*?"

"Yes, and don't turn up your nose like that. There's a great deal of money in commercials. Fred has a friend who's looking for someone to be the California Orange Juice Girl and he thinks I'm perfect for the part. I'll sing a little song about sunshine and vitamin C, and every time the commercial is shown, I'll get more money. Fred calls it residuals."

"But, Mom."

"There's no but about it, Jonno. We need the money, and that's why you have to go fishing with him. I want you to reel him in for me, darling. I need you to cement the deal."

"*Me*? For chrissake, what can *I* do?"

"There's nothing to it. All you have to do is be adorable and let him take you fishing. What could be simpler? Will you do this for me, Jonno? Please, please, please . . ."

In the end, she cajoled me. When words didn't do the trick, she kissed me and tickled my stomach and started laughing in her infectious way, until finally she got me laughing too. She bent me to her will.

My mother was irresistible, there was no way to get around her. You knew she was manipulative and selfish, and that she seldom told the truth. But there was something about her that made it impossible to say no.

Which was how I ended up spending one of the strangest days of my life with Congressman Fred Landson on his boat at Lido Isle while his wife Debbie and their two kids were out of town.

*****

Fred picked me up at exactly eight o'clock on Sunday morning, as had been pre-arranged. He came alone, driving a brand new sky blue Cadillac Eldorado Sedan de Ville, which I knew was the most expensive model Cadillac turned out that year. Like every kid in the fifties, I knew my cars, every model, every change of taillight design from year to year— Detroit cars, that is, because with the exception of the occasional Rolls or Bentley cruising Beverly Hills, there were no others back then.

Fred honked for me in the driveway and I scooted out the front door and slipped in next to him in the front seat. He was

An Almost Perfect Ending

dressed in a sports shirt with the top buttoned, dark glasses and a baseball cap pulled down low on his head. He was in an incognito mode. I understood this fact immediately because it was something my mother did as well, hiding in floppy hats and dark glasses when she didn't want to be recognized.

Of course, Fred was a politician and he had to be careful. His church-going constituents in Orange County wouldn't be happy if they found out he was courting Sonya Saint-Amant, the famous sexpot, on the sly. I doubt if Fred's wife, Debbie, would have been happy either. I had never met her, but I didn't picture her as someone beyond bourgeois constraints, like Mina and my mother. Fortunately, Debbie and their two kids were in some state with a lot of vowels to see her family. Ohio, I think. Or maybe it was Iowa. This gave Fred some leeway, but he clearly didn't intend to take chances.

"Gosh, Jonno! How you doing, son? Great day for fishing, huh?" His enthusiasm was painful, like the sun shining too brightly in your eyes.

"I'm okay," I told him. "Nice car."

"Hey, you bet it's a nice car! It cost a mint. It has a V-8 engine, hydraulic valve lifters, vertical front seat adjuster, E-Z Eye tinted glass . . . all the trimmings."

"Wow!" I managed. I'm not sure which one of us was more nervous, him or me, but neither one of us was what you'd call relaxed. Fred liked cars and as we drove, he regaled me with more technical details than I wanted to know about

103

his Eldorado. I suppose he thought this was boy stuff, that every eleven-year-old kid was dying to know about cast iron engine blocks and power brakes. He was trying to be nice, I see that now, but he didn't quite know how.

We drove for what seemed forever, hours and hours. Like a lot of people in Los Angeles, I only knew a very small part of the city. My personal L.A. had a boundary of the Pacific Coast Highway to the west, Wilshire Boulevard on one side, Paramount Studios on the other, and a small slice of the San Fernando Valley that included Burbank and the Warner Brothers studio complex. I think I'd only been in what people call downtown L.A. twice in my life. So, where we went that day was entirely new to me.

I don't remember what we talked about during all that driving, after we'd dispensed with the specifications of his car, except that our conversation was forced and sporadic. After a long time, the city came to an end and we were on a two-lane highway with orange trees on both sides of the road—acres and acres of orange trees as far as the eye could see, all in neat rows that were hypnotic to watch as they flashed by the E-Z Eye tinted glass of the Eldorado. I only realized later that this was Anaheim, pre-Disneyland, back in the Orange Age. I had no idea why we had come here, since there was no fishing and I certainly couldn't see any boats.

But then the orange trees came to an end, and suddenly there were hundreds of little houses, almost as many houses as earlier there had been trees, all of them lined up with military precision on tiny lots. A billboard on the side of the road said that this was Pleasant Valley Estates with homes starting at $5995, no money down for vets. Fred pulled to a stop at a turnout near the sign and brought down his electric window with a soft hiss.

"This is where I grew up, Jonno," he said unexpectedly. "I wanted you to see it."

I gazed out at the field of one-story houses, row after row of little boxes that were all the same beige color.

"Gee, you grew up in one of these houses, huh?" I asked.

He laughed. "Heck, no! I *built* these houses after I came back from the war. When I was a kid, there was nothing here but orange trees. You see, my daddy owned this land, three hundred and seventy-five acres. He wasn't one of the big growers, but we got by as long as we worked our butts off."

I didn't really know how to answer, so I said something stupid. "I guess you drank a lot of orange juice as a kid."

"Yeah," he said thoughtfully. "A lot of darn orange juice. My daddy was a mean son of a gun, never had a kind word for anyone. He passed away when I was overseas in the war and I didn't shed a tear, I can tell you that. You're lucky, Jonno, that you have a mother who loves you. You're a darn lucky kid."

I looked at Fred and suppressed a sigh. To be honest, sincerity was a more worrisome side of Fred than his earlier chatter about his car.

He kept gazing out the window at his empire of little houses, talking in a far-off sort of voice.

"Yeah, my old man . . . I wish he'd lived to see this. I planned it all out when I was overseas fighting the Krauts, every detail. There are three different models, see—one bedroom, two bedroom, and the deluxe townhouse that comes with a fun room downstairs. People like having a fun room, and it didn't cost me much more to add on. Building a bunch of houses almost all the same, I could cut way down on my costs—I was able to sell them cheap and still make a profit. I did it all by myself, Jonno, no help from anyone. I had a good idea, I worked my butt off, and now I'm richer than heck. Pretty amazing, huh?"

"Wow," I said again. Somehow with Fred, even being richer than heck didn't make me envy him.

"Now, I bet you're wondering how I got into politics."

I wasn't wondering that at all, of course. But Fred told me anyway.

"You see, I had to deal with a lot of county officials to get these houses built—zoning, roads, schools, you name it. There were a lot of government types I had to convince, sometimes slip them a little baksheesh to get things done. Know what I mean?"

I shook my head.

"It doesn't matter. The main thing was, over the years I started making the right contacts until soon I was having lunch with congressmen and senators. Before I knew it, people were saying I should run for office, that I had the right kind of American story, what the Republican party was all about. It didn't hurt that I got the Silver Star for what I did during the war. You know about that, I guess?"

I didn't know, so Fred told me his war story, how he and a group of saboteurs had parachuted into France in order to blow up a bridge. I'm not sure why Fred decided to make me his audience, but I suspected even then that he was a lonely man. In any case, he warmed to his story and I listened— reluctantly, at first, but in fact this was pretty juicy stuff, killing Krauts and living behind enemy lines, so gradually I didn't have to fake my interest.

From Anaheim, we drove for another eternity until eventually we came to the coast, the blue Pacific glittering in the sun. Fred's house was on Lido Isle off Newport Beach, a nautical part of Orange County with dream homes on a maze of waterways. It was the sort of place where nearly everyone had an American flag waving from a pole in their front yard, and a cabin cruiser berthed in a private dock out back.

Fred owned the biggest house around, a huge modern box that took up nearly every inch of his land. There were plenty of sundecks and tinted glass and sliding doors. We pulled up through an electric gate that he opened by pressing a button beneath his dashboard and parked in a courtyard alongside a three-car garage.

"Well, here's my castle!" he enthused. "Home sweet home!"

I think Fred found clichés restful. Conformity was the main requirement of the Fifties and clichés provided a kind of cookie mold for your thoughts that kept everybody within safe boundaries. He took me inside the house through a side door and gave me a quick tour, all three floors starting with the fun room in the basement that had just about all the fun you could ever want—a pool table, ping-pong, TV, and lots of other games and toys. There were photographs of his two kids on the walls, Chip, who was seven, and Sally who was four. As children went, they seemed generic, like they might have been ordered from the May Company. But maybe that was only how they looked in photographs.

We climbed upward through the house, past a huge modern kitchen, dining room, living room, then up to the next floor where the bedrooms were, five bedrooms in all—a master suite with a big deck outside overlooking the waterway and the boats below, two more bedrooms for Chip and Sally, and two guest bedrooms that looked as though no guest had ever slept in them. It was a nice house, I suppose, very impressive. But there was nothing in it to warm to.

We stopped to look at a framed photograph in one of the bedrooms of his wife Debbie. She was blond and slim and should have been attractive, but somehow she wasn't. There was something pinched about her. A club woman, I would have said at a later time in my life, though I didn't know the breed then: a pinched, sexless, well-scrubbed California club woman of the 1950s, not a hair out of place.

"It's important to marry the right woman, Jonno—you'll understand that when you grow older," Fred advised, studying the photograph with me. "Sometimes she's not the one you had your heart set on, but that's okay. The main thing is she needs to be steady, the sort of gal a man can rely on. My Debbie, she's as steady as a rock, I can tell you that. She's not the sort of gal who'll ever let me down."

It was a compliment, I suppose, for a wife to be steady as a rock. But Fred didn't look happy as he regarded the photograph of his wife, and I imagined there were drawbacks to not marrying the one you had your heart set on. He put his hand on my shoulder and led me to his special room, his den.

"This is where I hide out from the family," he told me. "Come on, I want to show you something."

Fred's den was a manly sort of room. There was a dead bear sprawled out across the floor, a fireplace, a wet bar, a gun cabinet full of rifles, several paintings of cowboys and Indians and a big telescope set up on a wooden tripod next to the picture window that overlooked the waterway in front of the house.

I watched as he unlocked a drawer in his gun cabinet and pulled out a pistol.

"Go ahead, you can hold it, if you want. Boys should get used to guns."

It was heavier than the revolver Zachary had given me, a solid piece of perfect machinery. I raised it experimentally, pointing it at the big picture window. "Neat!" I said, trying to get in the spirit.

"It's a German Lugar. What do you think of that, Jonno? I took it off a Nazi officer in France."

"He gave it to you?"

"Naw, they didn't give their guns away. I had to kill him for it. He didn't give me any other choice. It was war, Jonno. It was either him or me. So I blew his darn brains out."

I think Chekhov must have twitched in his grave—that rule again about story-structure—because I felt a shiver up my spine. Suddenly I didn't want to be holding the Lugar any longer. I gave it back and was relieved when Fred put it in the drawer.

"Hey, I bet the fish are biting!" I said, ever so brightly.

"Sure they are," he agreed. "Let's go get 'em!"

*****

Fred's cabin cruiser, *Debbie's Dream*, was docked in a wooden slip at the rear of his house, where the lawn rolled down to the water. It was a big white boat—fifty-five feet, Fred told me proudly—sleek and modern with a bridge way up high that you had to climb to on a ladder, and an American flag flying in the rear. It was an ultimate boy-toy, bigger than something you could fit into a bathtub but the same general idea. To be honest, I was looking forward to taking her out into the open ocean for a spin.

But Fred disappointed me.

"Maybe another time, Jonno," he told me. "It's kind of rough out there today, lots of big swells. I wouldn't want you to get seasick."

"I won't get seasick, I promise."

"Naw, I wouldn't want to chance it. Not today. Besides, we don't really have the time. It would take an hour to get out beyond the buoy, and another hour to get back, and I told your mother I'd have you home by five. Look, I tell you what. We'll fish off the rear deck. There are plenty of fish in the channel, believe me."

I felt cheated. I had thought that going out in Fred's boat was what this day was supposed to be about, and we would have had time for it if we hadn't made the long detour to Anaheim to see his stupid houses.

"Gee, how about just a short ride up and down the channel," I suggested. "I'd sure like to see how she goes."

Fred laughed uneasily. "You know, Jonno, to be honest, I get nervous taking her out. I mean, a fifty-five-foot craft isn't so easy to handle, especially in a narrow channel like this. Jeez, the other day I nearly ran down a catamaran that cut in front of me. I hate sailboats. They always act like they're morally superior somehow. Know what I mean?"

I didn't know then about the moral superiority of sailboats, but I got the general drift. Fred was terrified to take his fancy cabin cruiser out from the dock. *Debbie's Dream* was meant only to be an expensive appendage to his house, an extra room floating at the edge of his lawn.

He set me up with a fishing pole and bait and I lowered my line from the stern into the calm blue channel waters, watching gloomily as other boats with bolder captains came and went—sailboats, motorboats, sometimes little outboards, all of them full of people who were having a lot more fun than we were. One cabin cruiser sailed by with two teenage girls in swimsuits sunbathing near the bow, and I wished like hell that I was on it.

The only fish I caught that day was a tiny guppy that I threw back, not very thrilling. Fred made hot dogs for us on a small barbecue grill and tried his best to be cheerful, but I had become sullen and answered only in monosyllabic grunts. I was a shallow kid, I suppose. If Fred had only taken his big cabin cruiser out into the ocean that day and opened up the throttle—and maybe given me a turn at the wheel—he would have won my friendship in a heartbeat. But he didn't. We never left his silly backyard.

I guess he knew he wasn't scoring any points with me. Around three o'clock he said we'd better quit, and shortly after that he drove me home, this time with no detours and little conversation.

"Well, Jonno, it's sure been swell spending the day together," he lied, pulling up to the curb by my house. "I hope you tell your mother you've had a good day."

"You bet," I said, wanting only to get away.

"You see, I like your mother a lot," he confided. "And I want her to know she can trust me. I want her to know that I'm a friend."

"Right," I said.

"So you'll say we're pals, won't you? You'll stick up for me—you and me, Jonno, because friends need to stick together. I know she listens to you."

It was hideous. I wanted to weep for him because he was so pathetic. But mostly I just wanted to run from the car.

But he wouldn't let me go, not yet. "Listen, one more thing, since we're pals," he said, holding onto my arm. "I'm curious about something. I've been wondering if Max McCormick still comes around. To see your mother, I mean. You can tell me the truth, Jonno. Is she still stuck on that guy after all this time?"

This was a twist I hadn't expected and I wasn't sure at first how to answer.

"Look, I don't mean to put you in an awkward spot," he said, forcing a smile. "It's just I never much liked Max, you see. I knew he wasn't any good for your mother. Oh, sure, he has those fine namby-pamby manners, going to Harvard and all, and I guess that impressed your mother some. But I knew from the start that he was a weak sister. A lush, too, if you want to know the truth. So I just want to make sure she's free of him."

It was an awkward speech and it left both of us embarrassed. But it gave me time to think. Probably too much time, for this is where I made my big mistake. I got too clever for my own good. I told a lie . . . like mother, like son. But I wasn't as good at lying as she was, I was still an apprentice in the make-believe department, and it was a lie I should have left alone.

I put on my innocent kid voice and told Fred that sure Max still came around. Of course, he did. He came around a couple of times a week and my mother and Max were close as close could be. Sometimes I even wondered if he'd leave Mina and he and my mom might get married. I said I would like that, and I laid it on a little thick.

None of it was true, of course. My mother and Max hadn't spoken to each other for a while—one of their usual fights, I presumed. But I thought if Fred believed Max and my mother were still an item, he'd get discouraged and leave her alone. That's what I wanted. I wanted Fred to do a vanishing act from our lives. I didn't want to go fishing with him again, and I didn't want him coming around. I wanted him gone.

An Almost Perfect Ending

Fred's eyes turned inward as I spoke and everything about him seemed suddenly to sag. I hadn't known until then that mere words could be so hurtful.

"So, they're still at it, those two!" he said thoughtfully. "I guess I should have known!"

"Gee, thanks for taking me fishing," I told him ruthlessly, making my escape from the Eldorado. I ran up the path to the front door and didn't look back. I regret that now. I should have stopped and turned and taken a much closer look at Fred Landson as he sat by the curb to our house clutching his steering wheel and making plans. I should have seen the darkness in his eyes.

I should have known that lies have consequences.

*****

I can only imagine how it happened, because I wasn't there. But I have a good imagination, and I know the ending of this particular story, so I can picture it clearly enough: Fred driving home to Lido Isle working himself up over Max, getting angrier with every passing mile.

For Fred, it would have seemed that Max had come by everything so easy, all his charm and fancy ways, and this would have been infuriating to an awkward, envious man. Fred had struggled for every small advantage, no one had given him a thing. But he was the sort of guy a gal could rely on and he didn't understand why Sasha should love a weak sister like Max and not love him. It wasn't fair, it wasn't right. Luckily for Fred, he had a card to play.

A day later, on Monday night, Fred took the red-eye flight from LAX back to Washington, D.C., where he kept a home in Georgetown. He wasn't a man who required sleep—with enough self-discipline, he believed a person could do without sleep altogether—and he used the time, sitting in his comfortable First Class seat, to read through the script of a low-budget black and white movie called *Joe* that Max had directed a year earlier, in 1953. Max had put up part of the money for the picture himself and it was what a later generation would call an art film. Art hadn't been invented yet in 1953, but the movie had done unexpectedly well at the box office and the writer—an East Coast Jew named Ray Blau—had been nominated for an Academy Award.

Though Fred was only a junior member of Congress, he had risen to a position of prominence in the Republican party due to his determination to cleanse Hollywood of Communism. The concern was that Communists were placing subversive messages in Hollywood movies and discriminating against unsympathetic colleagues, right-wing actors and writers who only wanted to earn an honest dollar.

Ginger Rogers' mother, one of the first friendly witnesses to testify before the House Un-American Activities Committee, claimed her daughter had been forced against her will to say the subversive phrase, "share alike, that's democracy," in a 1943 movie written by Dalton Trumbo. Such outrages went on and on. In a 1943 war movie, *Action in the North Atlantic*, Russian sailors had the nerve to call American sailors "tovarich" —comrade—when an American ship was forced into a Soviet port due to a Nazi blockade.

You had to have a subtle mind to ferret out such examples of un-Americanism. But Committee members didn't mind grasping for straws, if that was all they could get. One of the most notorious examples they found came from the 1943 film, *Song of Russia*—the title said it all—a picture that had been made during a brief period when Washington needed to sell the Soviet Union to the American public as a temporary ally to fight the Germans. The complaint was that the movie showed Russians smiling. The novelist Ayn Rand, testifying as a friendly witness before HUAC, assured the Committee that "it is one of the stock propaganda tricks of the Communists to show these people smiling." Worse still, at one point in the movie, the actor Robert Taylor was forced to smile in return at a Russian farmer and say, "This is wonderful grain." As far as HUAC was concerned, this was subversion in its most insidious form, an example of the Communist threat that was eating away at the heart of America.

Joe, the script of Max's movie that Fred examined on his flight to Washington, was about an ordinary G.I. who returns home from the war and has problems readjusting to civilian life. A HUAC aid had gone through the screenplay already to vet it for un-Americanism but had come up empty-handed. The problem with *Joe* was that, although the overall tone of the story was blatantly unpatriotic, there was nothing in the dialogue that could be easily construed as Communist propaganda. Nevertheless, Fred was certain he would find something if he looked closely enough. He could almost smell the whiff of unapologetic liberalism in the ink and paper.

In the story, Joe comes home from the war to a small town only to find his girl has married another guy in his absence and his job has been given to someone else. Nothing goes right for Joe. He gets drunk, he keeps dwelling on the horrible things he saw in the war, he just can't get a leg back up the ladder. As far as Fred was concerned, the basic premise of the film was un-American, an insult to the spirit of can-do Yankee optimism. Yet never once in the script did Joe call anyone "tovarich," nor did he say anything quite as telling as "share alike, that's democracy."

Fred was finishing up his second reading of the script when he finally came to a small piece of dialogue he believed might have potential. It was toward the end of the story when Joe, after a night in jail, tracks down the girl he was supposed to marry and has it out with her. When she chides him for giving in to despair, he says, "I tried and tried, Mary. God knows I tried! But no matter what I did, I just couldn't get anywhere."

Fred used his pencil to underline "no matter what I did, I just couldn't get anywhere." Wasn't this implying that Capitalism didn't work, that America didn't take care of its own in the land of plenty? With a frown of concentration, Fred began making notes for Frank Tavenner, the chief consul for HUAC. It seemed to Fred that with a bit of courtroom theatrics, this line, "I just couldn't get anywhere," might be shown to be only a few steps short of the Communist Manifesto. How far was it, really, to jump from this statement to "Workers of the World Unite"?

Luckily, the hearings in Washington were arranged in such a way that HUAC witnesses could be bullied, interrupted, insulted, and never given a proper chance to defend themselves. Personally, Fred thought this was absolutely fair. He didn't like people who whined about America, nor did he see why these nay-sayers should be entitled to the benefits of a justice system they claimed to despise. Fred himself had done very well in America readjusting to civilian life and he had no sympathy for fictitious fellows like Joe, nor fancy directors like Max McCormick, who tried to show that his country wasn't any good.

"Your time is coming, McCormick!" Fred said to himself with satisfaction, closing the script in his lap. "You bet'cha britches, buddy . . . I got you in my sights and you're going down!"

*****

The following afternoon, Fred made a long distance call to Warner Brothers from his Washington office. He reached the central switchboard and told the operator that U.S. Congressman Frederick Landson wished to speak to Mr. Jack Warner on an urgent matter. Fred and Jack Warner had met several times at political functions and the call was put through.

"Jack, it's Fred Landson here in Washington," he said, once he had the great man on the line. "Look, I have to warn you about something. I'm afraid you have a Commie sympathizer on your payroll, Max McCormick, the director. We're going to be serving him with a subpoena and I wanted to give you a heads-up. You guys at the studio have always been swell, totally cooperative. And I wanted to make sure you didn't get caught by surprise . . ."

It was as easy as that in Hollywood in 1954, to destroy a person's life. A movie director, an actor, a writer . . . singers, too. When it came to the blacklist, no one was immune.

Abracadabra!

A single phone call and it was done.

Part Two

The King of Noir

Ten

California: Spring, Summer, 1954

Max McCormick began what was to be the worst day of his life on location at Trancas Beach, working only a few feet from the surf with a movie crew and many tons of heavy equipment—arc lights, cameras, generators, reflectors, dolly tracks, ladders, cables—struggling to move everything about in the sand, logistical problems galore. He didn't know yet how badly the day was to turn out, but he had his suspicions that things weren't going well.

Max had reinvented his career after the war, earning a reputation for gritty, low-budget black-and-white thrillers that he turned out at Warner Brothers by the truckload throughout the 1940s and early 50s, often four or five pictures a year. These were stories in which it rained a good deal of the time, the hero generally appeared in a trench coat with a cigarette dangling from his mouth, and the women were all dames, beautiful but deadly.

By 1954, he had done well enough with B-pictures—and with his own low-budget independent movie, *Joe*—that Jack Warner had begun giving him bigger budgets and bigger stars. B-plus movies, Max liked to joke. The picture he was directing today was called *Storm Tossed*, a gothic thriller about a young woman (Jean Simmons) who lived with her father (Leo G. Carroll) on a lonely beach that was supposed to be Cape Cod. One day, walking by herself on the beach, the girl accidentally witnesses a murder, one man drowning another in the surf. Predictably, as thrillers go, the killer soon discovers that his crime has been observed and now must rid himself of the girl, who escapes with her life after a climactic car chase on a winding road on high cliffs above the crashing surf below. The plot was far from original, but Max hoped to make a good picture. There was plenty of room for creativity—good acting, beautiful black and white photography, and enough tension to keep the audience on the edge of their seats.

Max preferred to work on location whenever possible, and he had chosen Trancas Beach in the wild northern reaches of Malibu County as the primary setting for the picture. With the extra transportation, the location meant long days for Max in which he generally left home at six in the morning and didn't arrive back in Bel Air until nine or ten at night.

The morning's work went well. Over the course of four hours, he shot the murder scene that was central to the story, an action sequence at the edge of the surf in which he used stunt doubles. Max filmed the entire sequence first in extreme close-up, hoping to bring the audience right into the action. And then he shot it again from a distance, two small figures struggling in the surf surrounded by a vast expanse of nature. Later in the cutting room, he would find a way to fit the two versions together, distant and close, for maximum effect. This was a key moment in the picture, and he wanted it to be both frightening and profound.

Max was a perfectionist in his work and it took him more than a dozen takes before he was satisfied. The production manager—Tommy Maher, a craggy old studio veteran—kept pointing impatiently to his watch because they had four pages of script to get through today in order to stay on schedule, and time was money. Max promised to hurry up and then went on working slowly, exactly as before.

"Okay, let's try it again, everybody," he said again and again, taking up his position alongside the camera.

Late in the morning, Mina made a surprise visit to the set, appearing with lunch in a picnic basket and two of her friends in tow, Peter and Helena Cross, a rich British couple who lived in Ojai. Max did his best to hide his irritation. Mina said he should just forget about them, they didn't require any special attention, but Max was too innately polite not to feel an obligation. He didn't like socializing when he was at work and would have preferred a quiet lunch in his trailer going over the script.

Mina arranged the picnic on a blanket in the shelter of a sand dune while Max finished the final shot of the morning, a close-up of a body floating face down inertly on the tide (the stuntman holding his breath). By the time he joined Mina and her friends, she had set out lunch on the blanket—a large salad, French bread, cheese, and several bottles of chilled German wine in a bucket filled with ice. Rain was predicted for later in the afternoon, but Mina and Helena were in their swimsuits, hoping the weather would stay decent long enough for a dip after lunch. They were all in a fine holiday mood, come to see a bit of movie work and enjoy themselves on the beach, unaware that their presence was an unwanted distraction on a busy day.

Max had mixed feelings about Peter and Helena Cross, Mina's friends. Peter was in his forties, an elegant wisp of a fellow with a deep suntan and a handsome face. He was a loud advocate of yoga and what he liked to call "advanced thinking," and was supposedly related to some famous British writer—Max was never certain if it was W.H. Auden or E.M. Forster, but it was someone with initials. His wife Helena was much younger, in her late twenties, and she was pretty in a frail, anemic English way. As Max understood it, she was the one who had the money—inherited—and Peter, for all his advanced philosophy, was happy enough to live off her.

"Ah, here's the wage slave!" Peter called loudly, as Max joined them on the blanket and kicked off his shoes. "Have you had yourself a glamorous morning churning out make-believe for the masses?"

"Actually, making a movie is hard work," Max replied, barely hiding his annoyance.

"Is it? Ah, well, life is all a grand picture show! We dream up our reality as we go along. We're the gods of our own stories. So we'd better enjoy the spectacle—eh, Max?"

Peter was a bully. He wouldn't let Max merely smile. He demanded an actual response.

"Yes, I suppose so," Max agreed, making an effort to be agreeable. "A tale for idiots, told by an overworked screen-writer."

Helena turned his way on the blanket, peering at him from beneath a big straw hat that protected her from the sun. She was quite sweet for a rich young woman, but self-serious and self-righteous, which ruined much of the charm.

"You know, Max," she said, "I saw one of your movies the other evening, *The Savage Night*. I hope you don't mind if I tell you something that might sound a little rude."

"Of course not, Helena. Go ahead and be rude."

"Well, it's just this. I couldn't help but be struck at how violent it was, all those people running about in the rain shooting guns at one another. Don't you think there's enough real violence in the world as it is? Wouldn't it be better if movies—art, in general—taught people to solve their quarrels peacefully? I mean, what would happen if all you cinema-makers decided to put away your guns and gave us stories about happy people instead?"

"Happy people?" Max suppressed a laugh. "That's swell in real life, Helena. But in drama, I'm afraid we storytellers require a few sorrows to nudge things along. Lust, greed, jealousy, anger, violence. It's passion and difficulties that make for a good story, something that audiences will plonk down their money to see."

"Yes, but these sorrows, as you call them, could be presented in a more enlightened way," Peter suggested. "For example, you could show how people overcome anger and work things out."

"Yes, I see what you mean," Max answered gravely. "Everyone getting along, working out their differences. You know, I'll have to speak to Jack Warner about this."

"I really do believe it would make the world a more positive place," Helena decreed.

"It would create a new reality altogether!" Peter cried. "We could change the basic mythology that people live by!"

"And why should it only be the movies?" Max suggested. "What about books? What about fairy tales? What if we could rewrite Little Red Riding Hood so that the Big Bad Wolf and Riding Hood sit down at the end and come to a happy compromise. If the Wolf is hungry, if he really must have something to eat, perhaps Riding Hood can offer him a sandwich?"

"Yes . . . yes, you've got it!" Peter said, frowning with thought. "The possibilities are enormous, transforming the very fairy tales we grow up with . . ."

Max was on his second glass of white wine and would have been happy to revise the entire canon of world literature as they sat there on the sand. But Mina shot him a warning look and he let it go.

Max often wished he wasn't such a skeptic. He was sure it would be lovely to believe in something, a religion or a cause. For Mina's sake, he tried his best to charm his way through the picnic and keep his irony under control.

Really, he had nothing much against Peter and Helena Cross. Except for the fact that they lacked a sense of humor, they were rich without ever working, and they were deadly dull.

*****

The weather was changing quickly, with gray-black clouds rushing past the sun and beams of sunlight playing in and out of the sky. Max was relieved when the second assistant director, a youngster fresh out of UCLA, came over to say that the dolly track had been set up according to his instructions on the wet sand at the edge of the surf. The DP, the Director of Photography, was saying they'd better get the shot quickly before the tide started coming in.

"It seems I must get back to work," Max announced cheerfully, making his excuses to Mina and her friends and returning to the set. The scene he was shooting this afternoon was between his heroine, Jean Simmons, and her reclusive father, Leo G. Carroll—a famous author, according to the script—a long tracking shot as they walked together along the beach arguing about the murder she claimed to have seen.

A metal track a hundred feet long had been set up on the hard wet sand to carry the camera dolly with the sound man and the microphone boom riding in the rear. The challenge was to get the various technical elements synchronized—the two actors walking down the beach with the big 35mm Mitchell camera moving smoothly down the track alongside them. The scene was a long one, with a page and a half of dialogue to cover, and it was Max's intention to get it all in a single fluid, unbroken shot.

Magically, everything seemed to come together on the first take. The acting was perfect, everything appeared to go well. But then the sound man shook his head and said the microphone had picked up too much noise from the wind and surf and the footage was unusable.

They shot the scene again with a different microphone that had a baffle wrapped around it to mute the sound of the wind, but on this take Jean Simmons missed a line. The next take went well until the very end, when the camera dolly hit a stretch of uneven track—the sand had shifted underneath—and they were forced to shoot the scene yet again.

It went on and on in this manner for more than an hour, one small problem after another ruining every take. Max was aware in a peripheral way that Mina and her friends had left after lunch, deciding it wasn't such a good day for a swim after all—they had waved goodbye from their sand dune, but he barely noticed. Adding to his problems, the tide was rising, and the surf had begun creeping up on each wave almost to the dolly tracks.

"Look, Max, maybe we should call it quits," the production manager said, coming over with an anxious expression. "We don't want to lose any equipment here. We can finish the scene back at the studio, maybe with headshots of Jean and Leo, cutting back and forth to what we already have in the can. No one will know the difference."

"Just one more take," Max promised. He didn't want to film on a sound stage with a painted backdrop, *he* would know the difference. He wanted the scene here and now, with Jean's hair blowing in real wind rather than a wind machine. The weather was perfect, a stormy sky that would look fabulous in black and white, just the atmosphere that a picture called *Storm Tossed* required.

The crew pulled the camera dolly back to its starting position on the track, and Jean and Leo were summoned from their trailers one last time. The rain began just as they were about to start, hard drops pelting down from the sky. Max wasn't about to let this stop him.

"Camera!" called the assistant director.

"Speed!" the cameraman answered.

"Scene forty-seven-A, take twelve!" cried the clapper boy, holding the slate in front of the lens and clapping the stick down hard.

"Action!" Max shouted.

The actors began walking down the beach with the camera dolly moving alongside them. Jean spoke her first line: "Papa, I wouldn't make up such a thing. I saw it, honestly I did. There were two men fighting, and one man held the other man underwater, I'm sure of it."

Leo was about to say his line—"My dear, you have too much imagination, that's your problem"—when disaster struck without warning. A sneaker wave came crashing down on them seemingly from nowhere, plunging the crew and the actors into a maelstrom of spewing foam and sand. Both actors were swept off their feet. Max was spun around but managed to stay upright until the wave began sucking backward, pulling everything in its path back into the ocean, sweeping him into the water. By the time Max struggled to his feet and got his bearings, the entire set was in disarray, with the debris of movie equipment floating at the edge of the surf around him—lights, reflectors, a sound boom, even the script that the continuity girl had been marking before the onslaught of the wave.

Worst of all, the expensive 35mm camera had been swept clear off the dolly and was lying on its side in several inches of surging water. By the time the crew dragged the camera back to dry land, it was clear that salt water had ruined the delicate machinery as well as the film stock inside, destroying the entire afternoon's work. Jack Warner was going to be furious.

The rain was coming down steadily now as the crew worked to salvage whatever equipment that could be pulled from the surf. Max stood on the beach watching helplessly. In all his years of movie making, he'd never seen such a disaster. There was nothing to do now except send the actors home and try again another day.

Max called a meeting in his trailer with the assistant director and the production manager and they spent two hours on the phone to Burbank trying to figure out where they would go from here. Tomorrow, a new camera would need to be brought from the studio, and a great deal of other things as well, causing a delay in the shooting schedule of at least two days, perhaps longer. By the time it was finished, the damage and delay would cost the company tens of thousands of dollars.

Max knew it was his fault. Working so close to the surf, he'd gotten too arty for his own good. He should have listened to his production manager and finished the scene back at the studio with a painted backdrop.

Wet, cold, and unhappy with himself, Max found a flask of Glenlivet in his briefcase and began drinking, compounding the mistakes that were about to overcome him.

Eleven

Sasha was having a bad day, too. A day that had gone wrong even before it started, with a nightmare while she was still asleep.

In the dream, she was young again, on board the *Mauretania* crossing the North Atlantic during the war. Only now, as she stood on deck, she watched terrified as a torpedo came speeding across the water from a Nazi submarine. The torpedo made a white line on the surface as it came at her with the inevitability of fate, closer and closer, until there was a great explosion. The huge ship shuddered and began sinking fast, bow first into the cold gray water. Sasha climbed frantically to the highest deck at the rear of the ship knowing she was about to die, desperate to put off the certainty of drowning a few more moments. To make things worse, the ocean was full of sharks circling round and round, eager to get their teeth into her.

It didn't take an expensive Beverly Hills analyst to interpret this particular dream, to find herself on a sinking ship in an ocean full of sharks. It was her Hollywood life in a nutshell. Sasha woke gasping for air just as the *Mauretania* was going under. She sat up with her heart thumping, amazed to find herself safe in bed.

"But it was only a dream!" she told herself shakily. She wasn't about to drown in the North Atlantic. "I'm fine," she said aloud, as though saying it aloud would make it true.

But she wasn't fine.

Sasha was squinting at her bedside clock, registering the uncivilized hour—ten-twenty in the morning!—when her phone began to ring. She picked up the receiver without thinking, still not entirely awake. Normally at this hour she would have let her service field the call. But last night— "slightly stewed," as she liked to put it—she had forgotten to turn off the ringer.

"Hello?" she said as brightly as she was able. Because you never knew who was calling. Perhaps someone important with the offer of a job.

At first there was only silence on the line.

"Who is this?" she demanded.

"Guess?" said a whispery voice she knew too well.

Sasha inhaled sharply. It was Ricky Bolano, more terrifying than any ocean full of sharks.

*****

She couldn't speak. Literally. Her throat was strangled, no words came. Ricky wasn't dead after all. She couldn't believe Zachary — dear Zachary! — had let her down. Perhaps it was revenge for something she had done to him. Or more likely, he had simply been too sick to take care of the matter before he flew to Denver. It was only later that she remembered he had made a point of not promising anything.

"Cat got your tongue?" Ricky laughed. "Well, don't worry. This time I'm going easy on you. You and me, we need to talk. I got some things to do earlier in the evening, but I'll be coming by your house tonight when I'm finished. Let's say midnight."

"No," she managed. It was the only word she had for him. *No, no, no!*

"*No*? You know, I'm disappointed to hear that from you. You don't want me to be disappointed, do you?"

"I . . . I won't be home. I have . . . a date."

"A *date*!" he mimicked. "Sure, you have a date. You got a date with me. Now, let me tell you something. You don't want to get Ricky upset, because you remember how Ricky is when he's angry. He's liable to fly off the handle. So you be there, if you know what's good for you."

"I don't have any money. I swear, I don't. And I can't get hold of any by tonight."

"Have I asked for money? Maybe you got something else I want. Maybe you and me, we're going to cut ourselves a whole new deal. I'll tell you about it when I see you tonight."

"I . . . I can't . . . I don't . . ."

Sasha couldn't think. Her brain had stalled.

"Sure, you can. And you will," he assured her. "Now, don't let me down, because I'm counting on seeing you tonight. You fuck up, you try any funny business, here's what I'll do. This time I'm not going to touch a hair on your pretty little head. You're off the hook, doll. It's that spoiled brat kid of yours I'll be coming for. You got that? You give me any grief and I'll cut off that kid's balls and stuff 'em down his throat. So you be there. At midnight!"

He slammed down the phone. Sasha sat stunned with the receiver against her ear listening to the dial tone.

Ricky Bolano . . . it was incredible, it was horrible! He was still alive and her world had just done a somersault.

She sat at first simply paralyzed, too numb to move. Finally, it was anger that set her in motion, a rush of fury that grew and grew and burned its way upward from her groin to her head.

That bastard! That horrible man . . .

There must be something she could do. She refused to be at the mercy of this monster any longer. There was a lioness in her, and it had just woken up.

She was good in a crisis. She reminded herself of that. She was the girl who had escaped Nazi Poland.

And her mind was ticking.

*****

The first thing was to get Jonno as far from Beverly Hills tonight as she possibly could.

Think, she told herself. What day was it, she wondered. Wednesday?

No, it was Thursday. Sasha needed to consult her calendar in the den downstairs to make sure, because generally speaking, days of the week didn't mean much to a woman in her situation.

"Thursday!" she said thoughtfully. Unfortunately, Jonno had to be at Paramount tomorrow to do his show, so she couldn't just put him on a plane.

Max, she decided. Max was the answer. She picked up the phone and dialed his home in Bel Air. She presumed Max would be working, but hopefully Mina would be there. She wasn't. Sammy, their all-purpose Chinese chef/house boy, told her that Max was on location in Malibu and wouldn't be home until at least nine, while Mina had gone off for the day with friends. Sammy had no idea when she would return and neither Mina nor Max were expected home for dinner.

This was a disappointment. Jonno often spent weekends with Max and Mina in Bel Air and it would have been a safe place for him to be tonight.

Who else could she call? With a shock, she realized that she had no real friends in California. She had lovers, yes. And there were people like Sol who made money off her, and musicians who backed her when she sang. But she didn't have friends.

Long ago, Julka had been a friend. And so had Zachary Wise, in his odd way. But they were dead.

The realization made Sasha feel so alone she nearly poured herself a drink. But she couldn't do that, not today. Today she needed all her wits and wiles. She had to get Jonno somewhere safe.

At last she came up with a name. Not a friend, exactly, but one of her admirers. A man who was always eager to be in her good graces. She picked up the phone and called Mort Jenkins at his office at Paramount. Mort was the producer of Jonno's show, *What a Life!*, and he had been chasing Sasha for years. She had no interest in him romantically—he was middle-aged with a face like a basset hound and the body of a penguin. But he was the sort of useful single man who generally could be counted on to meet your plane or take you to a party when no one else was available. As Sasha expected, he said he would be happy to have Jonno overnight at his home in the Malibu Colony. They'd have themselves a weenie roast on the deck, then maybe watch a movie in his home projection room.

"What fun!" Sasha told him, hanging up. With Jonno taken care of, she turned her thoughts now to how she was going to kill Ricky. There was no more time to dicker over the matter. Zachary had let her down and she needed to get this done. Tonight.

An Almost Perfect Ending

Ricky didn't know it, but he had sealed his doom by threatening to hurt Jonno.

That simply wasn't going to happen. Not ever.

*****

The problem wasn't the simple act of murder. There were plenty of ways to kill someone. The problem was getting away with it. Sadly, California sent convicted murderers to the gas chamber at San Quentin prison, an awful place north of San Francisco. Sasha had successfully avoided gas chambers in her native Poland, and she did not intend to encounter one here.

She had been researching real-life murders for months now, looking for ideas. She had even read a book on the subject—the one that Jonno had seen her drop in the driveway, *Famous Murders: How They Did it, And How They Were Caught*. But the end result was discouraging. Killers, she learned, were almost always caught, particularly if they had an obvious motive. Unfortunately, that was Sasha's biggest problem. Blackmail was one of the oldest motives in the book and the cops would nab her right away.

Even without the gas chamber, she couldn't afford for that old New York arrest report to come out. It would destroy her career forever. It was one thing to be sexy. Everyone liked sexy. But an arrest for prostitution in a movie theater was something else. Somehow the fact that it had been a movie theater rather than a penthouse on Park Avenue added an element of humiliation that made the whole matter worse. Sasha thought she'd rather die than have people know what she had done. It had all been so unfair, of course, that afternoon in 1943—pregnant, her money nearly gone, about to be tossed out onto the street because she couldn't pay her hotel bill—when a man had sat next to her in the dark and offered twenty dollars for a blow job. How was she to know that he was a vice cop?

What Ricky had done that afternoon was illegal, she knew that now. It was called entrapment. But this was no help to her now. She had done the deed, what had seemed necessary at the time in order to survive. And he had arrested her.

"Damn, damn, damn!" Sasha said aloud to the green walls of the den.

Could Fred help? The Congressman was a powerful man, just as Zachary had been. They hadn't gone to bed yet, though they had necked a bit. Sasha kept putting Fred off, sensing it was best to play him longer, keeping the line taut so he wouldn't get away. Perhaps it was time now to seal the deal. Once he was properly landed, she could ask his help with Ricky.

Surely Fred had friends who didn't mind a dangerous job, just a small murder to set her free. You couldn't be a powerful fellow in a city like Los Angeles without knowing your way around. But something made Sasha hesitate. The problem with Fred was he was such a Boy Scout. He wasn't a man of the world as Zachary had been. She couldn't be sure what his reaction would be if he found out she'd been arrested for prostitution. The idiot might be shocked.

Sasha spent nearly an hour at her desk pondering these difficult questions. In the end, she decided she wouldn't ask Fred for help. Not yet, anyway. Perhaps later. Besides, he was in Washington at the moment and could do nothing for her tonight.

What then?

There was only one glimmer of hope. The more she considered the matter, it seemed unlikely that a cheap thug like Ricky Bolano would have an attorney who was keeping her old arrest report in his safe. Ricky was a liar, of course. He had admitted that himself. He was bluffing, that's all. Sasha should have seen through it right away. Though it was impossible to say for certain. That was the maddening part of this. She didn't know for sure.

She sat thinking, going back and forth. Why not just kill the bastard anyway and take a chance on the consequences?

Why not?

God knew, she had to do *something*! If you worried too much about every small possibility of failure, you ended up doing nothing, and that simply wasn't an option.

At the end of all her thinking, she still didn't know what she was going to do. But she had found the starting point.

Before anything else, she needed to get herself a gun.

Twelve

She knew of a store on Pico Boulevard that sold guns. It was only a small wooden building, hardly more than a shack, with a sign in the window that said Guns & Ammo, but Sasha had noticed it several times driving by because it seemed such an oddity.

In the Europe of Sasha's childhood, they had world wars—armies and tanks and planes dropping bombs, death on a grand scale. But individual citizens generally were prohibited from owning firearms. Here in California, it was just the opposite: no war, but Americans loved their guns and wouldn't do without them. Sasha found it incomprehensible. Personally, she despised guns. As a child she had seen too clearly the misery they cause. But she needed one now.

She parked on the street, and since it wasn't a good neighborhood, she pressed the electric switch to raise the convertible top of her Cadillac. She walked into the store hoping not to be recognized, hidden behind dark glasses, her floppy black hat with wide brim, a tight black dress, stiletto heels, and a mink stole wrapped around her shoulders. Just another floozy. Nevertheless, the owner gave her an odd look as she came in the door.

"I want to buy a gun," she told him. Inside, the store wasn't much more than a cubbyhole with a window with a beat-up shade. The owner was a bald man with a stomach that bulged outward from his gold-colored sports shirt. He stood behind a dusty glass counter studying Sasha for some time before he answered.

"I see. You want to buy a gun." He paused to light the cigarette that Sasha had put into her mouth, using a book of matches. "Tell me something. Have you ever owned a gun?"

"No."

"And this gun that you want, is it to protect yourself or are you planning to shoot somebody?"

"What's it to you?"

"Well, it's nothing to me. I'm only trying to figure out the best weapon to suit your needs. You see, you gotta decide if you want a revolver or an automatic, and what caliber. With a lady such as yourself, I'd suggest a revolver because they're more reliable. And you'll want a small gun, I'm guessing. Something you can slip into your handbag. A twenty-two will probably be all you'll need. Because with a lady such as yourself, I'm betting you'll be able to get very close to the person involved, the one you want to shoot."

"I'm not sure I like your manner," Sasha told him. "But all right, a revolver. I don't care, as long as it works. I'll let you decide. I'll want some bullets, too. You'll have to show me where they go."

Sasha left the store with a snub-nosed .22 revolver, a little gun that fit into her handbag. The owner showed her how to put five bullets into the revolving cylinder, leaving the hammer on the empty sixth chamber as a safety precaution. The cylinder would advance, he assured her, when she pulled the trigger. When he was finished with his brief instruction, he told her not to come back to his store after she'd done whatever it was she had in mind to do, and he didn't bother to give her a receipt.

From the gun and ammo store, Sasha drove to a gas station on Wilshire and while the attendant filled the tank—and checked her oil, her tires, and cleaned the windshield—she used the phone book in the office to look up Ricky Bolano. She found him in the Yellow Pages under P for Private Investigators, with an address and phone number at 1743 Cahuenga Drive, Sherman Oaks, in the San Fernando Valley. Ricky had paid for a small-boxed ad: "Discreet Inquiries. Business, Personal. Fast, Honest Service." Sasha snorted her derision.

With the gun in her handbag, she thought she might risk a drive to the Valley to see where the enemy lived. She still didn't have a plan, but was feeling her way forward, inch by inch. She hoped a bit of reconnaissance would give her some fresh idea as to how she wanted to proceed.

She paid the gas station attendant $1.53—17 cents per gallon—and sat in her car studying the map of Los Angeles that she kept in the glove compartment. After a good deal of searching, she found Cahuenga Drive, a small squiggly line not far from Ventura Boulevard. It seemed to her an ugly name, Cahuenga. The sound of those slinky vowels filled her with dread. She was tempted just to go home and pour herself a drink. But this had to be done, like it or not. And she knew she must do it quickly before she lost her nerve.

*****

Sasha took Rodeo Drive to Sunset then made her way to Coldwater Canyon behind the Beverly Hills Hotel. The two-lane road climbed past mansions hidden behind high walls and wound up into the brown hills—to the summit on Mulholland Drive, then down the other side into the San Fernando Valley.

Sasha drove with the steering wheel clutched firmly in both hands and her neck strained forward to see the road. She wasn't a good driver. She had learned too late in life and the treacherous roads that snaked their way up into the California hills made her particularly nervous. Whenever she came to a curve, she slowed to 15 mph, certain her tires would slip, or the brakes fail, and she would be sent hurtling through the guard rail into one of the steep ravines below. Before long, she had a convoy of a dozen cars trailing behind her, faster drivers who were impatient to pass.

The road swooped and swerved around roller coaster curves until it finally widened into four lanes as it descended into the San Fernando Valley. Sasha came to Ventura Boulevard and spent half an hour finding Cahuenga Drive in the maze of small streets. Ricky's house was modest, a pre-war white stucco bungalow with a small patch of lawn out front. There was a sullen, temporary feel to the neighborhood, as though the people who lived here had only just arrived and would be moving on to other places as soon they could.

There was a car in Ricky's driveway, a grey '51 Ford Victoria, which Sasha assumed was his. She continued past the house for half a block, then turned around in a driveway and parked several houses away.

Now that she was here, Sasha had no idea what to do. Even with the gun in her handbag, she didn't want to risk a confrontation with Ricky. She lit a cigarette and turned on the car radio to the classical station, but she kept the key in the ignition and was ready to speed away at the first sign of trouble. Two boys of about Jonno's age were throwing a football lazily back and forth on the front lawn a few houses away, but otherwise the street was empty of life in a way that only L.A. streets can be. A heavy narcotic slumber sat on the land.

A half hour went by in this manner, then forty minutes. Eventually the two boys lost interest in throwing the football, got on their bicycles and rode away. Sasha was about to give up and drive home when the door of Ricky's bungalow opened and he appeared on the front step. He was dressed in his usual brown suit and hat low on his forehead. Sasha slumped lower in the seat, afraid he might turn and see her.

But his mind seemed to be on other things. She watched as he got in the Ford Victoria in the driveway and drove away.

Now what? she wondered. Should she try to follow him? She didn't think so. It was the house that interested her, and what she might find inside. Some secret, perhaps. Some vulnerability that she could use against him. It was hard to say.

She waited a few more minutes in case he had forgotten something and returned. Sasha was terrified at what she was about to do. But she couldn't come this far and not finish what she intended. She forced herself from the car and up the sidewalk to Ricky's front door.

There was a screen door that creaked open when she tried it. But the real door behind the screen was solidly locked. Sasha was more relieved than disappointed.

She crossed the front lawn and peered inside the living room window. But the curtains were drawn and she couldn't see a thing. She continued along the front of the house until she came to a gate of half-rotten wood that led to an over-grown path to the backyard.

Sasha found the revolver in her bag and held it tightly in her hand. The bottom of the gate sagged on the ground and she had to give it a good yank to get it open. She walked slowly along the path, every sense alert for trouble. The backyard was littered with trash—a broken kitchen chair, empty cardboard boxes, an old car battery, a pair of boxing gloves that had been chewed up by some animal. A few over-ripe avocados had fallen from a tree onto the ground and there was an unpleasant smell of decay in the air. Sasha made her way past a garden shed and a narrow deck with a barbecue on it. The wood on the deck was broken in several places. It didn't look like Ricky threw many garden parties.

She walked carefully along the back deck to a sliding glass door. Peering inside, she saw a section of kitchen and a dining room. On the dining room table, there was a half-finished bottle of bourbon, an empty glass, and a stack of envelopes and papers that were weighed down by an ashtray full of cigarette butts. It was the papers that interested her, what she might find out about Ricky from his correspondence.

Sasha tried the glass door, but it was locked. She was standing on the rear deck, trying to see better into the house, when she heard a low growl behind her. She turned and was startled to find a huge black dog with its teeth bared and slobber drooling from its mouth. Sasha froze. The growl came from deep inside the animal's throat and he looked as though he was about to leap and tear her apart.

"Nice dog!" she tried.

But he wasn't a nice dog, and he wasn't about to be fooled with pretty lies. The animal edged closer, his growl growing louder.

Sasha pointed her gun at the dog and he retreated several feet. He seemed to understand that she had a weapon. He began to bark.

Sasha aimed and pulled the trigger. There was a pop, not very loud, followed by a woody thwack as the slug hit the trunk of the avocado tree at the edge of the yard. The bullet had gone wide by nearly a foot.

The dog seemed to come to an understanding that Sasha was a lousy shot. He snarled, his eyes full of hatred. He was about to leap when she fired again. This time her aim was better and the dog fell to his side, squealing in pain.

She kept firing. The dog yelped but it refused to die. She moved closer and fired again, this time directly at his head. At last the dog went limp and there was no further sound from him. A trickle of dark blood began to flow from his head onto the grass.

"Oh!" she cried. For it was horrible.

And what would Ricky think when he returned home to find his terrible pet shot in the backyard? She had a wild idea to wrap the body in a blanket and get rid of it somehow. Perhaps dump it in the woods off Mulholland Drive. With luck, Ricky would think his dog had gotten out of the yard and run away. But the corpse was revolting and she didn't want to touch it. And there was no time to find a blanket. She knew she had to get away fast. One of the neighbors could have heard the gunshots and phoned the police.

An Almost Perfect Ending

Sasha stuffed the gun back into her handbag and walked quickly from the yard, closing the gate behind her. She was shaking all over but she forced herself not to run in case someone was watching from one of the houses nearby. She made her way down the street to where her car was parked, fumbled with the key, got the door open, and collapsed onto the driver's seat. At first the Cadillac wouldn't start, for she had pumped too hard on the gas pedal, flooding the engine. At last the motor came to life with a roar and she sped away. She didn't even dare light a cigarette until she was back on Coldwater Canyon Drive.

*****

Before reaching the summit on Mulholland Drive, Sasha pulled off the road onto a gravel turnout by the edge of a steep ravine too upset to continue driving. She kept remembering the terrifying animal on his haunches about to leap at her. She couldn't get the hellish creature from her mind. God only knew what Ricky would make of it when he got home to find his dog shot in the backyard! He would be furious, of course, beyond any anger she had seen in him before. Just the thought of Ricky's anger was more than her nerves could bear. She rested her forehead on the steering wheel and wept, overcome with the horror of the afternoon.

A light rain had begun to fall tap-tapping against the soft material of the convertible roof. Bad weather was moving inland from the coast. Sasha cried for a long time as the traffic on Coldwater Canyon Drive drove past, their tires making a swishing sound on the wet pavement. When she finally raised her head from the steering wheel, she felt marginally better. She sniffled and blew her nose into a handkerchief as an idea began working through her mind. Ricky would almost certainly drive home this way over Coldwater Canyon tonight after stopping by her house. It was the most direct route from Beverly Hills to his house.

Wouldn't it be nice, she thought, if there happened to be an accident? She could see it so clearly: Ricky on these wet, treacherous mountain curves, sailing off the road through a guard rail into a steep ravine. The car would tumble end over end, somersaulting down the hillside with a sickening crunch of metal and breaking glass, bursting into flames at the bottom. A murder that could never be proved.

Sasha didn't know yet how such a thing could be arranged. As ideas went, this one came to her unformed, in need of development, more of a vague feeling than anything else. But she liked it. *A murder that looked like an accident and could never be proved!* She liked it very much. And she was certain that somehow it could be done.

Bourbon! she thought suddenly. What if Ricky had too much to drink? What if he was so impaired that he failed to navigate one of the sharp mountain curves? It was one of the dangers of California, after all: those late-night automobile accidents you were always reading about.

Sasha hated bourbon herself. Even the smell made her sick. But she knew from past experience that it was Ricky's favorite poison.

Thirteen

At close to seven that evening—as Sasha sat at her dressing table carefully opening gelatin capsules of Nembutal with a sharp paring knife, pouring the speckled contents into a small glass bowl—Max was arriving at the Warner Brothers studio complex in Burbank in the back seat of a company car. The car brought him through the main gate and let him off in front of the Mill Building, where he walked upstairs to his cubbyhole office to find a stack of messages on his desk.

As a mere director, far down the ladder of studio consequence, Max shared a frumpy middle-aged secretary, Carol, with two writers and an associate producer who had offices on the same floor. Carol was gone for the day, but she had left a note saying that Buck Schulman wanted to see him the moment he got in from location, no matter what the time.

Buck Schulman was Jack Warner's left-hand man, as the saying went at the studio, an unsavory fellow who took care of the messy problems that came up from time to time—getting movie stars out of jams, forcing unions to accept harsh contracts, settling lawsuits before they went to court. It was said that Buck had once murdered a writer who had failed to finish a screenplay on time, but this was probably only studio gossip, the usual black humor of creative hacks. Still, Max knew he was in for a bad time for his mistakes today, losing expensive equipment in the ocean and putting *Storm Tossed* behind schedule.

Max took a snort of whiskey from his flask to brace himself, then walked upstairs to the fourth floor where the big shots had their offices. The building was nearly deserted since it was after hours and his footsteps echoed loudly in the empty halls. The outer office of Schulman's suite was dark, his secretary gone home, but the door to the inner office had been left open. Max found Buck sitting behind his desk in a small pool of light.

"Is that you, McCormick? Get in here!" Buck shouted through the door.

He was a great bull of a man, well over two hundred and fifty pounds, with a coarse, broad face and a nose that had been broken at some point in his life. He looked more like a prize fighter than a studio executive.

"Sorry about the camera," Max said with a nervous smile as he stepped into the room. He felt absurdly like a schoolboy called into the principal's office. "It was stupid of me to let the tide get so close, but I was dead set on getting a great shot."

"Sit the fuck down, McCormick," Buck told him, pointing a stubby finger at a leather armchair. Buck's office was paneled with dark wood and aspired to look like a gentleman's library from the last century. A single brass lamp with a

Tiffany shade cast a circle of light on the huge desk, leaving the rest of the room in darkness. Buck was immaculately dressed in a dark gray pin-striped suit, but the expensive outfit only emphasized the brutality of his face.

"I have another camera lined up," Max continued, afraid to stop talking. "A Mitchell that I've been able to borrow from the Fonda picture that's just wrapped on Stage Five. It's a damn shame about the accident, but I figure if we hustle tomorrow, we'll only lose one day of shooting. I'll be able to make that up next week when we get back into the studio for interiors, so I'm still hoping to have the picture in the can by April thirtieth, right on schedule."

While Max jabbered, Buck stared at him with dark, unfriendly eyes, saying nothing.

"Anyway, I'm sorry," Max apologized again, filling the silence. "I have no excuse for letting that wave sweep everything away. I can only say, it's going to be a hell of a picture. Wait 'til you see the footage. Jean is fantastic. Leo, too. You're going to end up making money on *Storm Tossed*, I promise. It's going to be a great thriller."

"You don't get it, do you, McCormick?" Buck asked, finally speaking.

"Get what?"

"You're fired, pal. You're off the picture, as of now."

Max was momentarily too stunned to speak.

"I want you to pack your stuff and get out of here tonight," Buck went on. "As of tomorrow, I'm leaving instructions with security not to let you on the lot."

Max took a deep breath. "Look, Buck, this doesn't make sense. I can finish the picture in two weeks. It'll take you that long to find a new director. So why don't you—"

"I already *have* a new director, you dumb prick," Buck interrupted. "Henry Hathaway's taking over. He's coming in tomorrow to clean up your mess. We should have hired him in the first place. You're through, asshole. Now get the fuck out of my office before I start to get mad."

Max rose to his feet. He was starting to be angry himself. "Okay, if that's how you want it. But look, I lost one damn camera to a wave, and some sound equipment. It's not the end of the world and you have no legitimate reason to fire me. I'm going to take this to the Directors Guild for arbitration."

Buck laughed unpleasantly. "Oh, yeah, I forgot, you're a *union* guy, aren't you? Well, if I were you, I'd forget your fucking union because they can't help you. You know, I never liked you, McCormick. I don't like your kind. Now get out of my office, before I pick you up and throw you out."

Max shook his head, suddenly exhausted as he turned away.

"I guess I never liked you either, Buck," he admitted, walking out the door.

Robert Westbrook

*****

It was after nine by the time Max left Warner's and drove home in the misty rain. He had a few personal belongings from his office riding in the back seat of his Packard—a favorite coffee mug, a framed photograph of Mina from the wall, several scripts, an Oxford book of English poetry, a few notebooks filled with ideas, nothing much.

The night was dark and slippery and wet as he made his way into Hollywood and then onto Sunset toward Bel Air. Max drove slowly, mechanically, while his mind raced, the windshield wipers slapping back and forth with the mad insistence of a metronome.

He'd been fired! It was hard to absorb. *His* movie had been taken from him, he wouldn't be getting up early tomorrow to drive to the set, there was no need to set the alarm clock. In all his years in Hollywood, he had never been fired from a picture before. He felt violated, brutally wrenched from his work.

But of course, it wasn't really his picture, that was what was so frustrating. The picture belonged to Jack Warner and the faceless men back East who paid the bills. It was a fine thing to be a motion picture director; Max had always had an idealized notion of his craft. But in the end, directors were at the mercy of the bosses who held the purse strings. He was paid well for his work, but he was only the hired help.

158

An Almost Perfect Ending

Still, it didn't make sense that he should be fired tonight. Not when the picture was nearly in the can. Changing directors at this late stage was going to cost Jack Warner thousands of dollars, even if they did have Henry Hathaway lined up to take over. Besides, Max had done well for the studio over the years. He had made money with a dozen movies. So yes, a lecture for losing a camera in the surf, a serious dressing-down for his foolishness, that would have been in order. But to be fired in such a brutal manner, he didn't get it at all.

Max turned off Sunset onto Stone Canyon Road and made his way up into the hills toward his house as the rain dripped steadily from the black sky. His headlights came around the final bend of the road, lighting up the electric gate at the end of his driveway. But when he pressed the button beneath his dashboard, the gate refused to open. Max groaned with irritation, wondering what else could go wrong today. Up ahead, he could see through his windshield wipers past the wrought-iron bars of the gate to his house at the end of the driveway. The outside light by the garage beckoned, shining with a cozy yellow glow. But the rain was coming down harder and he saw he was going to get wet. He hadn't thought to bring an umbrella when he'd left the house this morning.

Max stepped from the Packard with his shoulders hunched against the rain. He was standing in the headlights of his car, about to unlock the gate with the key in his hand, when he heard a voice behind him: "Max McCormick?"

The man seemed to step out of the night itself, an apparition. He stood under a black umbrella in a black suit and for a moment Max thought it was the Angel of Death come to carry him off. He wasn't far wrong.

"Yes, I'm Max McCormick," he answered uncertainly.

"Then this is for you."

The stranger handed Max an envelope that had been wrapped in plastic to protect it from the rain.

"You have been served, Mr. McCormick." With this, the man in black turned and walked away. Max watched as he crossed the road to a car that was half-hidden in a neighbor's driveway, got in and drove away.

At first, Max was too stupefied to understand what had just happened to him. But he got it quickly enough. "God damn!" he cried bitterly. Wet and miserable, he unlocked the front gate, slipped back inside his car, then drove the rest of the way up the driveway to the house. Before he turned off the engine, he switched on the overhead dome light and read the contents of envelope. It was a subpoena summoning him to appear in Washington, D.C. at a special meeting of the House Un-American Activities Committee. The hearing was set for ten o'clock on the morning of Friday, June 12, 1954, six weeks away.

Max sat for a long time with the engine running, holding the piece of paper in his hand. *HUAC*! It was a lot for any man, to be fired from a picture and then subpoenaed to go up in front of the dreaded House Un-American Activities Committee, all in the space of a few hours. At least he understood now why Jack Warner was willing to lose money by hiring a new director. In fact, getting fired today had nothing to do with losing an expensive movie camera to the ocean. That was only a convenient excuse. He had been blacklisted, and it might just as well be the Black Death. The blacklist was secretive and informal; some in Hollywood pretended it didn't exist. But once your name was on it, you were finished. You would never work again.

The house was dark with only the yellow outside light shining. Max wasn't certain if Mina was out or had only gone to bed early. He hoped she was out because he didn't feel like talking with her. Not yet. He didn't want to see or talk to anyone.

Max switched off the engine and walked indoors, weary and angry and wet. He had never been a Communist, the whole thing was ridiculous. He had supported trade unions, that's all. He had been a founding member of the Screen Directors Guild. He had opposed fascism in Spain and Germany and had signed petitions in support of civil rights for Colored people. But apparently these beliefs did not conform to what was currently allowed in America, land of the free!

Max climbed the stairs and came to the second-floor landing so deep in thought that it took him a moment to realize there were several voices coming from the other side of the bedroom door and sounds of laughter.

There was also a strange smell in the air.

Max opened the door slowly. Mina was in bed but she wasn't alone. The room was dim, lit with several candles. Max stared stupidly. It was a classic situation. The sort of situation that was almost funny when it happened to other people. But it wasn't funny when it happened to you.

There were three people in the bed under a loose sheet. Peter Cross was in the middle, laughing at some joke he had just made. Mina was on one side of him and Helena Cross on the other. None of them had a stitch on. Peter held a badly rolled cigarette in his hand and Max realized that the odd scent in the air he had smelled on the landing was marijuana.

"Oh, Max!" Mina said when she saw him, as though this were all quite normal. "Did you have a good day?"

Helena giggled awkwardly and raised the sheet to cover her small breasts.

"Ah, it's the maestro!" Peter called out, unbothered. "Come on in and have something more interesting to smoke than your usual tobacco! Don't be shy, my good man—I always thought you Hollywood people were supposed to be sophisticated!"

Without answering, Max shook his head, turned, and left the bedroom. He got only as far as the bench on the landing by the top of the stairs where he sank down, too weary to walk another step.

In a moment, Mina appeared on the landing with the sheet wrapped around her.

"Oh, Max!" she said. "You cause yourself to suffer so much! Don't you understand, darling—this is nothing! You're upset over nothing, my dear."

"Yes, Mina," he said heavily. "I see that. Still, it's not nothing."

She approached cautiously, as though he were an exotic animal she didn't wish to disturb. "Is there anything I can do for you, Max? Any way I can help you be happy?"

He shook his head. "No, there's nothing."

She brightened. "Max, listen! Come to bed with us, darling. Helena's very pretty. I know she would like to be with you."

Max moaned and put his head in his hands. "No, Mina. No, no, no."

"Oh, my poor darling. You take everything too seriously. That's your trouble."

"Mina, I'm all right. Just go back to them."

"But I can't leave you, dear, not when you're feeling so blue."

"I'm fine, Mina. I want to be alone."

"But Max . . ."

"I just want to be alone," he told her more definitely. Strongly enough so that Mina studied him a moment, and then turned back into the bedroom, closing the door behind her.

Alone in the hallway, Max sat and simply breathed for a while, incapable of doing anything more. He felt like such a fool, a ridiculous creature. Life seemed to be some sort of joke whose punchline everyone got except himself. He wasn't sure why he was so slow.

But it wasn't too late, he supposed. Even a fool could learn.

Max still had his car keys in his hand. Without another thought, he rose from the bench and walked down the stairs. He stopped only briefly to find a full bottle of Glenlivet in the den downstairs, and then he was out the door and in his Packard, driving into the rainy night in search of comfort.

He knew where he was going: to Sasha. He intended to get roaring drunk and fabulously laid. He hadn't spoken with Sasha for weeks. They'd been fighting, he could hardly remember why. But at this moment he knew that she was everything real and warm and true. The one love that would save him in the darkness of the world.

It was a fine, clear feeling. But Max should have telephoned first to make certain Sasha wasn't otherwise engaged.

Fourteen

Timing is a key element of life, often more important than it appears. There is good timing and bad timing. You can be ahead of your time, you can even be out of time. As any old comedian will tell you, timing is especially important when it comes to milking a laugh. On stage, as in life, the punchline needs to be delivered right on time.

In the comedy that was about to happen tonight—a situation comedy, the gods' favorite sport—Max passed through the Bel Air gate on his way toward Beverly Hills at exactly 11:47. He would have noted that if he had looked at his watch.

As for Ricky Bolano, he arrived at Sasha's house on North Maple Drive a few minutes later, at 11:58, almost exactly on time for their appointment. Sasha had spent the evening waiting anxiously in her living room, too nervous to sit still for more than a few minutes at a time. She had the television on to a late-night movie, *Casablanca*, but she had seen the picture before, and tonight she was too distracted to pay attention.

She had her small .22 revolver hidden in the pocket of her house dress, now fully loaded with six shiny little bullets. It was too late to think of safety on a night like this, a hammer on an empty chamber. If she needed the gun, she would need it fast and six bullets were better than five. Ricky could die like his dog for all she cared. But the dead dog increased her anxiety. She didn't know if he had figured out that she had been in his backyard that afternoon.

The living room curtains were tightly drawn and Sasha had lit a fire since it was a raw night. The logs flickered with an orange glow, lit by gas jets. The drink trolley stood a few feet from the television set with the bottles carefully arranged so that the bourbon, a quart of Old Grandad, was easily visible in the front next to her Smirnoff's.

On television, Sam was about to play it again, the show-stealing song—Sasha was a big fan of show-stealing songs—when she jumped at the sound of her doorbell ringing, a two-tone chime.

She turned off Sam at the piano and took a deep breath, trying to calm her stage fright. Now that the moment had come, she realized how many things could go wrong. There were too many variables, that was the problem.

She opened the front door with her gun in hand, holding it close to her body so that Ricky wouldn't be able to slap it aside. He stood in the portico in a tan trench coat with his hat low on his forehead looking like a character in the movie she had been watching. Behind him, the rain had stopped, but the trees were dripping and the night smelled of dampness.

He smiled when he saw the gun in her hand, not overly impressed.

"Well, how about that? You've gone and bought yourself a pea-shooter. Am I supposed to be frightened?"

"Not as long as you mind your manners, Mr. Bolano." She was pleased that her voice held steady. "You may come inside. But you will keep your distance. If you step anywhere near me, I won't hesitate to shoot. You need to be perfectly clear on that, Mr. Bolano. Frankly, I don't give a fuck about the consequences. You will never . . . *never* touch me again. Is that absolutely clear?"

He laughed. "Sure, Sasha, have it your way."

She backed away from the door and kept a wary distance as he moved past her through the foyer into the living room.

"It's nice to have a fire on a night like this," he remarked, looking around at the drink trolley and the cozy room.

"Why don't you just tell me what you want and be on your way."

But as Sasha had anticipated, Ricky was in no hurry to be on his way. He liked to draw things out. For a thug, he was pompous. He considered himself a wit. He settled on the sofa by the fireplace and took off his hat, balancing it on his knee.

"You might offer me a drink, Sasha. I'd like that. I'd take it as a sign of hospitality."

She snorted with derision. "This isn't a bar, Mr. Bolano, and you are not my friend. So tell me why you're here and then get the hell out."

He kept smiling. "Come on, doll. What'll it cost you to give me a drink? It's wet out there and my bones need warming. They don't tell you that about California when you're back East, how cold and damp it is in this fucking town. So be sociable, Sasha. Besides, what can I do? You're the gal with the gun."

She tried to look undecided. It was important that she didn't appear too eager to give him a drink. "All right," she told him. "Just keep your distance. You can join me with a shot of vodka before you go."

"Make that bourbon," he said, just as she had intended. He nodded at the bottle of Old Grandad on the drink trolley.

"Okay," she told him. "Ice?"

"Sure, on the rocks. No water though."

Sasha set down her revolver by the ice bucket in order to make their drinks. But she kept it close enough to grab should he make a sudden move.

"Relax," he told her. "I'm not going to hurt you, I've told you that already. Why, I'm thinking you and me—we don't have to be at odds. Maybe I could even help with things. See what I'm saying?"

Sasha didn't answer. The bottle of Old Grandad was half-full, more artfully arranged than it appeared. She put two ice cubes in an old fashioned glass and poured him a big shot, though not so large as to make him suspicious. She made her own drink, vodka neat, from the clear bottle of Smirnoff's.

She was careful not to let her guard down. When the drinks were ready, she picked up the gun and held it in her free hand as she brought Ricky his bourbon. She set his drink on the coffee table then returned to the trolley for her own glass.

"Sit down and we'll have ourselves a talk," he said.

"I don't think we have anything to talk about."

"Sure, we do. In fact, I have a proposition for you. Something you might like. A way you can get me off your back and maybe even make a few bucks, too. So humor me. Have a seat and listen."

Sasha took her drink and sat rigidly on the matching sofa on the far side of the coffee table. She lowered the gun but kept it in her hand.

"All right, I'm listening."

He raised his glass. "Skoal."

Sasha raised her own glass just enough to encourage him to drink. Now that they had arrived at the heart of the matter, she was nearly breathless with nerves. Earlier in the evening she had mixed sixteen Nembutal into the half bottle of Old Grandad, the prescription sleeping pills that she took at night. Sixteen was an arbitrary number. She didn't want the pills to kill him, that wasn't the plan. She only wanted him to fall asleep at the wheel on his way home, driving those dangerous hillside curves of Coldwater Canyon Drive back to his home in the Valley. But she knew she was taking a gamble. She hoped he wouldn't notice the taste. She sipped very lightly on her own drink, ready for anything.

Ricky downed his drink in a single swallow as he always did. He was a tough guy, but he was a creature of habit and that would be his downfall. Sasha had a moment of fright as he held up his empty glass and examined it against the light of the fire, as though he were looking for something suspicious. But it turned out to be nothing.

"Old Grandad has nice bite on a night like this," he remarked.

"What is your proposition, Mr. Bolano?"

He leaned back comfortably into the sofa. "You know, a curious thing happened today, Sasha," he mentioned. "Someone broke into my backyard and shot my dog. You wouldn't know anything about that, would you?"

Sasha gripped the gun so tightly her knuckles were white.

"I don't know what you're talking about," she told him. "Is that what you came to talk about? Your dog?"

"Naw. I was curious, that's all." He shrugged. "But let's let that go for the moment. Here's my proposition. Imagine for a second that I know somebody, a guy with money. Let's say he's not from around here, but maybe from some hick place like Cincinnati. Just some ordinary jerk. Maybe he runs an auto dealership or a bank, I don't know. But he's not in show business, and he's not the sort who would ever get a chance under usual circumstances to spend a night with a woman who's a famous star. Are you getting the picture?"

Sasha nodded. She was getting the picture.

"So the question is, how much money do you think a guy like this would pay for a once-in-a-lifetime roll in the hay with maybe the most famous piece of tail in Hollywood? A thousand dollars? *Five* thousand dollars? I mean, what are dreams worth? How much will a rich man pay for a fantasy?"

"I don't know, Mr. Bolano. You tell me."

He grinned. "Personally, I'd say the sky's the limit. Ten grand. You name it. But it would need to be marketed right. That's the catch. You'd need someone like me to arrange it."

"A pimp," she said unpleasantly.

"Names don't bother me, Sasha. It's money I'm thinking about, not my reputation."

"And what would I get out of this?"

Ricky took a few minutes to explain his vision, how the two of them would clean up. He would supply the customers and the security, as he called it. She would supply the fantasy. And they would split the proceeds fifty/fifty. As for the blackmail, that old matter from New York, they could forget that because they would be business partners, on a whole new footing. He would even give her his copy of the 1943 arrest warrant just so she'd know she didn't have to worry.

Sasha nodded, pretending a wary interest. But she had to keep things moving. She didn't want Ricky to pass out here on the sofa. She finished her drink and went to the trolley to freshen her glass, hoping it would inspire Ricky to ask for a second glass himself.

"I'll have to think about it, Mr. Bolano. I won't pretend the money doesn't interest me. I'm broke, you know that. But I'm not sure why I should trust you."

"Oh, you can trust me," he said easily. "You see, we could only work this as a team. You would need me just as much as I'd need you. Partners *have* to trust each other."

Did the bastard think she was stupid? Trust Ricky Bolano? No, thank you! But she nodded, as though she was thinking.

"And you would give me that old arrest report?"

"Sure. Let's say after six months. I mean, we'll have a trial period to make certain we're on the same page. Then if you're a good girl, that piece of paper will be yours."

It didn't take rocket science for Sasha to know that once Ricky got his hooks into her, he would never give her that arrest report and let her go. But she pretended to go along.

"Okay, let's say I'm maybe interested," she told him after a moment. "But the money would have to be seriously good. These guys you're telling me about, the ones with big fantasies. I won't take less than two grand for putting out. And that's my cut alone. The minimum of what I'd expect for the sort of night you're describing, not what we split. Is that understood?"

Rick's wolfish face lit up with a smile that was almost friendly. "Sure, doll. I wouldn't want you to sell yourself cheap. That wouldn't be in my interest. This is about big bucks for both of us. So what do you say?"

"I'll have to think about it. I wouldn't want anyone to know about this, not ever. It's a big risk for me."

His smile became even broader. "Hey, you can trust Ricky to keep a secret! Secrets are my bread and butter, you see. So why don'cha pour me another glass of that Old Grandad. Just because we're friends now."

Sasha crossed the room from the sofa to the drink trolley and turned her back to Ricky to hide her nervousness. She didn't see herself as a killer. In the end, it was up to Lady Fortune to decide what to do with Ricky Bolano. Maybe he'd fall asleep harmlessly in his parked car. It wasn't even certain he would take the lonely late-night ride back home along Coldwater Canyon to his house in the Valley. Anything could happen.

Let fate decide, Sasha told herself. She handed Ricky the drugged cocktail with almost a clean conscience.

"Here you are," she told him. "One for the road."

Fifteen

Max felt a pleasant flutter as he pulled up in front of Sasha's house on North Maple Drive. The street was dark, lined on both sides with big trees whose branches formed a tunnel, meeting in a canopy overhead—magnolia trees, in fact, not maple, because in Los Angeles few things were as advertised. Max was almost school boyishly horny, ready to unwind after an awful day. In his mind, he was already halfway in bed with Sasha, pulling her body close.

Which made for a serious disappointment as his headlights picked out a car in her driveway and he realized that she wasn't alone. It was a dark '51 Ford Victoria that he had never seen before.

"Oh, Jesus!" he swore aloud, taking in the unexpected sight. He was certain it was a man's car. A lover, obviously. Who else would be parked in Sasha's driveway at this time of night? Max's disappointment was so sharp he felt like someone had just punched him in the stomach.

He drifted to the curb and switched off his lights and engine, coming not so much to a stop as a state of paralysis. His very breath seemed to squeeze from his body. He didn't think life had ever stomped on any man quite so hard.

The only immediate thing Max could think to do was to take a long pull from the bottle of Scotch whiskey that was riding on the front seat next to him. He debated his options as clearly as he could see them: 1) Drive to the bar at the Beverly Brown Derby and get raging drunk. 2) Pick up a woman somewhere, any woman at all with a cunt between her legs and fuck himself silly. Or 3) Knock on Sasha's door and scream obscenities to her upstairs bedroom window, what a goddamn whore she was, and how he should have seen it coming, a girl like that who cheated at cards.

But Max didn't like scenes, he didn't like shouting obscenities, and the thought of picking up a strange woman made him feel so lonely he couldn't bear it. He was leaning toward Option One, the bar at the Brown Derby, when an outside light came on by Sasha's front door, shining a yellow glow into the misty night. Max was about to take another slug of whiskey when the front door opened and a man stepped out onto the steps beneath the portico. Before Max could get a good look at him, Sasha joined him on the steps and he turned to face her. Sasha was wearing a yellow house dress that Max recognized. She had often come downstairs to see him out of the house in just such a way.

The man and Sasha stopped to talk together on the steps. Max couldn't hear what they were saying but he recognized post-coital intimacy when he saw it. His side window had begun to mist from the warmth of his breath and he had to rub the glass with his hand in order to see better. Sasha's lover was dressed in a trench coat and there was a hat pulled down low on his forehead that looked more Chicago than Beverly Hills. A cheap hood, Max decided. There was something sinister about him. But maybe that was how Sasha got her thrills these days, hanging out with bad boys. Pretty women often found bad boys sexy. He had seen that before in Hollywood.

Max knew he should leave. It wasn't nice to sit in the dark like a Peeping Tom watching Sasha and her lover on the front steps. Though it was fascinating in a seedy way. There was an odd thrill to it. He couldn't tear himself away.

Were they going to kiss? He thought they might and he was determined not to miss the show. Without taking his eyes from the front doorstep, Max unscrewed the top of the Scotch and raised the bottle to his lips. But in the darkness he misjudged the distance to his mouth and the glass banged against his teeth. Everything was out of alignment today. The world had gone bad on him.

Sasha and the man didn't kiss. Maybe they'd had enough of that earlier. She turned and closed the front door and the fellow began walking along the path to the driveway. Before he reached his car, the outside light went off and the scene went dark. The effect was cinematic. Almost as though a director had cried, "Cut!"

Max was disappointed that he couldn't see anything more. A dim yellow glow came from behind the curtains of Sasha's living room, but that was it. He took another swig of whiskey, but it wasn't his lucky night. His hand hit the horn on the steering wheel as he was lowering the bottle to his lap. A loud brassy *choo-ga* bleeped from his Packard into the darkness, like the call of some exotic animal.

Max froze, certain he had given himself away. He didn't know what he would say if the guy came over demanding to know what he was doing there lurking in the dark. It wasn't how gentlemen behaved, and Max liked to think of himself as a gentleman. But the seconds ticked by and nothing happened. The rain had begun again, trickling down gently through the trees, pinging against the roof.

The Ford's interior dome light came on abruptly. The man in the hat had found his way to his car and the light was startling. Max watched as he slipped into the driver's seat and shut the door behind him, causing the night to go black again. Then the red taillights flashed on followed by the headlights, a harsh white glare. The Ford started backing out of the driveway.

Max was unprepared for what happened next. The Ford backed up onto the street and kept moving quickly in reverse until it was alongside Max's Packard, only a few feet away. The side window rolled down and Max found himself looking into the face of Sasha's late-night visitor. In the darkness, the face was spectral, half-lit in the green glow of his dashboard, more like a ghost than a person. Max jerked back from his own window, but it was too late, he had been seen. The man smiled, as though he knew who Max was and wasn't entirely surprised to see him here. He raised his middle finger in an unmistakable gesture, jerking his finger up and down obscenely, like people fucking. Then he laughed and raised his window and sped off in the direction of Sunset Boulevard.

A great hot rush of anger flooded Max's body like a drug. "Asshole!" he cried. Without thinking, he fired up the Packard and slammed the car into gear. He made a reckless turn in Sasha's driveway and accelerated hard up North Maple Drive in order chase after the Ford.

Everything had gone wrong today and Max was in a wild mood, far beyond his usual boundaries. Luckily, he had directed plenty of thrillers with scenes just like this one, one car following another in the rain.

*****

The back streets of Beverly Hills were dark and slick. Max raced through the stop sign at Elevado Avenue without slowing down. For a half a block he thought the Ford had gotten away, but then he spotted its distinctive taillights, red slits like horizontal teardrops, just as it was about to make a left turn onto Sunset Boulevard.

Max sped through the intersection, closing the gap between them. He had no clear idea why he was doing this, but he was drunk, he was angry, and it seemed urgently important not to let the Ford get away.

There was only light traffic on Sunset this time of night and Max was able to position himself one car back from the Ford. They traveled several blocks together at the speed limit, 35 mph, but just before the Beverly Hills Hotel, the Ford made a fast turn onto Beverly Drive and accelerated into the expensive maze of darkened streets behind the hotel. Max followed as close as he dared, keeping the teardrop taillights in sight. Unless Sasha's visitor had a date at one of the fancy mansions here, there was only one logical place he could be going—to Coldwater Canyon Drive, the hillside road that wound its way over the mountains to the Valley on the other side. Max settled down for the ride, keeping a distance of about a hundred feet between them.

Steering with one hand, Max managed occasional nips from the bottle nestled between his legs. The liquor filled him with a glow of confidence that somehow it was perfectly logical to race after a man whose name he didn't know. The night was fateful and he was glad to have a purpose, one simple goal that made the rest of his chaotic life tolerable. As they drove along the winding road, he saw the scene from a celestial distance—a long shot, the two cars climbing together into the hills. He had reached a fine stage of drunkenness where he believed he was invulnerable, riding in the hands of God.

Coldwater Canyon had no traffic at this hour. There was just the two of them on the road, Max's Packard and the man's Ford, the two of them bound together in a kind of late-night dance. Max stayed close on the Ford's tail as they glided along the long curves of the mountain road. It was oddly beautiful, the gravitational pull as you accelerated along a curve, the dashboard glowing, the engine purring. It wasn't until they reached the summit on Mulholland Drive and were descending toward the Valley that Max realized the driver of the Ford had begun drifting erratically into the wrong lane. He appeared to be having trouble staying on the road. Max grinned maliciously. The guy was drunk as a skunk! He was even drunker than the skunk that Max was. Which was saying something.

The Ford came into a long turn and drifted again into the wrong lane. The driver corrected his steering, but he did it too abruptly. He fishtailed and almost lost control before he managed to get back to the proper side of the road.

"Whoa, Nellie!" Max said merrily. "Shouldn't drink and drive, fella! It'll get you every time!"

They were still coming down the long curve, diving toward the distant lights of the Valley below, when the Ford slowed so abruptly that Max wasn't able to react in time. There was no flash of brake lights, nothing to warn him. It was as though the man in the hat had simply let his foot slide off the gas pedal.

An Almost Perfect Ending

The crash took Max by surprise. It happened all at once, out of nowhere. The Packard hit the rear end of the Ford with a loud crunch of metal and a hard thump. Max found himself spinning out of control on the pavement, drifting round and round in dreamy slow motion. He made three complete rotations until at last he came to a stop alongside the guard rail. His engine was making a ticking noise and there was a smell of burnt rubber and oil in the air.

Max sat clutching his steering wheel, breathing hard, remarkably sober. But where was the Ford? As far as he could see, he was alone on the road. He couldn't see the other car anywhere.

He stepped from the Packard and stood in the drizzle trying to make sense out of what had happened. His legs were wobbly and there was a taste of blood in his mouth. The puzzle at first was beyond his power to solve, how a Ford Victoria could simply vanish. Then in the glow of his headlights, he saw what had happened. There was a jagged break in the guard rail on the road fifty feet above him where the Ford had sailed through. Max had hit the car from behind like one pool ball smacking into another, sending the Ford shooting off the side of the cliff.

Max stood on the center line of the road, too stunned to move. He was bleeding from a small gash on his forehead, but otherwise he wasn't hurt. He knew he should get help. He should climb down the cliff to the wreckage and pull the fellow free. But meanwhile, miraculously, there were no other cars. No one had seen the accident, he was alone.

"God help me!" he said to himself as he stood alone on the dark road in the rain. "What have I done?"

It took Max only a few seconds to give into temptation. Remarkably, his car engine was still running. He had even spun around to face the right direction. The nose of his Packard was pointing toward home. All he had to do was get back inside his car and drive away. No one would ever know. It was so absurdly easy.

At first, he told himself that he was only going for help. It was his duty, after all. The man in the Ford might be still alive in the ravine below. But as Max drove back up the grade toward Mulholland Drive, he knew there would be no easy way to explain this accident to the police. Especially how he had been lurking outside Sasha's house in the rain, a peeping Tom.

He drove for nearly half a mile before meeting a car coming from the other direction. He turned his head from the oncoming lights and hoped the driver wouldn't get a clear look at him.

Max kept going, fully aware of his shame and weakness. And his fabulous good fortune to get away.

Sixteen

In the days that followed, Max often felt as though he had slipped into the hackneyed plot of one of his own black and white thrillers. He jumped every time he heard the telephone ring, certain it was the police.

It didn't help that he had nothing to do with himself except worry. For the first time since the war, he had no work, nothing to occupy his time. He stayed home, roaming from one room to another, avoiding Mina as much as possible. He knew he had killed a man—a stranger, a man whose name he didn't even know. He wasn't really sure how the night had happened. He had been drunk, of course, out of his mind. The memory wasn't entirely real. It floated in a kind of mist. But if he needed proof, all he needed was to look at the crushed front fender of his car. Guiltily, he kept the Packard hidden in the garage, hoping no one would find it there.

And he wasn't only a killer, he was a coward, too. He hadn't called the police, he had run away. For Max, this was so despicable that it changed his very conception of himself. He had always thought of himself as basically a decent man. Not perfect by any means. He drank too much, he knew that. He had let Sasha down in New York. In his work, he had often betrayed his artistic principals, caving in to crass men like Sam Goldwyn and Jack Warner. As a result, a cultivated man in his position needed to regard himself with a certain jaundiced sense of irony. But he had never imagined that he was the sort of person who could kill and run away.

A dozen times a day, Max nearly picked up his telephone to call the police. He longed to say, "I'm the one! I'm the killer! I'm the bastard who sent that Ford crashing through a guard rail . . . I hit him from behind and then I drove away!"

It would be a relief to confess. But then he would need to explain how he had sat in the rain spying on Sasha's house while she was with another man, and to Max this seemed somehow more shameful than murder. He thought he'd rather die than have people know what he had done, that he had been some kind of appalling Peeping Tom.

Max searched the newspapers relentlessly for news of the incident, and two days afterwards, he found a short article buried deep inside the *Hollywood Citizen News* that identified the victim of a one-car accident on Coldwater Canyon Drive as Ricky Bolano, a private investigator who had worked at one time for the New York Police Department. The Highway Patrol appeared to believe that the accident was due to alcohol and excessive speed on a slick road late at night, but they were asking anyone who might have information about the crash to come forward. This sentence alone filled Max with dread. Could there have been a witness? There weren't many homes on that stretch of Coldwater Canyon, but it was possible someone had seen him.

And now there was another question as well, a mystery: what had Sasha been doing with a private eye? It changed his idea of the night. Perhaps he had jumped to the wrong conclusion. It was possible that the man in the hat hadn't been Sasha's lover. And if not, it made Max's crime doubly wrong, that he should kill someone in a fit of mistaken jealousy. Max was filled with such intense self-loathing that he could barely sit in one place for more than a few minutes before getting up restlessly and wandering aimlessly to another part of the house.

He lied to Mina about the damage to the Packard. He said he'd clipped a tree on Stone Canyon Road near the Bel Air Hotel. Mina appeared to accept this fictitious tree without question, knowing he'd been drinking that night. But he had never lied to her before, and it seemed to him he had entered a downward spiral where the lies would never end.

*****

A week after the accident in Coldwater Canyon, Max poured himself a stiff drink and used the phone in his den to call an attorney in New York who specialized in political cases.

The lawyer, Jonas Isaacs, had been recommended to Max by his personal attorney, his old school friend Nate, whose number Max had once given to Sasha as they were arriving in

New York. Jonas had a gruff manner when he came on the telephone but there was an air of authority about him that Max found comforting.

The first thing the lawyer wanted to know was the date of his Washington hearing with HUAC, June 12th. "Good, that gives us nearly six weeks to prepare," Jonas said. "Sometimes they only give you a few days."

"Well, Mr. Isaacs, I'm not sure if I need a lawyer or an exorcist," Max told him. "I'm not even sure what crime they're accusing me of. As far as I can see, I haven't broken any law."

The attorney chuckled. "Oh, they'll find a crime if they want to, Mr. McCormick, believe me. For starters, they're going to ask you some very unpleasant questions and try to make you commit a crime, right there on the spot. For example, they'll ask you to tell them the identity of any friends who might have expressed subversive opinions over the years. If you don't answer in a way they like, they'll get you for Contempt of Congress. That's a crime, Mr. McCormick, and they can put you in prison for it."

"Subversive opinions!" Max repeated scornfully. "I remember when this country was a democracy where you could say and think what you liked!"

"You see, there you go. If you talk like that at the hearing, they'll throw the book at you. The first thing you need to remember, Mr. McCormick, is never mention the D-Word."

"Democracy? You're joking!"

"Not a bit. They don't like people like you lecturing them about the Constitution. Were you ever a member of the Communist Party, Mr. McCormick?"

"Never. I knew party members, of course. Back in the Thirties you couldn't throw a swizzle stick at any Hollywood function without hitting a few. But I was never a joiner."

"No, no, Mr. McCormick, don't say you were never a joiner, that's not a good answer. That implies you're some elitist snob who looks down on the rest of the world and probably went to Harvard. It also implies that even if you didn't join, you were sympathetic."

"I did go to Harvard, actually."

"Well, try to keep that to yourself. If it comes up, we'll deal with it. But don't volunteer it, please."

"What? It's a crime now to go to Harvard?"

"The crime," explained the lawyer patiently, "is that Joe McCarthy didn't go to Harvard. Nor did Richard Nixon, nor did any of the guys on the House Committee who are gunning for you. The first thing I have to impress upon you, Mr. McCormick—the most important thing of all—is that you mustn't mock these men on the Committee, or make them feel that you believe you're better than they are. If you patronize them, if you lecture them, if you make fun of them in any way, you might just as well slit your wrists and be done with it."

Max sighed. "This is a world I don't understand."

"Exactly. But I do. That's why you're going to hire me. Now why don't you tell me as much as you can about yourself and your political past. And then we'll go from there."

Max spoke for about twenty minutes, giving a quick sketch of himself, from his work to help establish the Screen Directors Guild, his association with the Hollywood Anti-Nazi League, and petitions he had signed in support of the Scottsboro Boys, a group of Colored men who had been unfairly accused of raping a white girl. In passing, he also mentioned the months he had spent in the Soviet Union during the war.

"It's a pity you were in the Soviet Union," Jonas said thoughtfully. "That's going to be a problem for us."

"I was in the Army, for chrissake—they ordered me there!" Max told him. "Russia *was* our ally back then, if you remember."

"Yeah, sure, *I* remember. But it's not a memory that a lot of people like to recall. Well, we'll just have to deal with it. All right, Mr. McCormick, that'll do for now—you've given me enough to get started. Meanwhile, I'd like you to make plans to come to New York sometime in the next month. We'll need to rehearse your testimony in person."

"Rehearse? I can't just tell them the truth?"

Jonas laughed at Max's naiveté. "Leave the truth to God, Mr. McCormick. In Washington, it's best to regard your appearance as a theatrical event. Only in this case, I'll be the director not you. If you do what I tell you, there's a good chance I can keep you out of jail."

"But then I'll still be blacklisted, won't I? Even if I'm cleared of any crime, I won't be able to work."

Jonas didn't answer at first. He cleared his throat. "Why don't we cross that bridge when we come to it. Nothing lasts forever, Mr. McCormick. Not the blacklist. Not even a Hollywood career."

*****

After hanging up the telephone, Max wandered restlessly outside onto the flagstone patio at the rear of the house, then along the overgrown path toward the hilltop meadow at the edge of the property. Not far from the tennis court, he came upon Mina who was on her hands and knees in a flower bed dressed in khaki trousers and one of Max's old shirts pulling weeds from the garden. She looked up at him and smiled hesitantly. They had been living at a cautious distance since the night he had found her in bed with Peter and Helena Cross.

"Have you seen the roses, dear?" she asked. "They're just coming into bloom."

"Mina, I'm not much in the mood for roses right now. Can we talk a moment? I'm afraid there are things I need to tell you."

"Well, of course, darling."

He gave her a hand up from the flower bed and led her to the edge of the garden where there was a wooden swing, large enough for two people to sit side by side, hanging on chains from the limb of a huge old oak tree. Max remembered that they'd sat here together drinking gin and tonics on the night before he left to go to war. Today the sunlight filtered through the canopy of leaves overhead, a green dappled shade of flickering light and shadow. Max had to take a deep breath to stifle a sudden urge to cry.

Mina took his hand. "What's wrong, Max? Why don't you tell me?"

He laughed unpleasantly. "What's *wrong*? Well, my dear, added to all the other things that are wrong, it appears my idealistic youth has finally caught up with me, all those crazy ideas I used to have about a society that was fair to everyone, rich and poor. Now there's a good chance we're going to lose everything and be poor ourselves. I thought you had better know."

She studied him sympathetically but didn't reply.

"It seems I've been blacklisted," he went on. "Plus, I've been served with a subpoena to go to Washington and appear in front of HUAC, to be a star witness at one of their witch trials."

As they rocked together back and forth in the swing, Max told her about getting fired from Warner Brothers and the conversation he'd had with his new attorney, Jonas Isaacs. Mina listened carefully, nodding from time to time.

"I'm awfully sorry, Max," she said when he was finished. "I know this must be hard for you."

"Mina, I'm afraid this is going to be hard on both of us. I'm not going to be able to work again in Hollywood, possibly not ever. We've earned a lot of money, but the way we've lived, we've never managed to save a penny. Unless I manage to get out of this somehow, we'll have a cushion of perhaps six months and then we're going to be broke. And I mean seriously broke. We'll need to sell this house, we'll lose everything."

Mina smiled in her sympathetic way. "Well, good riddance! Who needs a lot of stuff anyway?"

"Mina! You're not visualizing this very well. We could be living on the street. Or out of our car like Oakies."

"At least it's a Cadillac, darling. Or would you prefer your Packard? It's larger, I think."

"Mina, I'm serious. We're facing ruin."

"Yes, I know, I'm being silly. But I do understand." She was quiet for a moment. "Do you know what I've enjoyed most about being a movie star?" she asked after a while.

Max sighed. "What, dear?"

"I've had a chance to meet so many interesting people and do so many interesting things. That's my idea of a rich life. So now if we're broke—well, that'll just be a new adventure, won't it? Don't you see? That's the point of life, to be on a grand adventure. It's not supposed to be safe. It's supposed to be a fabulously interesting journey. So honestly, Max, I'm not afraid to live in our car. It's more the idea of it that one resists, the fear of change. But if we approach it day by day, I'm sure we will meet fascinating people and have all sorts of experiences."

Max laughed sorrowfully. "Oh, Mina—you've always had money. You have no idea of the kinds of 'experiences' people have when their money runs out."

"Well, then I'll find out, won't I? Max, listen to me. It's all right. I'm not afraid of being poor. You see, I'm lucky. I've faced my worst fears already. I was locked up in a mental hospital, and if I could get through that, I can get through anything."

"Oh, Mina!"

"No, you need to listen. I'm not sure if you ever realized quite how terrifying it was to be put in that place. But you know, one day I found myself strapped to a bed in a hospital in Santa Barbara and I said to myself—all right, Mina, you're going to get through this because you're a pilgrim. That's what life is about, it's a pilgrimage. And when you're a pilgrim, every river you cross is holy. Every challenge has been specially designed so that you can learn the next lesson. That's what life is about, Max, the real richness of it, the joy."

Max shook his head, for there was no way to answer Mina's impossible logic. "Of course, I could always be a friendly witness," he told her. "I could save us by naming names."

"Naming whose names, dear? I don't understand."

He laughed bitterly. Working in her peaceful garden, Mina had been inhabiting a different universe than his own. She didn't know about HUAC's obsession with names.

"There's Stuart Roth, for instance," he told her. "Do you remember Stuart?"

"The writer, that funny little man? . . . what was the name of that dreadful picture he wrote for me in 1938?"

"*The Lucky Cavalier*, and it was thirty-seven. That funny little man, as you call him, did happen to be a Communist Party member for several years. I know this for a fact because one night I was getting drunk with Bob Benchley at the Garden of Allah, and Stuart came over and cornered us with a whole lot of nonsense about the international proletariat. He was drunk too, as I remember. In any case, he invited me to an organizational meeting at his house and he was very disappointed when I declined. But you see, this is exactly the sort of fellow I could finger. When the Committee asks me, 'Mr. McCormick can you tell us if anyone ever approached you to join the Communist Party,' I could answer, 'Why, sure. A funny little guy named Stuart Roth asked me, and it was while I was getting blottoed with Bob Benchley, so most likely he was a pinko too.'"

"But surely Stuart's not a Communist anymore? No one is, are they?"

"No, of course not. Socially speaking, the whole thing's entirely passé. Poor Stuart's probably a golf playing Republican these days. The point is that I can name Stuart, and then the Committee will go ruin his life and leave me alone. I'll be considered a patriotic American hero who rats on his friends in order to save his own hide. What would you think of that, Mina?"

Mina studied him for some time.

"I love you, Max. I would never presume to tell you what to do."

"And that's it?"

"What more could there be? You're the love of my life, and my hero. And whatever you do, I'll always respect your decision."

Max laughed gently and let it pass. He was more moved than he could say. He was absurdly grateful to be Mina's hero, even if she was so completely wrong about him.

Seventeen

Max flew to Washington on a bright Wednesday morning two days before his HUAC hearing. Mina insisted on accompanying him and he was glad for her determined cheerfulness. As the time grew closer, he felt a growing dread, like a man about to go under a surgeon's knife for an operation whose outcome was far from certain.

They took a room at the Hay Adams, which Max feared would be the last expensive hotel he would be seeing for a long time. On the morning of the hearing, Mina tried to coax him into eating a good room service breakfast, but he was too nervous to put anything in his stomach except coffee and a Bloody Mary, a double.

"Is that a good idea?" she asked, watching anxiously as he drank.

"Sure it is. Think of all the vitamins I'm getting from the tomato juice."

This was such a convincing argument that Max ordered himself a second Bloody Mary to chase down the first. A half hour later, feeling almost human, he rode to the Old House Building in the back of a limousine with Mina and his attorney, Jonas Isaacs. Max decided he liked Mr. Isaacs, who was a burly, no-nonsense man in his mid-fifties. A Jew, of course. No one else would dare take on HUAC.

Flushed with vodka, Max had only an impressionistic sense of the hearing room: an ornate windowless room that was crowded and brightly lit with television lights and stuffy with the smell of stale tobacco. He was guided to the front where he was to sit at a table and answer questions. A man in a dark suit told him to put his hand on the Bible and swear he would tell the truth.

Max only had a vague idea of who everybody was. There was a swarm of faces, but they all seemed the same to him, identical men in identical suits. A small army of photographers snapped pictures, some from the back of the room, others seated in awkward positions on the floor near where he was sitting, their flash bulbs exploding like little bombs. Jonas Isaacs sat at a desk toward the front of the room watching Max with worried eyes.

Representative John S. Wood, the HUAC Committee chairman, brought the meeting to order and said a few words about the need to protect the security of our great nation, the United States of America. Throughout the morning, the nation was never referred to simply as the United States, but was always given its full patriotic title, the United States of America.

One of the identical men rose to his feet, a middle-aged man with dark hair and such an ordinary face that it took Max a few moments to understand that this was Frank Tavenner, the HUAC Chief Counsel.

Mr. Tavenner spoke. "Mr. McCormick, tell us, please, when and where were you born."

"I was born in Cambridge, Massachusetts in 1899. I attended the Groton School and later graduated from Harvard College."

Max watched as Jonas Isaacs winced. He had forgotten he wasn't supposed to say he'd gone to Harvard. Mina, who was seated by Jonas' side, smiled at him encouragingly.

"And what is your present occupation?"

"I'm a movie director. And I would like to say that I'm very proud to be associated with the motion picture industry. I count myself a lucky man to be able to do such interesting, creative work."

"And work that influences the thinking of many people around the world—wouldn't you agree, Mr. McCormick?"

"I suppose that's true," Max admitted. "The movies have become an important factor in our culture. They affect how people dress, even how they talk. But if you're trying to say that movies disseminate propaganda, you're wrong. For starters, we couldn't get away with it. The studio bosses who pay our salaries would have our heads on a platter. With my own movies, my only purpose is to entertain."

"I see. We'll get back to this point later, Mr. McCormick," said Mr. Tavenner. "You understand that we desire to learn the true extent, past and present, of Communist infiltration into the movie industry in Hollywood. There has been considerable testimony taken before this committee regarding a number of Hollywood organizations, such as the Hollywood Peace Forum, the Hollywood Anti-Nazi League—or Hollywood League Against Nazism, as it was sometimes called. Also, the Motion Picture Artists' Committee, Hollywood Writers' Mobilization, Progressive Citizens of America, Hollywood Committee of the Arts . . . you people in Hollywood, you seem to have a lot of extra time on your hands for different sorts of committees, Mr. McCormick."

"Oh, I don't know. We don't have nearly as many committees as you folks do in Washington!" Max answered with a grin.

There was a smattering of laughter in the room. Max had forgotten he wasn't supposed to joke. Chief Counsel Tavenner continued in an irritated tone.

"Have you yourself been a member of any of these groups, Mr. McCormick?"

Max smiled. "I'm sorry? Which groups were those again?"

"Progressive Citizens of America, the Hollywood Peace Forum—"

"Oh, no, no certainly not that! Peace, dear God, what an idea!"

"Mr. McCormick, you are trying our patience. Were you a member—in fact, one of the founding members—of the Hollywood Anti-Nazi League?"

An Almost Perfect Ending

"Well, sure, I was a member of the Hollywood Anti-Nazi League. In the nineteen-thirties there were a lot of us who were concerned about Hitler and Franco, and we didn't think that you people in Washington were taking the threat very seriously. Of course, many of you didn't like Jews any more than Hitler did. So probably you thought he had some good ideas. Make the trains run on time, and all that."

Max saw Jonas shaking his head, no, no, no. But Mina was still smiling.

"I'm asking the questions here, Mr. McCormick," Mr. Tavenner said. "Were you aware of any Communists who were members of the Hollywood Anti-Nazi League?"

"Not particularly. Though it wouldn't surprise me if there were. You have to remember what it was like back then in the Depression with bread lines and millions of people out of work. Many of us started wondering if there might be a better way to organize a society that would benefit everyone, not just a handful of millionaires at the top."

"I'm not asking you to give me a history of leftist politics in the United States of America, Mr. McCormick. I'm asking you if there were Communists in the Hollywood Anti-Nazi League of which you were a founding member. Yes or no, Mr. McCormick?"

Max shrugged. "Of course, there were. But there were many other political beliefs as well. It was a broad coalition of people who found Hitler alarming—"

199

"There you go again, Mr. McCormick. It almost seems as though you're trying to wiggle out of answering my questions. But all right, you've admitted there were Communists in this group. Who, to your knowledge, were these Communists?"

"You want their names?"

"Yes, I want their names. I want you to tell us exactly who these people were—these well-paid Hollywood individuals who turned their backs on their country."

"I'm sorry, Mr. Tavenner, but it seems to me that these weren't people who turned their backs on their country. Quite the opposite, Hitler turned out to be the threat to America that we predicted he would be, and I'd like to suggest to you that the members of the Hollywood Anti-Nazi League were in fact far better patriots than those of you who sat on your fat asses and did nothing."

Somewhere a gavel pounded. "Mr. McCormick, answer the question please." It was John Wood, the Chairman. "We want you to tell us the names of any Communists you knew who were members of the Hollywood Anti-Nazi League."

Max paused, momentarily unable to continue. They had arrived at the central purpose of the morning, the naming of names, and Max had intended taking the Fifth Amendment at just this point. But now that the moment was upon him, he found himself unable to speak. There was a confused ringing in his ears that made everything dreamy and a little distant.

An Almost Perfect Ending

"Mr. McCormick, would you like me to repeat the question?"

"No, hell with you—I'm not going to tell you names, you slimy bastard!" Max said quietly.

"*No*?" repeated Chairman Wood, banging his gavel again to quiet the room. "Are you taking the Fifth Amendment, Mr. McCormick?"

"No, I don't need the Fifth Amendment. I'm taking the only course open to me as a decent American. For me, Mr. Wood, it doesn't seem either honorable or fair to force a man under-oath to inform on friends and acquaintances. I'm happy to answer for myself, for anything I've done, and I don't believe I've done anything wrong. But I will not give you names. I will not toady myself to your low moral level and save my skin by destroying someone else—"

"Mr. McCormick—"

"No, let me finish. This isn't American justice. We in this country have fought hard to create our system of democracy and in fact, you are the enemy, Mr. Wood. You are the enemy of democracy. What you're doing here today is more the type of thing one would expect in Hitler's Germany or Stalin's Russia. I would call this a monkey trial, except for the fact that I have a great deal more respect for monkeys."

Jonas had covered his eyes with his hands, unable to watch Max's self-immolation. But Max didn't care. He was just getting going, enjoying himself immensely. With a clear-sightedness born of vodka and bottomless despair, he did everything that Jonas had so carefully coached him not to do. He lectured, he mocked, he made jokes, he refused to name names, he refused even to take the Fifth. As flashbulbs exploded, Max went on in this fashion taunting the Committee for nearly forty-five minutes. He himself lost track of time, he hardly even heard the questions any longer, or saw the faces bobbing up from the anonymous suits who were questioning him. He looked only at Mina. Throughout everything, Mina's smile only became more and more beatific until she filled up Max's vision completely. He had never loved her more than he did that morning in Washington.

In the end, Max was led from the witness table by a federal marshal when he refused to leave on his own. The Committee's verdict was unanimous and unsparing. In return for his morning of fun, he was sentenced to a year in federal prison for Contempt of Congress, fined $25,000, and he would never be allowed to work in his chosen profession again.

"Oh, Max, I'm so proud of you, darling!" Mina called to him from across the room.

Max was proud, too. All in all, he was pleased as punch. For the first time since the night on the road with Ricky Bolano, he felt himself to be an honest man.

And then he was led away in handcuffs. The storybook part of things was over and now the real misery began.

Part Three

The Dark and Stormy Night, Revisited

Eighteen

California: 1954 - 1956

Max did his time at Allenwood, a federal penitentiary in the foothills of the northern Allegheny Mountains outside of White Deer, Pennsylvania.

"I can't say it's a country club, Jonno," he wrote in a letter to me. "But people have an astonishing ability to adapt to circumstances, and I suppose I'm adapting too. I've even made a few prison buddies. There's a forger from Baltimore, a sad-eyed little fellow who likes to discuss philosophy, and a professor of English literature who decided robbing banks was more to his taste, and we've taken to having our meals together in the huge mess hall. It's not savory company, I suppose, and the food isn't exactly Chasen's. But you need to have a few pals in the clink, it's one of the first things you learn here. You can't make it in a place like this alone."

Despite this avowed need for pals, Max did his best to cut himself off from my mother and Mina and all his old Hollywood friends during the time he was in prison. I suppose it was his way to reconcile what remained of his pride with his changed circumstances. With the exception of me, he made a complete break with the past.

An Almost Perfect Ending

I had always called him Uncle Max—and he had always acted that particular role with me, more of an indulgent uncle than a father. But prison somehow changed the equation between us, and he seemed determined now to take me on more officially as his son.

He wrote to me dutifully once a week, offering amusing tales of "life in the clink", as he liked to call it, and my mother, eager for news, always made me read the letters aloud. I hated thinking of Max in prison—gentle, aristocratic Max in striped pajamas with a pickaxe over his shoulder. Or at least, that's how I imagined it, like a bad cartoon. It weighed on my spirits, a sense that the world was out of kilter, my first inkling that good people didn't always come to a happy ending on Planet Earth.

"Damn Max! Why did he have to be such an idiot?" my mother often demanded—drink in hand, a cigarette about to burn her fingers—after I'd read aloud one of his letters. "All he had to do was tell those bastards what they wanted to know! All he had to do was behave himself in Washington for one goddamn morning! I did everything I could, Jonno. But he wouldn't listen to me."

"You did your best, Mom," I assured her, even though I wasn't sure she had actually done anything except drink and sulk. I know it broke her heart that Max was in prison; it made her almost physically ill to think of him there. But his willful self-destruction in front of HUAC offended every ounce of her survivalist nature and she was furious with him for being such a fool. She took it as a personal insult, a rejection of everything she held dear.

"Why do I always fall for weak men, Jonno?" she wanted to know. "Goddamn dreamers! Oh, they look attractive enough at the start, but they always end up needing me to get them out of their jams. And I've had it, I swear to God! When Julka gets out from that damn place, he can go fuck himself for all I care!"

"It's Max, Mom. Not Julka."

"Isn't that what I said?"

No, it wasn't, and it disturbed me how in her rambles she had begun to confuse Julka with Max, substituting one for the other. At the time, I thought it was the booze addling her brain, but it was more than that. It was as though Julka and Max had become interchangeable parts of her own drama, the same weak romantic dreamer she was inclined to recreate again and again, a justification for her own ruthless cunning. Someone to take care of, someone who needed her. I sensed I could fall into that category myself if I wasn't careful.

Of course, my mother was drinking heavily during this period, starting each morning with a Polish martini, as she called them—vodka straight from the freezer with three maraschino cherries dropped into the glass. It's not a cocktail you'll find in any book of recipes, but my mother liked maraschino cherries so she didn't see why she shouldn't have them.

An Almost Perfect Ending

The liquid refreshment continued throughout the day. Often she'd pour herself a fresh drink, forgetting she already had one "working"—her word—and I'd come across half-finished cocktails in various parts of the house, upstairs and down, generally with smudges of lipstick on the rim of the glass. It wasn't that I ever saw her stagger around the house—all her movements remained very precise, exaggerated if anything—but her lovely green eyes seemed to be swimming in her head, as though she were looking at the world from underwater, and her enthusiasm for life had ebbed away.

It was hard for me to see her in such a listless state. She had always thought of herself as the ultimate survivor, the girl who had outsmarted the Nazis. But California defeated her. It's ironic, I suppose. In the end, it wasn't hardship, but rather the soft life in Beverly Hills that was so impossible to bear.

*****

It was around this time, while Max was in prison, that Fred Landson started coming by the house, whenever he was in California and could get away from Debbie and the kids on Lido Isle.

I first became aware that the affair had moved from fishing to fulfillment, so to speak, when I woke one night thirsty for orange juice—lovely frozen orange juice, like ice cream, the very symbol of the 1950s—and I padded barefoot downstairs to the kitchen to find Fred's bodyguard sitting on a couch in the entryway near the front door. He had made himself at home: legs crossed, smoking a menthol cigarette, reading the sports section of a newspaper. It was the plain-clothes cop with the mashed-potato face who had come for me on the set at Paramount to take me to Fred's car, so I recognized him.

"What are you doing here?" I asked unpleasantly. I didn't like him and now that he was in my world, I believed I had the right to be unpleasant.

"Never you mind, sonny-boy," he answered, putting down the paper and giving me an evil look. "Maybe you're dreaming. Maybe you're not seeing me at all."

"I'm not dreaming. I'm awake and I'm getting myself a glass of orange juice."

"Then you better get it and go back up to bed. A sonny-boy like you, he needs all the sleep he can get. So just forget about me. Some things, kid, are better not to know."

I got my orange juice and went back to bed. And to tell the truth, I did forget about him, or close enough. In the morning there was no sign of him, even the ashtray had been emptied, and I was glad to pretend he was only a bad dream.

But it wasn't a dream and from that moment on, I became aware that Fred was coming by on a fairly regular basis, though sometimes months passed when there was no sign of him. He always had the same bodyguard in attendance, and his visits were always late at night.

An Almost Perfect Ending

The bodyguard's name was Mike, I found out eventually. Sometimes I'd find Mike on the downstairs couch, other times there would just be subtle signs of him the next morning—a lingering smell of menthol smoke, the sports section of the newspaper. Once Mike played checkers with me when I had a stomachache and couldn't sleep. We became a little chummy, I suppose. I still didn't like him, but when you're a kid, you get used to things happening that you can't control and don't understand.

Occasionally, I saw the Congressman in person. The first time was a Sunday morning around seven, still very early, when I was coming out of the hall bathroom and he was coming out of my mother's bedroom with his tie off and his suit jacket over his bad arm, the one with the gloved hand. He was embarrassed to see me but recovered quickly enough.

"Hey there, Jonno! Good to see you, son," he said, as though we were great pals. "My gosh, I fell asleep on your mother's couch while we were talking about old times. Well, I don't want to be late for church. See you around."

Church! I wasn't fooled a bit. After that first encounter on the landing, Fred started bringing me small presents from time to time, trying to make nice. A football, a new baseball mitt, boxing gloves. He seemed to think that since I was a boy, I would automatically love sports. I didn't, but Fred didn't bother to ask. He had the world figured out according to a fixed blueprint in his mind, and he held on tightly lest the whole thing fall apart.

My mother always referred to him as "the Congressman," by his title rather than his name. A reminder, I suppose, of why she had allowed him entry to her bed. Occasionally she would point out his name in the newspapers. "Look at this, Jonno. The Congressman is in Paris having talks with NATO!" She said it musingly, as though it were hard to believe an idiot like that actually had a hand in running the world. "My God, here's the Congressman at the White House standing next to Ike!"

Personally, I'm not sure he was the idiot my mother took him for. Fred was smart when it came to his own slice of the pie, maneuvering his way through politics and business and such. He was a realist. He knew very well, for instance, that he was no girl's dreamboat. He didn't fool himself that way, as some guys might. Knowing that he lacked romantic appeal, he developed other strategies to keep my mother's interest. He made himself indispensable to her, dishing out useful favors, large and small.

In July, my mother spent three days on a sound stage at Desilu filming the California orange juice commercial he had gotten for her, nudging an old associate in Anaheim to give her the part. And in late September, better still, he managed to get her an invitation to sing "I Believe in Tomorrow" at a Republican fundraiser for Ike that was held at the El Mirador

Hotel in Palm Springs. Ike was there in person, combining the weekend fundraiser with a few rounds of golf, and my mother found this prospect so exciting—the chance to sing for the President—that her gratitude to Fred rose, briefly, to a kind of faux-love. Hollywood love, you might say. That is, love for better, never for worse, as long as a person proves useful to you, and until someone else more advantageous comes along.

Sadly, she wasn't paid for the evening in Palm Springs, not a penny. But Bob Hope was the master of ceremonies, he spent the night flirting with her and making funny jokes about how sexy she was, and the other talent included people like Ginger Rogers and Robert Taylor and John Wayne, the conservative face of Hollywood that had come out to show the world that not everybody in show business was pink. They all liked Ike, and Sasha did, too . . . as long as it was convenient to do so. Above all, she believed it was a big boost to her career to hobnob with A-List people and be noticed again.

Fred played his hand in these favors as well as a man might do who had one hand missing. Whenever he sensed the romantic fervor in my mother's eye starting to dim, he managed to drop another goodie.

"So, Sash," he would say—he had begun calling her Sash, which irritated her no end—"how would you like to open the Republican National Convention next year in San Francisco by singing the national anthem?"

"Oh, Fred! The Spangled Banger!"

"The Star-Spangled *Banner*," he corrected solemnly. It was a hard song title to say, much less sing, if you'd been drinking Polish martinis all day. "It'll be broadcast live by all the networks, coast to coast. It'll be great exposure, Sash," he assured her. "The whole country will be watching."

"Honest, Fred? You can get this for me?"

"You bet'cha. I'm on the committee that's putting the shindig together at the Cow Palace. So what I say goes."

"The Cow Palace . . . but what's that, Fred?"

"Just you wait and see. Believe me, when you see the size of that place, your eyes will pop out!"

Part of the problem was my mother's lack of knowledge of native history. She didn't understand the honored place of cows in the American West. She had a Polish notion of cows as large, smelly animals that left behind great molten puddles of shit. The very name, Cow Palace, seemed to her crude and second-rate. It wasn't her romantic vision of herself to sing in such a place.

She should have been more grateful. Fred was doing his best to help and the money from the orange juice commercial on TV was certainly welcome. Residuals were everything that he had promised. Yet it was a joyless time on North Maple Drive with Max in prison, my mother pickled morning, noon, and night, and Fred showing up late at night with his body-guard and a gleam in his eye that was becoming worrisome, risking everything for his secretive nights of sin.

An Almost Perfect Ending

Looking back, I think we all knew that the life we were living couldn't last.

*****

The fall passed and soon it was 1955, a new year.

I'm not sure how long our lives would have drifted along, our strained existence. But then a sex scandal courtesy of *Confidential* magazine brought an end to my brief stint as a child star, and change came tumbling in upon us, ready or not.

It's not easy to convey the power *Confidential* had in Hollywood in the 1950s, the flutter of worry that passed from one end of town to the other as each new issue appeared, everybody wondering if it would be their turn to be pilloried, all their secrets exposed.

The exposé that was about to change my life concerned Don Silver, the actor who played my TV dad, who *Confidential* decided to out as a homosexual—"a mincing queer," as they put it. *Confidential* took a particular delight in outing homos. They had recently exposed an effete State Department liberal by the name of Sumner Welles (once FDR's Under Secretary of State, an East Coast pansy who had attended Groton/Harvard, the works), and they were warming up to take on Liberace in 1957, their most famous exposé of all.

Over its decade long reign of terror, *Confidential* often stretched the truth, but, in this case, they had the goods, com-

213

plete with photographs of Donnie dancing in a gay nightclub with a sailor. "We can only wonder," the magazine moralized, "why a major television network should allow a mincing queer to appear in a family comedy, condoning a dangerous role model for our nation's youth." Moral sermons, it should be noted, were an important ingredient of *Confidential* exposés, a means of making readers feel they were getting more between the covers than salacious trash.

The issue appeared on a Wednesday in January. On Thursday, I showed up at Paramount baffled to find all sorts of people I had never seen before on the set lurking in the shadows and conferring in low voices. No one would tell me a thing, but it was obvious something was wrong. Annette Corning, my TV mom, sat in her folding chair drinking openly from a bottle. Even Guy Dearborn, the happy-go-lucky next door neighbor, moped about with a worried expression.

As usual, it was Penny who clued me in on what was happening.

"It's Donnie," she said with a shrug. "*Confidential* did this big article on him, and now everybody knows he's queer."

I shrugged also. For Penny and I, this was old news, hardly worth mentioning. We had been spying on Donnie giving blow jobs to buff stagehands for over a year.

"Big deal," I said, "but so what?"

"The big deal is the network is going to cancel our show."

Being older and wiser, Penny was perfectly right. We finished that week's episode, but halfway through the following Monday, a man in a suit walked onto Stage 17 and told us all to go home. Homosexuality was considered a serious moral lapse in the Fifties, and a family sit-com like *What a Life!* was vulnerable to even the smallest whiff of scandal. We were supposed to be the typical all-American family next door, and I guess it bothered people that perhaps we actually were. The show was cancelled, we cleaned out our dressing rooms on Monday afternoon, and I never returned to Paramount again.

To be honest, I didn't much mind the end of my acting career. I had begun to find TV boring, all the waiting around for grownups to set up cameras and lights and such. But soon afterwards, Penny moved with her mother to New York where she found work playing the troubled teenage daughter on a daytime soap, *The Restless Heart*, that was broadcast live five days a week on NBC. And as if it weren't bad enough to lose Penny, I was now forced to attend a real school, a sadistic place called the Harvard School on the wrong end of Coldwater Canyon in the Valley. My mother insisted that a good education was necessary for my so-called future, even though she herself had done quite well in the world with only her brains and good looks and complete lack of scruples.

Today the Harvard School is considered quite a posh institution. It has merged with the snootiest girl's school in town, Westlake, and is now known cleverly as the Harvard-

Westlake School. I'm sure the presence of girls is an improvement. But when I attended, Harvard was a military school for the male sex only—vicious, pimply boys—and I wasn't pleased to find myself once again in uniform, marching up and down a field with my sad toy rifle, still getting ready for the Russians. To make matters worse, Harvard believed it had a religious mission as well—onward Christian soldiers!—and we were subjected to mandatory chapel and Bible classes.

I entered the Harvard School in the seventh grade halfway through the year, which didn't make things easier for me socially, trying to fit in after everyone else had already settled into their cliques and thuggish gangs.

Father Chalmers was the headmaster in those days, a mild-mannered Episcopalian priest who probably had little idea of what really went on at his campus. I lived in terror of hazing from the moment I arrived, for at Harvard, the seniors had absolute power to do whatever they liked to us. One of their favorite pastimes was to put us in trash cans and roll us down steep hills. We had to wait on them hand and foot, bring them sodas, ice cream, stand on our heads if they told us to do so. Once during the time I was there, they stripped a seventh-grade boy naked, drove him up Coldwater Canyon and let him out on the road to make his way back to the campus the best way he could. This was supposed to build character for those of us who were being hazed. And of course, one day when we were seniors, we could look forward to the joys of becoming vicious bullies ourselves.

I had managed to skip a grade from all my private tutoring at Paramount, and it didn't help matters that I was the youngest kid in the seventh grade, about two inches shorter than anyone else. Nor did the fact that everybody knew who I was from *What a Life!* and I had to endure a good deal of mean-spirited humor over the way the show had been cancelled. So there I was, a has-been at the age of not-quite twelve—and in Hollywood, believe me, it's better to be a never-was than a has-been. My goal during the week was simply to survive, and on the weekends lounge around the house, hiding from the world, friendless and miserable, missing Penny so much I sometimes just stretched out on my bed and cried.

I really didn't think my awful Hollywood childhood could get any worse.

But that, as it turned out, was wishful thinking.

*****

Early in the fall of 1954, a few months after Max was sent to prison, Mina put the Bel Air house up for sale and traveled to India in order to "see humanity in all its colors," as she wrote to me in a postcard that she sent from the Taj Mahal. India wasn't an easy destination in those days—disease, partition, overcrowded trains, the upheaval of a nation still being born—but Mina, despite her frail appearance, had always been an adventurer.

Once in India, she made her way north to the foothills of the Himalayas where she joined an ashram, sat for hours at a time with her body twisted up like a pretzel, and experienced profound visions of Cosmic Truth—or at least, such truth as is reserved for movie stars who possess nearly all the treasures of the planet except peace of mind.

She became very ill there, as is often the case with Westerners unaccustomed to the hygiene, and by the time she returned to America, she had lost so much weight that there was hardly anything left to her but a pair of exceptionally bright eyes. Mina had become a strict vegetarian, what today we would call a vegan. And more surprisingly, she had embraced a new life of celibacy—no sex, no booze, not even the occasional ménage à trois. I'm not certain celibacy is strictly legal in California, but she did it anyway. She had always been a person to go to extremes.

Mina was away for nearly five months and didn't return to Los Angeles until late February, 1955, coming home by way of New York and Pennsylvania, where she managed to see Max in prison. Shortly after she returned to L.A., she took me to hear Krishnamurti, the Indian philosopher, who was speaking in Santa Monica. The talk left me dazed with boredom since it had no relevance to my life as a horny California pube. But I put up with it for Mina's sake and afterwards we walked to the Santa Monica pier where we took a ride together on the carousel.

Mina was an old woman by then, or so she seemed to me—in her mid-fifties, at least. Her hair was gray, she had wrinkles she didn't bother to hide, and so it was funny to see her small figure bobbing up and down on a painted pony as the calliope squeezed out its raucous waltz. She acted like she was having the time of her life, laughing and waving to me on the next horse over, and I found myself laughing and waving back as we went round and round, feeling carefree for the first time in a long while. Mina almost always had that effect on me. She was infectious.

"Oh, Jonno, let's walk to the end of the pier! Let's look at the wonderful blue ocean and breathe the air!" she enthused once our carousel ride was over.

We sat on a wooden bench at the end of the pier near a group of old men who were fishing, and for some reason I started crying and couldn't stop. It didn't make sense because it had been a great afternoon. But there was something about being with Aunt Mina that opened the flood gates, all the tears that I'd been storing up.

Mina held me while I cried but didn't comment or ask questions. She was someone who respected sorrow. She let it be. But in the end, perhaps for that very reason, I told her everything. It came blubbering out. All my miseries, starting with how my TV show had been canceled, and now I might just as well be dead because I was a Hollywood has-been.

"Oh, so am I, Jonno!" Mina commiserated. "I'm a Hollywood has-been, too! But don't you love it, darling? Isn't it a relief that no one expects anything from you any longer, and now you can let your hair down and be yourself?"

I did my best to explain to her that, no, it wasn't a relief. I didn't want to let my hair down and be myself. I despised myself. I wanted to be someone else entirely, a magical being who might be famous forever, adored and coddled by the world. But it was nice to have another has-been to share my misery with. So next I told her about Penny, how she had gone to live in New York and now my heart was broken.

"Oh, good for you, Jonno!" she said after I had spewed out the whole sad saga. "You've opened your heart. You've loved somebody. And now your life is rich and full."

"But it's not good at all!" I objected. "I'm so lonely I can't stand it! I'm in agony, Aunt Mina!"

But Mina wasn't having any part of my agony.

"No, no, dear—you're looking at this all wrong," she told me gently. "Let her go, Jonno. Let her go like a white bird so she can fly away. Love isn't about owning someone. It's just a wonderful feeling, that's all. And no one can take that away from you, that's the marvelous part."

You can see how difficult it was to have a normal conversation with Mina. She wouldn't go along with my drama and I was starting to feel frustrated. So next, just to impress her with how totally awful my childhood had become, I told her about the Congressman and how he had started coming by the house at night with his bodyguard, and how weird he was, and how my mother had become a kind of zombie, drinking vodka all day.

I was expecting Mina to offer some fluffy words of wisdom—fine sentiments, I'm sure, but not so easy to put into practice. But to my surprise, she frowned and didn't answer. She didn't tell me to let Fred go like a white bird. She didn't tell me that my life was enriched by how greatly I despised him. She actually seemed upset.

She was silent for such a long time that finally I gave her a prod.

"Aunt Mina?"

"Yes, Jonno. I was just thinking of all the trouble in the world . . . all the misery. You know, when I was in India, I saw a group of Hindus beat a Muslim family to death. They kept beating them with sticks—a man and a woman and two small children—until they were bloody and limp. Then they threw them into a river and let them drown. There was nothing I could do to stop it."

"That's horrible!"

"Yes, it was. It was horrible." Mina sighed and shook her head. But it wasn't her style to be gloomy long. In a moment, she smiled and her eyes grew bright. "But that's how things are on Planet Earth, Jonno. Take it or leave it! Shall we sit around and mope? Or shall we . . . find you a great big dish of chocolate ice cream!"

"But Aunt Mina, what about Congressman Landson?" I persisted.

"Oh, I wouldn't worry about Fred Landson, darling. Karma will catch up with that man, believe me. Perhaps sooner than he thinks. Let the universe do the job, that's what I always say. Now, let's find you that dish of ice cream . . ."

We ended up going to Will Wright's on Sunset Strip, where Mina watched me gobble down a hot fudge sundae with unbridled greed. It wasn't a bad way to soothe my sorrows and I went home that day feeling almost good.

Let the universe do the job. I thought about this as I was falling asleep because it was an appealing idea, one that had never occurred to me before: that there might be a force beyond my personal will, something in the trees and stars and planets that influenced the outcome of the story that I called my life.

I wasn't sure what I thought about this. It's still a matter I'm trying to decide. But at the time I found it frankly worrisome that my crazy Aunt Mina was the only one of us who seemed even slightly sane.

Nineteen

Sasha knew that Ricky Bolano was dead. Like Max, she had seen the paragraph in the *Citizen News* describing the fatal one-car accident in Coldwater Canyon, and for an entire day she had glowed with pleasure, grinning every time she thought of his broken body lying in a steep ravine.

She pictured a great deal of blood. She pictured a final moment of excruciating pain as he understood how she had killed him, mixing his bourbon with sleeping pills. She pictured his last breath wheezing from his lungs.

"My God, I did it!" she told herself, beaming. "He's dead! The fucking bastard is dead!"

It was almost hard to believe, such good news. Ricky would never, never come around again to frighten her and ask for money. He was gone forever. But the pure pleasure of his death lasted only a short while before anxiety began creeping in around the edges, worry about all the things that could still go wrong.

What if the police figured it out?

What if they did an autopsy and found Phenobarbital in his blood? What if they discovered that he had been blackmailing her? What if they learned that Sasha (like half of Hollywood) had a prescription for sleeping pills and that Ricky had stopped by her house that very night?

There were too many ifs, that was the problem. The list of worries went on and on.

What if there really was an attorney who had an envelope to be opened in the event of Ricky's death? What if word got out that Sonya Saint-Amant, the famous singer, had been arrested for prostitution—in a movie theater, a blow job for twenty dollars, as low as whoring got!

For Sasha, these what-ifs hung over her like an executioner's blade, and as the days went by and nothing happened, she only became more anxious.

Then a new fear, worse than the others, gradually took hold of her imagination: What if Ricky Bolano wasn't *really* dead after all? She had been fooled before in this matter, believing that Zachary had taken care of him.

So what if the phone rang and there he was again, his sinister whispery voice?

She began dreaming about Ricky, nightmares in which he came back to life. Horrible dreams where he showed up on her doorstep, his hair matted with mud and blood, his eyes burning with terrifying evil.

"You thought you killed me, didn't you? Well, guess what, doll? I'm back. And now it's your turn to die . . ."

In the dreams, he took a terrible vengeance. He came after her with knives, with guns, with sharp sticks. Once he used a pair of scissors to cut her open and pull out her intestines while she lay watching. Sasha had never had such awful dreams. They came night after night and the terror of them followed her through the uneasy half-life of her days. Soon she was afraid to go to bed at night.

The nightmares were so convincing that Sasha began seriously to consider the possibility that the *Citizen News* had gotten it wrong. Perhaps it was someone else who had died in that accident on Coldwater Canyon Drive. Maybe the police had deliberately given out wrong information in order to trap her. Perhaps the police and Ricky were working together to drive her mad . . .

Weeks went by and Sasha thought she would go crazy if she didn't know for certain. One morning after a particularly bad night, she drove to Westwood and used a pay phone to call the California Highway Patrol. She said her name was Doris Bolano and she was worried about her brother, Ricky, who had been missing for several weeks and she wanted to confirm that there hadn't been a car accident. It seemed a good ploy, but the Highway Patrol didn't give out that sort of information on the phone and the officer said she would need to come into the station in person and fill out a request. This wouldn't do, so Sasha hung up and tried to think of other options.

She telephoned the *Citizen News*, once again pretending to be the fictitious Doris Bolano, asking to confirm the paragraph she had read in the newspaper, but the person she reached was unable to provide any further information. She telephoned local hospitals to see if they had any knowledge of a Ricky Bolano, who might—or might not—have been a patient several weeks ago. With a thumping heart, she even phoned his number on Cahuenga Drive, the number listed in the Yellow Pages, prepared to hang up instantly if anyone answered. The number rang and rang until finally there was a recorded announcement saying it was no longer in service.

This was encouraging. She was thrilled that Ricky's number was no longer in service. All she wanted was for him to be dead, dead, dead and never come to life again. But was a disconnected number really adequate confirmation? She wanted to believe so. But of course people discontinued telephone numbers all the time for various reasons and she couldn't be sure.

At her wit's end, she drove to the San Fernando Valley and cruised slowly by Ricky's house. The house looked deserted, but how could she be sure? Nearly all suburban houses in California seemed deserted during the day.

I could ring the doorbell, she decided.

But the idea of ringing his doorbell sent chills up her spine. She couldn't do it. Physically, she couldn't force her feet to walk up the path to Ricky's front door. In the end, Sasha was unable even to slow down as she cruised past his house with the convertible top raised, crouched down low in the seat so that no one would see her. She didn't breathe easily until she was back on Ventura Boulevard.

She had a good laugh at herself when she was safely home. It was ridiculous to be so frightened, she knew that. Of course, Ricky was dead! Newspapers didn't lie. She was just being silly because her nerves were shot to hell. She had loaded Ricky's bourbon with enough Nembutal to put an elephant to sleep. He had driven off the road on his way home, she had killed him.

Yet when she dreamed of him night after night, how could she know for sure?

What was fact? And what was fiction? That's what it always came back to in Los Angeles, city of dreams. Suffering from too much vodka and too little sleep, Sasha could no longer tell the difference between the two.

*****

Weeks passed, months, and oppression settled about Sasha like a heavy cloud. Driving around the city, she often found herself gazing out the window at ordinary people on the street, wishing she were one of them. A housewife, perhaps. Or a secretary in an office. Or one of those teenage girls in pedal pushers who didn't have a care in the world except getting by at school and finding the right boyfriend. She couldn't bear the burden of being herself: Sonya Saint-Amant, the famous singer.

Oddly enough, the TV commercial she had made—the little ditty about orange juice—had been such a hit that the California Orange Growers Association wanted more, a second commercial. It was the first real success that Sasha had enjoyed in years. People had begun to stop her again on the street, as they had once done in the 1940s, asking for an autograph. But not for her wonderful voice. Not for "I Believe in Tomorrow" or her steamy version of "Ain't Misbehavin'," but for dressing up as an orange and doing a silly dance.

A kid at a gas station had actually asked if he could *squeeze* her!

The only good thing about orange juice Sasha could discover was that it wasn't too bad when you mixed it with vodka.

In the new commercial, Sasha would be required to dangle ten feet in the air from the branch of a giant papier-mâché tree dressed up like an orange, a prospect which she did not look forward to with any joy.

"Pretty darn funny stuff, Sash!" Fred told her. "Boy, you'll have the whole country laughing."

"Lovely, Fred," she answered gloomily. "I can't wait."

In March, Sasha spent two days in a sound studio in Burbank with a ten-piece orchestra prerecording the song for the commercial. The filming itself took place the following week on a stage at Desilu, the old RKO studio that was now owned

An Almost Perfect Ending

by Lucille Ball and her husband, Desi Arnaz. Sasha hoped they would be able to complete the shoot in a single day.

On the night before the filming, Sasha drugged herself to sleep with three Nembutal which left her groggy and irritable the next day. A limousine came for her at the absurd hour of 7:30 in the morning to take her to Desilu—Sasha had insisted on a limo, it was in her contract—and after three hours in makeup and wardrobe and getting fastened into a hidden harness, a crane hoisted her up onto the tree branch where she was left to dangle unhappily in her costume, glowering at the crew on the stage below.

"Okay, Sasha!" cried the director hopefully. "Let's give it a go . . . all right? Camera . . ."

"Speed!" called the cameraman.

"California Orange Juice, Take One!" cried the clapper boy.

"Playback!" called the director. "*Action!*"

The playback machine played the ditty that had already been recorded, while Sasha in the tree did a little dance with her arms and legs and did her best to lip-sync to the music:

"I'm a juicy, juicy orange hanging in a tree!
Happy, happy, happy,
full of Vitamin C!
Bursting full of flavor,
In the California sun,

Tasty and refreshing,
Good for everyone . . ."

The first take didn't go well. Nor the second or the third.

"Sasha, you gotta look like you're having fun up there," said the director. His name was Doug. He was an outdoorsy forty-something man in a sports shirt and jeans who looked like he might be a scoutmaster in his spare time. Sasha despised him. "You gotta give it more pizzazz!"

On the fourth take, Sasha gave it so much pizzazz that she began spinning on the branch until her back was to the camera.

On the fifth take, Sasha got halfway through when she told Doug that she had to stop and take a pee.

"Sweetheart, can't you hold it just a while longer?" Doug encouraged.

Sasha told him no, sweetheart, she couldn't. The spinning and dangling was playing havoc with her stomach. She seriously needed to wee. Which took more than forty-five minutes, to lower her down from the branch, get her out of the costume, then back into the costume, then hoist her up onto the branch again.

The sixth take was good enough to print. But Doug was hoping for still more pizzazz. To Doug's discerning eye, she still didn't appear to be a happy, happy orange full of flavor in the California sun.

On take number seven, Sasha burst into tears because she was so frustrated doing the routine again and again.

Take eight was great until the very end when she coughed and began spinning again in her harness.

Take number nine was interrupted when she had to be lowered again to use the bathroom . . . and have just a small guzzle of vodka in her dressing room.

And on and on throughout the day. For Sasha it was torture. She didn't like heights. She didn't like Doug. She thought she would go crazy if she had to listen one more time to the happy, happy orange song.

At four in the afternoon, she had a temper tantrum and told Doug and his crew that they could go fuck themselves. But at five—after a short break, more vodka in her dressing room— she managed enough simulated pizzazz that Doug was finally satisfied.

Somehow she got through the day. But was it worth it? she wondered as she rode home gloomily in the back of the limousine, frowning at Santa Monica Boulevard as it passed outside her window.

A mere six months ago, she would have been grateful for a chance to do a TV commercial, all that lovely money. But now that the money was flowing, taken for granted, she was furious that Fred had forced her into such demeaning work.

Yes, it was Fred's fault! She was certain of it. Fred had forced her into a life that was as second-rate and boring as he was. A life where nothing mattered, nothing was beautiful, and all her dreams had crashed.

As the limousine pulled into her driveway, Sasha scowled to see that she had company. Mina was standing next to Jonno by her car, an old dark blue Cadillac that had seen better days. Jonno was on some sort of vacation from school—Easter break, Sasha wasn't sure—and apparently he and Mina had spent the afternoon together and had only arrived home themselves minutes earlier. Sasha hadn't seen Mina since she had returned from India and she wasn't in any mood for a visit today. All she wanted was to pour herself a very large Polish martini and get into the bathtub.

"What a goddamn nightmare of a day!" she complained, stepping from the back of the limo. "I'd invite you in for a drink, Mina, but I'm ready to collapse. Honestly, I've been hanging from a tree all day long and I feel like screaming."

"I was just dropping Jonno off," Mina said, regarding Sasha with her bright eyes. "We've had a lovely afternoon, the two of us."

"We went on the carousel on the Santa Monica pier," Jonno added. "It was a blast."

"A *blast*?" Sasha inquired archly. In an obscure way, she wasn't happy that Jonno and Mina had spent the afternoon together. "Are you a rocket ship now?"

"You bet," said Jonno.

It wasn't jealousy exactly. But she hated the idea that Jonno might care for Mina in the same way he cared for her. In fact, she would just as soon have Mina leave Jonno the fuck alone.

"You know, I'm glad to run into you, Sasha," Mina said. "Because I think we need to get together and talk. If you're not busy, why don't we have lunch tomorrow?"

"Oh, Mina, not tomorrow. Honestly, all I want to do tomorrow is collapse. I've just had the most awful day, you wouldn't believe it. It's going to take me *weeks* to recover, I swear!"

"Yes, I see that," Mina agreed. "Why don't we make it the day after tomorrow so you'll have a chance to have a good lay-in. We'll go someplace nearby, the Beverly Brown Derby. It'll be my treat. Shall we say one o'clock?"

"Oh, Mina, I don't really eat lunch these days. I'm just getting up out of bed at one o'clock . . ."

"Let's make it two, then. Because honestly, Sasha, we *do* need to discuss a few things."

Discussing things sounded like work. Discussing things sounded boring. But Mina was insistent, which wasn't usual with her, and in the end, Sasha couldn't quite summon the energy to refuse.

But now she had something new to worry about. What in God's name did Mina want to talk about? For Sasha, even the simplest demands of the world had become overwhelming. More than a person like herself—a star—should have to bear.

"I swear, if people don't leave me alone, I'm going to start breaking things!" she warned her mirror on the wall.

Wisely, the mirror refrained from saying anything in return.

Twenty

The Beverly Brown Derby occupied a triangular shaped building that pointed from the southern tip of Rodeo Drive toward the Beverly Wilshire Hotel across the street. It was a cheerful room with windows on three sides and plenty of light pouring in—a rarity in that dark age of L.A. restaurants, when you generally needed a flashlight to find your table. Inside there were leather booths with high backs that provided seclusion for important people to have conversations.

It couldn't have been an easy occasion for Mina, who lunched on raw vegetables and a pot of tea, or for Sasha who gorged on a pair of lamb chops, a huge plate of French fries, and an entire bottle of Pouilly-Fuissé. She and Mina had shared Max for well over a decade, but they had little else in common.

Sasha pretended interest in Mina's trip to India while she attacked her lunch as though she might never eat again. When she had reduced her plate to skeleton bones, the waiter brought a bowl with hot water and lemon. Once her fingers were degreased, Sasha lit a cigarette and blew a cloud of smoke across the table.

"You're looking good," she told Mina, giving her a critical eye. "But honestly, you should put on some make-up. And, my God, why don't you color your hair? You could look twenty years younger, Mina. If I could only get you into Elizabeth Arden."

"Sasha, Elizabeth Arden doesn't matter. I stopped off in Pennsylvania to see Max in prison and I'm afraid he's not doing well. He's been beaten up several times and I'm not sure he can take much more. That's why I wanted to see you today. There are some things you need to know."

Sasha stared dumbly across the table and made an effort to concentrate. "Max . . . I don't understand."

"He's been beaten up, Sasha. It's not the guards, it's the other prisoners who are doing it. But the guards look on and don't stop it because they all say Max is a Red. Apparently being a Red is worse than murder, rape, or robbery, the things the other prisoners have done."

Sasha shook her head darkly. "Oh, Max, that idiot, it makes me so mad! All he had to do was cooperate with that awful committee. He only had to behave himself for one morning. He didn't *have* to go to prison!"

"Yes, but he *did* go to prison," Mina continued patiently. "And the last time he was beaten up, it was so severe they had to put him in the hospital. A group of inmates jumped Max in the shower room and they kept kicking him when he was on the ground. They kicked him so badly he ended up with a broken nose and three broken ribs and a concussion."

For Sasha, the room had gone swishy, not entirely real. She heard Mina's words, and mouthed words of her own in return, but none of it had any solid import. Meanwhile, the bottle of white wine was empty and she was certain that if only she had another glass everything would come into better focus.

"Oh, poor Max!" she managed, as her eyes scanned the room in search of a waiter. "But why, Mina? Why would anyone hurt Max?"

"I explained that already, dear. They called him a Commie, a traitor. That's what they said while they were beating him."

"But he's going to be all right, isn't he?"

"Sasha, to be honest, I don't know if he'll ever be completely right again. We'll just have to see. I'm building a small beach house with some money I put away years ago, and the house should be ready by the time he's released. I'm hopeful that a few quiet months at the beach will make him well."

"Oh, people are so dreadful! I swear, sometimes I just want to drop out of the human race!" Sasha shook her head at how awful people were. Meanwhile, she had succeeded in catching the waiter's eye. She gestured to the empty bottle on the table, signaling for more.

"Now, here's something else I want to say. I understand you're dating Fred Landson," Mina said pointedly. It was such an unexpected remark that Sasha couldn't at first answer. Never in their many years had Mina ever made a comment about Sasha's personal life.

"Who told you I'm seeing Fred?" she demanded.

"Jonno told me. And I have to say, Sasha, he's very unhappy about it. We spoke about this on the pier the other day."

"Oh, that child! I can't believe he told you!" Sasha shook her head angrily. "It needs to be a secret, you see. Because Fred's married. But he's awfully nice, really. Jonno just won't give him a chance. Do you know what Fred did? He got me invited to sing for Ike in Palm Springs. All kinds of important people were there. Bob Hope, John Wayne. Why Milton Berle showed up and they did the funniest little skit. I wish I could remember how it went . . ."

"Sasha—"

"No, you have to understand. I sang for Ike and all those people. It was just what I needed for my career!"

Mina leaned across the table and took Sasha's hand. "Listen, my dear. I have something else to tell you, because you need to know this. It was Fred Landson who got Max blacklisted and called up in front of that House Un-American Committee. He phoned Jack Warner and said that Max was a Communist. It's Fred who's responsible for this whole thing."

Sasha shook her head. "But that's impossible! Why, Max and Fred . . . we were all on the *Mauretania* together! We were all such good friends!"

"Sasha, I'm telling you the truth. I learned this from Jonas Isaacs when I saw him in New York. Jonas was Max's attorney at the HUAC hearing, and he got the information from someone who's a Congressional aide on the House Committee. You see, you can't really keep these things secret. They always come out in the end because people talk."

Sasha kept shaking her head. "But it can't be true!"

"It *is* true, dear. I imagine Fred was jealous. That's all it boils down to, really. He wanted Max out of the way so he could have you for himself. Now, you're the only one who can decide what to do. But it's important you know how things really are. For Jonno's sake as well as your own."

What Sasha wanted was another glass of wine. Fortunately, the waiter arrived at just this moment with a fresh bottle. "Oh, thank you!" she said as he poured the pale yellow liquid that was almost the color of pee. She drained most of the glass before returning her attention to Mina. "I'm sorry, Mina. What were you saying?"

"I'm saying Jonno shouldn't have to put up with a man coming by the house who got his father sent to prison by telling a lot of vicious lies," Mina said with a severity that wasn't usual to her. "I'm saying that if you ever cared for Max, you should think very carefully about what you're doing."

"But it isn't true! And Jonno . . . Jonno doesn't understand!"

"It doesn't matter what Jonno understands. As long as *you* understand."

"But it isn't true!" Sasha repeated, baffled that Mina should be saying such things. "You see, we all had such fun together on the *Mauretania* . . . we were all such great friends!"

"Sasha—"

"No, I won't hear another word. Do you know what Fred has promised? He's said he's going to let me sing the Spangled Banger at the Republican convention next year in San Francisco. Oh, Mina, it's going to be at the Cow Palace! I'll get to sing for thousands and thousands of people!"

Mina was a woman of compassion and nonjudgmental views. But her eyes went cold as she regarded Sasha. "Have you been listening to what I'm saying, Sasha?"

"Oh, let's not talk about it anymore! It's all just a bunch of nasty gossip anyhow. Now, I want to hear all about India."

Sasha did her best to steer the conversation to harmless matters. But she didn't feel well. She was suddenly so nauseous that her face had gone white and a bead of sweat rolled down from her hairline. The room began to swirl. She managed to escape soon afterwards, leaving Mina to pay the bill.

"What fun, Mina! We'll have to do this again soon!" she cried, nearly running from the restaurant.

The parking valet brought Sasha's car to the curb and she was so upset that she tipped him with a ten-dollar bill, thinking it was a single.

*****

An Almost Perfect Ending

Sasha drove the short distance from Rodeo Drive to North Maple as though there were demons on her tail, speeding through two stop signs and a red light. She thought she might be dying. She couldn't breathe properly. The sky itself seemed to be pressing down on her—the terrible Los Angeles sky, bright and empty—squeezing the air from her lungs.

Oh, she knew what Mina was up to! Mina was jealous, that's all. Jealous because Sasha still had a career . . . because she was going to sing at the Cow Palace for all those people.

And Mina didn't have any children of her own! *That's* what this was really about! She wanted to steal Jonno! But it wasn't going to work because Jonno loved his mother, not some old has-been actress from the 1930s who didn't even have the sense to use makeup and color her hair!

No wonder Max came to her for sex, not Mina. Who would want to sleep with a shapeless old witch like that?

But Max . . . thinking of him in prison . . . thinking of him crouched on a shower floor with brutal men kicking his dear body, breaking his ribs and nose, made her want to howl in protest. The image was unbearable. She didn't want to think of it, but it wouldn't leave her alone.

It wasn't possible that Fred had done the dreadful things Mina had told her. She knew that. Getting Max blacklisted. Calling him up in front of that awful Committee. They had all been such friends on the *Mauretania*! She knew it couldn't be true.

Yet as Sasha parked in her driveway and stormed inside her house, something flipped in her mind, like a coin showing its opposite face, and she knew with an abrupt certainty that it *was* true. She was stunned by the revelation. Of course, it was Fred! And now that she saw it, she didn't know how she could have ever believed otherwise. It was so obvious, really, just the sort of thing Fred would do, sneaky and conniving. Oh, he pretended to be such a Boy Scout, but he wasn't. She had always sensed something nasty beneath his oh-gosh ways, and now she knew for certain. What a slime! She could imagine all too well how Fred had phoned Jack Warner with his sneaky little lie that Max was a Red. That's how someone like Fred got what he wanted, with secrets and plots and guile.

Even in bed . . . Sasha was no prude, but it was disgusting, really the things he did. He liked to lick her toes! Once he'd even rubbed his nasty penis against her foot, letting out a moan as he shot a trickle of sperm across her ankle. It was like having sex with a toad. Max might be a schoolboy with his silly code of honor, but Fred . . . Fred was a thief. He had stolen Sasha by guile from the man she really loved.

"The bastard, the fucking bastard!" Sasha muttered as she continued into the living room, tossing her handbag and mink stole in the general direction of an armchair. "All these people . . . these fucking people . . . these fucking bastards, every goddamn one of them . . ."

An Almost Perfect Ending

She was glad no one was home because she hated them all, the entire human race. They were all the same. A bunch of dirty people in a filthy world!

Sasha stood in front of the drink trolley breathing hard. She wanted a drink more badly than she had ever wanted a drink before—wouldn't anyone, putting up with what she'd put up with today? But the fucking bottle of vodka had less than an inch in it, barely enough for a swallow. It was Claire the maid stealing from her. You couldn't trust anyone anymore.

Sasha found herself staring at the bottle of Old Grandad from which she had poured Ricky Bolano his two fatal cocktails. But now she was confused. Hadn't she gotten rid of that bottle? She was almost certain she had. She remembered rinsing it out and throwing it into the trash. In case the cops came snooping. Yet here it was again, like some bad magic trick. Though perhaps she'd replaced it . . . she half-remembered now, driving to the liquor store on Doheny Drive to buy another bottle, one without Nembutal, to put on the drink trolley where the doctored bottle had been. Just to be extra safe. But she wasn't sure. The world had become such a haze.

All at once, Sasha felt such a wave of self-disgust that without thinking she swept her arm across the drink trolley and sent a dozen bottles crashing to the floor. She had to take a second swipe in order to get them all. The cherry brandy in the very back that no one ever drank. The Drambuie. The syrupy cordial that some asshole press agent had sent her for Christmas.

She sent them all flying onto the floor in an orgy of breaking glass. A few bottles landed intact—the gin, the rye—but Sasha took care of that in a hurry. She picked them up and threw them across the room at the stone fireplace.

CRASH! SMASH! It was lovely!

And she wasn't finished.

She picked up a chair and threw it through the French door to the backyard with a smash and crash of more breaking glass.

She overturned the sofa where Ricky Bolano had sat drinking his goddamn bourbon.

She picked up the floor lamp with a silver base, raised it above her head and brought it down hard on the coffee table near the fireplace, smashing a porcelain vase full of flowers.

She tore a picture from the wall—a print of a Degas dancer, not an original—and broke the frame against an oak side table.

She toppled over the heavy cabinet with the television inside, end over end, until it lay broken in the middle of the living room floor, electric wires hanging from the back. But that was hard work and the effort finally brought an end to Sasha's madness. She sat down out of breath on the steps that led from the foyer to the living room, her left hand bleeding, gazing with wonderment at the destruction she had wrought.

She didn't care.

After resting a few minutes, more calmly, Sasha went to the other places in the house where she kept liquor—the wet bar in the Sunroom, the drink trolley upstairs in her dressing room. She gathered together all the bottles and carried them into the kitchen. Then, one by one, she emptied the contents into the sink and watched in fascination as they swirled away forever down the drain.

"I'm not going to let this goddamn town defeat me!" she said again and again as she carried out her work. "I'm not going to let this town defeat me!"

It was a kind of mantra that soothed her, though she didn't know precisely what she meant, or what it would entail: not to let this town defeat her. But she knew she had to do it in order to reclaim the person she had once been.

She refused to be second-rate. She refused to be defeated. She would be again—as she had been once before—a girl with poetry in her eyes.

Even if it meant going on the wagon.

*****

And that was how I found my mother, in a house full of broken glass and busted furniture, an hour later when I returned home from school. She informed me that she had stopped drinking and that life on North Maple Drive was going to be difficult for a few weeks, but we would get through it together, her and I.

Frankly, I was skeptical. I had seen my mother go on the wagon before, and I didn't expect it to last. But this time was different. She didn't drink that day, nor the next, nor the day following that. She did it, I think, out of pure anger. Anger at Fred, and Max, and Mina, and the whole unfeeling world. And most of all, anger at herself for letting California defeat her.

It was an enormous undertaking. But she did it. She went cold turkey, just like that.

It was a good thing, of course. Long overdue. But at the time I thought it might kill her.

Twenty-One

She couldn't do it on her own, not even with all the will-power in the world. Knowing she needed help, my mother checked into a fancy clinic for five weeks in the desert outside of Palm Springs, for what we would now call rehab.

During the time my mother was in the desert battling her demons—her forty days and forty nights—I went to live with Aunt Mina at the Garden of Allah, a hotel on Sunset Boulevard where all the writers liked to stay, the sort of overeducated East Coast writers who came to Hollywood to make bundles of money but refused to put down roots in a place they pretended to despise.

For Mina, a hotel was necessary just then because she had sold the Bel Air house to pay Max's legal expenses and settle with the IRS, a bill for back taxes that had appeared out of nowhere. That was another thing about being an un-American—the IRS generally came after you once the politicians in Washington were through, dishing out a little more pain.

Luckily, while moving out of the Bel Air house, Mina had come across an old treasury bond in her maiden name for $20,000, money that she'd put away decades ago from a small inheritance. She'd always been careless with money, having lots of it, but this half-forgotten sum came in handy now to build the beach house at Trancas that she had mentioned to my mother.

She bought the vacant beach-front lot for $5,000 which left a tidy $15,000 for the structure itself. In 1955, the average price of a new house in America was just over $10,000, so $20,000 was more than sufficient for her needs: a modest bedroom for her and Max, a living room with a kitchen in one corner, another small bedroom for me when I came to visit, and a sliding glass door that would open from the living room onto a sundeck and the beach. Mina and I often drove to Trancas to watch the carpenters at work, the walls quickly rising among the sand dunes as we lived our hotel lives on the Sunset Strip.

I enjoyed the Garden of Allah. Mina was a goddess to all the writers, and I developed a life-long addiction to room service, the pleasure of picking up a hotel telephone and asking the kitchen for anything my greedy heart desired. I became friendly with two screenwriters around the pool who taught me to play gin rummy, and there was a twenty-year-old sexpot starlet who sometimes asked if I'd be a darling and rub suntan lotion on her back. This was such an interesting prospect that I sometimes forgot Penny for a micro-second at a time.

When I returned home after five weeks, I found my mother looking better than I'd seen her for a long time. She had lost weight, her eyes were clear, and she was on a serious health kick, playing tennis almost every morning with the pro up the street at the Beverly Hills Hotel. It worried me a little how hard she hit the ball, as though she wanted to kill the thing. But I was glad to see her getting exercise, so I left the matter alone.

Along with tennis, I often found her sitting intently at the piano, the black baby grand in our living room, humming melodies and noodling her way through chord progressions. She was a singer, of course, so this shouldn't have been surprising. But in fact, throughout my childhood I had seldom seen her at the piano and not for many years.

"Jonno, come here and listen to something," she said one afternoon when I arrived home from school. "I've written a song. I want you to tell me what you think."

"I didn't know you could write music, Mom."

"Of course, I can. In Krakow I had piano lessons from the time I was five. My teacher was a dirty old man who had me sit on his lap while he touched me everywhere he liked, very shocking. But he taught me all the music theory a person needs to know. Now, listen to my song, darling, and give me your honest opinion."

I put down my books and sat next to her on the piano bench and watched her fingers roam across the black and white keys. To be honest, it always embarrassed me to hear my mother sing. Generally speaking, when you're a not-quite twelve-year-old boy, you want your mother to show more emotional restraint.

She called the song "September Intermezzo" and it was about two lovers who meet late in life, fall in love in Verse #1, quarrel in Verse #2, and somehow—the reason wasn't entirely clear—commit suicide together in Verse #3. The chorus went, "Oh, September love! . . . September love . . . doomed, doomed to die!"

I won't even attempt to describe the musical part of this sonic disaster except to say it was definitely not rock and roll.

"So, Jonno, what's your verdict?" my mother asked with a pert smile when the song was over.

I tried to come up with something positive to say, but it was a struggle. "You know, Mom, I bet this would have been a hit on the radio a hundred years ago. I mean, if they'd had radios back then."

"Oh, dear, a hundred years ago!" She narrowed her eyes. "You're saying it's old-fashioned?"

"Only by today's standards," I assured her. "A hundred years ago, I bet it would have been totally cool."

She sat with her hands in her lap, momentarily defeated. Then, to my surprise, she banged both her hands down abruptly on the keys, making a terrible explosion of sound. I hadn't realized until that moment how tense she was.

"Oh, Jonno, I absolutely must have a great ballad! I swear, I'll die if I don't!"

This wasn't about music. I saw that now. She glared ferociously at the piano like she wanted to take an axe to the thing and cut it up for firewood.

"Why can't Sol find you a ballad?" I asked weakly.

She shook her head sadly. "He just can't, that's all, so I have to write it myself. The problem is, Sol is even more old-fashioned than I am. We're both dinosaurs, Jonno—that's the truth of it. But if I can't come up with a great ballad, I'm not even sure it's worth the risk."

I missed the important part of what she was saying. I should have asked, "Worth *what* risk? What are you talking about?" Conversations are often like that, beasts with several heads popping up all at once in which you sometimes miss the proper mouth to feed. I was still considering the question of finding a ballad.

"Look," I said, "if you want a great song, why don't you just steal one?"

My mother turned her predatory green eyes my way and gazed at me with interest.

"What do you mean? How can you steal a song? They're copyrighted, Jonno."

"No, I know that," I told her. "What you do, you see, is you take a song you like and use the same chords but change it just a little. Mix up the melody, give it new words, a new title, and there you are. Everybody does it. All the songs you hear on the radio, they're all the same anyway. So it doesn't really matter."

"Where did you hear this?"

"From my friend, Chris, whose father is a producer at Epic. He says people steal songs all the time, it's just the way things are done."

Chris Lumburger was the only friend I'd made so far at the Harvard School. He was an outcast and a sex fiend, just like I was. We often skipped gym together to smoke cigarettes and talk dirty about girls in the woods behind the student parking lot where the seniors left their cars.

My mother kept gazing at me, like she had never really seen me before. "You're quite a fountain of information, darling. I think this is a very good idea. Perhaps I will steal an old Sinatra tune and see what I can do with it."

"*Mom*!" I cried in exasperation, "Don't steal an old Sinatra song. For chrissake, if you're going to steal something, steal something *new*."

I could see her brain turning over what I'd said. "I see," she said after a moment. "And where do you propose I find this new song?"

"Easy," I said. "Just listen to the Top Forty Countdown on KFWB. Saturday's the best time for it. They start with number forty and work their way to the top of the chart."

A smile touched the corners of her blood red lips. It wasn't a happy smile. It was more like the look I'd seen on her face playing tennis at the Beverly Hills Hotel, just before she was about to smash a ball to smithereens.

"Mom, what's this really all about?" I dared to ask.

She put her arms around me and held me hard.

"Revenge!" she whispered in my ear.

"Mom—"

"Shh!" She put her hand over my mouth so I couldn't ask any more questions.

*****

In the days that followed, I often found my mother in front of the big old-fashioned console radio in our living room (restored at some cost after her tornado of destruction), listening to my favorite Top Forty station, KFWB. Frankly, I wasn't optimistic. As much as I admired my mother, she just wasn't a with-it sort of person. She belonged to another age. But it was good to see her active and still on the wagon, so I ignored my apprehension that there was something dangerous in progress and I pretended that she was doing fine.

Of course, I was caught up in my own drama just then, writing letters to Penny in New York, pages and pages of heartthrob almost every night but receiving only occasional letters in return, all of them hurriedly written with many misspellings. She wrote only of casual things—horseback riding in Central Park, movies she had seen, her favorite ice cream sundae at Schrafft's—not an intimate word in the lot. The only good part of her letters came at the end where she always planted a cute lipstick kiss after her signature, an impression of her mouth. Many nights I held my real lips to her paper kisses, but they gave scant comfort. My heart ached. I believed my life was over.

Then one day in May, I got home from school to find that my mother had a present for me wrapped up in gift paper in a box.

"Mom, my birthday's not until November," I reminded her, since she was prone to forget such things.

"Go ahead and open it. It's an early present, darling. Because I love you."

I was suspicious from the start, sensing trouble, and when I opened the box, I was astonished to find an expensive 35mm camera inside with a separate light meter and a long telephoto lens. It wasn't new, I saw that quickly enough. But it was professional quality, a Leica, not the sort of thing you give as a first camera to a kid who has never expressed the slightest interest in photography.

I looked up at her for an explanation.

"It's only a present, silly," she said laughingly. "I thought you might have fun with it."

I didn't want to appear ungrateful, but fun had become a rare item in my life and I didn't see how this camera was going to make me suddenly carefree. "Gee, thanks," I told her.

"I'll take it outside and snap some pictures of birds, or something."

She laughed. "No, darling, this is an inside camera. I want you to learn how to take pictures at night inside a house. I've bought you a dozen roles of a special film called Tri-X which doesn't need hardly any light, so you won't need flashbulbs."

My suspicions were definitely deepening.

"Mom, you gotta tell me what this about!"

She took both my hands in hers and proceeded to tell me her Grand Plan. She had always liked plans, her schemes to get ahead in life, they gave her a sense of motion and conquest. But this was a doozie—multi-faceted, a plan that would get her career back on track and revenge herself on Fred Landson in the process, all in one fell swoop courtesy of *Confidential* magazine. All she needed were a few compromising photographs of herself and Fred to set the thing in motion. And for this she needed my help.

"No, no, *no!*" I cried, embarrassed and scandalized. "I mean, you're my *mother!*"

"Darling, Fred and I will barely be kissing, only enough to give *Confidential* a bit of proof. I'm going to send the pictures to them anonymously. Why, you've seen me kiss on screen a dozen times."

"I won't do it," I told her soundly. "Sorry, but definitely not."

"Look, Fred and I will be on the couch in the living room. You can hide in the den and take the pictures through a crack in the door. He'll never know. That's what the telephoto lens is for."

I kept shaking my head.

"I'll pay you. I'll give you a hundred dollars."

"No! Besides, what about Fred? I mean, the guy's creepy, sure he is. But he got you that orange juice commercial, he's helped out a lot. You can't just go and ruin someone's life. It's not right."

She took my hand and squeezed hard. "Oh, yes, I can! I hate that bastard, Jonno. I hate what he did to Max. I hate what he's done to me, thinking he can buy me with favors."

"Then tell him *sayonara*," I suggested. By 1955, I'd become a little fancy with my phraseology. "Say you won't see him anymore."

I was offering what I believed was sound advice. But she shook her head gloomily.

"Oh, Jonno, Jonno, it's not that simple! It's awful, but I still need the jerk, just for a while longer. He's promised I'll be able to sing at the Republican convention next summer. Think what that will do for my career! Don't you see? He has me trapped."

It seemed to me that my mother had trapped herself with her own ambition. But I didn't say that. I took a more practical approach. "Then wait until you sing and leave Fred once it's over."

"No, no . . . you've got to take those pictures, Jonno, it's the only way I can get out of this hole I'm in. It'll make everything wonderful again. I'll be famous just like I used to be. I'll have work, I'll have all my bunnies in a row."

It wasn't quite the right expression, bunnies in a row. Despite her years in America, my mother had never nailed her idioms. She was still subtly foreign, somehow wrong.

"I can't do it, Mom."

"Oh, yes, you can. You're my Little Man, you've got to help me."

"I won't!"

"Oh, yes, you will!"

Without warning, she was furious. She took me by both shoulders and shook me violently, so hard that my head bobbed back and forth like a punching bag on a pole.

"Listen, you brat, you're going to do this or I'm through with you forever! What makes you think you're so special? Don't you know the things I've had to do to get this far? Do you think you're some goddamn little prince who doesn't have to get his hands dirty?"

I was stunned. She had never screamed at me before, she had never shaken me. But the storm was over as quickly as it began. In a moment, she was hugging me and begging my forgiveness.

"Oh, Jonno, I'm sorry, sorry . . . oh, please, say you're all right! Oh, God, I didn't mean to shake you like that! But I have everything riding on this, you see. *Everything*! Tell me you forgive me!"

"I forgive you, Mom," I replied weakly.

"Oh, thank God! Thank God!" She kissed me violently on both cheeks and held me so tightly I could barely breathe.

"But I'm still not taking those pictures," I managed.

She held me at arm's length and regarded me intently, the way a cat might study a mouse. Her green eyes had a cunning glint.

"All right, here's my final offer," she said calmly. "If you do this, I'll take you to New York for a long weekend so you can see Penny. We'll stay at the Plaza, my lucky hotel. Would you like that, darling? I bet you would!"

My mouth fell open. It was unbelievable, incredible, but my mother had divined my secret, my most urgent wish. A smile came to her lips as she watched my struggle.

I hated her for knowing me so well.

Twenty-Two

Fred was away in Washington just then, doing whatever it was that Congressmen did, and I had a few weeks to learn how to use the camera before he was expected back in California for the summer recess.

My mother bought a book for me that had basic information about film speeds, f/stop settings, shutter speeds, depth of field, and so on. In those days, once you advanced beyond the Kodak Brownie, nothing on a camera was automatic, you had to fix all the settings yourself. But I turned out to have a small talent for photography and I got the idea fairly fast.

The biggest challenge was that I would be shooting indoors at night with a telephoto lens and no flash. The long lens, as I understood it, meant that I would need even more light than was normally required. Tri-X film was designed for low light, but it wasn't as fast in 1955 as it is today.

I spent several evenings experimenting with various combinations of f/stop settings and shutter speeds, photographing my mother as she sat on the living room sofa while I was in the den with the Leica, the door opened just a crack. For our purposes, it was vital that the photos were clear enough so that both Fred and my mother would be easily recognized, and I went through a dozen rolls of film, which I had developed at a camera shop on Beverly Drive, before I was satisfied. In the end, I told my mother that she was going to need a floor lamp switched on in order to provide enough light. Also, equally important, she and Fred would need to remain as still as possible due to the fact that I was going to need to use a slow shutter speed. I'm sure a professional photographer would have found easier solutions, but this was the best I could do. I wasn't looking forward to the big night itself, but the photography part was fun for someone my age. I suppose I got into it, just a little.

Fred didn't return to California until nearly the end of June, and with one thing and another, it wasn't until after the July 4th weekend that he found time to escape his family and come see my mother in Beverly Hills. I'd spent the day in antsy anticipation, imagining all the ways I could screw up. Fred wasn't due until after nine-thirty, but I was ready by eight, positioned in the den with the lights off and the door opened a crack onto the living room.

Along with the camera, I had two pillows, a milk bottle filled with water, and a bag of chocolate chip cookies in case I got hungry. My mother didn't plan to allow Fred to spend the entire night as he sometimes did—she promised to have a strategic quarrel sometime before midnight as an excuse to get rid of him. Nevertheless, I would need to stay hidden in the den for quite a number of hours so it seemed wise to make myself comfortable. I even had an old cooking pot to pee in, in case my bladder couldn't wait. In my anxiety, I tried to anticipate every problem that might arise.

Fred arrived half an hour late, at close to ten, with his bodyguard, Mike, coming up the path behind him. I listened as my mother opened the front door with a seductive hello.

"Hey, aren't you a sight for sore eyes!" Fred said smoothly. Success in Washington had lubricated his tongue considerably. He was almost slick. "You look swell, Sash. Boy, have I been waiting to get my hands on *you*!"

"Mmmm, likewise," she told him. "Listen, big boy, I want Mike to wait in the car tonight. Jonno's gone for the night and I've been looking forward to having you in the house all to myself."

"Gee, Sash, I can't really ask Mike to wait in the car all that time. I mean, it isn't fair."

"Then you'll have to come back and see me another time. I've got naughty things in mind, and I'm not the sort of girl who likes an audience."

"That naughty, huh?" I could almost hear Fred grinning. "Well, okay, then. Mike, you heard what the lady said. You mind waiting in the car, just this once?"

"I'm fine, Boss. No problem."

Phase One had gone off according to plan. I listened as my mother led Fred into the house and steered him toward the living room. I could tell that Fred wanted to get upstairs quickly so it was necessary to slow him down.

"Hey, what's your hurry, Fred? We have the whole night," she teased. "And there just happens to be a bottle of very good champagne on ice in the living room."

"Oh, yeah? Maybe I don't need champagne. Maybe I only need a big long drink of you."

My mother laughed. "Whoa, there, fella! Let's have a drink first. Maybe *I* need to get to know you again after all these weeks away."

Fred laughed. "All right, you win. Come here, you!"

This exchange was followed by a silence in which I presumed they were kissing. I didn't want to think about that too much, so I reached for the camera, determined to get my job over with. From the open crack of the door, I could see my mother was standing at the bar opening a bottle of champagne while Fred stood behind her with his hands on her waist. She had piano music playing on the record player, Chopin, her favorite composer and one-time ancestor. Earlier in the evening I had helped her stack three LPs on the spindle, enough music to help drown out any noise I might make with the camera. As I watched, she filled a glass full of bubbly and handed it to Fred.

"Only one glass? Aren't you going to join me?" he asked.

"Maybe I'll have a ginger ale later. I'm on the wagon."

"No kidding?"

"That's right. I'm on a whole new regime, Fred. I'm a new person entirely."

"Well, good for you," he said uncertainly. "You were hitting the sauce a little hard there for a while."

"Come sit next to me," she offered, leading him to the sofa, to a spot that was lit in the warm glow of a floor lamp. "I want to hear about everything you've been doing. Why, I saw you on television the other day. They said you're an up and coming star!"

Fred chuckled as he sat down next to her. "Yeah, that's me, all right. Up and coming. There's even talk I might be tapped for Vice President if Nixon runs in 1960. Everybody's saying that Senator Kennedy will be the Democratic choice—we'll beat the heck out of that Catholic son of a gun, I can tell you that! You're going to be glad to know me, Sasha."

"But I can't tell anyone about us, Fred. So it's rather sad."

He put his arm around her shoulder and drew her closer. "Yeah, it has to be our special secret or my goose is cooked, that's for sure. But we'll know, just the two of us. I shouldn't be seeing you at all, I know that. I'm risking everything for you, but I just can't stay away. Come on, tell me you like me, just a little."

"Sure, I like you," she agreed. "Just a little."

"Well, I'm crazy about you, honey. You light me up like a firecracker that just wants to go boom, boom, boom!"

For Fred, I suppose, boom, boom, boom passed as poetry. From my hiding spot, I watched as he set his glass down on the coffee table and began kissing and groping my mother in earnest. I didn't want to watch this any longer than necessary so I raised the camera and set to work.

I had a fresh roll of film in the camera, thirty-six exposures, and two other rolls handy in case I needed them. I had practiced changing rolls in the dark, so I figured I was ready for anything. I kept snapping away, trying not to think too much about what I was doing—click, click, click, one picture after another. In the end, I used up two and a half rolls of film, hoping for three or four useable photographs. But it was a depressing job and when Fred slipped his hand inside my mother's bra, I snapped a final picture and then put down the camera and crawled away from the door. I suppose I should have used up the rest of the film, but I figured the pictures I'd taken would do. I just couldn't stand to watch any more.

Some more time went by until finally, mercifully, my mother led Fred upstairs to her bedroom, leaving me alone in the den. I couldn't make any noise in the house, so I just laid on the carpet hugging my knees and feeling sick in my soul. I put my head on one pillow and held the other pillow in my arms, trying to imagine it was Penny that I was holding, and that my love for her made everything clean.

I'd be seeing her soon for the promised long weekend in New York, and I tried to tell myself that this made everything all right. She was my reward, the light at the end of this awful night.

An Almost Perfect Ending

I did it all for Penny. But life wasn't destined to get better for me any time soon, and when I finally got to New York later that summer, she was too busy to see me except for a single disappointing hour. We met for lunch at the Schrafft's near the NBC studio at Rockefeller Center and we didn't have much to talk about. She was dating some teen idol, a singer who had a big hit on the radio, but I didn't want to hear about it, his penthouse and cars and all the fancy places they went. After some forced hilarity remembering old times on Stage 17, we both fell into an awkward silence over our club sandwiches. I couldn't understand how once we had been so close, and now we had become strangers.

I was so depressed afterwards that I walked back along Fifth Avenue to the Plaza and collapsed onto one of the benches across the street by the edge of the park. I was about to have myself a good cry when I realized with a shock that it was the very bench where Zachary Wise had discovered my mother and made her a star. Her lucky-lucky bench, as she called it. She always pointed out this important landmark to me every time we passed through New York.

I sprang to my feet as though I'd been sitting on hot coals and took off down West 59th Street in a hurry. It didn't make logical sense. I knew there was no Zachary Wise looking to find me; my angels were different than hers, and my demons, too. Nevertheless, I walked clear to Columbus Circle before I dared sit again on a small grassy knoll where the past couldn't reach me.

Twenty-Three

Max got out of prison in early July 1955 and I was shocked when I saw him. He was fifty-seven years old, but his hair had gone white and he looked much older than his age. His nose had a new bend from where it had been broken, and he walked with a slight stoop, as though he didn't dare assert his former height.

Arthritis had crept into his bones and often it took him a few moments to stand fully erect from a chair. It broke my heart to see him. All his jaunty wit was gone, his fine sense of himself. I wouldn't have believed that a person could change so much in a single year. Often there was a baffled, child-like expression on his face, as though he didn't quite understand what had hit him.

Yet there was a sweetness to him that hadn't been there before. "Well, Jonno, my God, look at me—I'm as poor as a church mouse!" he told me with his sad, sweet smile one afternoon when he didn't even have the pocket money to take us to a double feature in Santa Monica, a matinee. I ended up paying for the movie, which embarrassed us both.

At least he had a place to live, thanks to Mina. It was only a small beach house, but after his year in prison, Max found it luxurious beyond belief. From the sundeck, you could walk directly onto the sand and over the rise of a grassy dune to the ocean itself—the blue Pacific, the most lovely of all oceans, where in the 1950s you could pull an abalone off a rock at low tide for dinner, and use the shell afterwards for an ashtray.

Max settled into his new life, relieved to be isolated from old Hollywood friends. Poverty and failure had left him feeling shy.

"Isn't it wonderful to live a simple life!" Mina often declared. "We have everything we need, don't we, Max? The sun, the sand, the ocean . . . why should anyone want more?"

"Yes, it's lovely," he agreed. But he was afraid that Mina protested too loudly the joys of their simple life. They were both accustomed to grander times.

They could no longer afford servants so they cleaned house for themselves. Max even learned to use a vacuum cleaner. They sold the Packard to a junkyard for parts (it was nearly as battered as Max and brought only $50), but they kept Mina's old Cadillac for trips to the market. Money was so tight for the first few months after Max got out of prison that they were only able to afford California wine and no champagne at all, except for special occasions.

Max took up the challenge of life as a poor man with good humor and determination. He became the principal cook of the family, showing an unexpected talent in the kitchen, helping himself to free abalone from the beach several times a week— "dinner courtesy of God," as Mina liked to put it. When I began visiting on weekends, I often helped Max find abalone on the rocks at low tide, and he showed me how to get the meat from the shell and pound it out with a hammer. We had fried abalone, baked abalone, abalone with white wine and garlic over spaghetti, even abalone *parmigiano*, a dish Max invented.

Max learned to fish, casting his line from the surf, and on the days when we didn't eat abalone, we usually had perch. Mina had been a vegetarian since her trip to India, but she began eating seafood again in order to enjoy God's free bounty. She also began to drink again, but only moderately— California wine somehow got included in what she saw as the blessing of the sun and the land.

I'm not sure that Max ever got to like being poor, not the way Mina did—sometimes she acted as though it were a positive relief to be poor after all the rich, complicated living they had done. But then, ironically, it was Mina who began to work again, getting hired for small parts in TV shows, bringing in some much-needed money. At first she worked under an assumed name, Hope Goode—a fitting pseudonym for Mina, I always thought—but after a few roles, her agent began sending her out under her own name and the parts suddenly got bigger. Generally, she played eccentric, older women. Character roles.

One time she was the guest star on *Cheyenne*, a Western on ABC, a big hit at the time. Mina played the mother of a young cowboy wrongly accused of murder, and Max and I had to rent a motel room in Santa Monica to see the show on the night it was aired because there was no reception at the beach in those days, barely any radio. Mina had not been blacklisted and a new generation of TV producers didn't know the story of how she'd had to be hospitalized during the filming of a long-forgotten movie. Once she started working again, abalone and perch were no longer on the menu quite so often, and they even bought a second car, a station wagon, so that Mina could drive to the studio without Max feeling stranded.

In order to fill his days, Max read a great deal—from the Malibu library mostly, to save money—and he began to write a script under an assumed name (Jackson Goode) that he thought he might be able to sell. A number of blacklisted writers were writing under assumed names at that time, and he didn't see why a director couldn't try this as well.

Of course, Max could have gone to Europe to work. This was always an option for the blacklisted, and in Max's case his *noir* thrillers were still very popular overseas, especially in France. In September of that year, a British producer, a friend, tried to set up a picture for Max to direct in London. But the U.S. government had taken Max's passport when he was sent to prison and they refused to issue him a new one. Apparently, he was still considered a security risk. They seemed to think Max would take off like a homing pigeon to Moscow with important state secrets the moment they let him loose, perhaps even the recipe to abalone *parmigiano*.

An Almost Perfect Ending

Max didn't mind, not really. There were always beautiful sunsets to watch over the Pacific, and the cries of seagulls to listen to, and on weekends when I'd come to visit, we'd play Scrabble far into the night. Max did his best to adjust to new circumstances. He wasn't bitter, but he was tired. It took a lot of energy to start again, and somewhere along the way Max's energy had been used up.

"Well, here I am," he'd sometimes say aloud, as though startled to find himself a stooped, white-haired man living on a lonely, wind-swept beach in California. "I've grown old, that's all."

*****

By the fall, Mina was gone most days working on one TV show or another, which gave Max a good deal of time on his own. He spent most mornings writing on an old Remington typewriter which he set up on the dining room table with a view of the ocean. It seemed important to have a creative project and not let go entirely of whatever it was that movie people needed to grip hold of.

In October he finished the first draft of the screenplay he'd been writing, a love story set in England during the war, but he never got around to a second draft. He couldn't imagine working up the effort to drive into town and pitch the story to a producer, the mock-enthusiasm he would need to come up with.

In place of the screenplay, Max began to write snatches of a memoir. He started with his childhood and intended to go on through the entirety of his life, the rise and fall of a Hollywood director. He didn't imagine his memoir would be published, but that didn't bother Max unduly. It just seemed a good thing when you lived at the beach to be writing something, and a memoir fit the bill, a mournful project for a mournful man.

At the end of each morning, he made himself a small lunch, a salad or a sandwich, and then he had a nap. Naps became such a key part of the day that he often wondered how he had survived fifty-seven years without them. In the afternoons when he rose, he liked to walk on the beach, either north toward the rocky bluffs where Trancas ended, or south across the many miles of open sand toward the public beach at Zuma. The walks were a deliberate attempt at exercise. Still, it felt strange for someone who had spent his life working to be so idle.

The days flowed along in this peaceful fashion, August and September. Then in October, Max met a woman on the beach. The ocean brought her to him like other things that washed his way, driftwood and sand dollars and seaweed. It was only a small encounter, but she left an impression.

An Almost Perfect Ending

By October, there were very few people at Trancas and Max sometimes walked for hours without coming across another soul. But he had begun seeing another lonely walker like himself, a woman whose path he sometimes intersected. She was perhaps thirty years old, dark haired, tall and slim and graceful, pretty enough that Max assumed she must be an actress, though he didn't recognize her. She walked barefoot in loose white beach pants that she rolled up at the bottoms to let the surf swirl around her toes. On cool days she wore sweaters that were fluffy and warm, casual attire yet there was an elegance about her, an aura of intelligence and money. She had a dog, an Irish Setter, who often ran over to Max to wag his tail and accept a bit of affection.

Coming from different directions on an empty expanse of beach, Max would see the mysterious woman from a long way off, a small dot. Then, over the course of twenty minutes, they would approach gradually closer to one another until at last they met. Visually, this made for a dramatic encounter, and since it was 1955, a more innocent age than ours, they generally smiled and said hello. Sometimes Max made comments about what a fine afternoon it was before moving on. Once he mentioned a dead shark he had seen further up the beach and suggested she might look for it if she were walking all the way to the end.

She was very pretty. Max appreciated this fact whenever he saw her. But he was relieved to be an old man. Age excused him, he believed, from the necessity to either flirt or not flirt, but in either case be faced with the sexual issue. There was some value, he saw, in growing old. One could be harmless. One could bow out from the difficulties of the dance.

But then one afternoon the Irish Setter brought Max a stick and he lingered long enough to throw it a few times. He had passed the attractive woman now half a dozen times and they finally stopped to have a longer chat.

"We seem to be the only two people who ever walk on this lovely beach," he said mildly.

"Yes, aren't we lucky?" Her voice was clear as a bell. "You're Max McCormick, aren't you?" she added unexpectedly.

"Well, yes. That I am," he answered, surprised to be recognized.

"I've always admired your movies," she told him. "I'm a huge fan of yours, actually."

Max smiled awkwardly and studied a sand crab who was making a dash for the surf. "Ah, well, movies!" he sighed. "That's the old days. These days I have a splendid new life as a beachcomber. It's given me a chance to work on my so-called character."

She didn't laugh as he had intended at his slight, self-deprecating joke. Instead, her clear eyes focused on him intently.

"I think you have a great deal of character, Mr. McCormick. I particularly admired how you dealt with the House Un-American Activities Committee. I was deeply moved by what you said to them at your hearing. I can't tell you how upset I was when those idiots sent you to prison. I even wrote a letter to the *New York Times*. They didn't publish it, of course."

Max was embarrassed and didn't know how to respond. This was more than he had bargained for, in his lonely walk for one on the sand.

"Actually, the *Times* was one of the first newspapers to make all their employees sign loyalty oaths swearing they'd never been Communists," he lectured, glad to be speaking about something besides himself. "Then came Harvard, my own alma mater. They did the same thing. It's astonishing how all the great American intellectual institutions rolled over at the sight of Joe McCarthy. They gave in without a struggle. Liberals are fine folk to share a shaker of martinis with. But they don't have much backbone, I'm afraid, when push comes to shove."

"But you did," she said pointedly. "You had backbone. You became an example for the rest of us in dark times, Mr. McCormick. I'm Mary Beth Caldwell, by the way," she added, perhaps a little shy herself.

Max knew the name. She was a novelist whose first book had won all sorts of awards and critical acclaim. Max hadn't read it only because these days he seldom read anything with a copyright after the year 1900. He studied her more closely. She was older than he had first imagined, nearer to forty than thirty. Her eyes were keen and beautiful.

"Then I imagine you're in Hollywood writing a screenplay for your novel," he said. "*The Promise of Light*, is that the name of your book? . . . I'm sorry to be so ignorant."

"Yes, that's the title. Metro bought the rights and brought me to California."

"And you hate every minute of it," he added pleasantly. "You probably can't believe how crass all these producers are. They change their minds every five minutes. One day they love the scene you've just given them. They say it's absolutely a work of genius. And the next day, they want you to rewrite it five different times."

She laughed. "You've got it. Is my story really as common as that?"

"At least you were smart enough to rent a house at the beach. Where did Metro want to put you? At the Chateau Marmont or the Beverly Hills Hotel?"

"The Beverly Hills Hotel."

"Good. That's more expensive for them, which means your book must have sold a lot of copies."

"But I hate it! All I want to do is go home."

"And where's that?"

"Wellfleet. Cape Cod."

An Almost Perfect Ending

"No wonder you gravitate to the beach. I know Cape Cod well. I grew up in Boston, but my family had a summer house at North Truro."

They had a great deal in common. Max liked Mary Beth Caldwell. She was smart, she was pretty, she was literate, and she seemed to like him as well. Mina, as it happened, was on location at Lake Tahoe for several days. Max saw how easy it would be to invite Mary Beth back to his house for a drink. He would draw her to him, kiss her sea-cold lips, pull her body close against his own. He felt a familiar stirring. It wasn't even sex so much as the adventure of sex, all the trimmings of the feast. All at once, he didn't feel like such an old man.

He sensed that she would say yes if he asked her. In fact, he saw yes quite clearly in her eyes, along with her mistaken belief that he was some kind of romantic hero just because he had made a few decent movies and HUAC had thrown him in jail. But Max let the moment pass. He lingered long enough to chat about Boston and Cape Cod and the producer she was working for, and then he lied and said he'd better get home because his wife would be waiting for him to cook dinner. He said he hoped he'd run into her again on another afternoon walk. But he said it in a deliberately neutral manner, unprovocative.

He walked off with a friendly wave . . . and wondered with every footstep down the beach why in God's name he had turned down a fleeting chance for human comfort.

"I just don't have the energy to begin all that nonsense again," he told himself as he walked away. "Besides, my memoir is too long already. I really couldn't fit any more in."

Twenty-Four

Fred Landson enjoyed the neat compartments of his separate lives. He led precisely three lives, as he saw it—just like that show on television, *I Led Three Lives*.

Fred's first life, the one that was most important to him, was to be a Congressman in Washington, D.C. It never ceased to fill him with awe whenever he thought of this, both the important work he did and the position he had attained.

He had never become cynical like some of the other guys he knew. There was nothing he liked better than to be addressed as Mr. Congressman. Or to see his name in the newspaper, "Congressman Landson, the Republican from California." He wasn't a fancy guy, it wasn't that at all; he had come from the land, a simple man of the people. But as a Congressman, he had earned the right to walk tall. He had earned the right to think well of himself.

That was his first life.

Then there was his second life, his family life with Debbie and the kids at the Lido. Fred loved his family. They were the basis of his strength, the structure that allowed him to be secure and powerful. Fred craved structure and he never for one moment forgot that he was a family man, not even when he was enjoying Life Number Three with Sasha.

Life Number Three, of course, was about sex, danger, and excitement. Fred had an unexpected craving for sex, danger, and excitement—it gave juice to life, and a bounce in his step, and as a 1950s man it did not strike him in any way unusual that Life Number Three with Sasha and Life Number Two with Debbie and the kids needed to be kept entirely separate from one another. Nor did it worry him unduly that Life Number One as a U.S. Congressman had to be kept at a far, far removed from Life Number Three, his wild, wanton ways.

Separation was what made everything work for Fred. Separation kept the whole show going, each thing in its place. Separate But Equal, that was the ticket—and when people knew their place, the very jigsaw puzzle of society was a happy fit.

It was snowing in Washington on November 25th, the day Congressman Landson flew home to California for the long Thanksgiving weekend. Growing up in Southern California, Fred still got a kick out of snow. Snow was exotic. It was one of the things that served to remind him how far he had come from the sleepy orange-growing hamlet of Anaheim where he had been raised.

At eight that evening, his chief-of-staff, Chucky Vonn, and his secretary, Babs, rode with him to the airport to catch the overnight flight to Los Angeles. At the airport, Fred was met by a special representative from TWA whose job it was to deal with VIPs like himself and make sure everything went smoothly. Fred enjoyed these perks of the job. He didn't have to wait in lines like ordinary people. He was put in a comfortable VIP lounge where there were other senators and congressmen like himself going home for the recess, all very chummy, and when the plane was loaded, he was ushered on board separately at the last moment and shown into his seat in First Class—which in the days of propeller flights was in the rear of the plane rather than the front, as it is now.

As soon as the plane was off the ground, everyone brought out their cigarettes, filling the cabin with a thick cloud of tobacco. Fred filled his pipe and then used his 24-carat solid gold Zippo (a present from a lobbyist in a tobacco growing state) to light the rich Balkan Sobranie blend. This was another perk of being an elected member of Congress. Generally speaking, only cigarettes were allowed on passenger planes, no cigars or pipes. But when you were a VIP, normal rules didn't apply. Many of his colleagues on the Hill had begun to call him "Doc" because of his pipe habit, and Fred had come to enjoy the nickname. It was important to have a nickname in Washington. It was a sign that you were an insider, running with the pack.

Fred ordered a highball from the pretty stewardess and was sucking contentedly on his pipe when he heard a woman's voice address him from across the aisle.

"Excuse me, young man, but would you mind putting out that disgusting pipe. It's not allowed, you know."

Robert Westbrook

Fred looked across the aisle to find a very small old woman in dark clothing glaring at him with disapproval.

"I beg your pardon?"

"I said, please put out your pipe. The smell is atrocious. Obviously, no one taught you manners."

Fred wasn't sure whether to laugh or be angry. Fortunately, the stewardess had heard the exchange. She hurried over and bent forward to whisper in the old woman's ear, setting her right as to Fred's special status.

But the woman wasn't impressed. "I don't care who he is," she said loudly. "I didn't vote for him, I can promise you that. I'm a Democrat!"

Now Fred *did* laugh. The stewardess shot him a helpless look and Fred put out his pipe, just to show what a good sport he was.

"Gosh, I didn't know you allowed Democrats on TWA," he whispered jokingly to the pretty stewardess a few minutes later when she arrived with his highball. "I'm going to have to speak to Howard Hughes about this!" Howard Hughes, the eccentric millionaire, was currently the owner of TWA.

The stewardess laughed pleasantly. "Oh, thank you, Congressman, for being so understanding!"

"That's my job, to be understanding," he told her. "It's what we do in Washington, we listen to the concerns of our constituents."

An Almost Perfect Ending

Even Fred knew this wasn't true. What they did in Washington was accept 24-carot solid gold Zippo lighters from lobbyists in tobacco growing states who wanted to silence the growing chorus of health concerns about their product. But it was pleasant to reel off a platitude to a pretty girl and see the admiration in her eyes.

Half an hour later, Fred closed his eyes hoping to catch some sleep, but the old woman's words echoed in his ears with the passing miles: *I'm a Democrat*!

Next year, in 1956, there were going to be elections in which Fred's seat was up for grabs. He was already planning his campaign, and though he didn't expect to lose, there were rumors that he might face an unexpectedly strong challenger, a war hero like himself, but one who happened to be a liberal.

I'm a Democrat!

Fred tried to put it out of mind. It was only a small encounter, something to laugh about. Yet small as it was, Fred remembered it afterwards as the first omen that the comfortable structure of his life—all three lives—was about to come undone.

*****

Fred's plane arrived in Los Angeles at 7:20 the following morning, Thanksgiving Day. Though it was a holiday, he was met at the airport by Mike, his all-purpose driver/bodyguard, and Steve Peterson, the head of his California office.

Steve rode with Fred in the back seat of the limo as Mike navigated the freeway toward the Lido at 80 mph, well over the speed limit. This was another perk of Fred's position. He had a card in his wallet from the Attorney General of the United States to warn any Highway Patrolman who dared stop them to not even think about a speeding ticket.

Steve had set up a busy weekend schedule—a Friday morning meeting with a church group and another meeting later in the afternoon with a local civic organization that was lobbying to have a nuclear power plant built in Orange County (jobs, a new freeway to convey nuclear waste, money for everybody).

Saturday was going to be a particularly busy day. If the weather held, Fred had arranged to take four important Republican donors out on his boat, *Debbie's Dream*, a fishing trip for bass, bonito, and campaign funds for the coming election. If the weather turned sour, they would just sit at the dock and drink beer. This would be Fred's first choice, since the actual operation of his huge cabin cruiser, taking the monstrous thing out past the buoys onto the open ocean, always worried him more than he cared to admit.

"I sure hope Debbie's got all the food together for the shindig on Saturday," he said to Steve as he glanced through his weekend itinerary. "There's no need to be fancy for these guys. All we need is plenty of fried chicken, potato salad, and lots of beer. But I don't want to run out."

"Right, Boss. To tell the truth, I tried to phone Debbie yesterday, but I couldn't reach her."

Fred glanced up from his to-do list with a frown of displeasure. "What do you mean, you couldn't reach her?"

Steve was a bright, clean-cut young fellow straight out of college. "Well, I tried to phone her in the morning, then later in the afternoon, then once again before I went home for the day. I left a message each time with the service. But she never called back."

"Gee, that's odd. Debbie knows these big shot donors are coming to the house on Saturday, right? She's ready for them?"

"Boss, I sure hope so. I spoke to her two weeks ago about this, but no one's seen her this week at all, so I just don't know."

Fred absorbed this information with a frown. Debbie wasn't the kind of wife who disappeared. She was reliable. She was someone who could always be reached. It was one of her main virtues. She was never moody or mysterious. She was always there with a cheerful smile when she was needed.

"Well, if you spoke to Debbie two weeks ago about the fishing trip, she'll remember," he decided. "You know how organized she is. She writes everything down."

It was true. Debbie was perfectly organized, she never surprised him in any way. So Fred wasn't sure why he felt a knot of worry, as he had with the unpleasant old woman on the plane who had told him she was a Democrat, a sense of the world out of kilter.

*****

Fred arrived at his house on the Lido to find Debbie and the children gone and a stranger waiting for him in the living room, a slim, middle-aged man with tortoise shell glasses who was dressed in an expensive gray suit. There was no sign of Thanksgiving dinner, no turkey in the oven, no preparations anywhere in sight. As for the stranger, he didn't look like a burglar. He looked slick. He had an air of self-possession that Fred found disturbing.

"Who the heck are you?" Fred demanded, stepping into his living room. Under normal circumstances, Fred made a point of being polite to strangers, because strangers voted. But he was tired from flying all night and starting to feel fed up.

The man stood and offered his hand. "Sorry to barge in like this, Congressman. My name's Wilson Manning. I'm your wife's attorney."

"My wife's *attorney*! What's going on here? Where's Debbie?" Fred was suddenly furious. Debbie wasn't the sort of person to have an attorney. Certainly not one with an uppity name like Wilson Manning! The whole thing was ridiculous.

Mr. Manning smiled apologetically. But it was the sort of apologetic smile that had a glint of unapology lurking around the edges.

"Congressman, the fact is Mrs. Landson is filing for divorce. She engaged me on her behalf to meet with you this morning when you returned in order to present her demands."

"Her *demands*?" Fred was nearly paralyzed with surprise. He was starting to feel like Alice falling down her famous rabbit hole. Nothing made sense anymore. In all their life together, Debbie had never made demands, not about anything.

"Perhaps it would be best to discuss this in private," said Mr. Manning, glancing over Fred's shoulder at Mike and Steve, who were standing awkwardly at the edge of the room.

"Look, Boss, we'll rustle up some coffee in the kitchen," Steve said quickly, a politic young man.

Fred could only shake his head in amazement. When they were alone, he muttered: "There'd better be some darn good reason for this, that's all I can say!"

"Oh, there's a good reason, Congressman. A very good reason indeed. When I show you the photographs your wife received last week, I think you'll understand."

As Fred stood watching, the attorney brought a large envelope out from his leather briefcase, and from the envelope produced four eight-by-ten glossy black and white photographs which he placed delicately on the coffee table for Fred to inspect.

Fred was so surprised by what he saw that it took his brain a moment to make sense of the images on the table before him. He felt his face going hot. The photographs were shocking, pictures of himself and Sasha, the two of them necking on her living room sofa in Beverly Hills. But it wasn't possible. There was no way photographs like this could exist. Fred remembered the night in question. It was last July. Sasha had told him that Jonno was away, so they had sat in the living room for half an hour or so before going upstairs, necking a little on the sofa.

Unfortunately, the photographs were astonishingly clear. There could be no mistaking who they were—Congressman Fred Landson and Sonya Saint-Amant, the famous singer in person, there for all to see, both of them getting hot and bothered. In one picture, he had his good hand slipped down the front of her dress into her bra. He remembered that, the feel of her nipple against his fingers.

Fred had to sit down. "Oh, Lord!" he said.

"I'm sorry, Congressman. I don't take any pleasure in showing this to you. But I hope you can understand your wife's reaction."

Fred tried to think, but for the moment he was baffled.

"You know what?" he said at last. "I'm going to tear these darn things up, Mr. Manning. They're dirty, and I don't want them around for my kids to see."

"Go ahead, tear them up, Congressman, if it'll make you feel better. They're only copies—we have the originals safe and sound." The attorney sat opposite Fred and spoke very calmly, which Fred found unbearable. "Your wife has had time to think most carefully about this and she doesn't intend to be vengeful. If at all possible, she wants to avoid harming your chances for re-election next year."

"Where is she? Where are my children?"

"I'm not at liberty to tell you that, Congressman. What I can tell you is this. Debbie is prepared to wait until after the election for the divorce. She'll keep your separation secret until that time, along with the reason for it. But in return, she wants five thousand dollars a month alimony to be paid for the rest of her life, even if she decides to marry again. You will grant her sole custody of the children. You will put this house completely in her name. You will also give her the boat out-side that's named after her, *Debbie's Dream*. In addition, she's asking for a one-time payment of three million dollars. If you consent to these terms, and sign the contractual agree-ment that I'll draw up, she'll agree to appear with you at specified campaign appearances next summer and fall. She has your interests at heart, Congressman. She's not vindictive. But she will not see you, nor allow you anywhere near the children, except in public circumstances connected to your re-election campaign."

Fred listened with growing incomprehension. Five thousand dollars a *month*! . . . a one-time payment of *three million dollars*! She even wanted the damn house and boat! The words droned on, an abstraction of sound, yet terrifying nonetheless.

"Do you have any questions, Congressman?"

"Look, I gotta see her," he said hopefully, man to man. "You can understand that, can't you? We can work this out, Debbie and me. I've always loved her. I mean, this thing with the woman in the picture . . ."

"Sonya Saint-Amant, the singer," said Wilson Manning, giving the woman in the picture her proper name.

"Right, Sonya. Well, look you're a man . . . you know how these things happen. I swear, it didn't mean anything! I have to see Debbie and tell her that. Debbie's my girl . . . she'll understand."

The attorney shook his head. "I'm sorry but my instructions are clear. Your wife doesn't wish to see you. I understand this is a shock so I suggest you take a day or two to think it over. Your wife knows how much your political career means to you so she's willing to be generous. But you must agree to all her demands or she'll go public about your affair with a singer of loose morals. A woman from an Eastern Bloc country, by the way, who has been rumored to have had a long-term liaison with the Communist movie director, Max McCormick, who your House committee sent to prison for his subversive views. I'm afraid this won't look good for you, Congressman."

Fred's mouth fell open. It had never occurred to him that the un-American card might boomerang and come back to haunt him. But none of that mattered. With the conservative voters in Orange County, divorce itself, for whatever reason, would ruin his chances next November at the polls. Divorce was not acceptable. A divorced man was not a family man.

"All right, I'll think about it," he said reluctantly. "I'll have to consult my own attorney as well, of course."

"Of course," said Mr. Manning, rising from his seat. "Think it over. But make the smart move, Congressman. Your wife is only asking for money, which you can always earn again. But if these photographs come out, you can kiss your career in politics goodbye."

*****

Fred prayed for foul weather, but Saturday dawned clear and warm with temperatures expected to reach seventy-five degrees. It was the sort of postcard-perfect late November day to turn frozen people back East green with envy. It was what sunny Southern California was all about: no winter, no pain. For Fred, there was no way now that he could escape taking his four donors out of the channel into the terrors of the open ocean.

With important guests coming, it was inconvenient that Debbie had taken just this moment to leave him. Fortunately, Mike and Steve had found a restaurant in Newport Beach willing to cook up the necessary chicken and potato salad, even a few trays of deviled eggs. A nearby liquor store delivered five cases of beer and plenty of ice, and the boys stowed everything away in the galley of the boat.

Fred's campaign manager, Dick Dodson, was the first to arrive at close to ten o'clock. He was dressed for the sea in blue canvas deck shoes, white pants, and a sports shirt with fish on it, a pattern of marlins flying through the waves. Dick was a short, chubby, middle-aged man, no movie star when it came to looks, but the sharpest brain in California when it came to getting a guy elected.

"Hey, Fred! Great morning to raise a whole lot o'cash!" Dick cried out in greeting.

"Sure is!" Fred answered. "Wonderful morning indeed!"

Fred had decided he wasn't going to tell Dick about Debbie leaving him. Not yet. Not ever, if he could help it. Nor would he dwell on the awful photographs and the threat they posed to his career, his life, to everything he had built and done. He wasn't even going to think about Sasha, who had to be involved in this picture-taking in some way. Oh, she was going to be sorry! But today he was going to smile and be cheerful. Today he was going to put the whole mess from his mind.

His guests began to arrive at eleven, one limousine after another pulling up into Fred's circular driveway. Fred greeted each one of them as though he didn't have a care in the world. The fishing party included the president of a bank, the owner of a baseball team, the heir to a newspaper empire, and a retired cowboy star who had bought up nearly fifty acres of prime Los Angeles real estate back in the days when prime L.A. real estate had gone for pennies. All the men shared a common hatred of FDR (who was dead, but not dead enough) and a burning desire that the noble destiny of America not be sullied by income tax, social security, or school integration.

They set out from the dock shortly after noon. Fred sat at the helm of *Debbie's Dream* high up in the ship guiding his huge power boat through the narrow channel, dressed for the part in a jaunty blue sea captain's hat, dark aviator glasses, and a blue windbreaker. On the deck below, in the open space at the rear, the rest of his party cracked open bottles of cold beer, laughing and joking, in the mood to have a good time.

Fred did his best to pretend that he was having a good time, too, though he was so tense he wanted to scream. Piloting the big boat through the narrow channel always made him nervous, even under the best of circumstances, and today there were hundreds of craft in the channel due to the fine weekend weather. The air was thick with diesel fumes, but the motorboats were the least of Fred's problem. He nearly ran down a small sailboat, some jerk who crossed his bow without looking. Fred had to throw the stick forward to put the engine in reverse. God, how he hated sailboats!

"How you doing up there, pardner?" the ex-cowboy star called from the deck below.

"Hey, I'm swell! Lots of traffic, though," Fred called back cheerfully. His throat was so dry he wished he had a lozenge. "I wish some of these guys would look where the heck they're going."

"Just don't run over any Republican voters," the baseball team owner shouted up. "We need the sons of bitches!"

Fred forced a laugh. "You bet'cha! We're only going to sink Democrats today! Hey, pass me up one of those beers, why don'cha? I'm not going to let you boys drink up all that brew on your own!"

Fred was relieved when he managed to get through the traffic jam in the harbor without running anyone down. Once he was in the open water, he was able to open up the throttle and enjoy the satisfying growl of the mighty engine beneath his feet. Behind him, the propeller vomited a plume of gray smoke and foam. But now there were ocean swells to contend with, real water. *Wham!* He was going too fast and slammed down hard into an oncoming wave. The bow sent saltwater splashing into the face of the newspaper heir on the deck below. Luckily, everyone laughed. The guys were in a relaxed

Saturday mood, among their own kind, ready to fish and drink and have fun.

Fred hated the ocean, the mountains of water that kept coming at him, one huge swell after another. It was terrifying to be in the bottom of a trough looking *up* at a wave that was higher than the boat. They didn't tell you these things at the boat show, what it was like to be on open water, the Pacific Ocean, with land dwindling behind you.

He aimed *Debbie's Dream* toward Skeleton Rock, a jagged protrusion of rock and bird life that broke above the surface a mile out to sea, a place where many ships had sunk in the days before radar and depth sounders. The rock was easy enough to find since all the other motorboats were headed there too, an armada of sport fishermen. For Fred, it was a terrible place, barren rock covered with bird shit, roiling with foam and spray from the waves that kept crashing against it. The armada of boats bobbing on the swells made Fred dizzy just to look at them, their motion exaggerated by the immobility of the rock. He stayed well off the rock itself, finding a spot about two hundred yards to the south.

"Here we are, boys!" he shouted to the gang below as he released the anchor. "Get your lines in the water! There are fish down there and, boy, are they hungry!"

Once the anchor was in place, Fred was able to stagger down the steps from the bridge, open himself another beer, and join the party. The fishing was excellent that afternoon, which put everyone in a good mood. Within ten minutes, the ex-cowboy star had caught a huge bonito, at least twenty-five pounds. The baseball owner got himself a big rock bass and the bank president snagged another bonito.

Fred's first catch was a tiger shark which he pulled up to the side of the boat and then cut loose, not wanting to bring it on board. This wasn't a lucky start, but then he caught a nice grouper and after that some weird rock fish that no one could quite give a name to. Soon they were all pulling in fish like crazy, harvesting the sea for their personal glory. They had a pool going; they'd each put a hundred dollars into the pot, which would go to whoever caught the biggest fish. So there was a lot of good-natured joking back and forth.

With the brilliant sun and blue-green ocean all around, Fred almost forgot his domestic problems. It was wonderful to find himself an equal among important men, all of them calling each other by their first names, forgetting their usual dignity, acting like a bunch of rowdy boys. *Here they are on my boat*, Fred kept saying to himself, awed at his own rise in the world. Politics might have been the reason they were gathered together, but no one talked politics on an afternoon like this, that would have been considered crass. The fishing trip *was* politics, the core of the beast, without any need to verbalize.

As the day wore on, they ate fried chicken and potato salad and drank so much beer they thought they would burst. All that beer had only one place to go, back into the ocean, and without further ceremony, the guys all peed over the side, off the stern, rather than use the head down below. For Fred, this was something—the sight of these multi-millionaires, powerful men, with their dicks out seeing who could pee the farthest. If there was any moment in all his life that symbolized his arrival among the elite, this was it. He gloried in their easy friendship, though he made a mental note to ask his Filipino gardener to hose off the stern tomorrow to get rid of any yellow streaking.

What a day! There came a moment when the ex-cowboy star put his hand on Fred's shoulder and said, "Well, pardner, this sure is a fine way to spend an afternoon!"

For Fred, these words were pure magic. Here was this cowboy star Fred had idolized as a kid on Saturday afternoons at his local movie house, this American icon who was so famous everyone even knew the name of his horse. And he was here on Fred's boat, with his hand on Fred's shoulder.

Well, pardner, this sure is a fine way to spend an afternoon!

It was at this moment that Fred decided he would do whatever Debbie's lawyer demanded. He would sign her agreement, give her the money, the boat, the house, whatever she wanted. It would be a huge bite from his fortune, but Wilson Manning had a point: money could be made again.

The main thing was to have this wonderful life forever, the intoxication of insider politics, of being one of the guys. All he had to do was keep the photographs secret, hide his pending divorce, and get himself re-elected.

*****

It took just over three weeks to get the paperwork completed, mailing the documents special delivery back and forth from Los Angeles to Washington, with Debbie's attorney and his attorney squabbling over the fine print. There had been a sticking point concerning Debbie's campaign appearances. At first, her lawyer insisted she would appear only three times with Fred in public, cheerful and smiling, for campaign events during the coming summer and fall, while Fred's lawyer held out for six appearances. In the end, they compromised on the number four, a compromise that favored Debbie. But Fred didn't mind. He just wanted to get the whole thing over with.

Fred signed the divorce agreement in Los Angeles on December 19, 1955, after he had returned to California for the Christmas recess. On the same day, he gave Debbie's lawyer a check for $5000, her first monthly alimony payment, and a second check for three million dollars—it wasn't the single largest check Fred had ever written, but it came close. He was not required to move out of the house on the Lido until after the election (this would have been a give-away as to the state of his marriage), but he would be living there by himself. It wasn't a cheerful way to begin the Christmas holidays, but Fred was optimistic that he had the situation under control.

That was the main thing, damage control. Meanwhile, he had received Christmas cards from the entire House of Representatives and most of the Senate, and even one from Ike and Mamie, personally signed. Fred was determined to keep his focus on what was important. Christmas week passed without incident and as the days passed, he became increasingly confident that he would survive the tempest that had shaken his life.

But the tempest had only just begun. Without any warning, the January 6, 1956 issue of *Confidential* magazine hit the stands with a lurid photograph of Fred and Sasha on the cover. The banner made Fred's stomach turn to jelly: SONYA AND THE CONGRESSMAN! HOLLYWOOD LOVE NEST SNARES CROOKED POLITICO!

That was him, apparently, the sort of man the public loved to hate: a crooked politician. Inside, the article itself was even more damaging, beginning with his philandering sex life but then moving on to expose a number of shady irregularities in his past business dealings, including mention of a bribe he had once paid to a city councilman. Fred was outraged to read this. Of course, he had paid bribes! It had been the only way to get zoning laws changed in order to build tract homes and shopping malls. Everyone slipped a bit of money under the table, it was how things were done. But this wasn't going to do him any good with the voting public.

And then, as though extra-marital sex and bribery weren't enough, the article went on to question his Silver Star, suggesting that he wasn't the war hero he had always pretended to be. A retired State Department official was quoted as saying that Fred had been awarded the medal despite army objections that none of his deeds were verifiable. "The war was going badly in 1943," said *Confidential*, "and Washington needed heroes to shore up public support. Even phony heroes like Fred Landson."

A phony hero! This was the last straw. Fred read the article in a state of shock. He knew without anyone telling him that no cowboy star would ever again put his hand on his shoulder and be his pal.

His life was over, finished. And to make it worse, he had just signed a binding divorce agreement with Debbie, paying out a huge amount of money to buy her silence . . . for nothing!

Twenty-Five

On the day the *Confidential* story broke, Sasha had an afternoon appointment with her manager, Sol Weintraub.

She was ready for Sol with a song that she had succeeded in writing (i.e., plagiarizing). It was a ballad that she called, "If You Ever Leave Me, I Will Make You Cry," and she had managed to make a primitive recording of it at her piano on a bulky reel-to-reel tape recorder with my help.

The recording was far from professional but it gave an idea, at least, of what the number might be if recorded properly in a studio with an orchestra. She was certain it was just what she needed to jump-start her career and be famous again.

For Sasha, it had been an agonizing wait for the *Confidential* story to appear, nearly going crazy each time an issue came out and she wasn't in it. She had sent her anonymous envelope of photographs to *Confidential* months ago, all the way back in July, and in November, at the end of her patience, she had sent off a second flurry of envelopes just to stir things along. Copies of the photographs had gone out in the second mailing to the *New York Times*, President Eisenhower, the Speaker of the House, and finally (for the sheer destructive hell of it) to Fred's wife, Debbie.

When the story finally appeared on January 6th, Sasha at least understood the delay. *Confidential* had used the time to make a full investigation of Congressman Landson's life. She didn't appreciate having her own central role shunted to the sidelines, but that didn't really matter. She was glad to see Fred so thoroughly exposed for the sneaky bastard he was.

Clear-eyed and sober, she showed up exactly on time for her three o'clock appointment at Sol's office in a new canary yellow outfit from Saks that showed a great deal of leg and emphasized the slimness of her waist.

The receptionist, Ruth, gave her an odd look as she walked in the door, and so did Sol when she entered his inner room. Sasha pretended not to notice, refusing to give herself away. She handed Sol the flat box of recording tape she had brought along.

"Play this, darling, and tell me what you think. I've just written a ballad that's going to make both of us oodles of money."

Sol raised his bushy eyebrows as he took the tape. "You wrote a song?"

"Of course, I did. And I don't know why I didn't think of it earlier. I play the piano very well, thank you. And I have an excellent education in music from my childhood. I don't need to wait for someone to write me a ballad when I can do it myself. Play it, Sol, please, and judge for yourself."

An Almost Perfect Ending

"Well, all right, Sonya," he agreed without enthusiasm. More and more these days, Sol looked like a gloomy basset hound. He took the reel of tape and threaded it on a bulky machine that stood on a bookshelf against the far wall.

"It's a very simple version, just me and the piano in my living room. But you'll get an idea," she assured him.

Sol pressed a button and they waited together as the reels began to turn and the speakers hissed with white noise. The music began, a brief piano introduction that swooped down to a jazzy minor-ninth chord. Sasha began to sing:

You think you can leave me, baby,
Well, go ahead and try,
But if you leave me, baby,
I will make you cry.

They say love is forever,
I say love is a lie,
But if you ever leave me, baby,
I will make you cry . . .

The melody jumped from the minor into a major key as Sasha belted out the chorus:

So don't you leave me, baby
Don't you ever try,

For if you ever leave me, baby,
You'll be the one who cries.

Sasha watched Sol's face as the song played, anxious to see his reaction. Did he like it? Did he hate it? Sol didn't give away a thing.

There was a bridge section eight bars long on just two words, "Oh, baby . . . oh, baby!" But she stretched out the vowels and played with them, like a surfer diving in and out of a wave—Oooo-ooohh, baaaaaya-ya-beee—moaning like she was in heat, an apt imitation of sex. Then she was onto the second verse:

You say you love me, baby,
Well, go ahead and try,
But if you don't love me, baby,
You'll be the one to cry.

So, who's crying now, baby,
Who has tears in his eye,
It's not me hurtin', baby,
It's your damn turn to cry.

Then it was back to the final chorus, repeated two times with all the power of Sasha's voice carrying the tune to an emotional climax. Musically speaking, it was very slight and the lyrics were far from brilliant. But Sasha's voice gave it a haunting sexy sadness that made it work. Sol listened while standing next to the tape recorder holding his hand to his chin.

"Well, well," he said vaguely when it was finished. "Let me hear this again," he said pressing the rewind. "You know, that's not half-bad, Sonya," he said after the second listening. "You need to get rid of the 'damn,' though. The last line of the second verse, 'It's your damn turn to cry.' They won't play that on the radio."

"Okay, Sol. I'll change it to 'It's your turn now to cry.'" It was astonishing that she could fake the sound of an orgasm but couldn't say the word damn. Americans were odd that way, not entirely rational. But Sasha was willing to go along.

"You like it though, don't you, Sol?"

"Sure, I do. It reminds me a little of . . . what's that song? There's a McGuire Sisters thing on the radio, I can't think of the title. But you might have something here."

"Oh, Sol! It *is* good, isn't it? And it's not really very much like the McGuire Sisters song. If you heard the two songs side by side, you'd see how different they were."

Sol gave her a penetrating look and sat down again behind his desk. "All right, Sonya. You have a song. Your voice sounds good. Very sexy. You'll have every guy in the country fantasizing about you. But what are we going to do about this?"

"This?" Sasha pretended puzzlement. She watched as Sol picked up the new issue of *Confidential* from his desk and handed it to her. "Oh!" she cried, looking at the cover. And then, suitably shocked: "Oh, God, how awful!"

"You didn't know about this?"

"Oh, no, Sol! What a shock!" she assured him. "What a terrible shock!"

She peered up from the magazine cover to find Sol's bushy eyebrows knitted together, studying her hard.

"This isn't good, Sonya," he told her quietly.

"I bet Debbie did this! . . . that's Fred's wife!" she explained, bursting with outrage. "That sexless little bitch! I bet she hired a private detective with a camera!"

"That doesn't matter now. They got them, that's all that counts. Look, Sonya, this story is going to get bigger before it goes away, so you need to be ready for it. There are politics involved. A lot of people don't like HUAC and what the Republicans have been doing. None of them dared say much about it for a long time, but now things are starting to change and there's an election coming up. My guess is that some Democrats are going to use this as ammunition, saying Republicans aren't the moral family guys they've been pretending to be. Which will leave you caught in the middle."

Sasha leveled her eyes in Sol's direction. "But my song . . . my career . . . what is this going to do?"

"Well, that's impossible to say exactly. It depends on how this plays out. Now, look, there's an old saying—there's no such thing as bad publicity. This isn't going to do much for Congressman Landson, that's for sure. But it could end up helping you. A singer is judged differently from a politician, and it's not such a bad thing for people to regard you as a sex siren."

"This could . . . *help* me?" Sasha repeated, as though the thought had never crossed her mind.

"Sonya, I don't know. I'm saying maybe. But you're going to have to be very careful what you say. You can't be seen as a homebreaker because then people won't like you. Now listen to me, you're going to have reporters on your doorstep and you need to say the right things. You've got to present yourself as a victim. You were helpless, see. Alone in the world, no one to guide you. It's not your fault that guys can't keep their hands off you. You let yourself be seduced by a big bad politician. People don't much like politicians so they'll be inclined to go along. But you have to play it right."

"So I can be sexy. But . . . I don't quite understand, Sol."

"Put it this way. You can be the sexiest thing alive, but deep at heart, you're a nice girl. You're sincere. You're vulnerable. And you're definitely not a homebreaker, that's the most important point of all. Underneath all that sophistication, what you want most is to bring a man his slippers."

Sasha had always thought it was dogs who were supposed to fetch a man his slippers. But she was willing to learn.

"All right, I'm nice. I'm sincere."

"And you're glamorous, too. Don't forget that part."

"I can be all that at once?"

"Sure, you can. Don't worry about it. Let me do the worrying. None of it's real, anyway. Men don't care about real when it comes to beautiful women, they want a fantasy. That's what show business is all about."

"Sure, Sol," Sasha told him delicately. "I can do that. But what about my song?"

Sol smiled for the first time. "I'll take it to Capitol. And if they don't bite, we'll go to Columbia. You're going to be the most famous woman in America for a week or two, until the next most famous woman comes along. And we can use that. This song of yours, Sonya, it's hot stuff . . . and that fits right in with all the free publicity you're getting from *Confidential*."

Sol held up the tape Sasha had brought him. "Now, you just go home and lay low. Don't talk to the press any more than you have to. I'm going to make copies of this tape and I'll get back to you in a couple of days. All right?"

Sasha nodded, keeping her excitement under control. Only Ruth, in the outer office, saw the triumphant smile twitching at the corner of her lips as she sailed out the front door to her convertible that was waiting at the curb, top down for all to see.

*****

Sasha pulled into her driveway to find half a dozen reporters with cameras waiting for her on the sidewalk.

"Sonya! Look over here!"

She turned before reaching the front steps, aimed her dark glasses their way, and managed a tragic yet poetic smile as the flashbulbs popped. She was glad she was wearing such an attractive dress.

"Sonya, will you take off the dark glasses, doll?"

Dutifully, she complied with the photographer's request, posing with the glasses held thoughtfully in her hand. She did her best to look glamorous yet vulnerable, the sort of woman who would be most fulfilled if only she might be bringing a man his slippers. It was a lot to imply in a single pose.

"Sonya, can you tell us when you first met Congressman Landson?" one of the reporters called to her.

"I'm really too upset to talk about it," she answered delicately. But then she answered anyway. "Fred is one of my oldest friends. We met on a troop ship in the war, when I first came to America. He's been very kind to me. I never intended to hurt anyone. You see, when I met Fred again in Hollywood, it was a time in my life when I was very vulnerable, all alone."

"Have you spoken to the Congressman since the story broke?"

She shook her head slowly. "No, no . . . I'm sure he's with Debbie now. I wish them both well. And I want to say, if I can do anything . . . *anything* to bring them together again . . . because, you see, I believe marriage is the most beautiful, sacred thing . . ."

Sasha was struggling to find the right words when another reporter, a handsome man in a linen suit, called to her.

"Sonya, Pierre Charbol, *Paris Match.* Are politicians good lovers?"

Sasha was surprised a French magazine would be interested in her, from all that way across the ocean. It was an unexpected question, very French. And because the reporter was handsome, she forgot herself. She answered more candidly than she should.

"Are politicians good lovers? Not at all," she assured him. "Politicians only love themselves."

The Frenchman laughed. "I see. But tell me this. Who do you think is the best lover—a left-wing politician or a right-wing one?"

Sasha smiled back coyly. "When it comes to love, wings aren't the part of the body women care about."

An Almost Perfect Ending

All the men laughed loudly. Sasha believed she was a big hit. It was only belatedly that she understood she had allowed herself to be drawn out. She hadn't done at all what Sol had asked her.

"Oh, you mustn't print that!" she cried. "I'm really not myself today . . . I'm so upset."

Sasha excused herself after only a few more photographs. She slid into her house and locked the front door behind her, her heart beating fast, pure adrenalin.

Pure joy!

Her phone kept ringing all that day, and the next day as well, and the day after that—dozens and dozens of lovely people requesting comments and interviews and photo sessions. How wonderful it was to be wanted again, to be in demand. Sasha let her answering service field the calls, but she returned every one that seemed promising and set up appointments in descending order of importance.

Locally, the *Hollywood Citizen News* gave her the biggest space. *SHE'S NO ANGEL*, said the bold print beneath her picture. This was followed with print only slightly smaller: "Sonya Says Wings Not The Important Body Part A Girl Looks For In A Man."

Sasha loved every small gush of attention. "I'm no angel," she said to herself with a smile, gazing into the mirror. And she knew for a fact that it was true.

*****

Three nights after the *Confidential* story appeared, Sasha broke down and had a drink, her first in many months. The attention was satisfying but stressful, and a small doubt had appeared to throw a shadow on her triumph—the thought of Max who had been out of prison for three months now, but still hadn't called. What would he think to see her photograph on the cover of *Confidential* with Fred? Would he find the whole thing tasteless and embarrassing? Would he despise her for being cheap?

At midnight, Sasha was still awake, sitting in an armchair in her bedroom with all the lights out, a cigarette in one hand and her third glass of vodka in the other, when her telephone began ringing stridently in the late-night stillness of the room. Sasha spilled her vodka as she hurried across the room to get to the receiver before the caller hung-up. It had to be Max, she was certain it was him. It was Max calling to say that he still loved her, that he understood.

Only Max knew the real person she was inside. Only Max knew the untouched purity of her soul.

"Max!" she cried, picking up the receiver. But it wasn't Max. It was Fred.

"You bitch!" he said. "I'm going to kill you, you fucking bitch. Do you hear me? I'm coming for you, bitch!"

An Almost Perfect Ending

His voice was slurred and he didn't sound his usual self at all. Fred had been drinking too, a lot more than she had. Sasha didn't dare answer. Without a word, she set the receiver back onto the cradle, cutting the connection.

In her self-absorption, scheming her way back to fame and fortune, she hadn't considered Fred Landson quite deeply enough, a man whose life she had ruined, what he might do.

It was a glitch in an otherwise perfect plan.

Twenty-Six

Max might easily have missed the *Confidential* scandal. With his isolated life at the beach, he had missed more important events—uprisings in Hungary, besieged French armies in Indochina, school integration in Little Rock. He didn't even know who had been nominated for the Oscars that year. But one afternoon he walked down Broad Beach Road to the Trancas Market in order to buy milk and cigarettes and he saw the magazine on a rack near the checkout counter. The cover was impossible to miss, Sasha and Fred in an embrace that left little to the imagination.

LOVE NEST IN BEVERLY HILLS!

Standing in the aisle of the store, Max skimmed through the article, loathing every word. He hated the bad writing as much as the trashy photographs. He wanted to rip the magazine in half and throw it in the garbage.

"Are you going to buy that?" the woman at the cash register asked pointedly.

He returned the magazine to the rack so quickly his fingers fumbled and it fell to the floor. He had to pick it up and try a second time. "Sorry," he muttered to the woman at the register, who was watching him closely.

Max had meant to walk home the way he had come, along the paved road, but he was so upset he crossed the highway onto the beach and took off his shoes, wanting the clean feel of sand and ocean on his feet.

He had thought that Sasha no longer had the power to upset him. A year in prison had given him some distance; he had believed he was purged. Yet here he was again, caught in the murky turmoil of her, a jumble of emotion, sex, and regret that had never been resolved.

Max stormed home angrily along the wet sand close to the surf, carrying his socks and shoes and his small bag of groceries. Everything in his New England soul found the *Confidential* story repulsive, to have the scandal of your private affairs emblazoned across the cover of a cheap magazine. He wondered how Jonno was taking it, the embarrassment at school to have the other boys see a photograph like that of his mother.

It was contemptible. Sasha and Fred! The poor jerk probably didn't realize that she was only using him!

Yet in the end, it was all part of a world that Max had left behind and his anger faded as he walked along the beach in the great expanse of the afternoon. The disastrous course of his life had brought him to a softer, sadder acceptance of things. He knew he was innocent of the charge that had sent him to prison—un-Americanism! But he was guilty nevertheless. He had killed a man and run away. So how could he be angry at Sasha when he was worse than she, by far?

The sun beat down. The vast panorama of ocean and sky absorbed all that remained of his self-importance. As Max walked along the beach, he felt himself engulfed in a deepening sorrow. It wasn't depression exactly. It was more profound than that, a vivid sense of Sasha's humanity and his own, both the beauty and the pathos of their lives—a failed movie director and a second-rate singer.

Yes, I'm a failure, he said to himself. He had made a few good movies, he knew that. But somehow he hadn't had the skill—the moxie, the cynicism—to come out a winner. He had let life defeat him. He had made wrong choices and wrong turns. Halfway home, Max stopped to regard a sea lion who was peering at him curiously from the crest of a wave. Her eyes were oddly appealing. Max was certain she was a lady sea lion from her dainty air of coquetry. She seemed to find him as fascinating as he found her. He wished they could communicate more fully, from her ocean realm to his, have a good chat. He wanted to ask her what life was like beneath the waves, and if she found it all as sad and beautiful and senseless as he did. But then another wave came and she was gone, leaving him alone on the beach.

"Hey, don't leave!" he cried. "Come back here!"

Max knew it was absurd to shout at a sea lion. He was glad there was no one around to see how eccentric he had become living his solitary life at the beach. Yet it seemed urgently important that he find her again. He didn't want to let her go.

Max was walking into the surf trying to get closer to where the sea lion had disappeared when a wave he hadn't seen swept him off his feet. For several long seconds, he found himself underwater in a whirl of raging foam. Then the wave receded, leaving him on his hands and knees on the wet sand. But just as he was trying to rise to his feet, a new wave rushed in on him and knocked him over. He was caught up in the water and couldn't get away. He had a ridiculous sense of déjà vu, that here he was again, swept up by the Pacific—just like that afternoon when he had lost his movie equipment to the surf. A man who never learned.

Max was a reasonably good swimmer—a vestige of boyhood summers on Cape Cod and California swimming pools. Still, it took him a number of tries before he got himself free of the surf. He kept standing up then getting knocked down again. At last, the surf retreated and he found himself on his stomach, like a piece of kelp washed up on the shore. He was wet and cold and the bag of groceries from the Trancas Market was gone. His shoes and socks were gone also. Swept away, as he had nearly been himself.

"Jesus!" he said. It was ridiculous, but he had nearly drowned.

Then something else happened more surprising still. Max was getting to his feet clumsily—still disoriented from his roll in the waves—when he felt a shock of pain slam against his chest, as though someone had punched him hard. His legs wouldn't hold him, he couldn't breathe properly, the afternoon began to fade into a mist. He had to sit down again on the wet sand, he couldn't move. His heart was out of rhythm, beating wildly fast.

Was he going to die? He thought he might. It was astonishing, but here was death come to find him, on this unlikely stretch of beach, on an average afternoon. It seemed so inconclusive, to be in the middle of one of his usual muddles, getting everything wrong. But gradually, very gradually, his heart returned to normal, and the mist cleared.

Good God! he wondered. What was that?

He knew, of course, exactly what it was. But he was fine now, that was the main thing. His heart had carried him this far through life, so why not carry him a while longer?

Within a few minutes Max felt well enough to stand up carefully from the sand, find his balance, and set off slowly home. He was cold, he was wet, and he was tired. But he was okay.

Back home, he took a hot shower, changed into dry clothes, and poured himself a large glass of whiskey. He put a Brahms symphony on the record player and began looking in the kitchen among his recipes for a new sauce to go with the abalone he had pulled off a rock earlier in the day. Cream, he decided. Abalone with a light cream sauce and mushrooms. A squeeze of lemon, a touch of garlic, perhaps a dollop of white wine.

An Almost Perfect Ending

Max lit a cigarette and poured himself a second glass of whiskey with a pleasant sense that he wasn't going to die today after all. He still had time to reach a better ending.

Mina would be home soon, and they would have dinner. Luckily, the abalone were so plentiful that year in California, Max was certain they would last forever.

*****

Sasha's love nest scandal took on a political dimension, as Sol had predicted, which kept the story alive.

The storm gathered momentum throughout January as Congressional Democrats fired off predictable barbs about the hypocrisy of Republicans. Many of them demanded that Representative Landson resign. But it was *The New York Times*, which at first had ignored the scandal, that eventually added a new element to the story by pointing out that Congressman Landson had come to office vowing to "cleanse Hollywood of Communism," and had served in this capacity as a special motion picture advisor to HUAC, the Congressional committee which had sent Max McCormick to prison. The *Times* had been as cowardly as all the other newspapers when McCarthyism still had a bite, but now the tide had turned, it was no longer quite so dangerous to express outrage.

Everyone in Hollywood knew that Sonya Saint-Amant and Mr. McCormick had been romantically involved for years.

Some even claimed that the movie director was the real father of Sonya's son, Jonathan, the child actor who until recently had appeared on the weekly CBS sit-com, *What a Life!* With a love triangle between Max, Sonya, and the philandering Congressman, the *Times* dared to suggest what most people already knew: that the HUAC hearings were often used to settle personal scores. At the very least, it was shockingly improper that Congressman Landson had been allowed to have any part in a House hearing that had sent a romantic rival to prison.

After the *Times* editorial, accusations flew back and forth between pro-HUAC and anti-HUAC factions. Once again, Sasha was disappointed to find her own role in the matter relegated to the sidelines. She remained the sexpot who had launched a thousand ships, but now that this particular Trojan War was raging, she was no longer the central issue. For the next several weeks, reporters continued to lurk outside her house, but there were fewer each day and gradually they disappeared altogether.

Sasha continued to drink secretly, doing her best to hide it from Jonno, barely acknowledging even to herself that she had fallen off the wagon. "It's really nothing," she said to herself. "Only two . . . well, perhaps three drinks a day." It was a temporary measure because everything was so unsettled just then.

Occasionally, she would find Jonno studying her suspiciously, and she made an effort to be bright and chatty and not slur her words.

"What is it, darling?" she would ask with a laugh, then give him a tickle and a kiss before he could reply. In her experience, a tickle and a kiss were a girl's best tool to keep men from asking awkward questions.

Each day, she picked up all the newspapers and magazines from a kiosk off Hollywood Boulevard that reminded her of the kiosk near the Plaza Hotel in New York long ago where she had bought *Variety* in order to go out on auditions. There was even a funny little old man in a cap, a twin of his New York counterpart. Only now the little man brought the newspapers to her as she sat incognito in huge dark glasses in her Cadillac by the curb, passing them to her through the window.

"Well, am I in the news today?" she would always ask, for she had made the little man her confidante.

"Oh, yes, Miss Saint-Amant. You're just as famous today as you were yesterday," he answered, always the same reply.

It was a nice reply, and she generally gave him a few dollars beyond the cost of the newspapers as a tip. But *was* she as famous today as yesterday? It was hard to say, because fame was a thing with a will of its own, and there was no telling when you might be forgotten.

There was still no word from Sol about her song. She refused to call him, she didn't want him to know that she was worried. But she kept watch on her telephone, waiting for it to ring, taking only a small nip of vodka from time to time to ease the awful insecurity.

It was all she could do not to take Jonno and run for their lives.

Twenty-Seven

At last, something decisive happened.

Toward the end of January, Sol came to see Sasha at home. It was a sign of her renewed importance that now he came to her, rather than she to him.

She bombarded him with questions from the moment she met him at the door. "Oh, Sol, I'm going crazy! What's happening with my song!" She took his arm and pulled him into the living room, hardly giving him a chance to answer. "Do people like it? Will I be able to record it properly in a studio?"

"Whoa, my dear!" he said with a laugh. "All right, I have good news and bad news. The bad news is that Capitol listened to the tape and they passed. They lost money on you in the past, Sonya, so they're gun shy. But there's a producer at Columbia who's very interested, a guy named Jake Halloman. He loves the song, he loves your voice."

"Oh, Sol! Columbia! They're better than Capitol. That's wonderful!"

"Yeah, but hold on. He's waiting to get the final okay from the big boss in New York. The way it's looking is Columbia wants you, but they need to be certain the situation with Landson doesn't take any new twists. A little bit of scandal never hurt business. You're hot stuff right now, but they don't want any more surprises."

Sasha sat down across from Sol on the living room sofa, not certain she understood what he was telling her.

"Surprises? But what else can happen, Sol?"

"What else? Sonya, how do I know? Maybe Landson will be forced to resign from Congress and the schmuck decides to kill himself. I'm not saying this will happen, it's just an example. Something like that would set the public against you, then they wouldn't buy your records no matter how hot you are. Big record companies like Columbia err on the side of caution, especially when there are politics involved. So my sense is they're going to sit tight for a week or two before they commit, to see how everything plays out."

For Sasha, a week or two seemed forever. She wasn't sure she could bear any more waiting. "Can't we go to another company?"

"Sonya, Sonya . . . just be patient. Avoid the Congressman, behave yourself, don't speak to reporters, and I can almost guarantee this deal will go through. Jake and I have been talking about a three-record contract with a signing bonus of twenty grand. You'd like that, wouldn't you? Jake's itching to get you inside a studio. Meanwhile, I have another little goodie to throw your way. How would you like to spend April in Paris?"

"Paris!"

"Sure, why not? They like you in France. They're not so prudish on that side of the Atlantic and you've had a lot of press over there recently thanks to *Paris Match*. You've been quoted all over for what you said about politicians as lovers—they like that sort of thing in France, they think you're quite a woman. Now, here's the deal. The job will be headlining at a place called the Crazy Horse Salon. It's a strip joint, frankly, but don't let that put you off because it's very expensive, very chic, probably the most elegant strip club in the world. This is Paris, remember, and the rules are different. They'll dress you up in some gorgeous outfit, sexy, but nothing you couldn't wear in Vegas. I promise, you won't be expected to take off your clothes, only sing. They'll pay all your travel expenses, put you up in a suite at the George V, and pay two grand a week for a three-week run. Best of all, it'll open up a market for your records in France. Does this interest you?"

"I could do the job in France and still get the Columbia contract?"

"Why not? Columbia loves this. I've already mentioned it to Jake and he's talking about a live recording, 'Sonya Saint-Amant at The Crazy Horse Salon.' It's a natural. Like I told you, sex sells. As long as it's handled in a tony way so that nobody's offended. What do you say, Sasha?"

It was all lovely: $2000 a week, a chance to travel to Europe, and best of all, an album. 'Sonya Saint-Amant at The Crazy Horse Salon.' She was already imagining the cover, a photo of herself on a fancy stage with maybe a hint of a few discreetly bare showgirls nearby, very French. It would be risqué, but fabulously so. The sort of risqué that would make the public see her again as they had ten years ago and say all over again, Ooh-La-La.

Yet, she hesitated. A strip club. *What would Max think?* Sasha knew it was absurd. After the *Confidential* story, Max must have given up on her altogether. Yet she couldn't help but feel a stab of anxiety imagining how this would appear to him. He could be awfully prudish. She knew without asking that he wouldn't approve.

"Just think about it for a few days, Sasha," Sol said, reaching over and patting her hand in a fatherly way. The sort of father who would pander his little girl for a ten percent cut without the slightest stab of conscience.

*****

Sasha was still considering her options a week later, when she was surprised by an invitation to attend the premiere of a new movie, *Giant*, with the actor Troy Brandon.

Troy was a blond pretty boy on his way up the Hollywood ladder, not a big star yet, but rising fast. She had met him playing tennis at the Beverly Hills Hotel and was surprised when he asked her to be his date for the premiere. Troy was dull and egotistical, at least ten years younger than herself, and she didn't find him remotely attractive. She knew the invitation was a calculated move on his part to get himself noticed, to appear in public with the notorious Sonya Saint-Amant and see his name in all the gossip columns tomorrow.

Sasha accepted the invitation with calculations of her own. As the scandal over the *Confidential* photographs continued to simmer day after day, she wanted to show Hollywood that she wasn't afraid to be seen in public. The premiere was to be at Grauman's Chinese Theater and it promised to be a huge A-List event. Everyone who was important would be there, which would provide a perfect opportunity to show the world that she was back.

Troy picked her up at seven in his Corvette, a bright red sports car that was like a spoiled child's toy. Sasha wasn't sure what they would find to talk about, but this turned out to be the easy part. What Troy wanted to talk about was himself.

As they drove toward Hollywood, he asked her advice about two different roles he had been offered—the lead in a teen movie set on the beach in Malibu, or a part in a Biblical epic in ancient Egypt where he would be playing one of the Pharaoh's two sons. The Bible epic was the bigger picture, more status, but he would have a smaller part than in the Malibu movie, where he would be the star. Thus, the difficulty of his decision.

Sasha was able to listen with considerably less than half her attention. She advised him to take the Malibu picture, mostly because it was ridiculous to imagine Troy Brandon as Egyptian. But she hardly gave it any thought. What Sasha was really thinking about was her own life, her own decisions that needed to be made.

Driving along the Sunset Strip, they passed a motel where Sasha had once had an afternoon assignation with Max—years ago, back when she had first arrived in California and success was brand new. Now, remembering that afternoon and the person she had been, Sasha felt so bleak and lonely she could hardly bear it. Where had that magic gone?

At the Chinese Grauman, bleachers had been set up on the sidewalk for the hundreds of screaming fans. Two giant searchlights sent roving beams of light high into the sky, reminding Sasha absurdly of wartime London. The Corvette was taken by an attendant and she held onto Troy's arm as they walked together up the red carpet toward the lobby.

"Troy . . . *Troy*!" someone screamed. "Oh, *God*, it's Troy Brandon!" Sasha was astonished, but the idiot appeared to have an actual following. A group of pubescent girls tried to duck under the velvet rope and mob him and had to be held back by a line of police. Sasha fixed her gala smile firmly on her face as they made their way past cameras and fans.

Halfway up the red carpet, a gossip columnist, Sheilah Graham, was standing with a microphone doing a live radio broadcast of the event, and Sasha was happy to pause for a few questions.

"Sonya, what did you think when you saw yourself on the cover of *Confidential*?" Sheilah asked.

Sasha laughed breathlessly. "Oh, Sheilah, it was awful! I just don't know how *Confidential* got hold of photographs like that. I don't care for myself, but it was a horrible thing for Fred."

"Is Congressman Landson going to divorce his wife? And if he does, will the two of you be married?"

"Oh, I hope not!" But this didn't sound right. She laughed at her *faux pas*. "I mean, Fred and I are very old friends, but I wouldn't want to come between him and Debbie."

It was satisfying to be interviewed on the radio, and Sasha had a great deal more she wanted to say. Perhaps she would mention her new recording contract with Columbia, though it wasn't completely set. But Cary Grant had just come up the red carpet behind her, and even with her scandal, Cary was a much bigger fish in the Hollywood pond.

"Thank you so much, Sonya Saint-Amant!" Sheilah said with ruthless finality, turning her attention to richer fields.

Sasha continued along the red carpet with an edgy sense of having been interrupted before she could make an impression. At her side, Troy was smiling terrifically, but Sasha could tell he wasn't pleased that Sheilah Graham had ignored him.

"You didn't let me get a word in," he said sulkily without letting his smile dim. "I wanted to plug my new picture."

"Darling, there was barely time to plug a sink. We got edged out by Cary Grant, my pet."

"Still, you could have brought me into the conversation."

What conversation? In the past, Sasha had always loved Hollywood premieres, the excitement of being among those who counted. But tonight it seemed empty, not like the real glamour of an opening night at the Krakow Opera, the lost world of her childhood. Inside the lobby, Grauman's Chinese Theater was more like a sultan's harem than a Chinese palace, over-decorated in garish reds and golds. Making their way through the nearly impenetrable crowd, Sasha waved frenetically to several people she knew—an orchestra leader, the head of the music department at Metro, a press agent, but no one really important. Beneath her smile, she felt a terrible isolation. Somehow she was forever the outsider, never comfortable, excluded from the easy camaraderie of those who took success for granted.

And then she saw Bob Hope, who had been so friendly to her at the Palm Springs fundraiser for President Eisenhower. She remembered how Bob had flirted and joked. He had even suggested that they might go on tour together overseas to entertain the troops.

"Bob!" she cried happily, coming up alongside him. "How good to see you!"

Bob's eyes scanned her way briefly, then glazed over and kept moving, pretending not to see her. "You know, I haven't played there for years," she heard him say to a man at his side, discussing golf.

Sasha was left with her mouth open, facing the back of his dinner jacket. Bob Hope had cut her! He had cut her dead! He had treated her as though she were nothing, not in his class, only a cheap girl who broke up marriages and got her picture put on the cover of scandal magazines. She hoped desperately that no one had noticed the slight.

"Let's find our seats," she said urgently to Troy, taking his arm. "It's impossible to talk to people in this awful crowd!"

*****

Sasha sat in the darkness of the huge movie theater in a state of wretched embarrassment, barely watching the movie that played incomprehensibly on the screen. Bob Hope had cut her dead! He had treated her as though she were beneath contempt!

Oh, Max, Max . . . Max! Sitting in the darkened theater, she found herself yearning for the one legitimate part of her life: smart, gentle Max. If Max were sitting here with her now, how they would laugh together at this silly Hollywood premiere! Bob Hope would mean nothing. Max had always been her ally in this terrible town.

Halfway through the movie, it came to Sasha exactly what she must do. She must win back Max. She must have him, there was no other way to find again the poetry that had bled from her life. Without poetry, life was nothing. She saw that

331

now. There was only an empty shell. There were only people like Troy Brandon pushing and grasping their way forward. As *Giant* flickered by on the huge screen, Sasha decided a number of things. First thing tomorrow she would phone Sol and give him a definite yes to the job in Paris at the Crazy Horse. Of course, she would accept it. It would be crazy not to. She could hardly wait to be in France. She would take Jonno and they would settle in Paris. The French loved her, she would be able to work as much as she liked there. Jonno would learn French and pick up some real culture. A year from now, he would be listening to Puccini instead of his terrible rock and roll. They would be bohemians together, the two of them enjoying late suppers in little cafes. It would be almost like her own childhood.

She could still have her recording career with Columbia. Why not? She would record in New York, that was all, rather than Los Angeles. TWA had just inaugurated a marvelous new airplane, the Super-G Constellation that flew from Paris to New York non-stop, a matter of ten or eleven hours. She would go back and forth whenever necessary. But France would be her home. France would welcome her.

And Max would come with them. That was the most essential part of the plan. Max would be able to work in France, the blacklist couldn't touch him there. All she had to do was convince him. Jules Dassin, Carl Foreman, Lionel Stander, even Charlie Chaplin and Bertolt Brecht . . . there were dozens of blacklisted actors, writers, and directors who were doing well in Europe. If he had trouble getting his passport back, he could cross the border into Canada and travel from there. Europe would welcome him.

Sasha believed she had found the answer. She and Max would live together in a little house in Paris, perhaps in Montmartre where *La Bohème* was set. Mina could visit whenever she liked. In France they didn't mind odd domestic arrangements. In France you didn't have to worry about being un-American.

But how could she win back Max? That was the sticky part. How could she get him to love her again? It wasn't until the movie was ending, with the titles playing on the screen, that the final part of the equation fell into place for her, exactly what she must do.

Their anniversary was coming.

Seven days from now, it would be Valentine's Day, February 14, 1956, the thirteenth anniversary of their first night spent together on the *Mauretania*. Max was sentimental, he was nostalgic. It was one of his endearing flaws that he spent too much time mooning over the past. If she invited him to see her that night, surely he would come. If he hesitated, she would say she needed to discuss Jonno. She would think of something. Once he was with her, the rest would take care of itself. The law of attraction, one body to another, that had always been so strong between them.

This was a lucky break, the arrival of their anniversary just when she needed a special occasion to win Max back.

February 14th, the day of lovers. Thirteen lucky years!

Twenty-Eight

Fred resigned from the U.S. House of Representatives on Friday, February 7th. He announced his resignation at a hastily arranged press conference in Washington, in front of a gathering of microphones, cameras, and shouted questions from the press.

He kept to his prepared statement, a typewritten page that he "held with a trembling hand," as the *Los Angeles Times* described it. In his statement, he apologized to his family, the voters of California, and the nation at large for his own behavior, while at the same time implying that he had been set up by political enemies who lacked "the true American spirit" and so were reduced to "filthy tricks and subterfuge."

"I am a simple man," he concluded. "I came to Washington to serve my country, and I am willing now to step off the great stage of history if that is what my country requires of me. God bless America."

With that, Fred fled the room for the men's room down the corridor, where he burst into tears and pounded his fists against the outside of a metal stall, frightening half to death the representative from Alaska who was inside with his pants down.

*****

Fred returned to Southern California on the Super-G Constellation the next day, after putting his Georgetown House up for sale. On the plane, he sat with his face to the window in the First Class section hoping no one would recognize him.

In California, Fred took a taxi from the airport to his empty house on the Lido, unwilling to face Steve and Mike who would normally have met him. The silence of the expensive house reinforced his sense of disgrace. According to the terms of his divorce settlement, he could remain in this tomb of his former life until November 4th. The divorce settlement, of course, was one more cause for misery, a final joke to seal his failure. He'd been generous to Debbie so that she would conceal their personal situation until after the elections. But now that didn't matter. The leaders from his own party had drummed him out of politics forever.

Fred had never imagined that his entire life could collapse so quickly. He was still a wealthy man, though not nearly so wealthy as before. But money without respect was little consolation. For Fred, that had been the purpose of success, to be regarded as a fine fellow, someone the other guys looked up to.

On Monday, Fred closed his California office and dismissed his entire staff, including Mike, his longtime bodyguard and driver. He gave everybody three months' salary, a generous severance, and then he wept in front of them, causing much embarrassment. Fred was beyond caring.

An Almost Perfect Ending

He returned to the Lido, driving his big Eldorado, a car that had once seemed to him the pinnacle of success. At home, he shut the curtains and began drinking, hiding from the world that no longer admired him. He watched television, mindless comedies and cop shows that he forgot the instant they were over. He phoned the local market for food when he was hungry and had it delivered so that he wouldn't need to show his face and risk the possibility of being recognized.

As the days passed, Fred forgot to shave, he stopped washing dishes, he didn't bother to take the garbage out. He began smoking cigarettes because it took less effort than fiddling with a pipe. Before long, there were full ashtrays and empty glasses scattered about the house and beer bottles with half-finished cigarettes floating inside. For Fred, to be a bachelor again after years of marriage was like a jungle repossessing a clearing that had once been domesticated.

And all the while, he brooded over Sasha, trying to understand why she had turned against him. Hadn't he gotten her that orange juice commercial? Hadn't he arranged for her to sing for Ike? He had been good to her. He had risked everything to love her. So why had she ruined him? *Why?*

And the worst part was that, despite everything, he still wanted her. The thought of her kiss—her smile, her body, her touch—nearly drove him mad with a desire that only seemed to grow with the passing days, until it took over every corner of his being.

How could a person want someone so badly . . . and be denied?

It wasn't fair, Fred decided. It wasn't right.

*****

Max had come to accept that the working part of his life was over, a thing of the past. But then in the second week of February, something remarkable happened. His telephone rang and to his astonishment, he was offered a job.

Max had an agent, Terry Grunwald at the William Morris Agency, who had negotiated his contracts since 1946. They weren't friends particularly, but Max respected Terry's professionalism and they had always gotten along. After nearly two years of silence, Terry phoned early on a Monday morning when Max was at the kitchen sink washing up his breakfast dishes. He dried his hands on a towel and picked up the receiver.

"Good morning, Max!" Terry said in such a bright, hearty manner that Max immediately knew his fortunes were about to change. "Hope I didn't wake you."

"Not at all."

"How's life at the beach?"

"Tranquil," Max lied.

Terry didn't bother to apologize for his silence of two years, and Max didn't mind. In the movie business, when your career was stalled, your phone didn't ring. Meanwhile, agents didn't make telephone calls on Monday morning unless there was money involved. They chatted for a few minutes about inconsequential matters, then Terry got down to business.

Carlo Ponti, the Italian movie producer, had phoned from Rome over the weekend hoping to hire Max to direct a picture that was scheduled to start filming in May. The movie would be a French-Italian co-production shot at Cinecittá studios outside of Rome with several weeks of location work in Naples. It would be an English language film, to increase its commercial viability, and Ponti wanted a trustworthy Hollywood director. The story was a bittersweet comedy about a lonely American G.I. in Italy at the end of the war who falls in love with a Neapolitan girl, with many cultural obstacles between them to stir the plot. The American actor Richard Basehart was signed to play the G.I. and a pretty young Italian actress, Sophia Loren, was to play the girl.

Max would receive a salary of $1500 a week plus first class roundtrip airfare, L.A. to Rome, and all living expenses paid in Italy. The film would be shot in black and white with a budget of $1.2 million dollars—an amount that would be lavish in Rome where everything was cheap. Carlo Ponti was a great fan of Max's work and vowed to give him complete artistic freedom to work as he pleased.

There was more. Signor Ponti knew about Max's "political problems", and like many Romans, respected Max more than the boundaries of the Italian language could adequately express. With this in mind, the U.S. Ambassador to Italy (a personal friend of Ponti's) had already been contacted in order that Max should not have any further problems obtaining a passport. The Ambassador promised that Max would have his passport as quickly as the mails allowed, remarking that McCarthyism in the United States was happily a thing of the past.

And so it was a done deal. What could Max say except yes? He knew Richard Basehart's acting and admired it greatly. As for the new Italian girl, Sophia Loren, he imagined he could work with her as well.

Terry promised to send a messenger to the beach that day with a script and a contract for him to sign. Max put down the phone with a sense that he had been swept off his beloved beach by a hurricane. He stared out the windows at the waves, incredulous.

He hadn't been to Italy since his honeymoon with Mina in 1936, twenty years ago. By 1956, Hollywood movie makers were increasingly heading off to Europe in search of glamorous backgrounds. Max understood very well the opportunity this job presented. If he played it right, this could be the start of the long road back.

Max wandered out the sliding glass door onto the sand dunes in front of his house and stared at the ocean. He had reinvented his career once already after coming home from the war, but he had been a much younger man then. He wondered if he had the energy to do it again.

Well, he would try. That was all he could do. Given an opportunity, a man had to give his best effort. The wheel of his life was spinning still, it hadn't stopped here at this peaceful beach in California as he had supposed. He would go to Rome, he would make the best movie he could manage with Carlo Ponti's $1.2 million dollars.

But there was one thing he needed to do before he could leave America. He had to call Sasha and somehow make a better closure with her. It wouldn't be easy; he didn't have any clear idea of what he wanted to say. Yet he knew it had to be done.

*****

But to his surprise, it was Sasha who phoned him. She phoned that evening just as he was sitting down with a glass of Jameson's to read the script that Terry had sent over.

She sounded nervous on the phone, almost shy. "I don't suppose you were expecting to hear my voice," she said.

"No, but I'm glad you called. I've been thinking about you. In fact, I've been working up my nerve to call."

"Really?" She laughed awkwardly. "Oh, it doesn't take any nerve to call *me*, Max. I think it's the other way around. I'm . . . I'm so glad you're out of that horrible prison. I always ask

Jonno for news of you. It sounds like you're doing well at Trancas."

"Yes, the beach has been good for me. How are you, Sasha?"

"Better. To tell the truth, I went through a bad period for a while. But I'm better now. Even with all . . . all the craziness recently. You probably saw the *Confidential* story."

"Well, yes." Max felt awkward too, especially now that she had brought up *Confidential*. He fell silent, not knowing quite what to say.

"Anyway, the reason I called," Sasha said, pushing the conversation along, "I thought we might get together some-time, just to talk. Would that be okay, Max? It's been so long since I've seen you."

"Yes, I'd like that. I tell you what, why don't we make a date for lunch. I could drive into town sometime this week."

She cleared her throat uncertainly. "Well, actually, I have an idea," she said with a laugh. "You'll never guess what this Friday is."

"What's this Friday?" he asked, laughing in return.

"It's February fourteenth. It's Valentine's Day."

"Well, that's fine," he answered vaguely, though in fact he hadn't made the connection. He had forgotten.

"Oh, Max . . . it's our anniversary! Valentine's Day. Don't you remember?"

An Almost Perfect Ending

"Of course!" For Max, the memories came flooding back: that night on the *Mauretania*, Sasha in her nightgown, the old man dead down below. "My God, can it really be? Let's see, how many years—"

"Thirteen," she told him gaily. "This will be our thirteenth anniversary. Isn't that marvelous?"

"Well, yes. Of course, thirteen generally is not considered the world's luckiest number."

"That's nonsense! In Poland, I assure you, thirteen is guaranteed good luck. I love the number thirteen."

He laughed again at her enthusiasm. Her voice sounded young on the telephone without the weariness he had often heard in recent years.

"Max, I thought we might go out and do something together that night. I . . . I just haven't seen you for such a long time."

"Yes, let's get together," he agreed quickly. "I want to see you, too. And what better day for it than our lucky thirteenth anniversary? What do you say I pick you up at your house around seven and take you out to a splendid dinner somewhere. We'll go to Chasen's or Romanoff's. We'll make a gaudy night of it."

"Perhaps it would be better to find someplace quiet, Max. Would that be all right? Someplace where we could talk and not have a bunch of Hollywood idiots gaping at us."

"Okay, I'll look in the yellow pages under quiet restaurants. I bet I can find some really stodgy joint in Pasadena."

She laughed. "I've missed you," she said.

"I've missed you, too, Sasha. I'll see you Friday at seven."

Max hung up the telephone with an unbearable sense of time. It wasn't going to be easy to part with Sasha on their thirteenth anniversary. But he understood that this was what he had to do.

It was too late to start all over again. The old fires were best left as ash. What remained was a final conversation to set things right between them. And then a loving goodbye to close that turbulent chapter of his life.

Twenty-Nine

The rain began on Wednesday, February 12th. It was a hard, cold rain, the sort of winter storm that sweeps in from the Pacific to flood streets and bring hillsides sliding down. From his house at the Lido, Fred stared out his huge picture window and decided he liked rain. The weather matched his mood. Gradually, new thoughts began to stir in his head.

On Friday afternoon, Fred showered, shaved, and put his appearance back together. It seemed to him that some cycle had been completed and he was ready to come out from hiding. He didn't care who saw him, a disgraced congressman who had been drummed out of office. He was beyond that now.

He dressed carefully in an expensive grey suit. He put on a belted trench coat, a gray homburg hat, and took his 9mm Lugar out of a locked drawer in the den. He made sure it had a full clip of bullets then slipped it into his trench coat pocket. The last thing he did before leaving the house was to fill his wallet with money from his safe, ten one hundred dollar bills. For years, Fred had always kept a thousand dollars in cash on hand for emergencies, the proverbial rainy day that had come at last.

Night had fallen by the time he was ready. Fred backed his Eldorado out of the driveway and drove north along the Coast

Highway. He had a vague plan, but he wasn't sure. He decided to approach the evening one step at a time and see where it was that everything ended.

*****

The night was dangerous with howling gusts of rain. Fred drove carefully, his windshield wipers slapping back and forth on their fastest setting. After two days of rain, there were a number of low-lying places where the highway was flooded, but Fred didn't mind. It was satisfying to have a heavy, expensive car that could plow through the puddles with plumes of water flying in his wake.

He drove until he reached Santa Monica, where he decided to stop at a restaurant on the beach side of the highway, a place called the Jolly Buccaneer that had been designed to resemble an old sailing ship. Fred had no particular reason to stop here except he hadn't eaten since breakfast and the restaurant caught his fancy. It didn't seem real, it looked more like an amusement park ride.

He parked and hurried inside out of the rain. The interior of the Jolly Buccaneer was dimly lit and over-decorated with kitschy nautical knick-knacks—fishing nets hanging from the walls, brass sextants, a captain's wheel, old instruments from old ships, even a carved wooden mermaid. There was a bar on one side and booths of dark red leather on the other. It was a slow night due to the storm and the room was nearly empty, only a single customer at the bar. A Sinatra song played on a juke box that glowed orange and red. Two waitresses and a bartender with nothing to do were huddled together at the far end of the bar talking among themselves.

Fred slipped into the booth closest to the bar and did a double-take as one of the waitresses came his way. It was Sasha! He had no idea what she was doing here, or why she was working as a waitress. His blood raced at the sight of her. But when she came closer, Fred saw it wasn't Sasha after all, only a pretty California girl. She had Sasha's blond hair, Sasha's build, but her face was more elongated and there was something a little common about her.

"You know something? You remind me of a girl I once knew," he told her when she stopped in front of him.

"I guess I've heard that line before!" she answered with a laugh. "So, what can I get you, mister?"

"Oh, I don't know. You still serving dinner?"

"Sure, we are. On a wet night like this, mister, you can have anything you want."

Fred grinned. "Then I'd better take a look at the menu. Bring the wine list too, why don'cha."

She turned and left, posing for him a little as she walked away. She had a nice figure and Fred found himself warming to her. He liked it that she was a working girl, a waitress. It seemed to him that a girl like this wouldn't destroy a guy, she would be grateful.

"So, what's your name?" he asked when she returned with a menu and wine list.

"Why do you wanna know?"

She was flirting in a tough way, a streetwise girl. Fred was liking her more and more. He found himself keeping his bad hand out of sight in his lap, hoping she wouldn't see that he was damaged goods.

"I just like to know people's names, that's all," he told her.

"Well, the name's Betty, if you gotta know."

"Okay, Betty. My name's Fred. What do you have that's good on the menu tonight?"

"You hungry?"

"Oh, you bet I'm hungry. I'm always hungry, Betty."

She giggled. "Then I'd say the Surf 'n' Turf. That'd take care of a big fella like you."

"Surf 'n' Turf? What's that, a mermaid on a bun?"

Fred had never been able to joke like this before with women. He was feeling witty. He was feeling free.

"No, you big palooka! It's a ten ounce New York steak and a lobster tail, choice of fries or a baked potato. Comes with a salad, your choice of French, Italian, or Thousand Island dressing."

"Okay, I'll have that. You make all the choices for me, the potato and such. I'm in your hands, Betty. Just make sure the steak is well-done. And bring me a bottle of champagne. You got French champagne?"

"Sure we do."

"Then bring your best bottle."

"Okay, but it's gonna cost you. Aren't you gonna take a look at the wine list to see the price?"

"Naw, I don't care what it costs."

She laughed. "So what's the deal, Fred? You just win the Sixty-Four Thousand Dollar Question or something?"

"Yeah, that's it exactly. The Sixty-Four Thousand Dollar Question. Look, Betty," he said, letting his voice go soft. "I can see what a slow night it is here at the Jolly Buccaneer. I bet they don't need two waitresses on a night like this. So why don't you sign out, or whatever it is you need to do, and have dinner with me instead. You can put in an order for another Surf 'n' Turf and help me drink that bottle of French bubbles."

She laughed. "My, my, you're a fast worker, aren't you, Fred? But I don't know a thing about you."

"What's there to know? I'm a guy with a wallet full of cash looking to have a good time, and you're a very pretty girl."

"Oooh, you *are* fast! So tell me, is that your big Cadillac in the parking lot, Fred?"

"Yup, that's mine."

"You know, you look famous somehow. Ever since you walked in here, I've had the feeling I've seen you before. What are you, some sort of Hollywood type?"

Fred smiled, happy suddenly not to be a congressman anymore. Congressmen had to worry about what they said and did. But he didn't have to worry about anything, not anymore.

"Naw, I'm no one," he told her. "I'm just a guy who got lucky in real estate. I made a bundle turning orange groves into houses and shopping malls. I'm what you'd call a millionaire."

"Oooh!" she squealed. "A millionaire! I like that! So tell me, Fred, are you like that guy on the TV show who goes around giving away a million dollars every week?"

"Sure," he told her. "I'm just like Ray Milland. Only my wife left me and I've been a little blue. To tell you the truth, I could use someone to help chase away those blues. But don't do it if it doesn't feel right to you, Betty. Maybe you're shy."

She laughed. "Naw, I'm not shy."

She left him to speak to the bartender, a whispered conversation. A few moments later she returned with a bottle of Moet & Chandon in an ice bucket and two champagne glasses. She opened the bottle, poured the glasses and then slid into the booth across from him.

"Happy Valentine's Day," she told him as they clinked glasses.

"What? You're kidding!"

"Naw, didn't you know that? It's February 14th. So you better look out, Fred. Cupid's on the prowl!"

An Almost Perfect Ending

*****

While Fred ate Surf 'n' Turf with Betty, Max drove north on the Pacific Coast Highway, struggling to see the road through the blowing sheets of heavy rain.

He left Trancas at five-thirty to give himself plenty of time to get to Beverly Hills by seven, but the afternoon had faded into a premature night and he could barely see beyond the smeary streaks of his windshield wipers as they slashed back and forth.

Just south of the Malibu Pier, part of the hillside had slid down, blocking one of the lanes. Two cops from the Sheriff's office were there to guide traffic through with flashlights but Max felt tense all over. He continued slowly, hunching forward in his seat to see better. There wasn't much traffic, but when the occasional car or truck lumbered by in the northbound lane, the headlights left him momentarily blinded.

He turned off the Coast Highway at Sunset Boulevard and headed inland. But Sunset was even worse, one bad curve after another with the rain so heavy he could barely see the road. Several times he splashed through deep puddles that turned his car into a skittering boat. He slowed to a crawl until another car came up behind him, its headlights shining hard into his rear window. This made Max so tense he sped up again to put some distance between them, but the car stayed close on his tail.

In Pacific Palisades, Max was able to pull over into a driveway to let the car pass. He lit a cigarette then maneuvered carefully back onto the road. The rain was coming down even harder now, pinging loudly on the metal roof. Max considered turning around and phoning Sasha to say he couldn't make it, but by this time he was halfway to Beverly Hills and there was as much danger behind as ahead. It seemed best just to go on.

He continued slowly past Brentwood, past the gate to Bel Air where he had once lived, and on through the final curves into Beverly Hills. It was a relief to turn off Sunset onto North Maple Drive, but halfway down the 700 block, he had to slam on his brakes to avoid a tree limb that had fallen across the road. Max put on his emergency blinker and got out of the car to pull the tree aside. But the limb was heavy, larger than it had first appeared, an awkward weight to drag aside. By the time he made an opening wide enough to drive his car through, he was soaked to the skin and shivering cold. Pulling on the branch, he had strained a muscle in his chest so badly he could barely move his left arm.

He slipped back into his car and drove the final block to Sasha's house. His teeth were chattering as he made his way up the front steps and rang the doorbell. He was afraid he wasn't going to cut an elegant figure.

Sasha opened the front door for him with a smile that changed instantly to concern.

"Oh, Max!" she cried.

"Got a little wet," he told her. Despite his condition, he smiled goofily at the sight of her. She had lost weight and she looked very good, youthful and buoyant. She could have been twenty years old, almost the girl on the *Mauretania* a lifetime ago.

"Oh, Max, you look awful! Come in. Let's get you out of those wet clothes!"

"Now, there's the best offer I've had in a while," he told her, trying to joke. His teeth chattered so badly it didn't come off as funny. Sasha had taken him by the arm and was leading him through the house towards the stairs.

"Can you make it upstairs?"

"Honest, Sasha, I just got a little wet."

"We'll get you into a hot bath," she said, leading him up the stairs, not letting go of him for a second.

"With a big glass of whiskey, please."

"All right, a big glass of whiskey. Anything you want."

"Then you, too."

"Me?"

"In the bathtub with me and the whiskey."

She laughed, despite her concern for his condition. "You're incorrigible, aren't you?"

"Well, it is Valentine's Day," he told her. "We wouldn't want Cupid to have all the fun."

This wasn't what Max had planned to say to Sasha. But as she ran the bath and helped him out of his wet clothes, he remembered very well that this wasn't the first time his words had changed course at the sight of her.

It was all right, though. As he watched Sasha undress and join him in the tub, there was kindness in her eyes and such a perfect familiarity that something gave in him, and his resistance slipped away.

It was crowded in the tub facing one another, an ungainly tangle of limbs, not entirely elegant. Naked, he saw in her more fully the slippage of years. Her body sagged in places where it had never sagged before. But it didn't matter. It seemed to Max that time had carried them to a fullness that was like the golden light of a late summer afternoon.

"To the years," he said, raising his glass of whiskey to her glass of vodka.

"To us, Max," she answered.

Thirty

So here we are returned at last to where we started, St. Valentine's Night, February 14, 1956. Like the T.S. Eliot poem, back to the beginning, but knowing that place for the first time.

In a more perfect world, I would direct my readers to the first page, back to the make-believe ending of this tale that I have told all these years with a straight face. It's a more sensible ending, truly. A tidier package: furious Fred breaks in on the woman he loves, finds her in bed with her lover, and shoots them both dead. Then, unable to bear the grief and the responsibility, he turns the gun on himself. This was the story that was eventually accepted by the police, even by *Confidential* magazine, because it's as American as apple pie, almost folk legend in form.

But the night didn't happen that way. Truth isn't as tidy as fiction or as easy to describe. Which is why people like my mother often choose to disregard it altogether.

*****

The rain came pouring down. I always come back to the rain, because it's what I remember most. The sound of rain and the smell. It could have been a *noir* night from one of Max's thrillers, rain falling from a black and white sky.

I'd spent the day at home because school was closed due to the storm and I was in a bored, niggly mood. I had dinner about six by myself in the kitchen, a plate of fried chicken and mashed potatoes that our maid Claire had made up for me before leaving for the day. Afterwards I tried to call Penny in New York to wish her a happy Valentine's Day. But I got her mother instead, an unpleasant woman who had never liked me, and she informed me maliciously that Penny was out on a date, knowing it would hurt. And of course, it did hurt. It hurt a lot.

All I could think to do was creep upstairs, hide in bed, and escape into a book. I spent the rest of the evening deep in the pages of *Red Planet*, a Robert Heinlein novel about a colonial boy on Mars who goes to an unpleasant boarding school that didn't sound too different from my own unpleasant school on Earth.

I became aware of Max's presence in the house around eight-thirty when I went downstairs to the kitchen for a glass of Bosco—chocolate syrup that you put in milk, sickening stuff that all the kids loved back then. I was surprised to see that my mother and Max were having dinner in the living room in front of a blazing fire, eating on the coffee table, and that Max was dressed inexplicably in one of my mother's oversized terrycloth robes, which was small on him and ridiculous. Earlier, my mother had said that they would be going out to a restaurant, but I imagine the storm had made them change their plans. It didn't look like the kind of dinner I would enjoy—eggs and bacon, more like breakfast. But there was a bottle of champagne in an ice bucket and they were laughing, obviously enjoying themselves.

It worried me a little to see my mother drinking. But I hadn't seen Max in our house for a long time and I decided it was probably all right. They made a nice picture, sitting across from each other by the fire. They didn't see me as I skirted barefoot past the darkened end of the living room toward the kitchen. I got my Bosco and headed back upstairs as unobtrusively as possible, not wanting to interrupt the progress of romance. But I couldn't resist lingering on the stairs to listen.

"Do you remember the terrible kidney stew in that gloppy brown sauce?" Max was asking. "Oh, and those stale buns!"

"I thought they were quite edible, Mr. McCormick! It was better than what we were eating in Poland at that time, I assure you."

"Yes, I remember you said that."

"What ever happened to that British actor? Shelton Graves?"

"He died shortly after the war. 1948, I think it was. Cancer."

"And his wife? That horrible woman! What was her name?"

"Biff. She's dead too, I heard. A car accident outside of Philadelphia."

"Oh, Max—the *Mauretania!* How could so much time pass? Where did it all go?"

"It hasn't gone anywhere, Sasha. It's still with us, as long as we're here to remember it. And you know, I can still see you as though it was yesterday, the way you came into the Officer's Canteen that night."

"My father, he is sick, please. He sends me, please for cognac," my mother said in a foreign accent I had never heard before.

Max laughed. "That was the moment I fell in love with you."

"Did you?"

"Of course, I did. How could anyone resist you? And I've loved you ever since . . . with just a few bumps in the road."

"I'm sorry for those bumps, Max."

"No, no, don't be. For us dramatic types, bumps keep life interesting. Bumps are what make love stories compelling. In fact, my dear, you really can't have a good love story without them."

I didn't linger any longer. As much as I liked spying, this seemed to me a private land for two from which I was quite properly excluded. I disappeared back into my bedroom, closed the door behind me and read about life on Mars until my eyes grew heavy and I couldn't read any more. On the edge of sleep, I heard a final burst of soft laughter from the living room below.

I was feeling happy with the sound of the rain on the window and the far-away assurance of adult laughter drifting up from the living room. For months now, I'd been caught up in a whirlwind of worry. But now, I'm not sure entirely why, I felt a deep sense of everything being okay. Peace crept over me. The rainy night itself seemed to be calling: Give in, give in, close your eyes and let your troubles slip away.

I suppose it's funny that the one night when I should have worried, I fell asleep with an easy heart, innocent in my faith that the world takes care of its troubled children.

*****

I must have drifted off into the sound of the rain because the next thing I knew, I was startled awake, brought violently back to consciousness.

But I wasn't woken by a pistol shot, as I have always claimed. I was woken by a scream.

It was my mother, and her scream was terrifying, like nothing I'd ever heard. I jerked up in bed and reached for my bedside light. But the light wouldn't come on. The electricity was off because of the storm. I kept clicking the switch but nothing happened.

The darkness seemed somehow darker now that I knew I couldn't make it go away. I was wondering what to do when my bedroom door flew open to reveal a near-hallucinatory image of my mother with a candle in her hand. The glow was uncertain, a single flame that danced erratically. She had a sheet wrapped around her, but I could tell she was naked underneath.

"Oh, Jonno, come quickly!" she cried. "I need help!"

I got out of bed in my pajamas and followed my mother back into her bedroom, not knowing what to expect. She led the way with the candle casting weird moving shadows against the walls. There wasn't a sound anywhere except the wind and the rain whipping down on the house. I can't adequately describe my sense of dread. The shadows, the terrible rain. I think I followed my mother only because she held the only light, and, if I turned back, I would have been left in the dark.

"Mom, what is it?" I kept asking. "What's happened?" But she didn't answer, I'm not sure she even heard me.

I followed her along the hallway that led past her closet, her dressing room, her bathroom. There was a dim, flickering glow coming from the bedroom ahead, and when I turned the corner, I saw several candles burning, two in silver holders and one that had been stuck merrily into an empty champagne bottle.

An Almost Perfect Ending

Max was on his side in the center of the bed, unnaturally still, and there was a sheet up to his waist. He was naked, at least the part of his body I could see. He had pale skin with dark hairs on his arms and back, an old man's body that was far from attractive. One terrible eye was frozen open, unblinking.

My mother set her candle on the bedside table and clutched hold of my arm so hard her fingernails dug into my flesh.

"You see, he's fainted," she said, speaking in a voice that was oddly calm. "I know he's all right . . . but he's fainted such a long time."

"Mom—" I began. But my words stalled, I didn't know what to say.

"We'll call a doctor. The phone's out, so you must go to the neighbors . . . oh, Jonno, go quickly!"

The neighbors? This was Beverly Hills, we didn't know our neighbors, not even their names. No one was going to open their door to me, not on a dark and stormy night that even Lord Bulwer-Lytton, the inventor of dark and stormy nights, would have found appalling.

"Mom—"

"Go, Jonno! Please, oh, please . . . you're a big boy now, you must get help for your father."

My father! How strange it was to hear those words at last, after so many tales of imaginary French flyers shot down over the Channel, so many lies. But it was too late for help. I'm not sure how I knew that Max was dead because I'd never seen a dead person before, but I knew. There was something absolutely different about the inert form on the bed. It wasn't a person there anymore, only a kind of shed skin.

"Mom, he's—"

My mother wouldn't let me finish, she didn't want to hear. She screamed and leapt toward Max on the bed in order to hold him. Her sheet came off in the sudden movement and she began to gibber in Polish, a language I didn't understand. Fortunately, kids have a way of taking charge in situations when the adults have fallen apart.

"Mom, you got to calm down," I told her, averting my eyes. "I'm going to get help."

Help? It was easy enough to say, but *was* there help for a situation of this sort? I didn't think so. But I ran downstairs anyway, ready to dash out barefoot in my pajamas into the rain and scream at a neighbor's door for help. Call a doctor, call the police, call someone who might do something . . . anything at all, just so I was doing something.

Downstairs, I had to slow down as I made my way through the darkness, my hands stretched out before me like antennae. My progress was far from smooth. I kicked over a chair, I banged into a side table in the foyer. I knew the front door was somewhere ahead of me, but I couldn't find it. Everything was different from the way it normally was. After a good deal of blind groping, I found the doorknob several feet from where I imagined it to be and opened the door.

Outside, the noise was deafening, the pouring onslaught of rain. There was a smell of moisture in the air so thick it was hard to breath. The lights were out everywhere up and down the block, a darkness that was almost Biblical, as though I had traveled backward to an ancient time.

I hesitated in the doorway with all my bearings gone, afraid that if I went out beyond the threshold of the house, I would never find my way back again.

Unexpectedly, I heard a sound from somewhere in the front yard. It was a car door opening. I couldn't see the car, but the sound was familiar, comforting. It meant someone was there, help was at hand. I was about to cry out when I heard a woman's drunken laughter, shrill and high. It was so eerie, coming out of the darkness and the rain, that my cry died in my throat.

"Fred, honey, where the fuckin' christ are we?"

"Beb'ly Hills, baby," came the slurred reply. "Good friend mine you gotta meet. You'll love her . . . c'mon, baby."

"Honey, it's fuckin' wet out. Like a big fuckin' swimmin' pool!"

"Wet don't goddamn matter. C'mon now, let's move it, doll."

It was Fred, though not anything like the stiff, golly-gosh version of Fred I had always known. As for the woman, I didn't have a clue who she might be. From the sounds they were making, I could tell they had driven onto the front lawn, missing the driveway by a dozen yards. They were making plenty of noise, laughing and staggering about in the dark. I had a wild hope that maybe they'd head off in the wrong direction and get lost. But their voices were moving closer.

I think the woman slipped and fell on the lawn. That's what it sounded like, at least. They were both laughing as Fred helped her up.

"Wha's that in your hand, honey?" I heard her ask.

"Jus' a lil' ol' pistol, sweetheart. Don' pay it no mind."

"Wha' you need a pistol for, honey?"

Fred answered with something I couldn't make out, a joke. I think it was dirty because they both laughed uproariously.

I was glad they couldn't see me. My mother and I had ruined Fred's life, I knew that very well. And when you've ruined somebody's life, you can assume it's bad news when they arrive in the middle of the night with a gun, driving their car onto your front lawn.

No one had to tell me that we were in trouble.

Thirty-One

I was inching back inside the house, preparing to slam the door and lock it tight when the beam of a flashlight hit my face.

"Who's there?" Fred demanded.

I managed a sick smile. "Uncle Fred, it's me! It's Jonno! Thank God you're here!"

I regret that now, that I called him Uncle Fred. But I was frightened and not beyond a little subterfuge. I stood in the doorway as the flashlight careened closer, a bright circle of light that was shot through with streaks of rain. I was wondering if I could still duck back inside and slam the door before he got to me. But he had already reached the front steps.

"S'okay, Jonno. Wet night, huh? . . . meet my good fren' Betty."

"Oh, ain't you a cutie!" the woman said. Enough light from the flashlight was reflecting back beneath the portico that I could see them both now more clearly. The woman was blond and young and unsteady on her feet. My first impression was shock. She looked almost exactly like my mother, a twin image, except when I studied her more closely, I could see that she wasn't as pretty. Even at the age of twelve, I realized Fred was probably trying to fill the gap my mother had left, but finding a woman who looked like her wasn't going to work.

The gun was in Fred's good hand.

"Stand aside, boy," he said quietly. He didn't sound so drunk anymore. "I gotta see your mother."

"Look, you'd better not. There's been an accident," I told him. "I was just on the way to a neighbor's house to phone the police."

"What sorta accident?"

"It's Max and I think he's dead. So you'd better go away, Uncle Fred. I mean, someone in your position—you don't want to be mixed up in this when the cops come."

"My *position*?" He laughed unpleasantly. "I don't *have* a position! So get out of the way, Jonno."

I backed into the foyer thinking I might still have a chance to slam the door in his face, but he pushed past me roughly, pulling the woman in behind him. The woman grunted and more or less tumbled through the doorway. They both smelled of rain and liquor.

"Hey, honey," she said to me, trying to be friendly. "How old'r you, sweetheart?"

I didn't pay any attention to her. My focus was on Fred, who had already made his way across the foyer to the bottom of the stairs.

"C'mon, Betty," he growled, shining the flashlight at her face. "Leave the kid alone. I told you, I have someone for you to meet. Your goddamn twin."

"But, Fred, I . . . I mean, we're bargin' in—"

"C'mon now!" he bellowed. I could see the woman was frightened, and more sober than before. She did what Fred told her. When she reached him, he slipped his gun into his raincoat pocket, hooked her arm with his fake hand, and pulled her up the stairs behind him. The flashlight was in his good hand leading the way, shooting wild beams of light into the darkness of the house.

"Fred, please!" she whimpered.

"Just do what I say!"

I knew I had to stop Fred before he reached my mother. I ran up the stairs and made a lunge at Betty who was ahead of me, about halfway to the upper landing. I got hold of her ankles and pulled her feet out from under her. She screamed and fell with a thud. The moment she was down, I scrambled over her to get at Fred.

I caught him just as he was reaching the top landing and tried the same move I'd done with Betty. But I could only find one ankle, and I didn't get a good grip. He kicked back at me violently and I went plummeting down the stairs with one of his shoes in my hand. It would have been a nasty fall—a cracked skull, a broken neck—only I collided with Betty just as she was rising to her feet on the stairs below me, and she acted as a cushion. We fell together the rest of the way to the bottom landing, where she took the brunt of the fall. Even so, I had the breath knocked out of me and my knee hurt, and we ended up in such a tangle of limbs that I was caught fast and couldn't get up right away.

I wasn't sure if Betty was dead or unconscious or just playing possum, but she wasn't moving. I didn't know where Fred was. He had disappeared upstairs with his flashlight, leaving us in darkness.

I struggled free of Betty and ran up the stairs as fast as I could go. A weapon, a weapon, I was thinking—God knew, I needed a weapon. A baseball bat, maybe. And then as I reached the top landing, I remembered the gun with the silver bullets that Zachary Wise had given me years ago, the sort of bullets the Lone Ranger used to shoot Bad Guys. Over the years, I'd worked up the nerve to fire the gun exactly twice—once at the beach, and once far up in the Hollywood Hills—but there were four bullets left in the chambers, and I was ready to use them on Fred if I had to.

I was clumsy in the darkness of my bedroom, rushing about. I banged into my desk, I knocked over a floor lamp, I stubbed my toe hard against the armchair that stood near my closet door. It took me more time than I liked, feeling blind through old toys and the half-forgotten junk that was piled on my closet shelf. But the revolver was where I'd left it, still in the wooden puzzle box that Zachary had given me, hidden with a few girlie magazines behind a stack of games that I never played anymore. I wasted more time getting the box open, feeling my way over the smooth surface to find the slat that needed to be slid backward.

At last, gun in hand, I rushed across the landing toward the candle glow that was coming from my mother's bedroom. I was about to charge in, silver bullets flying, when I decided I'd better slow down to get the lay of the land. Inching forward, I came to a stop at the end of the hallway and peered into the room.

I expected mayhem, but I was surprised by what I saw.

My mother had put on a dressing gown at some point and was huddled on the bed with her back against the wall, as far from Fred as she could get. Max lay where I'd last seen him, oblivious. As for Fred, he stood near the foot of the bed with a look of bewilderment on his face that might have been comical under other circumstances. I don't know where the flashlight had gone, but he didn't need it now with the candles burning, so maybe he had tossed it aside. He was talking quietly to my mother, and except for the gun in his hand, he appeared almost reasonable.

"I just don't understand why you did it," I heard him say. "I was good to you, Sash. I gave you money when you needed it, I got you jobs. God knows, I tried to make you happy."

"Yes, you did . . . you *did* make me happy, Fred!"

"Then why? Why did you destroy me?"

"Fred, I didn't do it! I swear I didn't! Those pictures were as much of a shock to me as they were to you."

"Oh, Sash! It had to be you. You must have hired somebody. There's no way anyone could have got inside your living room to take pictures like that unless you were in on it."

"It was . . . it was Max!" my mother said wildly.

"*Max*?" Fred seemed as surprised at this as I was.

"Of course, it was Max! He hated you, Fred. He was getting even, don't you see? He hired someone with a camera and they must have snuck in here when I was gone. I bet they hid in the den, waiting for us . . . it was Max!"

My mother certainly deserved an A for effort, blaming the whole thing on Max, who lay conveniently dead, unable to deny the accusation. I watched as Fred stared morosely at Max on the bed, trying to decide what he thought of my mother's tall tale. I sensed he wasn't buying it.

He shook his head. "You think you can fool me with nonsense like that? Ever since I've known you, you've given me nothing but lies."

"But Fred, darling, honestly—"

"Don't lie any more. I swear, I just can't bear it. I loved you so much, and what have you ever given me in return? Do you know what that's like for a guy? To love and love and then have a gal just jerk him around."

"Fred, put the gun away and we'll have a drink, and we'll talk about this," my mother said earnestly.

"It's too late," he said gloomily, shaking his head. "It's just too damn late!"

"It's never too late, Fred. Look, we can start all over again. We won't have to sneak around anymore. We can work on our relationship, we can make it right this time."

The idea of "working" on a relationship was just coming into vogue in 1956, what with psychotherapy and bestselling self-improvement manuals. I'm not sure how long my mother and Fred would have gone on in this vein, the two of them working things out while Max was lying dead on the bed. It was a scene to remember, I'll say that. But I must have stepped too far into the room because Fred's eyes suddenly jerked my way, and he saw me standing in the shadows with the silver .38 revolver that I held pointed at him with an unsteady hand.

To my surprise, he smiled. "Look at you," he said. "Come to protect your mother!"

"You bet!" I growled. "And I'll blast you into the next galaxy if you move a muscle!"

I liked the phrase "blast you into the next galaxy"—I'd just come across it in Robert Heinlein. But my tone didn't appear to impress him.

"Jonno, put down the gun, son," he said calmly, facing me. "We're all friends here, and nobody's going to hurt anybody."

He began to walk slowly my way with his hand out-stretched to take the gun from me. "Let me have the gun, son. You're too young for this kind of thing."

He advanced step by step, avoiding any sudden move that might spook me. He didn't seem particularly drunk any more, or even angry. I was so hypnotized by his aura of authority that I nearly let him take the gun away.

"Jonno! Don't let him have it!" my mother cried.

"Don't listen to her, son," Fred told me. "I'm not going to hurt anybody. I guess I came here thinking I might, but that's all over now. Give me the gun, son."

I wanted to pull the trigger, but somehow I couldn't. Instead I backed off and began side-stepping around the room, careful to stay out of reach. He turned and followed me, keeping his own gun, the Lugar, at his side while he held out his gloved hand to receive my weapon.

"Give me the gun, son," he kept saying calmly, again and again. "Give me the gun."

We did a little dance, me edging around the room, my back to the wall, and Fred following me every step of the way.

"Stop right there, you son of a bitch!" my mother said unexpectedly. "Drop that gun or you're dead. Drop it now!"

I was surprised to see a pistol in my mother's hand, a little revolver that I'd never seen before. It was a woman's gun, almost cute, and it didn't look like it could do much damage. The drawer of her bedside table was open, so I image this was where she'd had it stashed. I hadn't known my mother owned a gun until this moment. Small as it was, its appearance was a game-changer in our late-night tableau.

Fred turned his head and he appeared as surprised as I was. Unfortunately, his Lugar was now half-pointed in my direction. I'm not sure he was aiming at me deliberately, it was more just the position of his arm when he had turned to look at my mother.

We were all frozen in place, like one of those children's games where you say "Red Light," and everyone freezes wherever they are in a silly position. It was a stalemate, my mother with her gun aimed at Fred, and Fred's gun pointed at me, and my silver revolver wobbling nervously in the general direction of Fred. I'm not sure how long we might have stood like this, but then someone started screaming. At first I couldn't imagine who it was or where the scream was coming from. But it was the worst scream I'd ever heard, high and shrill. I wanted to put my hands over my ears to make it stop.

We all turned toward the terrible noise. It was Betty, the woman Fred had brought to the house. I'd forgotten all about her. She was dazed, her nose was bleeding, I'm not sure she knew where she was. She had wandered into the room and was pointing a finger at Max who was dead on the bed, one eye open. I'm not sure if she thought Fred had killed him, or whether she was thinking coherently at all. Whatever the cause, Betty was hysterical, out of her mind.

"Stop that screaming!" Fred told her.

But she kept on, too wound up to stop. Probably she thought she was in the House of Death. Or Hell.

I'm not sure I can adequately express how unbearable it was to have this strange woman screaming in my mother's bedroom after everything else that had happened. We were so tense anyway, keyed up. It was the last straw. But I recognized this as my best chance. Fred had lowered the Lugar to his side and all his attention was on Betty.

So I did it. I pulled the trigger of my Lone Ranger pistol.

God help me, I aimed at Fred and tried to kill him. But nothing happened, only a dry metallic click. The hammer had come down on an empty casing, one of the shells I'd already fired. Somewhere I knew there were four live bullets left in the gun, but over the years I'd spun the cylinder a few times for the hell of it, and this round of Russian roulette had come up empty.

Fred turned my way, stunned that I had tried to shoot him.

Then I heard a pop. It was my mother's little pistol, hardly louder than a cap gun. But either she had missed him or the gun was too small to do any harm. I didn't wait a second more. "Yeeaaahhhh!" I cried, leaping forward. I didn't have any real plan except to use my gun as a club and knock him silly. He brushed me aside without any trouble, but I got my teeth on the wrist of his gun hand and I began biting hard, rabid with terror and anger, more like a wild dog than a kid.

An Almost Perfect Ending

Fred's Lugar went off, a searing roar close to my ear. I didn't know what he was firing at, but as far as I could tell, it wasn't me.

"Yeaahhhh!" I cried again, biting down so hard on Fred's wrist that I got a mouthful of blood. He screamed in pain and flung me aside with so much force that I couldn't hold on. I flew across the room and landed near an armchair, one of my mother's uncomfortable antiques. At first, I was too dazed to move. I saw stars, bright flashes of light. My back hurt, my head hurt, and I wasn't sure whose blood was bleeding in my mouth, whether it was Fred's or mine. I was completely disoriented.

I heard another pop from my mother's little gun, and then another. I knew I had to sit up. I spat out blood onto the carpet and rolled over. When my eyes could focus, I saw that Fred was still on his feet, standing in the middle of the room with a goofy expression on his face, as though he couldn't figure out what was hurting him. My mother kept firing, advancing on him with her tiny revolver, walking from the edge of the bed.

Pop! I think it was the fifth bullet, and it brought him finally to his knees.

He tried to speak. Believe it or not, I think he was trying to tell my mother that he loved her.

But a lot of men had told my mother that and she kept firing. Bullet number six seemed to do the trick. He collapsed head first onto the carpet and didn't move again.

My mother's robe had come open and she was kneeling on the floor by Fred's body, still firing at him, though the revolver was empty.

It was a terrible scene, insane, beyond anything I could imagine. And this was the moment the electricity came back on. A bedside lamp sprang into life, a surprised yellow glow, and another light as well from my mother's bathroom down the hall. From all over the house there came the whirr of small electrical devices returning to their usual state of being.

"Yeeaaaahhhhh!" I cried. Which was an understatement, under the circumstances. The returned electricity illuminated all the gory details. Fred was lying in an unnatural position, still as stone, one arm twisted to the side, his nose in the carpet. Betty lay face-up in a heap a few feet away with a gooey puddle of blood oozing from the back of her head. And, of course, Max, one eye open, hadn't budged from his spot on the bed.

I figured that it was Fred's gun that had killed Betty, because half her head was blown away. Maybe Fred hadn't meant to do it. Maybe it was my fault, biting his wrist like that and making the gun go off accidentally. It was impossible to say. Many years later, when I became an author of thriller novels, I tried my hand at writing scenes like this one with guns going off and dead bodies everywhere. But in fiction, the action needs to happen in a logical sequence or your New York editor—who's never seen any real violence either—will have your hide. This, on the other hand, was total chaos. From beginning to end, there was no logic to it. It was more a kind of psychotic convulsion, a series of accidental spasms gone wrong.

Meanwhile my mother kept firing her empty gun again and again, unable to stop, making dry clicks as the hammer came down on the empty casing.

I crawled to where she was kneeling and took the gun from her hand.

"Mom," I said, "it's over."

*****

It was a while before either one of us moved or said another word. We were exhausted, emptied out.

I sat in my mother's armchair watching her on the bed as she held Max, cradling him in her arms. Max had been more than her lover, he was her link to the past—to Julka, the *Mauretania*, Krakow, and the girl she had once been. She wept, she held Max for a long time, she was inconsolable. But at last she sat up and kissed his lips.

"*Do widzenia*, Max," I heard her say softly in Polish, telling him goodbye.

I waited, wishing she would hurry up. Fred and Betty didn't make a pretty sight on the floor. Betty in particular had emptied out all her vital juices onto the carpet. There was an increasingly bad smell in the room of blood and shit and goo.

"Are you okay, Mom?" I asked stupidly. Clearly, she wasn't okay. I was not okay, Fred wasn't okay, Betty certainly wasn't okay. I doubted if any of us would ever be okay again. But it helps sometimes to say dumb things. Stupidity restores a sense of normalcy.

"Look, maybe I should call the cops," I said hopefully when she didn't answer. "I bet the phone's working again."

"Not yet, Jonno," she said quietly, sitting on the edge of the bed. "I need to think."

"But, Mom—"

"Just let me think."

Think? I didn't see what there was to think about. We had come to the end of everything, as far as I could tell. But my mother sat very still, almost primly, on the edge of the bed, and I knew the wheels of her conniving brain were spinning round and round.

I've had years now to wonder about the thoughts that must have been passing through my mother's head. I've revisited this scene again and again, in memory and dream, seeking its meaning. When I was younger, I always presumed my mother was working out the problem, how she was going to get away with killing Fred. It was a puzzle to be solved, and she was good at puzzles: Max dead, Fred shot, the candles still burning, three guns on the floor. And finally, most intriguing of all: a dead blond waitress who bore a striking physical resemblance to herself.

It was only years later that I realized my mother had come up with the solution almost from the start. She had always been clever when it came to getting out of a jam, and the answer in this case was not hard to see—it simply took nerve, and she'd always had plenty of that, audacity born of desperation.

No, I'm convinced that the reason she sat there so long was because for the first time in her life, she was wondering if survival was worth the price. She had been running all her life. Now, I believe, she was tempted simply to stop and let whatever ghost was pursuing her catch her at last.

Her eyes flickered my way—her lovely green eyes—and she seemed to return from wherever she had gone. She looked surprisingly good considering the ravages of the night, for there was a wild innocence inside my mother that life never touched.

She reached for a cigarette from a pack on the bedside table and I could tell that she had come to a decision.

"Jonno, go and pack," she told me quietly, exhaling a thin stream of smoke. "We've got to leave and we're not coming back."

"But, Mom—"

"Shh," she said, as she put her arms around me. She kissed my forehead. "I have it all figured out."

She held me tightly and whispered in my ear: "It's going to be all right, darling. I have a plan!"

I did as she told me because when it came to survival, I knew she was the best there was. Even after a night like this, I still thought of my mother as somehow invulnerable. She was a cat with nine lives.

I was in the hallway, walking toward my bedroom in order pack a suitcase—one suitcase only, my mother had warned, only the most important things—when I heard from behind me the sharp, loud crack of gunfire.

A single shot.

I was too surprised to cry out. The shot reverberated through the house and lingered like distant thunder, fading slowly into the stillness of the night.

Until at last there was only the sound of rain.

Epilogue

The Golden Triangle: Laos, 2007

I have one more story and this long tale is done: something remarkable that happened many years later when I was sixty-four years old and on a whim, dissatisfied with life, looking for answers—I checked into a Buddhist monastery in Laos for a three-week meditation retreat.

I was in particular need of enlightenment that year. A wife had recently left me (not the first wife to do so) and of my two children, with one I was barely on speaking terms and the other treated me like a buffoon.

After a shaky start, I had made a quasi-success of myself in the many years that had passed since that stormy night in 1956. I had lived for extended periods in exotic places: Greek islands, Spanish islands, Hawaiian islands, and more islands still off the coast of Thailand. Once I'd had my fill of islands, around the age of forty, I moved on to more sober places: New York, London, Buenos Aires, and finally New Mexico. To support myself, I followed my family's inclination for make-believe. In short, I became a fiction writer. I wrote several thrillers under various pseudonyms, and while none of them were blockbusters, they did well enough for me to afford my modest pleasures in the far-flung reaches of the world.

I was a man with a smile and a quick laugh, an arty fellow who traveled easily in different social circles, high and low. But I wasn't happy. I had spent my life as an exile, a rootless man on the run—worse still, the sort of man on the run who doesn't even know precisely what he's running from. My sorrow was intangible. It seemed to me as I grew older that something important was eluding me and that I'd better go and find it if I was ever going to find it at all.

Thus Laos.

I had been something of a Buddhist for years, ever since listening to Alan Watts on the radio back in the 1960s. Perhaps, I thought, a meditation retreat would help me deal with the feeling I had, waking sometimes at two in the morning, that I was a hollow man, stuffed full of worry, who couldn't bear to live another minute inside his skin.

I found my Buddhist monastery on the Internet, that modern gateway to enlightenment. The Internet provided me with a huge offering of spiritual possibilities throughout the world—and I quickly realized I wasn't the only one searching for peace of mind. For a time, I debated between a retreat in Australia, thinking I might do a little diving on the Barrier Reef afterwards, and another place in Argentina in the mountains of Patagonia.

An Almost Perfect Ending

In the end, I chose Laos because I'm fond of elephants and there happened to be an especially good price just then on air tickets to Bangkok, which would be my jumping off place. Beyond that, the path to enlightenment provided by my Laotian monastery promised to be especially severe. I would be expected to rise each morning at four for untold hours of meditation. There would be no tobacco, no drugs, no sex, no alcohol, no unnecessary talking, and certainly no meat. We weren't allowed to bring books, writing materials, musical instruments, iPods, laptops, or ibuprofen. Even exercise was discouraged.

The idea was that there would be no distractions, period. Nothing to sidetrack the serious seeker from meeting "reality" head on. I was intrigued. I was curious about "reality." In fact, I was ready to remove the glib quotation marks I'd always put around the word. Besides, it seemed to me that if one is going to enter a monastery, it might as well be truly monastic.

These were my reasons, more or less, for going to the Golden Triangle. But in the end, it was a blind choice, something akin to pin-the-tail-on-the-donkey. Or in this case, choose between the crowded offerings of spiritual tourism around the world. I need to emphasize this because of what happened later, the completely arbitrary nature of my decision.

I flew to Bangkok and made my way by bus and train to Vientiane, the Laotian capital. From Vientiane, another long bus ride through spectacular mountains brought me north to Luong Prabang on the Mekong River, a city of ancient temples and tourist traps half-lost in the mist.

The next part of my journey took me deep into the Golden Triangle, a place where guide books advise tourists to proceed at their own risk. I traveled on one of the long, narrow cigar-shaped boats that ply the Mekong, with the pilot keeping a sharp lookout for floating trees and other debris. After a day-long journey, we stopped at a small village for the night, since this part of the Mekong River is so dangerous for navigation you can only travel by day. The next morning we set off again. A little after noon, the boat set me and a young Swedish couple off at a bend in the river where an international organization was running a camp to care for unwanted elephants, an endangered species in Laos since their work in the lumber trade has been made redundant in recent years by gasoline powered engines. This is especially sad for the elephants, of course, since, like me, they never forget.

The Swedish couple remained in the village by the bend in the river—they had come for the elephants—while I continued another five hours in the back of an ancient pickup truck, a tortuous ride over misty hill and soggy dale, past the occasional poppy farm (very pretty) until reaching a monastery that was on the banks of yet another river. Rain was falling gently when I arrived, dripping through the high canopy of huge teak trees overhead. The monastery was a gaudily painted complex of wooden temples with crazy pointed roofs that looked like they might flap their wings and fly off at any moment. Everything smelled of mildew and slow decay. Jungle is the word Westerners generally use to describe this land, though rain forest is more accurate—"seasonal monsoon forest" more accurate still.

A German man with a well-trimmed beard greeted me in calm tones and showed me to the men's quarters, a long shed-like building with open sides and screens instead of glass windows. The building contained twelve simple cots for twelve simple pilgrims, and I soon got into the flow of things. There were currently ten of us men in residence, all Western-ers. There were three Australians, two Brits, a German, a young man from Holland, a Canadian, a Kiwi, and me. I was the only one there over the age of thirty, but beyond that I discovered very little about my fellow seekers. We weren't there to socialize.

There was another shed a short distance away on the far side of the temple complex where the women slept, but I had even less contact with them. There appeared to be twelve women, a full contingent, and they were likewise young and tended to be (as far as I could tell) from the same sort of advanced Western countries where lost souls were especially in need of enlightenment.

We all wore loose white clothing, the required dress, a fashion statement of spiritual endeavor. I dove right in. I gave it my best shot. I rose each morning at four to the temple bell, washed my face in cold water, and sat on my pillow in my late-life imitation of a half-lotus position.

The type of meditation we practiced is what is known as Vipassana, or "insight" meditation. As I understood Vipassana, the idea was to simplify one's mental terrain in order to see clearly all the passing thoughts, without judgment. You watched your thoughts as they appeared like fluffy white clouds floating by in a clear blue sky. You said to yourself, "Ah, there I am, thinking again" . . . and then, on the exhale, you let the thoughts go. Personally, I had a great many passing thoughts, so many thoughts they howled at me like monkeys. (But of course, there *were* monkeys in that rain forest, plenty of them, so perhaps those weren't my thoughts after all.)

I won't go through the details of our long meditative day, for this is not a book about Buddhism—and if you were looking for a book on Buddhism, you certainly wouldn't want one written by the likes of me. Basically, we sat on pillows and breathed in and out, that's the sum total of it. Often it was extremely boring. We sat hour after hour in the main temple among dozens of brightly painted statues of Buddha. The walls of the temple were covered in murals, every square inch, cartoonish pictures of fire-breathing demons with bulging eyes, and Buddhist saints with their hands raised in blessing. The monsters and saints watched over me on my cushion, as I watched my passing thoughts and memories fleeting by. In the jungle the monkeys howled. Every now and then someone rang a gong.

Such was our schedule, hour after hour, day after day. In the late afternoons, we had the opportunity for a short private interview, if we wished, with the people who ran the program, two Westerners—the bearded German man I had met on my arrival and an older woman who wore a maroon robe of the Pure Land Sect and who I sensed might be an American. There were local Laotian monks as well in the monastery complex, but we had nothing to do with them. I never discovered exactly how our program was set up, but it was clearly geared to foreigners.

The German man was in his forties, a very austere fellow with a gloomy way about him. Clearly, dealing with people like myself, a crass beginner, irritated him intensely. He wore the same white, loose-fitting clothes as the rest of us and I didn't like him very much, nor I sensed did he like me. His dark eyes were piercing dots of disapproval. I think he knew intuitively that I was a shallow fellow who had grown up in Southern California, not his kind of place at all.

But the Buddhist nun in the maroon robe was another matter. She appeared to be slightly older than me, in her late sixties, and she had a pleasantly round, wrinkled face, a shaved head, and the kindest eyes I think I've ever seen in a human being. I often found her watching me with a gentle, compassionate smile as I sat on my cushion in front of her and the German man during my individual sessions.

We weren't supposed to debate theology during these personal interviews or discuss abstract matters—we weren't here to debate or ponder but rather to ask practical questions concerning how we were getting along. Generally, I addressed the man, whose name was Hans. I told him things like how my legs kept falling asleep in painful ways during meditation, and he would reply with specific advice.

"Try not to move," he told me. "Just keep breathing and you will pass beyond the pain."

"What if a fly lands on my nose?"

"You may brush off the fly," Hans said wearily. "But gently. The fly is a living creature, too. You certainly don't want to slap yourself on the nose. That would be counterproductive, eh?"

He was a mean son-of-a-bitch. Really.

But the woman, the American Buddhist nun, whenever I turned to her, her eyes only grew kinder. She always seemed to be sending me waves of gentle encouragement. Her name I discovered was Ayya Nyidron. She rarely spoke and I sensed somehow that I wasn't supposed to address her. She was there only to observe.

But as the days passed, there was something about her eyes that began to haunt me. As I say, the glow of kindness in them was almost overwhelming. I had never met anyone before who I thought might know "the answer," but this woman—I thought she might. Most strangely of all, there seemed to be something almost familiar about her, something in her eyes that I had seen before.

I began to think about her constantly, this wonderful Buddhist nun with lovely eyes who seemed to laugh at me so gently and understand me so well. I couldn't have met such a person without remembering, yet I was increasingly certain that I knew her from someplace else. Perhaps a previous life . . . you start to think this way in a Buddhist temple in the jungle. Perhaps I knew her from a dream.

And then one day after lunch, I was walking from the kitchen back to my dormitory for a meditation-nap when she happened to pass near me in the courtyard. I turned and addressed her. I felt I shouldn't, for there was something so holy about her. But I couldn't help myself.

"Excuse me, Ayya, may I ask you something?" I said.

"Yes, of course," she answered, turning to me. Her voice was as clear and lovely and calm as her eyes.

"It's just the feeling I have sometimes that you're so familiar. That I know you from some place. I know this is a strange question, but have we ever met?"

Her smile became kinder, deeper. "Why, yes, Jonno, we have."

Jonno? I stared at her in confusion. I hadn't gone by that old nickname in years. No one knew me by that name here.

"I'm Penny," she told me gently. "Don't you remember?"

"Penny?" I cried. "Penny!"

She blushed. Which was odd to see in a Buddhist nun of a certain age, with shaved head and maroon robe. But in this case it was a blush that was particularly well deserved. Frankly, I have seldom opened a can of tuna fish over the course of the last fifty years without thinking of her.

Penny!

*****

We couldn't talk just then, since we were entering a silent part of the monastic day when talking was not allowed. But Ayya—Penny!—agreed to meet me later. She told me to go to the river at sunset that night where I would find a path along the edge of the bank. If I turned left and kept walking a short way, I would come to a small pavilion where she would be waiting for me.

I can't adequately explain how excited I was to find Penny again after all these years, my TV sister from *What a Life!* And not only to find her again, but to discover that she had evolved into an advanced being with the kindest eyes I'd ever seen. This was amazing. Here was someone who had come from the same dysfunctional world as my own Hollywood childhood, and yet she had found her way to enlightenment.

An Almost Perfect Ending

Could it be that Buddha had guided my steps to this far jungle outpost? I was sure that Penny had appeared by miraculous design to show me The Way. There was such symmetry at work here, I could hardly bear it—a veritable orgy of synchronicity. After all, she had been my teacher fifty years ago, though in very different skills (which I didn't want to ponder in too much detail, stuck as I was in the chaste present).

I meditated with all my might for the rest of the day in order to be ready for her . . . inhale, exhale, watch all those thoughts fly away into the cosmic sky. And then, at sunset I made my way eagerly to the riverbank, stepping around a huge pile of elephant dung until I found a narrow dirt path that seemed to have been made over countless centuries by the passage of bare feet.

The river was wide and sluggish, full of little whirlpools that spluttered and sucked. I walked for nearly ten minutes until coming to a small peninsula that jutted out into the water. Penny—that is to say, Ayya Nyidron—was waiting for me on a bench in a small wooden pavilion with open sides that someone had built here in order to take advantage of the peaceful view. Across the river, the sun was just lowering itself into the endless forest. A lone fisherman in a narrow boat, with oars laid gently across his lap, floated by on the current, heading home. The exotic beauty only added to my eagerness.

I sat on a bench across from her and tried to find in the face of this late-sixties woman some trace of the thirteen-year-old girl I had known. She was still beautiful, though it was a very different sort of beauty than what she'd had before. And yet I could tell somehow that it really was Penny. It was her eyes, I think.

"Penny!" I said, "I can't tell you how totally blown-away I am to find you here. Ayya, rather . . . it's a miracle, really it is!"

She laughed at my enthusiasm. "Please, call me Penny if that makes you more comfortable. Even though I haven't been Penny for a long time."

"So now, my God, you're a Buddhist . . . nun?"

To be honest, it was hard even to say the word nun in connection with Penny. Her smile, I saw, became a little sad, and I know she was remembering what I was remembering.

"Jonno, I'm very glad to see you again. For many years now I've wanted to apologize to you for what I did."

"What you did? You didn't do anything you need to apologize for."

"I sexually abused you." She looked me directly in the eye. "Jonno, I was sexually abused myself continuously from early childhood, and I passed the cycle on to you. That's what people do when they're unconscious of their actions. And I'm deeply sorry. I've suffered greatly thinking about what I did to you, and I beg your forgiveness."

"Penny! You were the prettiest girl ever! I was dying for you!"

"You were eleven, Jonno."

"Listen," I said, "many things have happened in my life that I regret, but not that. You got me through that show."

Penny's smile was disarming. "Really? That's how you remember it?"

We had so much in common, so many memories. I almost forgot what an exalted being Penny had become. She just seemed like an old friend.

She told me a bit about herself, how for a number of years her life had gone from bad to worse. After the 1950s, of course, came the 1960s, a time in which a troubled person could get into vastly more trouble still. Like me, Penny had had a rough ride. She had taken every drug known to man (and a few drugs known mostly to horses) and had gone fairly crazy. In the seventies, she found Jesus for a while, but that didn't last, and she was soon back to her wild ways. Finally, toward the end of the seventies, she stumbled across yoga and meditation and her life gradually calmed down. Buddhism interested her and she began to do various retreats. She spent a year in northern India listening to the Dalai Lama, and then in France she encountered the Vietnamese monk, Thich Nhat Hanh. She stayed with Thich Nhat Hanh at Plum Village, his teaching center in France, until she eventually took monastic vows and rose to a position in his organization.

She wanted to hear my story too, of course, what I'd been doing all these years, and so I told her. It took some time to tell my tale, more than one night—we began to meet regularly at sunset at the pavilion on the river, which was not quite allowed in the retreat program, this sort of personal contact, but Penny apparently was such a high personage that she could do what she wished. Over the course of three evenings, I told her my complete story, the revised edition, all that I have related in these pages and other things as well that happened afterward, marriages and children and such.

Most importantly, I told her the story of what happened on that night, Valentine's Day, 1956.

*****

"That final gunshot," I said, gathering my courage to continue. "You remember where we left off?"

"The gunshot? Of course. You'd left your mother's bedroom and you were in the hall when you heard it."

"She'd told me to pack a few things, that we were leaving and wouldn't be coming back. I was headed to my bedroom thinking the horror was over. But it wasn't. As soon as I heard the shot, I knew what she'd done. She had a plan, you see, but unfortunately it didn't include me. She was selfish to the end."

Penny was watching me intensely but didn't say a word.

"I ran back to the bedroom but I was too late. She was dead on the bed next to Max. She'd shot herself in the temple with Fred's Lugar. There wasn't much left of her face and it was terrible. I totally broke down. I collapsed on the floor and screamed and wept."

It was hard talking about these things, even all these years later, and I had to force myself to go on.

"You see, my mother had come to the end. She'd outrun her demons for years, but this time she saw no way out. So she made her great escape, a gun to the temple, leaving me behind to take care of the mess. I was angry that she would jump ship like that, just when I needed her most. And I stayed angry for years. I still feel a touch of it now remembering how she abandoned me."

Penny nodded very slightly, encouraging me to go on. But she remained silent.

"But maybe anger is good. It was what got me through that night. It gave me the strength to do what I had to. Betty was the big problem, of course. I wasn't sure if I had killed her, or whether it was Fred. But I knew I needed to think up something fast if I didn't want to end up in reform school. So I made up a story. I rearranged the scene. I made it look like a love triangle gone bad. I set the stage for what I wanted the cops to find. It wasn't so hard. I only had to get rid of Betty because she didn't fit the script. I made it look like Fred had come upstairs and found Max and my mother in bed and shot them in a fit of jealousy. It made sense that a guy like Fred, an overgrown Boy Scout, would kill himself in remorse. It's why people believed it so easily.

"I was sorry about Betty because none of this was her fault. She was just in the wrong place at the wrong time. But I didn't have time to worry about her. I dragged her downstairs to my mother's car. It wasn't easy because she was heavy, but I didn't have any other choice. I wrapped her in a blanket and stuffed her in the trunk.

"Once I got rid of Betty, I went back upstairs, I propped up Fred in a chair across the room and I put the Lugar in his hand. Then I set the house on fire. That felt good, actually. I used a can of gasoline that was in the garage for the lawn mower. I lit the curtains by my mother's bed. I didn't want to make it easy for the cops to figure out what really happened. And they didn't, though they were suspicious for a long time. This was the mid-50s, of course—forensics was still fairly primitive back then so I got away with it. The fire was so hot, it didn't leave much behind. I had to move fast to get out of the house in time.

"Max had taught me to drive and I knew where my mother's keys were. So I took the Caddy and drove up the Pacific Coast Highway like some crazy person. I had the .38 that my Uncle Zachary had given me riding on the seat beside me and I knew I had to get rid of it. I threw the gun into the ocean somewhere around Pt. Mugu. Then sometime before dawn I dumped Betty's body over a cliff onto the rocks below. I left her naked without any identification. I'm sorry about that. The last I saw, she was getting swept out to sea. It wasn't very nice.

Penny still didn't say a word. But the look she was giving me kept getting sadder and deeper.

"Well, I was desperate," I continued, as though that made it all right. "The world I knew was over. I kept driving until I ran out of gas in this dinky little beach town north of Santa Barbara. A Sheriff's deputy spotted me, a little kid behind the wheel of an expensive car stuck at the side of the road pounding the steering wheel in frustration.

"They brought me back to L.A. and I was quite a celebrity for a while, my picture on the front page of the newspapers. Everyone wanted to know what happened that night and I got a lot of sympathy. I told a pretty good tale, all in all. It thrilled the gossip columns for months."

After a pause, Penny finally spoke. "Well, that's quite a story. You're amazing, Jonno! You're like Scheherazade. You come up with a new tale every time you need it!"

I wasn't sure I liked what Penny had said. It didn't sound like a compliment.

"What do you expect?" I asked. "I grew up in the land of make-believe. Just like you did, on Soundstage 17. There was nothing real about any of it."

"Oh, I don't know about that. We were real enough once the cameras stopped rolling. Our fears and longings and insecurities. We weren't so different from other people, not really."

"You think so? Well, maybe you're right. I went to live with Mina after the cops and the courts were finished with me. Mina sold the house in Malibu, and we moved to New York so we could start fresh in a new place. She became a big success on Broadway, one play after another. It was either the third or fourth reinvention of Mina's career, I forget which. She sent me to a New England boarding school—Choate, a very snobby place. I didn't like it much, but I kept my head down and worked hard. Frankly, I'd had enough of getting into trouble. On vacations I'd return to the city where we led quite a sophisticated life together. Late dinners at Sardis. Lots of theater and music and art. She took me everywhere."

"Mina was a very kind woman."

"Yes, she was. She lived to be 91, and when she died I missed her very much. I missed Max, too, of course. I missed him a lot. I even missed my mother, to tell the truth. Though she was probably the worst mother in all of Los Angeles. Which is saying something."

I shrugged. "So that's my story, Penny. The good and bad of it. What do you think?"

It was dark by the time we finished talking. A heavy tropical mist had settled on the river and the forest. There were a thousand sounds of bugs and monkeys and strange birds. I could barely see Penny's face in the darkness though she was only a few feet away.

There was a growl of thunder and the rain began all at once, with the suddenness of the tropics, a downpour. We were quickly soaked. Still, neither of us moved.

"What do I think?" There was another flash of lightning and I saw her more clearly. She was sitting in a full lotus position impervious to the rain. "I think you're like one of those Russian dolls that you open up and there's always another doll underneath."

It took me a moment to absorb this. "You don't think I'm telling you the truth?"

"I don't know, Jonno. That's for you to say, not me. Make-believe is fine as long as you don't fool yourself."

"You think what I told you is make-believe?"

"Jonno, I think you're the absolute saint of make-believe. But it's okay. You're my oldest friend and I love you deeply."

"I wish you'd told me that when I was eleven!"

There was another flash of lightning and I saw her face more clearly. Her eyes were soft with compassion and sorrow so deep I felt I could drown in it.

"We were naughty children, weren't we?" she said softly.

"Children of the damned," I agreed. "In the land of lust!"

"That was California back then. Paradise or bust!"

"And what a life it was!" I added, remembering our old show.

She laughed, and I joined her. We laughed because suddenly it all seemed so ridiculous. We laughed for what we had, and what we lost, and our laughter was full of love. We laughed until we cried.

And that's the final image I'll always have of Penny, the two of us sitting on that riverbank in Laos laughing in the rain, because the next day she was gone, and I never saw her again.

*****

I returned the way I had come, five hours in the back of a pickup truck to the elephant camp, and from there I caught a ride on another cigar-shaped boat. This time I traveled downriver to Vietnam. The opposite direction from Penny.

From Saigon, as people call it to this day, I flew to Bangkok, and from Bangkok to Buenos Aires.

I like B.A. It's a sophisticated European city set down in the New World. Tango, good wine, outdoor cafes, every table full of animated conversation. But I didn't linger.

From B.A., I took a 72-hour bus ride south to Comodoro Rivadiva on the Patagonian coast. Argentina's long distance busses are pleasant. They have seats that lie down flat, and they feed you and even give you champagne. Quite a difference from Greyhound, which I've taken as well.

An Almost Perfect Ending

I rented a car in Comodoro Rivadiva and drove on small roads west into the desert toward the huge mountains in the distance. The Andes have peaks higher than 20,000 feet and they make the Rockies look small. As you approach the mountains from the desert, they get bigger and bigger until you can hardly believe their size.

I think of this part of Argentina as the Fugitive Zone. It's home to people who have made a run for it. Nazis, Jews who didn't want to end up in a concentration camp, thieves, killers, crooks, runners of all kinds. Even Butch Cassidy and the Sundance Kid ended up here at one point when they were on the run from the law.

After many hours of driving, I reached a village I won't name in order to protect the guilty. A few miles further on, I came to a private road that passed through one of those too-grand entrances in the middle of nowhere that anyone with an ounce of sense would wonder about.

I rang a bell, spoke into a speaker, continued through the gate and into the high desert for several miles more. The road gradually rose in elevation to a grassy pampas.

This was the Estancia Cordova, one of the great haciendas of Argentina. The road went on so long it felt like being in a separate kingdom. I passed a large herd of cattle and fields where horses were grazing. Like many of the large estancias, the Estancia Cordova had its own polo team.

The owner of this small kingdom, Carlos Cordova, died two years ago at the age of 87, a very wealthy man. His real name was Ernst Blumfeld and he was both a Nazi and a Jew, which is certainly a special category of villain. The Nazis had allowed him to remain in Germany because he was so useful to them. But in 1944, sensing the gig was up, Ernst made his great escape from war-torn Europe to South America, managing to take nearly all his money with him. It wasn't easy getting out of Nazi Germany at this point in the war, but survivors nearly always find a way.

I came at last to the main house, a sprawling hacienda that sat among pleasant shade trees and green well-cut lawns. Marcelo Cordova, the present owner—son of Carlos—was in the front yard inspecting a horse which one of the grooms had brought on a lead into the driveway. Horses in Argentina are a deep part of the culture.

"Jonno!" he called when he saw me. "I didn't know you were coming!"

"Spur of the moment," I told him.

He stopped what he was doing with the horse and gave me a big bear hug because we hadn't seen each other for nearly two years.

"How is she?" I asked.

"Remarkable, as always," he answered. "It's hard to believe she's 84. She rides, she gardens, she's still a beautiful woman. She defies time."

An Almost Perfect Ending

I smiled. She defied a lot of things.

I left Marcelo and walked on a path around to the back of the house to the swimming pool. A spry, elderly woman was doing leisurely laps in the pool. She wore a rubber bathing cap so I couldn't see her blonde hair underneath, but I knew there wouldn't be a hint of gray in it.

Such are the joys of reinvention. In this case, it hadn't been difficult to pull off. Two women who looked very much the same, one dead, one a survivor. A simple substitution. For a girl with a big imagination, it was a piece of cake. All it needed was nerve, a bit of luck, and my help.

The old woman turned my way and smiled.

"Hello, Mom."

Coming Soon!

ROBERT WESTBROOK'S
Walking Rain
A Howard Moon Deer Mystery
Book 8

Driving home from Utah, Howard Moon Deer is passing through an empty stretch of New Mexico desert when a young Chinese woman staggers onto the highway, seemingly out of nowhere, and collapses before his onrushing car. Howie screeches to a stop and gets her to a hospital, but it is too late. She is dead on arrival.

Who was this woman and where did she come from? When Jack Wilder and Howie are hired by a non-profit organization, The Committee to Abolish Human Trafficking, they are soon embroiled in the most dangerous case of their career: a huge illegal cannabis growing operation on Indian land, financed by Hong Kong money, worked with trafficked labor.

To complicate matters, Howie is making preparations for the visit of his 17-year-old daughter, Georgina, whose existence he only recently discovered. Georgina grew up in Scotland and it's a good thing she's an adventurous girl because she's about to get a real taste of the Wild West.

Inspired by true events, *WALKING RAIN* is a tale of corruption, international crime, and the challenges of parenthood as Howie finds himself an unexpected father to a teenage girl.

For more information
visit: www.SpeakingVolumes.us

Coming Soon!

MARDI OAKLEY MEDAWAR'S
Murder at Medicine Lodge
A Tay-Bodal Mystery
Book 3

In 1867, the Kiowa travel to Medicine Lodge, Kansas, along with the Comanche, Arapaho, Apache, and Cheyenne to meet with representatives of the U.S. government and to sign peace treaties. But not all of the Kiowa agree that the peace treaty is a good thing, and tensions between them and the U.S. Army ("The Blue Jackets") are running high. So, when the army bugler disappears and White Bear, chief of the Rattle Band, finds his bugle out on the plains, the army command assumes that White Bear has killed the man to steal it. To make matters worse, the bugler's body is later found—murdered—out on the plains. With the army set to try White Bear for murder, and the Kiowa set to declare war if he is not found innocent, Tay-bodal—a healer amongst the Kiowa—is charged by the Principal Chief to investigate and clear White Bear's name. With very little time before an army tribunal is to be held, Tay-bodal must find out the truth about the bugler—a man he doesn't know—and what might have actually happened out there on the plains.

For more information
visit: www.SpeakingVolumes.us

On Sale Now!

ROBERT WESTBROOK'S
SUSPENSE / MYSTERIES

**For more information
visit:** https://svpubs.com/2S7Svfr

On Sale Now!

JAMES V. IRVING'S
JOTH PROCTOR FIXER MYSTERIES

"Irving's writing is relaxed and authentic and takes readers inside a compelling world of legal and social issues..."
—Bruce Kluger, columnist, USA Today

For more information
visit: www.SpeakingVolumes.us

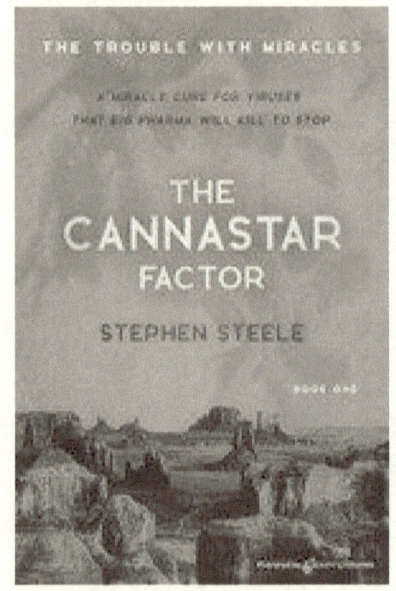